FORT
POINT

Center Point
Large Print

Also by Susan Page Davis and available from Center Point Large Print:

The Priority Unit

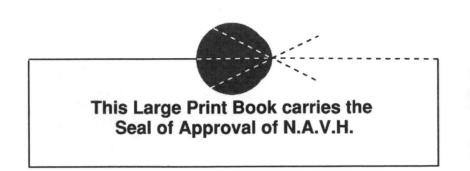

This Large Print Book carries the Seal of Approval of N.A.V.H.

FORT POINT

MAINE JUSTICE
• BOOK 2 •

SUSAN PAGE DAVIS

CENTER POINT LARGE PRINT
THORNDIKE, MAINE

Library of Congress Cataloging-in-Publication Data

Names: Davis, Susan Page, author.
Title: Fort Point / Susan Page Davis.
Description: Center Point large print edition. | Thorndike, Maine :
    Center Point Large Print, 2018. | Series: Maine justice ; book 2
Identifiers: LCCN 2017051152 | ISBN 9781683246824
    (hardcover : alk. paper)
Subjects: LCSH: Large type books. | GSAFD: Mystery fiction.
Classification: LCC PS3604.A976 F67 2018 | DDC 813/.6—dc23
LC record available at https://lccn.loc.gov/2017051152

Chapter 1

Monday, June 21

Detective Harvey Larson drove out of the airport access road and headed toward the police station. Ahead of him, a black-and-white braked sharply as a pedestrian darted into the street in front of it. Harvey hit his brakes too.

His young partner, Eddie Thibodeau, braced against the dashboard. "What's going on?"

"Someone's in a hurry." Harvey pulled his Explorer up behind the squad car. To his relief, he saw that it hadn't hit the runner. The man stood next to the car, talking animatedly to the officers, waving his arms and pointing wildly.

"I'll check it out." Eddie jumped out of the vehicle and walked up to the police car, spoke to the pedestrian, and then bent slightly to speak to the patrolmen inside. After a minute, he nodded and strode back to where Harvey waited.

"That guy says there's a body down over the riverbank." Eddie swung into the front seat. "Can you pull off here?"

"Sure." Ahead, a small park edged the Fore River beside the road, before the junction with Congress Street. Harvey pulled around the squad car and drove into the small lot for the park. "Who's in the car?"

"Hal Downey and Joe Clifford. The civilian says he thinks someone drowned. He went down there and looked, but he didn't touch him."

Harvey had Eddie call the desk sergeant and tell him they would handle the unattended death and ask him to call the medical examiner. They got out and walked quickly to where the two uniformed officers stood on the sidewalk, talking to the man who had stopped them.

"I was going to call 911," the man said, a little breathless, "and then I saw your car."

Officer Joe Clifford was taking notes. Hal Downey turned to nod at Harvey.

"Detective Larson, this is Mr. Tipton."

"You're a detective?" Tipton asked. "I took my coffee out on the deck and I saw that guy just lying there, down on the mud flats." He wore jeans, a T-shirt, and moccasins, and he looked wide awake now, even if he'd missed his morning coffee.

"Low tide?" Harvey asked. The river was an estuary that emptied into Casco Bay.

Tipton nodded and pointed toward the bank. "He's right down there."

Harvey said, "We'll take a look." Downey and Clifford would get the man's full statement and keep people out of their way. They walked across the lawn. Tipton's home on the riverbank was

6

an older wood-frame house in a great location.

When they reached the bank, Harvey could see the body lying below him. No footprints, other than Tipton's, or drag marks.

"He must have washed up here."

"Sure enough," Eddie said at his elbow. The man lay face down with water swirling around his feet, his wet clothes darkened, except for white sneakers. Eddie pulled out his smart phone and began clicking rapidly. "Can we wait for some guys with gear to come out here?"

"No, the tide's turned. In another half hour, it could carry him downstream. Come on. We're going to have to move him."

Harvey edged down the bank and slogged out, glad the riverbed wasn't too soft, and knelt by the body. He put a hand to the man's throat, but there was no doubt. He took out his phone and snapped several photos.

Eddie came behind him. "Low tide was forty minutes ago."

"Grab his other arm so we can get him out of the river. We're losing evidence."

They dragged him close to the bank and turned him over. The middle-aged face was wrinkled and mud-smeared. The water had plastered his short hair to his scalp.

"Get Joe to help us lift him," Harvey said, and Eddie scrambled up the bank.

Harvey pulled on sterile gloves, patted the

man's pockets, and pulled out a waterlogged wallet. He flipped it open and studied the driver's license, then peered closely at the man's face. "Really?" he said softly. "Terrific."

"Need us both down there?" Joe called from above.

"No sense all of us getting wet," Harvey said. "Eddie, get down here."

Eddie jumped down, and Harvey passed him the wallet. Eddie swore under his breath in French and squinted down at the corpse. "We got Maine's most famous man?"

"Looks like it." Harvey shook his head. He loathed investigating celebrity deaths. They'd be tripping over reporters every step they took, and with internationally acclaimed author Martin Blake lying lifeless at his feet, he could bank on a long day.

He looked upstream to where Route 9 crossed the river. The place was known as Stroudwater Crossing. A lot of traffic passed over that bridge day and night. If only he'd kept going and crossed over it, and let Downey and Clifford call for someone else. But no, he'd stopped, and he was stuck with it now.

Clifford helped them lift Blake's body up onto the bank, and Harvey told the patrolmen to keep bystanders away. He didn't want the dead man's identity leaking out while they were still working here, or they'd have a circus on their hands.

While they waited for the M.E., Downey brought a tarp to cover the body, and Harvey knelt beside it. His initial examination revealed a wound high in Blake's abdomen. It looked like a knife wound; the medical examiner would tell them for sure later.

"Not a straightforward drowning," he murmured to Eddie.

He wasn't an expert, but he guessed Blake had been in the water a few hours. The body was fully clothed in a brown tweed sport coat, striped shirt, dark brown pants, and white athletic shoes. Very ordinary clothes for such a rich guy. He emptied the man's pockets and dropped each item into a bag Eddie held: a key ring with a dozen keys, a waterlogged pocket notebook, three pens, a dollar twenty-two in change, a pocketknife, and a soaked business card.

He opened the soggy wallet again. Besides Blake's driver's license, it held three credit cards, a medical insurance card, four library cards, eighty-seven dollars in bills, three photos, and a year-old fishing license.

"Not a robbery," Eddie said.

Harvey studied the driver's license, effortlessly memorizing the address and vital statistics. Blake was 53, and his house was half a mile away. Harvey glanced toward the street. A couple of cars had stopped, and several people now watched from the lawn of the nearest house.

Clifford and Downey were doing their best to move people along.

Harvey called for a mobile crime unit. The medical examiner arrived within minutes. Eddie went to have a word with the homeowner, to make sure the patrolmen hadn't missed anything, while Harvey talked to the M.E. After making his preliminary exam, the doctor prepared the body to be taken to the morgue for an autopsy. Harvey took Blake's watch and wedding ring. The clothes would be sent over to the police station later. No cell phone. Had he left it home, or was it in the river?

He checked the time. Almost nine-thirty. His fiancée, Jennifer, would be immersed in her work. How would she like him getting handed such a high-profile case a month before their wedding? Of course, she had no idea yet what that would entail. She would get the Cop's Wife Crash Course.

Eddie came back. "Nothing new."

"Okay." Harvey looked up and down the river. The body had lodged in a grassy little cove on the west side of the Fore, just below the park. "That bridge is the most likely point of entry."

They walked along the riverbank toward it. On the downstream side of the bridge, riprap tumbled into the water on both sides of the channel. They waited for a lull in traffic on Congress Street and crossed to the other side, where a brick sidewalk melded into concrete over the bridge. That side had a higher railing. Harvey pulled out a tape measure. Forty inches. He walked along the sidewalk, looking closely at the railing. He stopped about two thirds of the way across.

"This could be dried blood."

Eddie hurried to him and looked at the brown smear on the painted steel railing. "Yeah, it could."

"Flag it for the techs." Harvey took some pictures of it and the bridge on his phone.

There wasn't much more they could do at the scene, so when the mobile unit arrived at ten, he instructed them to take a good look at the bridge and the park, as well as the cove. The two detectives headed for Martin Blake's house to see if his widow was home.

The huge old mansion was surrounded by a high, wrought-iron fence, and the gate was locked. Harvey spotted a switch on one side. He got out of Eddie's truck and pushed the switch. Nothing happened that he could see, but he waited. Thirty seconds later, a young woman came out of the house and walked down the driveway toward them.

"May I help you?"

"I'm Detective Larson, Portland P.D." Harvey held up his badge. "We're here to see Mrs. Blake."

She hesitated. "What is it about?"

"Are you a relative?"

"No, I'm Mr. Blake's assistant."

"I'll need to talk to Mrs. Blake."

She frowned. "I'll take her a message." Harvey got back in the truck.

They sat there a good ten minutes, and Eddie drummed his fingers on the steering wheel. Finally the woman came back down the driveway and opened the gate.

"You can drive up to the house."

Eddie eased the truck through the gate and up the driveway. It was quite a house, a huge white Queen Anne with three different styles of shingle siding, brackets under the eaves, and a turret on one corner. They didn't build houses that way anymore. Harvey wished Jennifer could see it. She liked antiques.

The assistant opened the front door for them. They stepped from the porch into a large entrance hall, with stairs rising to a landing above.

"I'm Barbara Heflin," the young woman said. "You can wait in here." She ushered them into a side room and left them.

Harvey looked around. The room looked comfortable in an upscale way—two sofas, armchairs, antique tables, a fireplace, oriental rugs on an oak floor. A huge landscape on one wall, and an abstract over the fireplace. He squinted at that one and decided it was genuine, and expensive. In the bookcase were copies of guess whose books, in regular, large print, and foreign editions.

Eddie was looking out a French window, and Harvey stepped over beside him to see what was so interesting. He gazed at a fenced-in swimming pool that could be reached via a wide deck outside the French window.

"Why do you suppose Martin Blake kept working as a reporter, when he was raking in millions from his books?" Eddie asked.

Blake had started as a reporter for the *Portland Press Herald*, then went on to become one of Maine's most celebrated novelists. He wrote fat, passionate family sagas, churning out at least one a year, but continued to hold his job at the paper.

"I dunno," Harvey said. "Maybe he used his job as fodder for his books." He read a lot of books, but not Martin Blake's.

"Gentlemen, how may I help you?"

They turned and faced Thelma Blake. Harvey had never seen her before, but had noticed her picture in the paper a few times. She was said to be a middle-aged eccentric, and he believed it. Her platinum blonde curls looked so precise, he decided she wore a wig. Her eyebrows and lashes were very dark, and her eyes were brown. She wore green eye shadow, bright red lipstick, and matching nail polish. Her toenails were red, too, peeking out of her sandals, and she wore a purple blouse and white capris.

Harvey introduced Eddie and himself. "Would

you please sit down, ma'am? We have something to tell you."

She looked mildly concerned, but not upset. She sat in one of the armchairs, and he sat on a sofa corner-wise to her. Eddie stayed by the window.

"Mrs. Blake," Harvey began, "I have some bad news for you. Your husband has met with an accident."

Her eyes widened in alarm. "Martin? What's happened? Is he hurt?"

"Yes, ma'am. Well, you see, he's dead." Harvey usually gave a smoother presentation than that. The toenail polish and the wig distracted him.

For a moment she sat still, seeming ready to laugh if he said, *Just kidding.* Then she said, "Oh, dear," as though perturbed with her inconsiderate husband.

Harvey said, "I'm very sorry."

"I can't believe it. He was fine last night."

"It's true, ma'am. I've just seen him. His body."

She let out a little sob and tears streamed down her cheeks. She pulled in a shaky breath. "What happened?"

"We're not exactly sure. His body was found in the Fore River. Did you see him this morning?"

"No, I thought he must have gone out early."

"What about last night?"

"We went to his class reunion yesterday. We got home about nine o'clock and had a couple

14

of drinks. I went to bed, but Martin said he was going to write for a while."

"Where does he do his writing, ma'am?"

"In his study, upstairs."

"Is that the last time you saw him?"

"Yes, I guess it is. I slept soundly, and I didn't hear him come into the bedroom, but sometimes he stays up all night or falls asleep in his study. And sometimes he goes out and walks at night to think about his plots."

"I wonder if we could see his study, ma'am?"

"Of course. Do whatever you need."

She stood up and wobbled a little. Harvey put out his hand to steady her, but she crumpled into his arms.

"Eddie, get that assistant girl." Harvey laid her on the couch.

Eddie stepped quickly into the hall, calling, "Ms. Heflin?"

They stayed until they could see Mrs. Blake was coming to, then left her in Ms. Heflin's care and went upstairs.

The study was in the tower room. The three windows overlooked the front yard, and the low windowsills were a foot deep and cushioned, so people could sit on them. Against one wall was a huge, oak roll-top desk, and a modern computer desk faced the door. Between them was an oak swivel chair with red cushions.

"Pretty cool setup," said Eddie.

The computer was the newest thing, the kind Harvey would love to have. While Eddie checked out the four oak file cabinets, Harvey scanned the overflowing bookshelves. They ranged from *Writer's Market* and standard references to genealogy and medical books. There were several volumes on China, and another clump on Mexico.

Since Mrs. Blake had given her permission, he sat down in the chair and turned on the computer. He went quickly to the word processing program and viewed the titles of the last few documents opened: "Border Feud," "Cover letter," "Shanghai Sequel," and "McDougal Family."

He opened the first one, "Border Feud," which would be the one Blake had accessed most recently. It appeared to be a rough draft of a new novel.

"Finding anything?" he asked Eddie.

"Well, this first cabinet seems to be drafts of his fiction, research material and correspondence."

"What kind of correspondence?"

"Uh, book proposals, synopses, contract negotiations."

"Check the other files." Harvey did a rapid search of the text files on the computer. He'd probably better ask for a warrant if he wanted to take the machine away, but he felt Mrs. Blake's statement gave him the green light to look through the documents. If he wanted to peruse the e-mails and instant messages, he'd probably need some time with the computer.

"Everything here seems to relate to his books and the business end of writing," Eddie said, closing the bottom drawer of the third file cabinet.

"Nothing to do with his newspaper job?"

"Not yet."

Harvey went through both desks. The computer desk held mostly office supplies. The roll-top held some personal items, bills, and notices. No phone.

"I've got paid bills, filed by the month," Eddie said, bending over the last cabinet. "Warrantees for appliances, deed to the house." He opened the bottom drawer. "Newspaper clippings."

Harvey looked. The drawer was full of news articles, filed alphabetically by subject. Aston Exposé, City Council, Clukey Murder . . .

He remembered reading Blake's front page stories on the Clukey murder. Someone else would be writing this one.

"Okay, we'd better seal this room," he said. "We may not need any of this stuff, but if we do, I don't want to come back and find out the widow's been cleaning house."

They went downstairs and found Barbara Heflin in the foyer.

"Where can I find Mrs. Blake?" Harvey asked.

"I took her to her room to lie down."

"I'll need to see her for just a moment," Harvey said.

Ms. Heflin took them upstairs and along a hallway. She knocked softly on a closed door then opened it.

Mrs. Blake lay on a queen-sized maple spool bed, with a pile of pillows under her head and shoulders.

"I'm sorry to bother you, ma'am," Harvey said, "but we'll have to seal your husband's study until we finish our investigation. May I have the keys?"

"I don't understand."

"Until we know what happened to him, we need to make sure all his records and papers are undisturbed."

Ms. Heflin brought the keys, and Harvey sent Eddie to the truck for yellow tape, then upstairs to do the job while he talked to Mrs. Blake.

"We haven't found Mr. Blake's phone," he said.

"He would have taken it with him." She sat up straighter and looked across the bed at the other nightstand. "I don't see it here."

In the river, Harvey thought. She gave him the number, so they could ping it from the police station.

He told her where the body would be taken, and that her husband's personal effects would be returned when they no longer needed them. He emphasized that no one was to enter the room Eddie was sealing.

He also got a list of people living at or frequenting the house. Mr. and Mrs. Blake lived there, of course, and Ms. Heflin had a bedroom on the third floor. The cook and a cleaning woman came in daily. The Blakes' two married children lived out of state. There had been no overnight guests for two weeks.

While he was getting this information, Ms. Heflin took a phone call and interrupted gently, telling Mrs. Blake the medical examiner's office wanted to know what funeral home she would be dealing with.

She lay back on the pillows, her face very white, and closed her eyes for a moment. "Coopers', I guess. You'll have to help me with the arrangements, Barbara."

"Of course."

"We'll leave you," Harvey said, "but we'll want to talk to you again soon."

Eddie drove to the police station, at the corner of Middle and Franklin, and parked in the garage. They went up the stairs to the third-floor Priority Unit office. The main room was large for a small unit, but full of computer equipment and files and desks. The brick building had a lot of glass, and Harvey's area looked out over Franklin, at a legal office across the street.

He had moved up from the regular detective squad eight years before, when the Priority Unit was organized. Captain Mike Browning was the driving force behind the unit, and they had proved its worth many times to the skeptical city officials who scrutinized the budget with a microscope every year.

Harvey liked his desk. He spent a lot of time there on the computer, and he'd made it comfortable, more comfortable than his apartment. The outstanding feature was an eight-by-ten photo of Jennifer on the breakwater at Rockland, her blonde hair blowing out in the wind around her. When he saw that, he sat down in his chair, took out his cell, and speed-dialed her.

"Hey, gorgeous." It was her second week working in the records department, in the basement of the police station. Her temporary job was only for the summer, a stopgap between her software designing job that fizzled and marriage. "Eddie and I got a new homicide case this morning. Can I see you?"

"No time now," Jennifer said. "Lunch?"

"Sure."

Mike Browning approached with coffee mug in hand.

"You guys up to your elbows in the Blake case?"

"At least," Harvey said.

Eddie had made a list of Blake's effects and tagged the items, and he came over to join them.

"The press is onto it," Mike said. "You'll have to talk to them."

Eddie swore, and Harvey felt like it. He

20

would rather look at a corpse than a TV camera.

"What have you got so far?" Mike asked.

"Not much," Harvey said. "I'm thinking Blake went out for a walk in the neighborhood last night and got mugged on the bridge at Stroudwater. He had an abdominal wound. Could be a stabbing."

Mike scrunched up his face, thinking about that. "You might get a prelim autopsy report by this afternoon."

"Yeah. We'll try to get more on his movements last night."

Harvey went downstairs and logged Blake's possessions into the evidence room, then asked the liaison to set up the press conference for three o'clock. Some hotshot reporter had already heard that the medical examiner had been out by the bridge that morning, but as far as Harvey could tell, Blake's name hadn't leaked out.

He and Eddie got coffee and went over their notes on the case.

"Well, we've got to talk to the widow again," Harvey said at last. "We need to know more about that class reunion and where else he might have gone last night."

"Maybe a neighbor saw him go out," Eddie suggested.

"Could be. We'd better get some patrolmen to help with this."

Harvey asked the patrol sergeant to loan him Nate Miller and his partner for the day. He'd worked with Nate before. He was methodical and good at recognizing significant details. His partner, Jimmy Cook, was still on leave from a wound he'd received a few weeks earlier, and Nate had a new recruit riding with him.

"That okay with you?" Sergeant Terry Lemieux asked. "It would give him some experience—first homicide for him. Nate will keep an eye on him."

"I guess." It wasn't the case Harvey would pick to train a rookie on. "When's Jimmy coming back?"

"Not for another week. He needed physical therapy for his leg."

Harvey felt bad about that. Jimmy had been hurt while trying to arrest a man hired to kill Harvey.

"All right, we'll take Nate and the new guy. What's his name?"

"Tony Winfield."

"Oh, boy." Did it have to be the governor's nephew? The P.D. was already taking flak for hiring him, but he'd come through the Academy with flying colors and had supposedly been judged by the same standard as everyone else.

"You can have Benoit and Yeaton instead."

"No, give me Nate and Wonder Boy." Harvey liked Sarah Benoit all right, and Eddie liked her better than all right, and Cheryl Yeaton seemed competent. But Harvey also wanted Eddie to concentrate on the job. He'd take his chances on Nate and the rookie.

Chapter 2

When they drove back to the Blake mansion, Nate and the rookie followed in a cruiser. Winfield looked about sixteen, a sandy-haired kid with a toothy smile and dimples. Harvey hoped he was as smart as his uncle, whom he considered a pretty good governor.

Barbara Heflin gave him two of Blake's publicity photos, and he passed them to the patrolmen so they could canvass the neighborhood, asking if anyone had seen Martin Blake the night before.

Ms. Heflin showed him and Eddie to a cozy sitting room, where Mrs. Blake was talking on the telephone. She had on a different wig now, auburn waves to the earlobe, and wore a black border print skirt and a green blouse. She looked almost normal.

She glanced up at them and quickly ended the conversation. "I'll be going to the funeral home right away, Detective."

"That's all right, ma'am. We'll be working upstairs in the tower room, and we'll try not to disrupt your household."

"Thank you. My son and daughter are coming this evening."

"Before you leave, ma'am, I wanted to ask you

23

more about the reunion you went to yesterday."

"It was up at Fort Point. Too far away."

"Fort Point? Where's that?"

"It's clear up Route 1, by Stockton Springs. It took us over two hours to get there. They should have had it here in town."

"And this was a high school reunion?"

"Yes, Martin's thirty-fifth."

"Can you get me a list of the people who were there?"

"I certainly can't name them all. It's not my class, but the invitation is on my dresser upstairs. The people who organized the reunion might be able to help you."

"What did Mr. Blake wear to the reunion?"

"A navy blue polo shirt and gray slacks. He had a tan jacket along. It was cool on the shore."

"Did you see him after he changed his clothes last night?"

"No, I didn't know he'd changed."

Harvey described the clothes he was found in, and she pursed her lips. "Oh, that ratty old tweed jacket. I've tried to get rid of it, but he says it's comfortable." She sobbed a little and shook her head.

"Why did they have the reunion at Fort Point?" Harvey asked.

"His class has a thing about state parks." She dabbed at her eyes with a tissue. "Every five years they go to a different one. The first one, thirty years ago, was at Baxter, and they all climbed Mount Katahdin. Nowadays they just pick one with easy access and a nice picnic area. That one didn't have a decent beach, though. The shore access is steep, and it's rocky."

"Historical spot?"

"Yes, there are ruins of some old fort. Picturesque, but not spectacular."

He wrote it in his notebook.

"My class has a banquet and a cocktail hour," Mrs. Blake said. "I like to be able to get a martini and sit in a comfortable place indoors and talk to people."

He followed her into the hall. Ms. Heflin was waiting for her.

"Oh, Ms. Heflin," Harvey said, "I wanted to ask you, did you go to the reunion?"

"Me? Goodness, no. I went to an art opening yesterday and met a girlfriend for dinner." She named the gallery, restaurant, and friend for him, and he wrote it down.

"Did you come back here after that?"

"Yes. I was here when the Blakes got home."

"About nine o'clock?"

"A little after, I think. I only saw them for a moment before I went to my room."

He let them go after getting permission to look in Martin Blake's wardrobe. In the bedroom, the invitation was where she had said it would be. Harvey pulled out his phone and dialed the number listed on it for Cyndi Rancourt Reynolds, committee chairman. After identifying himself, he asked if she could provide a list of guests at the class reunion the day before. She was curious, but agreed to copy off the list and fax it to him at the office.

Several sport jackets and three suits hung in the closet, with half a dozen sweaters, twenty-one shirts, a bathrobe, eight pair of pants, and a tuxedo. A tan poplin jacket hung at one end.

Harvey checked the jacket pockets, but they were empty. He also checked the two pair of gray slacks that hung there, but found nothing. There didn't seem to be any dirty laundry in the room.

On the nightstand sat a lamp and a novel—someone else's. In the drawer he found some pens and paper clips, a dime, a memo pad, and a fingernail clipper.

"Anything?" he asked.

"No," said Eddie, turning away from the dresser.

"Same here."

Eddie glanced out the window.

"Hey, Nate and Tony are coming up the drive-way."

By the time they got downstairs, Nate was ringing the doorbell. Harvey and Eddie went out onto the driveway, and Harvey said to Nate, "You guys get anything?"

"A Mrs. Potter down the street was out walking

her poodle last night, about ten-thirty. She saw Martin Blake—passed him on the sidewalk."

"Great! Which way was he headed?"

"Down the hill, on this side of the street. She showed us the exact spot where she met him."

"Did she speak to him?"

"She said, 'Hello, Mr. Blake,' and he said, 'Good evening.' She's not sure he even knows who she is, but of course all the neighbors know him by sight."

"Anything else?"

"He was wearing dark clothes, a sport coat of some kind, and white tennis shoes."

"That fits what he had on when we found him."

"And after they passed, she turned around and looked back at him," Nate said. "He had stopped at the corner, under the streetlight. She wasn't sure, but she thought he was writing something."

"He had a pocket notebook," Harvey said. "I'll see if it's dried out yet."

Eddie asked, "Did she see which way he went from the corner?"

"No, she and poochie moved on."

"Okay," Harvey said. "You and Tony extend your inquiries and see if you can get a line on where Blake went from the corner. It wasn't that late. Someone else might have seen him. We'll be back at the office. Call me if you find anything interesting."

"I was just thinking," Tony said. "If he died last

night between ten and midnight, say, the tide was probably pretty high."

"It would have been midway between," Harvey said. He took out his phone and did some quick searching. "High tide at 2:26 a.m., low at 8:35, which is just about when the body was spotted."

"Okay," Tony said. "So, he hung up in that cove instead of being dragged out toward the harbor."

"Yeah. Lucky us. I'm banking on him going off the bridge, but if we can pinpoint the time of death, it will help."

Harvey and Eddie headed back to the police station, and Harvey got the envelope of Martin Blake's effects from the evidence room. When he got upstairs, a fax lay on his desk—the list of reunion guests from Cyndi Rancourt Reynolds.

"They couldn't get a fix on his phone," Eddie reported from his desk a few feet away. "It's turned off, or maybe waterlogged."

"Hmm." Harvey carefully slid the items out of the envelope. The small notebook was still soggy. "We'd better leave this out to air dry." He opened it gingerly. It contained several pages of scrawl. The last page Martin Blake had used said "M confronts TN—TN is defiant."

"Notes for a book?" he hazarded.

Eddie came over and looked at it. "Maybe that's how he plans his plots."

"I wonder if that's what Mrs. Potter saw him writing under the streetlight." Harvey leafed back a couple of pages, but it was more of the same, "RJ crosses border, C follows," and the paper was beginning to separate at the spiral binding.

"Sarah's probably got a hair dryer in her locker," said Eddie.

Harvey eyed the damp paper. "It's pretty fragile. We'd better not push it."

Eddie had picked up Blake's watch. "Still running. Nice watch."

"Yeah, an expensive one," Harvey picked up the thick, plain gold wedding ring. "We can probably take his watch and ring back to Mrs. Blake. She'll want the ring on him for the funeral."

"What's the business card?" Eddie asked.

Harvey picked up the limp card he'd found in Blake's jacket pocket.

"Mervin H. Dawes, attorney at law, Maple Street, Belfast." A thought struck him, and he looked at the reunion guest list. "Bingo. He was at the reunion. An old classmate. Blake probably got his card there."

Eddie bent to look over his shoulder at the list. "Hey, check this out." He pointed to the name David R. Murphy.

"The congressman?" Harvey asked.

"Last time I checked."

"So, the class has some pretty distinguished alumni."

"Murphy lives in Portland." Eddie straightened. "Congress isn't in session, so we should be able to get hold of him."

Harvey folded the list and put it in his pocket, then put the effects back in the manila envelope. "I'll get this back to Evidence."

His phone beeped. Jennifer.

"Hi. Are you ready for lunch?" she asked.

He smiled hugely. Eddie smiled too.

"Yeah, I'll meet you downstairs," Harvey said.

Eddie left to get an outside table at the café down the block, and Harvey went to the ground floor and logged the envelope back in, but permanently logged out Blake's watch and ring. He met Jennifer on the stairs that led to the basement.

"Hey, gorgeous!" He kissed her.

"Harvey, they have security cameras in here." She looked up toward the landing above them.

"So?" Jennifer was modest, and a bit insecure. He put up with it. "Eddie's getting us a table." They went up to the landing, down the hall, and past the front desk.

"How are things in Records?"

"I'm starting to get used to it," she said. "There's a lot to remember."

He held the door for her, and they stepped out into the June sun. Jennifer wore a blue linen blazer over a print dress. Her long, blonde hair hung down her back in a braid. On her left hand was the diamond Harvey had bought her two weeks before. She was always good to look at, and he grabbed her hand, hoping everybody in the department saw them.

Jennifer smiled when she saw Eddie sitting in front of the café, where they had tables out on the brick sidewalk. A cute waitress stood talking to him. The girls all liked Eddie. He was sweet and unassuming, despite his killer good looks. Jennifer liked him immensely, now that she knew him, but she realized Harvey sometimes had to rein in his young partner's wandering attention. Still, Eddie's devotion to Harvey was a comfort to her. Being in love with a police officer was new and a bit frightening, but she worried less about Harvey when Eddie was with him.

"Hey, Larson," a man in uniform called, and Harvey returned the greeting.

She was getting used to the stares she and Harvey got when they were together in the vicinity of the police station. It had bothered her at first. Harvey was modest and self-effacing, but he had a lot of friends, and apparently they were fascinated when he started dating again after his ex-wife died.

"Hey, Jennifer!" Eddie's smile was irresistible, and she forgot the stares.

"Hi!"

Harvey pulled out a chair for her between him and Eddie. They chose their sandwiches and drinks, and the waitress went inside.

"New waitress?" Harvey asked.

"Couple of weeks."

Harvey shrugged. He wouldn't notice a new waitress unless she was a witness to a crime, but Eddie always did.

Eddie leaned toward her. "So, Jennifer, how are the wedding plans coming?"

"Pretty good. We're supposed to get the invitations by the end of the week." She turned to Harvey. "We need to work on the guest list." The wedding was set for July 17, less than four weeks away. She'd agreed to a short engagement before she realized how much work she would have to squeeze into the intervening weeks.

Harvey said, "How about if I come over tonight and we work on it?"

"Great." Jennifer grinned. "Beth will be there."

"Haven't seen your roommate for a while," said Eddie. Beth was a pretty young kindergarten teacher with shoulder-length dark hair and a great smile.

"It's her last week of school, and she's been really busy," Jennifer told him. Not the best time to invite Eddie over. Their sandwiches came, and they started to eat. Mentally, she ran down her to-do list. "We need to order the wedding cake, too."

"Just get whatever you want." Harvey took a bite of his sandwich.

"It's not that simple," she said. "There are all kinds of options."

"Chocolate," said Eddie.

"No, not chocolate!" Harvey scowled at Eddie. "And no little bride and groom on top."

Jennifer gulped. "Well, what do you want then?"

"I don't care."

"Yes, you do," she said carefully. "You just said no chocolate, and no little bride and groom."

He was silent for a moment, then smiled sheepishly. "Okay, so anything but that."

"Could you go by the baker's after work with me?" She hated to ask him to get involved in the wedding minutiae when he was so busy, but when their wedding day came she wanted everything to be right. She didn't want to embarrass him, even a little, in front of all his friends and relatives.

"Okay, and then we'll go to your place and work on the guest list."

She smiled in relief. "The bakery is down on Exchange Street. Patricia Lundquist."

Harvey blinked. "Lundquist?" He pulled a sheet of paper from his pocket. "Michael and Patricia Lundquist, Exchange Street, Portland. One of them was Blake's classmate."

"You're kidding," said Eddie.

"What?" Jennifer looked from Harvey to Eddie and back.

"She's on a list of people we need to question about the homicide we're working," Harvey said. "She and her husband were at the deceased's class reunion yesterday."

Eddie shrugged. "Coincidence."

"I'll ask Mrs. Lundquist a few questions after we sample the cake," Harvey said. "You take the jewelry to the widow, Ed, then start calling other reunion guests and ask if they talked to the victim yesterday. I'll try to get a preliminary autopsy report and hold the press conference at three."

"You're holding a press conference?" Jennifer felt a little lost. She wasn't sure yet how much he would share with her about his work once they were married, but the mention of a press conference leaped out at her. Harvey hated dealing with the media.

"Yes, our dead guy is famous, and I have to."

"Who is it? Or am I allowed to ask?"

Harvey looked at Eddie, and he lifted his shoulders. "It's going to be public knowledge in a couple of hours anyway," Eddie said.

"Martin Blake," Harvey told her, and sipped his coffee.

She stared at him. "Martin Blake? You're not serious."

"Yup."

"Oh, no, not Martin Blake." She couldn't understand how he could be so nonchalant about it.

"You a fan of his?" asked Eddie.

34

"Yeah, I've read several of his books, and he's a great writer. And he has a huge readership. Everybody loves him. He's always giving money for something, like the park, or the university, or the hospital. Most people who get rich leave the state and don't put their money back into Maine like he does."

"Did," said Eddie.

Jennifer grimaced.

"So, which of his books have you read?" Harvey took out his notebook and a pen.

Jennifer thought about it. *"West of Buckfield, The Irish Sun, Time Adrift, Morristown.* That's my favorite."

"Morristown?" He was writing quickly.

"Yes, it was his first book. They say it's his best. I think so. Of course, I haven't read them all. But it's about Maine. I know they're all well researched, but in *Morristown,* you know he lived there."

"I wonder if Morristown is Portland incognito," Harvey said.

"Maybe. It's a coastal town." She thought about it. "It's smaller than the real Portland, but it could be, I suppose. He grew up here." She swallowed hard. "Am I a witness?"

Harvey laughed. "No, gorgeous, just an informant." He leaned over and kissed her on the cheek, and she glanced around quickly as her face heated.

Eddie grinned at her. Apparently his life was a lot easier when Harvey was happy.

Back at his desk, Harvey called the medical examiner. Several designated M.E.'s shared the work within the state, with the chief one located in Augusta. Harvey reached the office of the Portland one, Dr. McIntyre, who had been out at the scene that morning.

"You'll have to call Augusta," the receptionist said.

"The body went there?" Harvey asked.

"Celebrities always do. Dr. McIntyre's up there with the chief M.E., doing the autopsy."

Harvey called Augusta, and after a short hold, Dr. McIntyre came on the line. "Can't tell you much yet, Larson. Sorry."

"I know, but I have to give a press conference at three."

"Well, he was stabbed once, and it punctured his right lung. He was still breathing when he hit the water. Cause of death, drowning, but the knife wound could have killed him, unless he'd gotten help immediately."

"So, he went into the water right after he was stabbed."

"I'd say so."

"Time of death?"

"Tentatively, between ten and midnight last night."

"Someone saw him alive around ten-thirty," Harvey said.

"Okay, between ten-thirty and midnight, then. That's all I can give you now. I'll fax you the official report when we're finished. We're expediting this one, but it may be a few days. We're being thorough, as you can imagine."

"All right. Tox screens?"

"Oh, yes, all of that, but it takes time."

Harvey thanked him and hung up, then went over his notes and wrote a few sentences in preparation for the press conference.

Mrs. Blake had given him the family attorney's name, and Harvey called and made an appointment for nine o'clock the next morning. Then he called Blake's agent. Mrs. Blake had notified Bob Hoffsted. He would come to the police station office at 11 a.m. the next day. Harvey's schedule for Tuesday was filling up.

Mike came to his desk. "How you doing, Harvey?"

"Pretty well. The M.E. says Blake was stabbed, but probably drowned."

"Did you go over that bridge? If you wait, any evidence will be gone."

"The techs were on it this morning. I looked around early, and I tagged a spot that could have been blood."

Nate and Tony came in.

"How did it go?" Harvey asked.

37

Nate said, "Someone else saw Blake through a window, a block over."

"What time?"

"He says quarter to eleven, but he wasn't sure. Then we may have lucked out with a woman who lives in Stroudwater. She was driving home last night, and she saw two men standing on the bridge, talking."

"Did she identify Blake?"

"Not exactly," Nate replied. "She said at first she had no idea who they were, but after I showed her Blake's picture, she said it could have been him. The other man had his back to her, and all she could say was that he was shorter than the one whose face she saw and had on dark clothes. Short hair, nothing that stood out in her mind. The taller guy was middle-aged, she said. No beard, no glasses. She really didn't describe him very well, but she said it could be Blake."

"And what time was this?" Harvey asked.

"She said she got home at 10:55. She's sure about that. She would have crossed the bridge about two minutes earlier. It's only a few blocks."

"All right, good work."

Tony Winfield had stood quietly, listening to Nate recite the facts.

"Tony's the one who found her," Nate said. "I didn't want to take the inquiry that far, but he said we'd ought to keep on, and that people who lived over there had to cross the bridge. He was right."

Harvey nodded. "Good work, Winfield. Did you guys get lunch yet?"

"No, sir," said Tony.

"Okay, go eat, then I need you to get back on it. And make sure the techs got any trash that was on the bridge."

Harvey put in a request for a warrant for Martin Blake's computer, even though Thelma had given him verbal carte blanche. It was getting close to time for the press conference. He went to the locker room and shaved and put on a tie.

The press conference was brutal. Eddie came in as the reporters were filling the foyer, and Harvey had him stand close by. Just as he began speaking, Mike came down the stairs and stood by the wall with his arms folded.

Most of the reporters already knew Blake was dead. The police had questioned so many people that day that word had gotten out. Harvey described the discovery of the body and presented Dr. McIntyre's limited information, stressing that it was preliminary and the final autopsy report might contain different data. Then the questions started.

"Do you know who killed Blake?"

"We're actively investigating every lead, and we'd like to speak with anyone who saw Mr.

Blake after nine o'clock last night," Harvey said.

"Has the family been notified?"

"Yes. Mrs. Blake is making arrangements, and her children are coming in as soon as possible."

"When is the funeral?"

"I don't have that information yet."

"Are the police protecting the crime scene?"

"We don't know where the crime took place." He winced. He shouldn't have let that slip. He didn't want to mention the tentative blood smear he'd found, but he explained to them that Blake's body was found in the estuary and might have entered the water at a different point during the night.

"Have you found the murder weapon?"

"I can't discuss that."

"Do you have a suspect?"

"I can't say."

"How about witnesses?"

"We have a few witnesses, and we're working on finding more."

"Anything to indicate the motive?"

"It's too early for that."

"Who benefits by Martin Blake's death?"

Harvey looked over at Mike. He was just leaning against the wall with his arms folded up tight, watching. They locked eyes, and Mike shook his head just a little.

"I don't have that information."

He decided it was time to shut off the questions.

"Do you expect an arrest soon?"

"As soon as possible," Harvey said. "And I think—"

"Do the police have anyone in custody?"

"No. That's it for now. When we have more information to share, we'll notify you."

They shouted more questions, but Harvey didn't answer. Mike turned toward the stairway and punched the keypad by the door. By the time Harvey reached it, he had the door open. Eddie and Harvey went through and Mike followed, closing the security door behind him. They went silently up two flights of stairs. When they got into the Priority Unit office, Harvey sat down at his desk. He rubbed his chin with one hand, then looked up at Mike.

"Not too bad," Mike said.

"I shouldn't have said anything about the crime scene."

"It's awfully hard not to get rattled. You did okay." He slapped Harvey on the shoulder and walked away.

Chapter 3

Harvey typed up all his notes from the day and wrote his official report. He was just about to leave it on Mike's desk when Nate and Tony came back.

"We didn't learn anything new," Nate said. "The techs had already picked up a bag of trash off the sidewalk and they said they'd log it in."

"Good." Harvey rubbed the back of his neck. "You guys can go home, but report to me after roll call tomorrow, okay? I'll fix it with Terry."

He went searching for Mike.

"That bridge looks like a good possibility," he told the captain. "No sign of activity at the park. Should I ask for divers? We don't have a weapon."

"It's a long shot, but, yeah, you might as well try."

The divers couldn't do it that night; by the time the men and equipment got there, the light wouldn't be good. Tuesday morning was the best he could get.

Time to meet Jennifer for the cake foray. Eddie went down the stairs with him.

"Hey, Harvey," said Terry Lemieux, the day

patrol sergeant. He was heading from the foyer toward the parking garage, keys in his hand.

"Hi, Terry."

"You did okay with the press conference."

"Thanks," Harvey said. "Could have been better."

"Oh, well, could have been worse. Say, have you seen the new girl in Records?"

Eddie and Harvey looked at each other.

"We've seen her," said Eddie.

"Some looker, hey?"

Harvey said, "She's my fiancée."

"No! Really?"

"Really."

"Hey, congratulations! You're really getting married?" Terry looked at Eddie. "He's not pulling my leg, is he? I thought Harvey was a confirmed bachelor."

"He's getting married, and I'm the best man," said Eddie. "I have to wear a tux."

"No kidding. Is everyone invited? When's the wedding?"

"July seventeenth," Harvey said. "Sure, everyone's invited. I'll stick an invitation on the bulletin board."

Eddie and Terry went toward the garage, and Harvey started punching the keypad at the basement door, where the stairs went down to Records and Human Resources and all those other windowless underground offices. He got the code wrong, which happened too often, and was starting over when the door opened and Jennifer came out.

She smiled, but wouldn't let him kiss her in the foyer. "Are you ready for some cake?"

"Guess so." He took her hand and headed for the garage.

In her car, she handed him a piece of paper.

"What's this?"

"A list of things we really need to talk about tonight."

He looked at it. Cake, guest list, apartment, honeymoon, vows, tuxedoes, motels for guests.

"Okay," he said. "We're having the tuxes fitted tomorrow after work."

"Great. Cross that off."

"Maybe I should wait. Mike and Eddie will go, but I'm not sure Carl will make it. He might have an emergency appendectomy or something." Carl was Harvey's doctor, and also his friend. Harvey had recruited him and Mike as groomsmen.

She drove over to Exchange Street and pulled into a parallel parking spot. The street sloped down toward the Old Port and the harbor. The stores were old brick buildings, each with its own style of window arches. The varied brickwork patterns satisfied something in Harvey. Jennifer led him down the sidewalk to a bakery with doughnuts and a flag-striped cake in the window. A bell rang as he opened the door. Inside, the air smelled sweet and yeasty. Patricia Lundquist was putting things away for the night, getting ready to close shop.

"Jennifer?" she said brightly.

"Yes, and this is my fiancé, Harvey Larson."

Patricia eyed the badge on his jacket. "Portland P.D."

"That's right," Harvey said.

She smiled. "When the groom comes in, I know he wants to taste the cake."

"I don't care, really. Whatever Jennifer wants, as long as it doesn't taste like cardboard."

Jennifer looked a little embarrassed. "I need some help deciding on the decorations. One of us has an antipathy to little bride and groom cake toppers."

Patricia laughed and took them through a door at the back of the shop, through a professional kitchen with huge ovens, broad butcher block islands, and lots of stainless steel, into a smaller office. They all sat down, and she brought out a three-ring binder and opened it to display pictures of wedding cakes.

"I've got photos of about two dozen styles of cakes I've done. Take a look at the pictures and see if there's something that appeals to you. If not, give me your ideas and I'll tell you if I can do it."

Jennifer flipped the plastic pages slowly, studying creations with frosting flowers and columns and plastic doves and teddy bear brides and grooms.

"This one," she said at last. "What do you think?" She held it out to Harvey.

It was a simple cake, compared to some, four square layers, with fancy frosting that looked like braid on the edges, and flowers that looked real on the top and at the corners of each layer.

"Looks fine," he said.

"All white frosting, and flowers to match my bouquet," said Jennifer.

"What will be in your bouquet?" Patricia asked, writing on a tablet.

"I don't know yet." Jennifer looked at Harvey. He shrugged.

"Just let me know as soon as you can. And how many people will you be serving?"

Jennifer looked at him. He shrugged again.

She smiled apologetically. "I'm not exactly sure. We were going to finalize the guest list tonight. Could I call you tomorrow with an estimate?"

The two women discussed the decorations, the date, time and location, and two dollars a slice. Pretty expensive cake. At last, Patricia went into the kitchen and came back with two plates, each of which held three small slices of wedding cake, white, yellow, and chocolate.

"Dessert first tonight." Harvey picked up his

plastic fork and tried the white cake. It tasted much better than cardboard. The chocolate wasn't bad, either.

Jennifer was saying, "Harvey prefers that we don't have chocolate."

"Well, this chocolate is pretty good," he said. Jennifer stared at him in shock. He couldn't help laughing. "I'm sorry. Get whatever you want."

She nodded, smiling. "Maybe we can have one chocolate layer and the rest white."

"Of course," said Patricia. She wrote it down. "So, it's all set. Just call me by Friday with the number of guests and the final choice for flowers to match your bouquet."

"Pink roses," Harvey said.

Jennifer turned and stared at him.

"Pink and white for your bouquet, pink for the cake," he said. "Unless . . . you'd rather have something else?"

"No, I'd love that." A smile spread across Jennifer's face, and he knew he'd said the right thing for a change.

"Okay." Patricia wrote it down.

Jennifer stood, so he did, too.

"May I ask you something, Mrs. Lundquist?" he asked.

"Certainly, Harvey, and call me Patricia." They were all on a first-name basis now that they'd survived the cake crisis.

"Were you a classmate of Martin Blake's?"

"Yes. How did you know?"

"Unfortunately, I've had to investigate Mr. Blake's death today."

"His death? Martin is dead? But I just saw him yesterday."

"Yes, ma'am." In his official capacity, Harvey dropped back into the formal mode. "That would be at the high school reunion at Fort Point."

"Yes." Her face was as pale as the white wedding cake. "What happened to Martin?"

"Apparently he went home last night, then took a walk and got himself killed."

"Was he hit by a car?"

"No, ma'am. It was homicide."

"Oh, dear. Poor Thelma."

"Yes. I'm in charge of the investigation."

"I see."

"That's not why I came here—I mean, we really do need the wedding cake—but I saw on the list of reunion guests that you and your husband were present, and I thought maybe I could ask you a couple of questions."

"Of course." She sat down on a stool. Jennifer and Harvey resumed their seats.

"Did you talk to Martin Blake at the reunion?" he asked.

"Yes. He and Thelma were both there. Thelma was all gussied up in a sailor top and navy blue Capris and a red wig. She seemed to think the picnic was a little rustic. Martin was great.

He's so down to earth. I see him here in town sometimes, and he's always friendly."

"Do you see them socially?"

"Not really. Michael and I are very busy, and I'm sure the Blakes have their own circle. I run into them once in a while."

"Do you read Martin Blake's books?"

"Always. Our class is very proud of him."

"What did you talk to him about yesterday?"

"Oh, the usual catching up things. The children. I did ask him when his next book will be out. He said in the fall. It's a story about Mexico and California."

"*Border Feud*?"

"That sounds right."

"Is your husband Michael also a member of the class?"

"No, he's from New Jersey. It was members and spouses yesterday. Thelma's not a Portland High alumna, either. She grew up in Farmington."

Harvey took his notebook out and began writing. "Did Mr. Blake have any sharp words with anyone?"

"Not that I know of. Martin is pretty easygoing. I've never seen him fight with anyone, not even Thelma."

"Is there anything about the reunion that sticks out in your mind?"

"Well, David Murphy was there. A lot of people were talking politics with David."

"How about Martin?"

"He's quieter. He talks one-on-one, but doesn't usually hold forth to a throng like David does."

Harvey nodded. "Anything else that you think might help me?"

She frowned. "I can't think of anything." She gave him her business card for the bakery. Harvey gave her his.

"Call me if you or Mr. Lundquist have anything to add."

They parted cordially, and Jennifer promised to call the next day about the cake.

Jennifer called her roommate, Beth Bradley, and alerted her that there would be three for dinner. When she and Harvey arrived at the house together, Beth had beef stew and biscuits cooking. Harvey took off his jacket and tie and sat down at the kitchen table while Jennifer helped Beth lay the place settings.

He looked tired, which was no surprise. Jennifer was tired, too. The long day on the new job had worn her out. Compared to the upscale software design firm where she'd worked previously, the police station was noisy and hectic. Beth looked as though she needed to sleep off the entire school year.

"Time for the news." Beth turned on a small TV that sat on the kitchen counter.

"Harvey doesn't like to watch himself," Jennifer said.

"Oh, sorry." Beth reached to turn it off.

"Maybe I'd better today," Harvey said, so she left it on. Martin Blake's death was the lead story. They all sat at the table and watched. The editors had obviously cropped the tape and used two clips, one of Harvey's initial statement and one of him saying, "We don't know where the crime took place." He groaned.

"What's wrong?" asked Beth. "You look great." The reporter was going into a retrospect of Blake's life and gushing over his books, from *Morristown* to the unfinished Mexico book, due out in the fall.

"I shouldn't have said we don't know where he was killed," Harvey said.

"But if it's true . . ."

"It just gives the press a chance to make us look incompetent."

Jennifer squeezed his hand in sympathy. Harvey wasn't concerned about his own image, but making the police department look good was important to him.

He ate appreciatively, but Jennifer could tell he hadn't gotten over the news broadcast. After the meal, she settled on the living room couch with him and her bridal planner, to work on the guest list. She was determined to make the tedious process as quick and painless as possible for him.

"All right, relatives first. Your two sisters and their families."

Harvey nodded. "And Aunt Linda and Uncle Robert, and Aunt Billie—"

"Aunt Billie?"

"Well, her name is really Agatha, but no one calls her that. And my cousins. Let's see, Stewart, Peter, Melvin, Anna, Heather and Gary."

"Do you have addresses?"

"I'll have to call my sister Gina."

"Okay, why don't you just have her send all the addresses to me?"

"Good idea." He wrote himself a note.

"Now, what about friends?"

"Carl and Margaret. And Grandma Lewis. She may not be able to come, but I want to invite her." She was Harvey's first wife's grandmother, and Jennifer knew he was fond of her, although he didn't see her often.

"Do you want to invite Tim Lewis?" He'd told her about Carrie's younger brother.

"No, we haven't kept in touch. I'll just let Grandma tell him about the wedding."

"Old school friends?" she asked.

"Hmm . . . I don't think so. It's been so long. But I would like to invite my neighbors, the Jenkins family."

"Sure." Jennifer knew Mrs. Jenkins. The family had the apartment below Harvey's.

"And all the Thibodeaus. Eddie's folks are always good to me."

She wrote it down.

"And the P.D. Do you think I can just post it on the bulletin board?"

She tried to keep her jaw from dropping while she processed that. "That will make it hard to count cake slices. Will they RSVP?"

"Some will. Most won't. But we're both working there now, and the guys downstairs are already asking me about it."

"Okay," she said, against her better judgment. "But you'll want to give individual invitations to the men in your unit. Mike and Eddie are in the wedding, but give them one, anyway, and Arnie and Pete. Anyone else who needs their own?"

"How about Sarah Benoit?" She had been to the lighthouse on a double date with them and Eddie.

"All right," Jennifer said. "Who else?"

"Nate Miller and Jimmy Cook. Maybe Tony Winfield. He's on this investigation with me. Guess we'll see how things are when it's time to mail the invitations."

"How about the chief?"

"The police chief?" Harvey looked surprised at her suggestion.

"Sure."

"He goes to all the men's funerals, but I don't know about weddings."

"Well, we don't want to insult him by not inviting him."

Harvey frowned. "Maybe I should ask Mike about that." He made himself another note.

They went on through his part of the list. Their church would get a blanket invitation, except for a few special friends they had made there in the last month. Pastor Rowland was doing the ceremony, and the reception would be held in the church hall.

Beth, their unofficial chaperone, had been working on her cross stitching while she listened to them. She got up and folded her handwork. "I'm sorry, you guys, but I'm really tired. I'm going to get ready for bed."

"When do you get out of school?" Harvey asked.

"By three o'clock Thursday, I should be free for the summer."

"Sounds like paradise," Harvey said. "I hope things go smoothly for you until then."

"Thanks." She said goodnight and headed down the hallway.

Harvey looked at his watch. "Guess I'd better get going." He still sat there, eyeing Jennifer uncertainly.

"Don't go yet," she begged, although Harvey had deep shadows beneath his eyes. "We don't know how many people the cake has to feed, and I promised Patricia I'd call her tomorrow."

He seized her hand and kissed her fingertips. "Get your list out, gorgeous."

Jennifer had already pondered over her list. It included a large extended family, a few old friends in the Skowhegan area, and some former coworkers. They tried to count a total, but with the uncertain numbers from the church and the police department, it was hard. They hadn't been at Victory Baptist Church long, so she doubted all the church people would come, but a lot of the cops might show up with their wives and girlfriends.

Harvey sighed wearily. "Guess you'd better be prepared for two hundred. If only half that come, we'll freeze the leftover cake and eat it all summer."

"What if three hundred come?" she asked. It was entirely possible, given the size of the congregation and the city's police force.

"We're not paying six hundred dollars for a cake."

"My father's paying for it."

"Well then, George isn't paying six hundred dollars for a cake."

"But if there's not enough—"

"There will be. There's always cake left over. Half the people who go to the wedding won't eat it."

"Think so?"

"Know so. Diabetics, people on diets . . ."

She nodded hesitantly.

55

"Couldn't you have just gotten one of the church ladies to make us a cake?" he asked.

"No. They're all willing to make salads and finger sandwiches and help serve at the reception, but nobody there seems to make cakes professionally."

Angela Williams at the church was heading up the food committee for the wedding, and Jennifer's parents were footing the bill. It was going to be a lot cheaper than a caterer, but she knew Harvey was still thinking about her father paying all that money for a cake.

"We still have the list of topics that we need to make decisions on." She hated bringing it up, but Harvey didn't complain. He found the list in his jacket pocket and squinted at it.

"Cake, guest list, and tuxedoes are covered. That leaves apartment, honeymoon, vows, and motels for guests." His brow furrowed. "Do we have to do all this tonight?"

"Well . . . Maybe we can go over what we want for vows with Pastor Rowland Friday night when we have the counseling." They had attended one premarital counseling session and were scheduled for the next three Friday evenings.

"Great. And I can make a list of motels on the computer. You can mail them to out-of-state guests with the invitations, or is that tacky?"

"No, I think it's okay," she said. "That would help me a lot."

He nodded. "So now we're down to apartment and honeymoon. What does *apartment* mean?"

She stared at him. "It means, where are we going to live?"

"Oh."

She swallowed and wished she hadn't brought it up, but they had to decide. "Beth would like to keep the house, but she said if you and I want it, she'll find another place. I'd hate to make her move out, though, when she just moved in."

She watched him anxiously. He glanced around, and she could almost read his thoughts. The little rental house was characterless, a box in a ho-hum neighborhood. The kitchen cabinets were stained plywood, and the bathroom fixtures were old and water stained. He'd never criticized it, but she couldn't imagine it as his home.

"Do you want to keep living here?" he asked.

"Not really. So, what do we do? Move into your apartment?"

"No way."

She bit her lip and waited. He had lived in his apartment for fifteen years, since the days of his first marriage. The thought of living with him in the same place Carrie had made him miserable troubled her, and she knew it would bother him even worse.

"I think we should get a new place," he said at last. "Neutral territory, so to speak."

She exhaled. "Okay, but that's going to take time. Our schedule is already jammed."

"Well, I don't want to live in the apartment with you." His blue eyes were grave and pleading.

"Me either." She put her hand on his, and he slid his arm around her. Nobody said Carrie's name, but she was there.

"So, I guess we check the classifieds," he said.

"For a new apartment?"

"Yes. But I hope we can find something that's not too far from Eddie." He and his partner ran together three days a week and carpooled to work.

"That's fine. Wherever you want."

"Let's not go through that routine again," he said.

"What do you mean?" Jennifer asked.

"Well, I did it to you on the cake, and it turned out I had stronger opinions than I'd realized."

She smiled. "I mean it. I'll be happy with you, wherever we land."

He looked deep into her eyes. "Jenny, where we live will be important to you, especially when the summer's over and you're not working. You'll be home a lot more than I am. I want it to be a place you like." He kissed her, and she clung to him.

"Okay, then we should look together," she whispered.

"I think so." He straightened suddenly and looked at her with more animation than he'd shown all evening. "It doesn't have to be an apartment. We could buy a house."

"On your salary?"

"I have some money. My stocks."

He had mentioned his investments to Jennifer before, in a modest way.

"You mean we could make a down payment?"

"Sure. Or, depending on how much the house was . . ."

She cuddled in against his shoulder. "Well, I guess we could look, if you think we should."

"I think I'd like to have a house of our own to come home to."

"That sounds good. I'll see if I can find a real estate agent who can show us houses after work one of these days."

"What's left on the list?" he asked.

"The honeymoon."

"I thought that was my department." He smiled, and her heart lurched.

"That's fine, as long as you have time to plan it."

Two days after he'd bought her the ring, he'd started paperwork on a passport for her. Just in case, he'd told her. Jennifer had had a passport as a teenager, for family trips to Quebec and Prince Edward Island, but it had expired.

He had his already, because he flew on business occasionally. Mike had sent him to Montreal the previous winter, and to Paris two years earlier for a week-long session on sharing international crime data via computer. He claimed he'd loved the conference, hated Paris, and she hadn't pressed him for details. It was during the time he'd been depressed and drank heavily, and she'd believed him when he said he never wanted to see Paris again.

A crafty glint came into his eyes. "I have some ideas for a trip."

"Fantastic. Do I really need a passport?"

"Well, that depends. I thought we'd better have it ready, but I'm not sure it will come through in time. Although I did request to have it expedited."

That probably cost him more than she wanted to know about.

"Okay," Jennifer said. "I'll leave it to you."

He smiled wider, and the corners of his eyes crinkled as he leaned in for another kiss.

He left soon after, and Jennifer headed for bed. She drifted off to sleep thinking about Martin Blake. The most famous man in Maine was dead, and it was up to her fiancé to find the killer.

Harvey was known as a relentless detective who wouldn't give up. He rarely left a case unclosed. But that could take time. Harvey had more patience than anyone else she knew, but if he couldn't find Blake's murderer before the wedding, would he still want to take time off? She tried to banish it from her mind. Pink and white roses in her bouquet—that was a more pleasant train of thought.

Chapter 4

Tuesday, June 22

Harvey drove by the bridge Tuesday morning, and the divers were in the water. So far they hadn't turned up anything but trash, so he and Eddie went on to the office. Harvey entered the names of all the high school reunion guests into his computer. Jennifer had written a flagging program for him that would notify him if any of those names appeared in city, county, or state law enforcement reports.

He was due at the lawyer's office at nine o'clock, so he left Eddie with the reunion list, to start calling Blake's classmates and see if they could shed any light on the situation.

Harvey walked into Chester and Clayfield's law office on Forest Avenue. Upscale old brick building with bay windows and fancy molding. Edwin N. Clayfield honored him with an appointment. He was the senior partner, white-haired and paunchy.

"I have an appointment with the family on Thursday, after the funeral, to go over Mr. Blake's will with them," he told Harvey.

Harvey nodded soberly. "Thank you for agreeing to give me a preview."

"Well, in view of the homicide investigation . . ." Clayfield pressed his lips together and opened a folder. "Of course, this is confidential."

"Of course." Harvey poised his pen to write.

"Martin left several bequests to his favorite charities," Clayfield said. "Two hundred thousand dollars to the local Humane Society—he was always an animal lover. Five hundred thousand to the medical center for its cardiac unit, and fifty thousand to the local senior citizens' center."

A writers' colony up the coast was getting another fifty grand, and the Portland Public Library half a million. Blake's son and daughter would each inherit an even million outright, and Thelma got the rest.

The rest? Clayfield was vague, but estimated forty million.

"That's a big chunk of change," Harvey said.

"Oh, Mr. Blake's books were highly successful. He got a million-dollar advance for the last one, and five million for the movie rights to *The Irish Sun* last year. With good handling, he piled up quite a lot, as you can see."

Harvey saw, all right. What he saw was motives. Big ones. But they didn't seem to fit the crime. He couldn't picture the librarian knifing Blake so they'd get the money for the library quicker.

Back at the office, Eddie briefed him on the Blake classmates he had questioned. They had all talked to Martin Blake at the reunion, some more and some less. Blake had been friendly to everyone. The Belfast lawyer had talked to him quite a bit and given Blake his business card. They had been friends in school, and they'd talked about old teachers and things they had done together after school, riding bikes and digging clams.

It was almost time for Blake's agent to arrive. Harvey brought in his e-mail and checked the crime updates. No flags came up.

Terry got off the elevator with the agent, Robert Hoffsted. Harvey introduced himself and ushered him into the interview room. It was a small room with a rectangular table and four chairs, a couple of cheap prints on the walls, and a video camera near the ceiling in one corner. The large mirror was one-way glass, and a tiny observation room the size of a pantry was next door. They used the interview room for questioning suspects and witnesses. Harvey got right to the point.

"Mr. Hoffsted, I understand that you handled most of Martin Blake's contracts and book marketing for him."

"I handle the contracts and any business with his publisher," Hoffsted said. "He has a publicist for the marketing."

"I see. Can you tell me about the new book that was supposed to be published in the fall?"

"You mean *Border Feud*. He signed the contract

last year. It was their standard language—no surprises. The book will be published on schedule."

"Really?"

"Yes, the manuscript was complete, if a bit unpolished. Martin had worked on it for eight months, and the rough draft was in hand two weeks ago. He had been making some revisions. His publisher will take it as is, make any corrections that are obviously needed, and send it to press. It should sell very well."

"And his widow will get the royalties?"

"Yes."

"What do you get?"

"Fifteen percent—the industry standard."

They talked for a while, and Hoffsted gave Harvey more information on their working relationship and the publicist's name and contact information, so Harvey could touch base with her if he wanted. When he left, Harvey joined Eddie in calling more reunion guests.

Jennifer waited patiently beside Harvey's desk. He was talking on the phone, his back to her. When he hung up, she touched his shoulder lightly, and he swung around.

He jumped up with a smile. "Hey, gorgeous, lunch time already?" He leaned toward her, but when she shot a glance toward Mike's desk, he drew back. She didn't like disappointing him, but there were half a dozen other people in the room, and it really didn't seem appropriate to let him kiss her in front of his boss.

"You want to go someplace?" he asked.

"There's not really time. We'd better stick with the café."

They walked down the stairs together.

"Jeff called," Jennifer said. Her brother Jeffrey had been in Portland the week before to interview and test for a fire department job. He was an EMT in Skowhegan and wanted to move south. He had stayed at Harvey's apartment for two nights, and they'd become good friends.

"What did he say?" Harvey asked. "Did he get it?"

"He doesn't know yet. They called him to come interview again Thursday."

"When's he coming down?"

"Tomorrow night. I told him to call you. Maybe he can stay over with you?"

"Sure."

"He said they've narrowed it down to six, for the two spots." There had been about fifty applicants taking the practical test when Jeff did.

"Hey, that's great. Sounds hopeful."

At the bottom of the stairs, Jennifer reached out hesitantly and touched his sleeve.

"Harvey, I love you."

He turned toward her with a melting smile and slipped his arm around her waist, pulling her close. Suddenly she wished the cake and invitations and florists' appointments were behind them.

"I love you, too." He brushed her forehead with his lips. "Can we just relax tonight?"

Jennifer flinched. "You're getting the tuxedoes fitted, remember?"

"Oh, yeah."

"And I'm going to talk to Mom and see if she's got the food and the girls' dresses under control."

"Jenny, I know all this is going to be terrific, but doesn't it seem like we're going to an awful lot of trouble for this wedding?"

"Well . . ." She tried to gauge his mood. Was this just fatigue, or was he annoyed?

"I know you want it to be nice, but you're running yourself ragged." He drew her closer and leaned back against the wall beside the door. She snuggled against his shirt front, trying not to think about the camera up in the corner. Harvey would probably scrap the big wedding gleefully and walk over to city hall to stand in front of a justice of the peace for five minutes. The hectic preparations were his fault, though, for insisting on such a short engagement.

She was quiet for a few seconds, enjoying his warmth and the secure feeling she had when he held her. Then she looked up at him.

"I know it's kind of a headache, but it's important to me. I want to have all our friends there, all the people we love, and I want the church and all the traditional things. Is that okay? I don't want it to be torture for you."

"Yes, of course it's okay." He kissed her tenderly and stroked her hair. "I'll come over tonight after the tux fitting, if you don't mind."

"Yes," she said softly. "Now, come on. We won't have time to eat lunch if we stay here any longer."

As usual, the café was full of cops. Eddie had an outside table with Sarah Benoit and Cheryl Yeaton. Harvey waylaid a waitress and gave their order, and he and Jennifer sat down with the others.

Sarah immediately turned to Jennifer. "So what color are the bridesmaids' gowns?"

"Blue," said Jennifer.

"Oh, nice."

"Can I see your ring?" Cheryl hadn't seen it yet. "Oh, that's beautiful!" Jennifer extended her left hand and admired her ring again. It was a diamond with a small sapphire on each side. Harvey had picked it out, and she loved it.

"What's your dress like?" Sarah asked.

Harvey and Eddie looked at each other. Eddie made a face and resumed eating.

Jennifer described her wedding gown. Harvey took out his pocket notebook and was soon absorbed in notes, sporadically taking bites from his sandwich.

Two patrolmen walked up to the table. Jennifer recognized Nate Miller and the governor's nephew, Tony Winfield.

"The divers were leaving when we got to the bridge," Nate said to Harvey.

"Did they find anything?"

"I don't know. Sorry. Any word from the lab on the blood yet?"

"Not yet," Harvey replied.

Cheryl broke off in midsentence. Jennifer had a moment of slight queasiness.

"Do you guys have to talk about blood while we're eating?" asked Sarah.

"Sorry," Harvey said.

Tony didn't talk. He just smiled at the women.

"So, did you see Ms. Heflin?" Harvey asked Nate.

"Yes. The Blake children arrived last night. The daughter's husband and two children are with her. The funeral will be Thursday at one. And they're upset about not being able to go in the tower room."

"Oh, boy," Harvey said. "I'll go out there this afternoon and talk to them. You guys get some lunch."

"Are you two going to a lighthouse Saturday?" Eddie asked, and Jennifer smiled. At last, a topic they could all enjoy.

She and Harvey had a summer project of visiting the state's old forts and lighthouses.

They had been to Fort Scammell, Fort Williams, Fort Western, Portland Head Light, and Rockland Breakwater Light. The previous Saturday, they had visited Spring Point Ledge Light and Fort Preble. It was a bigger project than they'd realized when they started, and there were more lighthouses and forts than they could possibly get to in one season.

Harvey said, "Funny you should ask. I was just thinking Jennifer and I ought to visit Fort Point."

"The same thought occurred to me," said Eddie.

Jennifer supposed she should have expected it, since their investigation involved a reunion at the park. "Business or pleasure?" she asked.

"Both," Harvey said.

Sarah looked at her watch. "Gotta run. See you, Jennifer." She and Cheryl gathered up their things. Eddie was giving Harvey a hangdog look.

"You think you need to come along on the trip Saturday?" Harvey asked him.

"Wouldn't hurt," Eddie said with a smile.

"Why not?" asked Jennifer. Eddie was always fun on an outing.

Sarah and Cheryl headed for the station.

"Can I bring Sarah?" Eddie asked.

Harvey arched his eyebrows at Jennifer.

"It's okay with me," she said, watching for his reaction.

Eddie went running after Sarah, and Harvey shrugged.

"Did you not want to take them?" Jennifer asked.

"Oh, it's okay. I just like having Saturdays alone with you." They hadn't gone far last week, but they'd had a quiet day together, with time to sit and talk about private things. They would miss that with Eddie and Sarah along. Harvey took her hand and held it under the table.

"Hey, Harvey!" The patrol sergeant stopped at their table, staring at Jennifer.

"Hi, Terry," Harvey said. "My fiancée, Jennifer Wainthrop."

"The new girl in Records, too?"

"That's right. Jennifer, this is Terry Lemieux."

Terry sat down and started talking to Jennifer about the wedding. She almost laughed at Harvey's expression. The poor man couldn't have lunch with his own fiancée without all kinds of people horning in. She would have to see that they had time to get away during the lunch hour tomorrow.

Harvey drove to Westbrook Road to see Thelma Blake, leaving Nate, Tony, and Eddie to call more of Martin's classmates.

He had to spend five minutes or so commiserating with Thelma and listening to the funeral plans. She thanked him for sending Martin's jewelry over by Eddie.

70

"I need to get into the tower room to get some papers from Martin's files to send to the insurance company."

Harvey apologized for not thinking of that and took her upstairs.

When she'd located the papers she needed, Harvey glanced through them.

"That's fine, Mrs. Blake." They went out, and while Harvey replaced the tape on the door, she went downstairs.

He tried to comprehend what Thelma had lost—her life companion, her husband of nearly thirty years, her place as the wife of a prestigious author, her source of income. Of course, forty million wasn't bad, and with care, it should last her.

But still, he couldn't see that she gained anything from his death. By all accounts so far, the Blakes had gotten along well, and Martin had been generous in sharing his wealth with her and their two children.

Harvey met the son when he went downstairs. Martin, Junior. Marty, they called him. He was tall and favored his father, with wavy brown hair and direct brown eyes. He spoke slowly, with a voice that might break at any moment. Harvey left, more conscious of the brevity of life and more determined than ever to build his own family while he had a chance.

He got back to the office later than he'd

intended. Eddie met him with significance bursting from his eyes.

"Look what the divers found." He nodded toward an evidence bag on Harvey's desk.

It was an old Buck hunting knife, a nice one, with a four-inch blade that had been sharpened a lot over the years. It had lodged below the bridge, its tip between two rocks beneath the surface. The divers had found it when they'd just about decided to give up. No fingerprints. He looked it over closely through the plastic, then sent it down to the lab.

Eddie had talked to more of the classmates and came up with one interesting exchange. A woman from Camden had heard Blake say to David Murphy, the congressman, something like, "I know all your secrets." She said Murphy got a strange look on his face when Blake said that.

Harvey was still mulling that over when Jeff Wainthrop called, saying he expected to arrive around 6 p.m. Wednesday. He was excited about the job interview, and Harvey hoped he would get it.

"Great, Jeff. I'll be there when you get here, and we can go over to Jennifer's after you unload."

Next, he called the home of the honorable David Murphy, but was told that the congressman was unavailable.

He and Eddie were on the phone for hours, chasing people down at their desks, in their cars, and in stores. They pulled one teacher from a classroom and a horse trainer from the barn.

"Makes me feel unwanted, bothering all these people," Eddie said.

Harvey nodded. "Don't forget, reporters are probably hounding them, too, looking for a story on Martin Blake's last day, spent with his high school buddies."

The news crews hounded the detectives, too, calling about the autopsy and the divers at the bridge. Terry, downstairs, hadn't given them anything, and Harvey was cagey with the few that got through his screening, but since the diving area was so close to the place where Blake's body was found, the reporters drew the natural conclusion that the police were after evidence in Blake's murder.

Forty-two classmates had gone to the reunion, and twenty-five of those had brought their spouses or dates. The detectives went on down the list, but hadn't talked to half of them by the end of their shift.

"We'd better quit for now and get to the formalwear store," Harvey told Eddie. They were due there at five-thirty, and it was already ten past. Mike was just walking out the door, and Harvey called to him.

"Oh, right," Mike said. "Almost forgot."

Harvey gave Carl's office a quick call, but no one answered. He and Eddie went to the parking garage and followed Mike up the street a couple of blocks, to the store on the corner of Franklin Avenue.

Jennifer had been in the week before and selected the style and color. Considering the outfits he saw on mannequins that day, Harvey decided she hadn't done too badly. No pink cummerbunds or long tails. She'd chosen a conservative, medium gray tux with a black vest, white shirt and black bow tie.

The men gave their sizes, and the clerk got out the outfits and shoes. Carl came in just as they were about to hit the dressing rooms.

Eddie's tux fit perfectly, and he was heartbreaker handsome, but no one said so. Even the clerk's eyes lit up when she saw him in the outfit. Harvey could only imagine what the girls wanting to catch the bouquet would do.

The clerk told Harvey he'd have to come back for another fitting. Great. Just what he needed, another appointment. Mike and Carl got fitted, and they all went out to the parking lot.

"Margaret told me to remind you that you and Jennifer are coming to our house Sunday," Carl said.

Harvey pulled out the pocket planner Jennifer had bought him when she bought her wedding planner. "You're right. If it's in here, it's official." He took out a pen and scribbled in the next fitting for the tux.

"You and Jennifer have every minute planned until the wedding," Eddie said sadly.

"That's right. If you want to see us, you have to make an appointment."

Mike and Carl headed for I-295, and Harvey drove Eddie home. He stopped at the grocery store and bought a few things, then went home and made himself sit down at the table and eat. It was a habit he'd long neglected, but Carl had told him at his checkup the week before that he needed to start taking care of himself, especially if he didn't want his bride to outlive him by fifty years or so.

That was an unwelcome thought. At their first premarital counseling session, Pastor Rowland had gone over some financial considerations with them. Harvey already knew Jennifer was sixteen years younger than he was, but when the pastor started talking about how women live longer than men, he started to feel old and decrepit.

He knew the pastor was being practical. He had to change his W-4 form soon, too, and make sure Jennifer's name went on his medical insurance at work, but the life insurance thing was the one that really got him down. It was the standard policy they got through the department, and if he got killed in the line of duty it paid double indemnity. He hated to think about it, but the sooner he made Jennifer his beneficiary the better.

He opened his laptop. He hadn't checked his

stocks in days, but they had all closed in an acceptable range. He started thinking about the honeymoon and did a little online reconnoitering, then called Jennifer. He always called Jennifer. He couldn't breathe long without hearing her voice during those weeks.

"Can I come over?" he asked her.

"Did you get the tuxedoes fitted?"

"Yup, all four of us."

"Great! I guess you can come."

"Are you sick of me?" he asked.

"Never. Well, Beth might be."

Jennifer and Beth were folding laundry in the living room when he arrived, and Jennifer hurried to let him in.

He kissed her in the doorway.

"I put the cake order in with Mrs. Lundquist, for two hundred people, and pink roses on top."

"Great."

She looked up at him through her lashes, suddenly self-conscious. "Are you sure about the flowers? Because we should order them soon."

"Well, yeah, if you like the idea."

"I love it. The girls can have pink roses and greenery, and I'll have pink and white. It just surprised me that you came out with it so decisively at the bakery."

He shrugged. "Sometimes I think of things. It

hit me all of sudden how beautiful you would be carrying those."

Beth smiled. "I think it's cookie time." She headed for the kitchen.

Harvey moved in closer to Jennifer. "She's my kind of chaperone."

She folded a hand towel precisely and looked up with anticipation. He bent down and kissed her. All of the day's headaches faded.

She heard Beth at the kitchen door and broke the embrace, reaching for another towel, but smiling at him.

"Here we go, chocolate chip cookies and milk," Beth said.

"So, you think a white rosebud with a fern behind it is okay for the boutonnieres?" Jennifer asked.

Harvey winked at her. "Terrific." He scooped up two cookies. "You girls are feeding me too well. I think I'd better kick in on the grocery bill."

"You need to eat," Jennifer said. He was too thin, since he'd been in the hospital. His on-the-job injury the previous month had given her a scare, and his health was always a concern of hers now, although he didn't seem worried about it. "Did you ask Carl when you can start running again?"

"He said I'm good to go. I'd have run yesterday if Eddie and I hadn't gotten called in early on a minor crisis at the airport."

"Don't rush it," It was true he was in great shape for a man his age. Still, he was alive only because of the Kevlar vest and God's mercy. Jennifer blinked back tears. Harvey was watching her keenly, and she knew that if Beth hadn't been in the room, she'd have been back in his comforting arms.

"On the news, there were divers looking for evidence in your case," Beth said.

Harvey swung her way. "Did they say if they found anything?"

"No."

"Good." He reached into his pocket. "Jenny, here's that list of hotels you wanted. I put down a range of price, but stayed within a couple miles of the church."

She took it and glanced at the list. "Great. Thanks."

"I was hoping we could go down to New Hampshire, so you could meet my sisters before the wedding," he said, "but that was before Martin Blake left this earth. I don't see how we can fit it in now."

"I wish we could. But Leeanne wants to come down this weekend." Leeanne was the younger of her two sisters, and since Jennifer had moved away from home, she never got much time with Leeanne and Abby.

"Just have her come down with Jeff tomorrow," Harvey said.

"Well, I have to work all day."

"I'll be off Thursday afternoon and Friday," Beth said. "She can stay with me."

Jennifer eyed her doubtfully. "Oh, Beth, you need a break."

"This might work," Harvey said. "Eddie told me Sarah can't go to Fort Point with us. Have Leeanne come tomorrow and stay over the weekend. We'll take her with us on Saturday and drive her home afterward."

"You really want to do that?" Jennifer wasn't convinced he wanted her kid sister tagging along, or the extra miles after the outing.

"Sure. There won't be another chance for Leeanne to visit before the wedding, will there?"

"I don't think so."

"So, do it this weekend." Harvey seemed sincere about it.

"Okay."

Beth said, "You two need some fresh air. Go walk around the park or something."

"Sounds good." Harvey's eyes pleaded, even though Jennifer knew he was exhausted.

She got a light sweater, and they went out into cool air. The sky was overcast. Harvey grabbed his sweatshirt from his Explorer.

"It's sweet of you to say Leeanne can go with us Saturday."

"I love your family. It will be a good chance to get to know her better." He put his arm

79

around her, and she slipped her arm around his waist. It felt daring, but she knew he was pleased.

The park wasn't exactly private, but the sun was going down and kids were pointing their bikes toward home. He guided her lazily toward a large stand of pine trees, and her stomach fluttered. He'd scouted a secluded spot where he could really kiss her.

"I miss living in the country," she said softly.

"Maybe we should look for a house outside of town."

"Then you'd have to commute, and you'd lose your time with Eddie."

He sighed. "I guess things are going to change, whether we like it or not."

Jennifer looked forward to the changes eagerly, but she realized Harvey took his time adjusting to new things in his personal life.

She couldn't help running down her mental wedding-prep checklist. "I forgot to call the real estate agent."

"You can't remember everything."

"But we need a place when we get back from . . . wherever."

"There's time."

"Where are we going, anyway?"

"How do you feel about Paris?"

She caught her breath. "I thought you hated Paris."

"Well, I thought you might like it."

"No, I'd know you were wishing you were someplace else."

"You're probably right. I have another place in mind."

"You're not going to tell me, are you?" Her family had made forays into Canada. Other than that, she had never left the country, but she supposed anyplace would be an adventure with Harvey.

"Is there one place you've always wanted to go?" he asked. "Someplace you'd really like to see, but it seemed out of reach?"

"Anyplace, honey."

"Okay, then."

She smiled. "But I wish I could read your mind."

"Do you know what I'm thinking right now?" He walked her toward the pines.

"Let me guess." She stopped in the shadow of the trees and turned to face him. "You're thinking . . ." She stepped closer and slid her hands up around his neck.

"That's it," he said and kissed her.

On the way back to the house, she wheedled, "Give me a hint."

"How about hula girls and leis?" he asked, his arm tight around her waist.

"Hmm. I don't need a passport for Hawaii. You've got something up your sleeve, haven't you?" She leaned away so she could see his face, but he just smiled.

In the morning, Harvey and Eddie ran their route in sweatshirts. The clouds were thick and dark. A sharp pain started beneath Harvey's right shoulder blade, and he couldn't do the whole run, so they walked the last half mile.

"You'll be okay in a couple of weeks," said Eddie. "It takes time to get it back."

Harvey was breathing fairly hard, and his side ached. Carl had said he was all right, but he thought maybe he'd get him to listen to his lung when he and Jennifer went to his house for dinner, just to be sure.

"So, Sarah's not going to the fort."

"No, she'd already told Cheryl she'd do something with her." Eddie kicked at a dandelion that had grown up in a crack in the sidewalk.

"Well, Jennifer's sister Leeanne is coming down with Jeff tonight. We thought we'd keep her over and take her with us Saturday, then drop her off at home."

"Okay," said Eddie.

"You sure? I mean, it's not like a date for you or anything. She's young."

"How young?"

"I don't know. Maybe 20. She's in college. Going to be a sophomore, I think. Or maybe a junior."

"Where's she going?"

"UMF. She goes home weekends. She's a nice girl, Eddie." Harvey wasn't exactly warning him, just setting boundaries. He hadn't considered how Leeanne might react. Eddie was unquestionably handsome and talked a good line with girls. He could barely keep track of the women he'd dated. He seemed to enjoy being single, but lately Harvey thought he showed signs of being ready to settle down. Sarah had sobered him a little.

Leeanne, on the other hand, could use some laughter. She was small-boned and pretty, with dark hair and blue eyes. She had a shyness, like Jennifer, that was appealing, but might get in the way of a friendship. The middle sister, Abby, was more outgoing. Leeanne, from the little Harvey had seen of her, was just plain sweet, but slightly introverted. Maybe putting her and Eddie together for a whole day wasn't such a great idea.

"Eddie," he said, "Leeanne is . . . well, she's Jenny's sister."

"So?"

"Please don't try to start anything with her."

His eyes opened wide. "Am I so awful?"

"No. You're my best friend."

"So, Jennifer told you to warn me off, or what?"

"No. Jennifer loves you, too. I'm just telling you. It doesn't seem like the best match. Leeanne is too young."

"You should talk."

"Oh, come on, Eddie. I shouldn't have said anything. I know you wouldn't misbehave." Not when it was important, anyway.

"Does she look like Jennifer?" Eddie asked.

"Not really."

"Oh. Is she homely?"

"Not at all."

"So, what are you saying?"

"There's more than one kind of beauty."

After a moment, Eddie said, "Okay."

They split up to get ready for work. Harvey wished he'd kept his mouth shut and just let things take their course, or not told Jennifer to ask Leeanne to come down. Now Eddie thought he didn't trust him. Well, maybe he didn't. In the five years he'd known Eddie, he'd been kind of wild. Even so, Harvey didn't want bad feelings between them.

On the way to the police station, they hashed over what they needed to do that morning. At the top of Harvey's list was getting an interview with Mr. and Mrs. Murphy and other reunion guests they hadn't already reached. He also needed to touch base with the medical examiner about the autopsy report.

He checked the e-mail and crime updates when he got to his desk. The flag icon appeared in the corner of his computer screen. He opened the message and sat still, staring at it.

Chapter 5

Wednesday, June 23

Harvey read the update again. *Unattended drowning, body found 8:05 a.m. on north shore of Islesboro, identified as Luke Frederick, 52, of Portland. Taken to Augusta for autopsy.*

He took out the reunion guest list. Luke M. Frederick, Shore Road, Portland.

"Eddie, look at this. I just got a flag on one of the reunion guests. He was found drowned on Islesboro this morning."

"You're kidding."

"Nope. Luke Frederick. I'll call the M.E. and see what I can find out about it. You call the Islesboro P.D."

Eddie immediately started clicking on his computer keyboard to get the phone number. Harvey tried the M.E.'s office in Augusta but got a busy signal.

"This is really weird," Eddie said after his phone call.

"How?"

"Well, Frederick was divorced. His 30-year-old son was living with him. The son, Ben, reported him missing to this department Monday morning."

Harvey frowned. "That was before I flagged the names. Did Islesboro P.D. interview him?"

"Yes, once the body was found. I guess the cops downstairs told him Monday that his father was an adult, and they weren't getting too upset about him being missing yet."

"But his father went to the reunion Sunday."

"Right," Eddie said. "Ben Frederick knew that was where he was going. But his father never came home."

"Two guys from the reunion found in the water within 48 hours," Harvey said. "Sounds like Islesboro will be calling all the same people we call, asking when they last saw Frederick, and what he did at the reunion. Maybe we'd better coordinate this thing."

Harvey called Islesboro and had a ten-minute conversation with Chief Philson. The upshot was, Philson's case seemed to be a straight drowning, and Harvey's was a homicide. Philson had not tried to get a reunion guest list. He was trying to establish whether or not anyone had seen Frederick after the reunion, from Sunday evening until Wednesday morning, when the body was found.

"Do you know how long he'd been dead?" Harvey asked.

"No, we don't have the autopsy report yet," Philson replied.

They agreed to keep each other posted, but it

seemed Harvey was on his own, unless the M.E. gave Philson reason to believe Frederick's death was not accidental.

The flag appeared on his computer screen again. He opened it and hollered to Eddie to come look. Luke Frederick's car had been found abandoned in the parking lot at Fort Point State Park.

Eddie's eyes flared. "Why didn't they find it two days ago?"

Harvey called Augusta and got a somewhat unsatisfactory answer, which he relayed to Eddie.

"They don't have Parks and Recreation people on duty all the time. The state budget's tight. On Sunday and Monday, they didn't even have anyone there to take money from people going into the park."

"So how did they find the car?"

"An employee went in yesterday morning and noticed a car in the parking lot. She thought it was just an early nature lover. She didn't notice whether it was there when she went off duty, but this morning it was there again, or still there. She heard about the drowning on the radio and called the state police. They ran the plate number and found it was Frederick's."

"They should have checked the park Monday morning, when his son reported him missing," said Eddie.

"Forty-eight hours for a missing adult. Can't investigate every little thing."

"They are so afraid to waste a buck or two."

"Sounds to me like Frederick never left the reunion," Harvey said.

Eddie sighed. "We haven't found anyone who saw him eat lunch there."

"Right." So far, Harvey had no explanation. "We've got to go back over the list of people who were there. Ask the ones we talked to earlier if they saw Frederick and pinpoint the last time anyone saw him."

"But we're investigating Blake's death, not Frederick's."

"If Islesboro won't investigate, we've got to," Harvey said. "There's some connection there."

"The reunion. Anything else?"

"I dunno." Harvey ran a hand through his hair. "I just don't know."

Eddie offered to call the medical examiner's office again, and Harvey dialed the Murphy home. He talked to the congressman's wife, Alison, for a few minutes first. She was also a Blake classmate. She and her husband had sat at the Blakes' table during the picnic.

"I don't think I saw Luke Frederick that day," she said, "but I'm not positive."

When David Murphy finally came on the line, he was curt. Yes, he'd heard about Martin. Terrible thing. Did the police have any leads?

The implication was that they'd better have. He planned to attend the funeral. Yes, he'd been at the reunion. He'd talked to Martin Blake some. They'd discussed politics, and he'd asked Martin to consider endorsing him during next year's campaign. For what? Big pause. He hadn't made his announcement yet and wasn't at liberty to discuss it.

"Mr. Murphy, did you see Luke Frederick at the reunion?" Harvey asked.

"I don't think I did."

"What time did you arrive?"

"Oh, it was eleven-thirty at least. I couldn't get away in the morning."

"So you never saw Luke Frederick on Sunday?"

"I don't recall. There were a lot of people there. But Luke and I were never close. He might have been there."

"Did you see a blue Chevy Cavalier in the parking lot at Fort Point?"

"Not that I recall."

"Sir, could I make an appointment with you for tomorrow? I'd like to talk to you and Mrs. Murphy after the funeral."

"I'm very busy," Murphy said.

"I'm sure that's true, but so am I. Could you come to the police station afterward?"

"Well, I don't—"

"It's important, sir." Harvey wasn't sure why he was pushing him so hard, but something didn't feel right. "If you'd rather I went to your office downtown—"

"No, I don't want cops showing up there."

"You do want to see this case solved quickly, don't you?"

"Of course."

He gave in, and Harvey instructed him on finding his office. When he hung up, he felt battered. The bout was a draw, but he'd scheduled the rematch.

"Eddie, we've got to be at that funeral. A lot of the classmates will be there. The fact that they just saw him Sunday will make it more poignant to them, and they won't want to miss it."

"What do we do? Interview all the mourners?"

"No, I want to concentrate on people who were at the reunion. We can get around to the ones who live in town eventually, but we need to see the ones who are coming from away while they're here."

"Don't tell me. We've got to call them all again and tell them to come here after the funeral."

"I hate to say it, but we'd better. A lot of them will be in town tomorrow. We've got to take advantage of it."

He requisitioned Nate and Tony as if they were paper clips and put them on phones in the Priority Unit office. Pete Bearse and Arnie Fowler, the other two detectives in the unit, were working on another assignment with Mike and were out of the office, so he put Nate and Tony at their desks.

The four of them tackled the list, and by noon determined that, of the forty surviving classmates at the reunion, at least twenty-eight of them and ten of the spouses or dates from the reunion were planning to attend the funeral. They asked everyone they talked to about Luke Frederick. Had they seen him, and when? They set up appointments with the out-of-towners for after the funeral.

The rain broke just before noon, pouring down and beating on the large windows that made most of two walls in the office. Harvey called Records and told Jennifer he would take her someplace away from the office for lunch. They got in his Explorer in the parking garage attached to the station, but had to get out when they got to the restaurant. They didn't have an umbrella, so he grabbed his bomber jacket out of the back seat and held it over Jennifer until they got inside. He got a little wet, but it could have been worse.

They'd just gotten their chicken when the power went out. Their table near the window was better lighted than most, and they kept eating. Some people left. The waitresses came around with candles and lit them on the tables.

"This is turning into a romantic lunch," Jennifer said. The rain sheeted down the glass beside them, and lightning flickered, followed by a crash of thunder that rattled the window.

Harvey reached for her hand across the table. "I'll be glad when I can get you off someplace where there's no office, and no floating corpses, and no limit on the lunch hour."

"Is this case getting you down? I know it's hard to deal with the public."

"There are so many people to interview, not to mention the press."

The restaurant was emptying, and the employees weren't letting anyone new in, because they had no electricity in the kitchen. Harvey and Jennifer finished their entrées in peace, and the waitress refilled Harvey's cup with lukewarm coffee.

"We've got two bodies now," he told Jennifer. He'd avoided the topic during the meal, but now he needed to tell her. She understood how his work burdened him, how he couldn't not think about it until the case unraveled.

"Two bodies?" she asked.

"Another member of Blake's class drowned."

"That's pretty strange."

"I think so."

The waitress cleared the tables around them and stood near a sideboard that held the cooling coffeepot, watching them. The manager had probably told her that she could go home when they left. Harvey looked at his watch. Five more minutes, he decided.

"I called the florist," Jennifer said. "Is there anything else I'm forgetting?"

"Is everything all set for the reception?"

"Yes, food, decorations, it's under control."

"Photographer?"

"Done."

"Your gown?"

"Hanging in my closet."

For some reason, that was an emotional trigger. She had the dress. It was really going to happen. He turned her hand over so he could see the ring.

"Jenny, I love you so much."

Her smile was a bit watery. "Rob Nelson is going to sing Bing's song for us."

"Great." Rob was the lead tenor in the church choir, and he was good. Harvey had requested "True Love," the song Bing Crosby sang to Grace Kelley in *High Society*. When Jennifer wore her hair up, she looked so much like Grace Kelley he was tempted to call her Princess.

The waitress approached. "Can I get you anything else?"

"No, thanks. We've got to get going." He took out his wallet and laid a generous tip on the table, then walked with Jennifer to the door. The rain was still falling hard. He left her in the entry and ran out to the Explorer, driving it right up to the door. He was going to go back in and put his jacket on her, but she ran out and jumped in the passenger side as soon as he had it in park.

She was dripping a little, and she threw her arms around him.

"Your hair's curly!" She slid her fingers through it and kissed him with an abandon she didn't usually practice. The wind shook the vehicle, and the rain pounded down on the roof. He turned the lights and wipers off, and they sat in their refuge for another five minutes, holding each other.

"We're going to be late getting back," Jennifer murmured. He was crushing her against the front of his shirt.

"Couldn't help it in this weather." But the downpour had softened. He kissed her one last time and started the engine.

He went once more to Thelma Blake's house. Eddie had stayed at the office to try to get the M.E.'s initial report on Frederick and check with the lab on the blood sample from the bridge. Nate and Tony were back from lunch and trying to contact the last few class members on the list. The power was still off, but the P.D. had a generator to keep the lights and computers up.

The Blakes' yard was soggy when Harvey arrived, and the bushes dripped. Water shot out of the downspout at the end of the porch. Mrs. Harrelson, the day maid, opened the door. Their power was out, too, and the interior of the old house was dim.

The daughter, Ellen Blake Trainor, greeted him. Trim and pretty, but solemn, she took him to the room off the swimming pool, where she talked to Harvey about her father with affection and humor.

"He would always make Marty and me read his works in progress when we lived at home," she said. "We'd go through the manuscript, and he'd ask us what was the best thing we'd read, and the worst. Then he'd go back and hack out the worst and replace it with something better."

"Did he often go out and walk when he was writing a new book?"

"All the time. He'd be gone for hours. If he thought of something on the way, he'd scribble notes in a little notebook, so he wouldn't forget when he got home."

"You mean, like 'M confronts TN'?" Harvey asked.

"Yes, things like that. And sometimes, he'd come home all excited and say he'd seen one of his characters."

"So, a character in one of his books might be someone he didn't know, but he'd use a model, so to speak?"

"Lots of times, I'm sure."

"How about this Mexico book?"

She shrugged. "I don't know. I haven't been home since Christmas, and he was just starting it then."

"So, are any of the characters in his books actual people?"

"Some are probably composites of many people he encountered. He said some of the people in the first book were real, but with different names. Of course, he wrote that before I was born."

"When?"

"He always said he started writing *Morristown* when he was in high school and finished it in college, when he took a writing class. But it wasn't actually published until ten years or so later, after he'd established himself as a journalist."

Her mother came in, and Harvey prompted Mrs. Blake to think again about the reunion. "Do you know if Martin talked to a man named Luke Frederick?"

She showed no recognition. "Maybe. I met so many people. A few I'd met before, like the Lundquists, and Dave and Alison Murphy, but most of them are a little hazy to me now."

"One of Martin's classmates, Luke Frederick, was found dead this morning," he said.

Thelma caught her breath. "How extraordinary!"

"That's terrible," Ellen said. "Mom, are you okay?"

"Yes." Thelma peered at Harvey. "What happened to this man?"

"It looks like a drowning. His body was found on the shore in Islesboro."

"And he was at the reunion?"

"Yes, ma'am. It's important to remember if you saw that man Sunday."

"I don't—wait." Her brow furrowed in concentration. "Maybe he was down on the beach."

"When was that, ma'am?"

"Just before lunch. Martin and I had gone back to the car after we looked at the fort and the lighthouse, to get the lunch things, and we took them down to the picnic area. The men were trying to move the picnic tables closer together, so we could all sit near each other. There wasn't enough seating in one spot."

"And you saw Luke Frederick?"

"Well, there was a man with no jacket, in a white, short-sleeved shirt. He was down on the beach with David."

"Congressman Murphy?"

"Yes. I said to Martin, 'Isn't that David down there?' and Martin said 'Yes, and so-and-so's with him.' I can't say for sure, but it may have been this Frederick fellow. We both saw them."

"So you were up above them?"

"Yes, the picnic area overlooks the shore. It's very rocky. The bushes and trees block part of the view, and the path going down is very steep. I didn't want to go down myself, but some people did. My shoes weren't made for it."

"But you're positive it was David Murphy you saw down below you?"

"Oh, yes. I'm sure about him."

"What time was that?"

"Before lunch. Between eleven-thirty and twelve, I'd say."

"Was it the first you'd seen of Murphy that day?"

"Yes. That's why I asked Martin if it was David, because some of us had just been talking about whether or not he would show up."

"And when he did, was he alone?"

"No, I saw his wife, Alison, helping set out the food. They both ate with us."

"Did you see Murphy come up the shore path?"

"No, I got distracted, talking to some of the other guests. But I noticed him later, in line for the food with Alison."

"And when you and your husband saw him on the shore below you, what were he and the other man doing?"

"Talking. They were facing each other at first, then they turned toward the sea. David always talks with his hands." She mimicked a sweeping wave outward.

"Did they walk?"

"Not when I saw them. They just stood on the rocks near the water, talking."

"Tide was pretty high then?"

"It was higher later, when we sat in lawn chairs looking out, near the bell tower. That was after lunch and the meeting. People were just hanging around talking. It started to cool off, and we packed up around three o'clock."

"Then you didn't come straight home?"

"We made a stop on the way, in Searsport. Martin has a cousin living there. We went in on the way home, and he and his wife asked us to have a bite of supper."

He took the name and address of the cousin.

"What time did you leave the house?"

"About seven-thirty, I think," Thelma said. "We came straight home then. Oh, and we stopped for gas."

"Where?"

She shrugged. "I don't remember. Martin said he'd better fill up before it got too late. It must have been around Northport or Lincolnville."

Harvey thought back over all the information he had gathered, and one nugget of Eddie's stuck out.

"Mrs. Blake, did you at any time hear your husband say to David Murphy, 'I know your secrets,' or something like that?"

"Let's see . . . David had said something to a friend of his about high school. There was a time when the two of them broke into the gymnasium through an air duct. Nothing serious. They were locked out and wanted to go in and get something they'd left behind. Martin said he knew all about it. 'See, I know all your secrets.' He was teasing them."

"What did Murphy say?"

"I don't remember."

Harvey went back to the office, and Eddie had the medical examiner's report on Blake at last, and the prelim on Frederick. Harvey looked at Blake's first. Cause of death, drowning. Knife wound, upward thrust between the ribs to the right lung. Blood alcohol .05. No surprises, really.

The preliminary report on Frederick was more riveting. The man had received a blow on each side of the head, probably before entering the water. The skull was fractured on the right temple, and there was bruising on the left. The body had been in the water 48 to 72 hours. The tox screens weren't in yet. Harvey called Chief Philson in Islesboro again. They had reclassified the death as a possible homicide, and the state police were taking it over.

He called the state police headquarters in Augusta and shared a little information with Captain Wadleigh there, to save them some time. Wadleigh knew about Frederick's car being found in the parking lot at Fort Point, and Harvey told him several reunion guests had seen the man there before lunch, but no one they'd talked to could remember seeing him after noon Sunday. Wadleigh was wavering on whether Frederick had fallen and hit his head on the rocks or been killed.

"I'll fax you a copy of the reunion guest list," Harvey said.

When he hung up, the lab's report on the blood smear was in, confirming that the stain on the bridge railing was human blood. The sample would be hand carried to Augusta, so the chief medical examiner could compare it with Martin Blake's blood. They could expect a "no match" or a "maybe" the next day. A conclusive "yes" would take longer.

"If it's Blake's blood," Eddie said, "he probably went off the bridge around eleven o'clock."

"Yes, if the Stroudwater woman driving past can be depended on."

"So, what else can we do now?"

Harvey blew out a slow breath. "Ask everyone you talk to from now on if they saw Luke Frederick talk to Blake, and I'd like to learn more about that conversation Frederick and Murphy had on the shore."

They got back on the phones, with Tony and Nate helping. Several people had seen Frederick early in the day, but no one had seen him during or after lunch.

"I think he had to leave early," said one man. "I saw him when we first got there, near the old fort, but I never saw him after that. I'd wanted to talk to him, too."

By quitting time, they had located a few more people who had seen Frederick Sunday morning. Shelly Parker and her husband both remembered him being at the fort and the bell tower around 11 a.m., before the picnic started. She had spoken to him, and she remembered him saying his ex-wife lived in Pennsylvania. They'd been divorced a long time, she wasn't sure how long. The son, Ben, lived with Luke.

She described the man's clothing at Harvey's request, and it matched Thelma's statement and the medical examiner's report. Mrs. Parker said Luke had headed for the parking lot. She thought he was going to his car for a jacket, as it was a little cool near the water. She hadn't seen him talk to David Murphy.

Harvey hadn't had a break all afternoon, so he got a cup of coffee and checked his stocks. The Dow was having a great day, and things were looking good. He opened a travel site he'd bookmarked and checked frequently over the last week. They were offering a good deal on the destination he had in mind for the honeymoon. If only Jennifer's passport was a sure thing, he'd have bought the tickets.

Mike stopped by his desk for an update. "You're doing fine, Harv. Keep up the questions, and you're sure to get some answers."

"It's so hard chasing all these people down over

the phone. At least a lot of them are coming here for the funeral tomorrow."

Mike helped him set up a schedule of interviews, to get Blake's classmates in and out as quickly as possible. He volunteered the entire unit to help with the questioning. Paula, their part time civilian secretary, would come in to help with the guests. Harvey made a short list of people he wanted to see personally and divided the rest up for Mike, Eddie, Pete, and Arnie.

"Mrs. Blake is tapping the department for security at the funeral and traffic control," Mike said. "They're detailing a dozen uniformed officers for it."

"Shouldn't she hire private security?" Harvey asked.

"The mayor thinks Blake is a big enough dignitary to merit it, and it's our duty to handle the traffic, anyway. But tomorrow's going to be a headache for us. They've already told some of the reserve officers to report for the day."

It was near five o'clock, so Harvey headed for the locker room to shave. He'd been leaving his razor at work, and half his wardrobe was hanging there, too. Since Jennifer had started working at the police station, he sometimes saw his apartment only for sleep time. He expected her brother Jeff by six, so he asked Eddie to drop him off.

In the truck, he told Eddie, "Jenny and I have

decided we don't want to keep the apartment. Neither of us wants to live there."

"But you've been there for ages. It will be a big change for you."

"I'm ready." It was still raining, and the wipers swung back and forth steadily.

Eddie eyed him with skepticism. "I don't know. You're not so good at making changes. I'll bet you're still carrying the keys to your old car that blew up."

Involuntarily, Harvey put his hand to his pocket, where his key ring rested. "You're right. It may take me a while to get acclimated."

Eddie smiled and shook his head. "So, have you started looking for a new place?"

"Jennifer's going to try to get a real estate agent to show us some houses after work next week."

"Houses? Not an apartment?"

"I've been saving up for a long time, Eddie. I didn't know what for at first, but I guess it's for a house. I was thinking we might look out in Deering or someplace."

"Out of town, maybe?"

"I don't know. I think we'd both like to live outside the city, but not so far it would be a pain for me to get to work. I think I'd miss living near you, though."

"Yeah." Eddie swallowed. "We've been running together and carpooling for years."

"I know, Ed."

"She doesn't want to live in town?"

"Well, she has for a couple years, and she doesn't seem to mind it, but her folks live on a farm, and I think she misses the country."

"You want to make Jennifer happy."

"Yes, I do, more than anything."

As Eddie pulled up in front of the apartment building, power was restored in the neighborhood, and the heavy overcast brought the street lights on.

Eddie grinned. "It's about time. See ya tomorrow."

"Right," Harvey said. "Have your suit ready for the funeral."

Jennifer waited eagerly for Harvey and her siblings to arrive. The rain had let up, and when the Explorer drove in, she went out on the steps. Jeff climbed out, and she flew toward him.

"You made it!"

"Yeah." He scooped her up in a bear hug. Leeanne hugged and kissed her next.

Harvey smiled big and held out his arms for a hug, too.

"How was traffic?" Jennifer asked Jeff.

"It was okay. It poured all the way down, but other than that, no problems."

She hustled Leeanne inside and introduced her to Beth while Harvey and Jeff brought in Leeanne's luggage. The men looked around suspiciously. Refreshments, a Scrabble game, and videos were set out, and floor cushions and a sleeping bag were heaped on the floor.

"You having a party?" Jeff asked.

Beth laughed. "We are, but if you be good, you can stay long enough for some popcorn and fudge."

"Was the drowning on the local news?" Harvey settled in on the couch.

"Yes, and they're still talking about Martin Blake," Jennifer said. "They had a segment about the reunion at Fort Point. I recorded it for you."

She clicked on the DVD player, and they saw Cyndi Rancourt Reynolds, the reunion organizer, gushing away about Martin and how friendly and relaxed he'd been Sunday, and how much everyone would miss him. Then they interviewed Shelly and Vincent Parker, both class members, and they seemed sad about Martin, but excited about being on TV.

No one mentioned Luke Frederick in connection with the reunion. Beth said the station had led with the story of Frederick's drowning, but it was separate from the Blake story. If the reporters had realized Frederick and Blake were classmates, they'd have played up the connection. Jennifer was glad that frenzy hadn't begun yet, but she supposed it was bound to happen soon.

"I'll probably have to hold another press conference tomorrow," Harvey said glumly.

"Wear your new jacket," said Beth.

Jennifer squeezed his hand. "You'll do great."

Harvey gave her a wan smile, clearly not believing her.

"So, you teach kindergarten?" Jeff asked Beth. His eyes had barely left her since he'd arrived. She was sitting in a rocking chair, and Jeff had the armchair. Leeanne sat in the corner of the couch, beside Jennifer.

"Yes, tomorrow's my last day for the year," Beth said. "When I get home, I'll take Leeanne over to the police station, so she can see where Jennifer and Harvey work."

"I'd like that." Leeanne sipped her lemonade. Her eyes were a dark, serious blue. Jeff had the same light hair and gray-blue eyes as Jennifer, but Leeanne favored their father, with rich brunette hair.

"Well, on Friday we can really have fun," Beth said. "I'll be free all day, and we can go shopping if you want."

Leeanne took a deep breath. "I'd like to go to the art museum, but you wouldn't have to go with me. If you could just tell me how to get there . . ."

"Of course I'll go with you," said Beth. "I've only been once, and I loved it."

Jennifer let the conversation flow around her and turned her attention to Harvey. He was watching her intently and gave her an inviting half smile. She considered herself a novice flirt, but she'd been watching Eddie for several weeks and tried to imagine what he would do. She picked up her bowl of popcorn and started feeding it to Harvey, one kernel at a time.

Beth asked Jeff about the fire department interview, and he told his new audience about the practical test he'd taken earlier and how tough it was.

"Jeff's one of six they picked out of fifty," Leeanne said proudly.

Harvey grabbed Jennifer's hand and held it to his lips. She pulled away, smiling, and started throwing the popcorn at him, piece by piece, and he threw it back.

Beth said, "Okay, you two. If you can't be mature, we'll send Harvey home."

Jeff scowled at his sister. "Quit it, Jennifer."

Jennifer straightened, slightly abashed, but still caught up in the sensuous mood. Jeff obviously didn't want Beth to toss him and Harvey out yet, so she gathered up the loose popcorn and set the bowl down.

"I saw Mark Johnson the other day," Harvey said, and she was glad he was also making the effort to put Beth and the others at ease. Mark was one of the EMTs Harvey knew. "He says two of the six finalists are women."

"No kidding." Jeff frowned.

Harvey shrugged. "He says they're not supposed to fill quotas, but you never know.

Somebody might be pressuring the chief to hire more women. Mark says they have three already."

"I hope they'll look at qualifications," Jeff said. "There were a couple of girls that were pretty good at the practical, but I couldn't see that they were better than any of the men."

"Do the best you can to sell yourself at the interview," said Beth.

"And don't go in there scowling," Jennifer added. "You have to project confidence!"

She was not the most confident person in the world, but when it counted, she usually managed to keep up a good front. She remembered her near-disastrous first date with Harvey, and how she'd put him in his place when she learned he'd done a background check on her. She was sure Jeff could muster the same bravado if he wanted to badly enough.

Leeanne was beginning to look droopy-eyed.

"I guess you guys had better leave," Jennifer said to Harvey. He got the dreamy, wistful look that told her he didn't want to say goodnight yet.

"I'll help you clean up." He started picking up glasses and popcorn bowls.

She took his cue and followed him into the kitchen. As soon as the dishes were out of their hands, he put his arms around her.

"I got the invitations today," she said. "There was a message on the answering machine when

Beth got home from school, and she went and picked them up."

"Great! No passport yet?"

"Not yet. Where are we going?"

"You really want to know? You'll be disappointed if your passport doesn't come in time."

"No, don't tell me."

He ran his hand over her flowing hair. Not so long ago that would have terrified her, but not now. She shivered, but not from fear. Her initial edginess with him was gone, and she felt only joy and a ray of decadence as she snuggled contentedly into his embrace. Harvey was no slouch at getting down to the real business of being in the kitchen.

After a couple of minutes, Beth knocked on the kitchen doorjamb and stuck her head in. "Visiting hours are over, Harvey."

"I hear you."

She went away, and Jennifer smiled up at him. "You'd better go." But she rose on tiptoe to kiss him again.

Chapter 6

Thursday, June 24

Mike called Harvey at seven the next morning.

"Press conference this morning, Harv."

"Oh, great. I knew yesterday was too good to be true."

"I put the word out. It's set for 8:30."

"That's too early. I'm not ready."

"Come in as soon as you can. I'll brief you."

Jeff was up, and he had dressed for his interview at the fire station. "Wish me luck," he said when he was ready to go out the door.

"I'll pray for you."

Jeff looked him in the eye for a second. "You and Jennifer really believe in that, don't you?"

"Yes."

Jeff shook his head. "I just don't get it. You're a reasonable man."

Harvey smiled. "Maybe we can talk about it sometime."

Jeff went out the door, and Harvey called Eddie.

"I'm picking you up in ten minutes, Ed."

"I'm not dressed."

"Well, get dressed."

When Harvey got to his house, Eddie came out in jeans and a black Henley shirt, with a garment bag over his shoulder. Harvey was already wearing his suit, because of the press conference.

Mike was waiting and the coffee was ready when they got to the office.

"The reporters are all over the Luke Frederick story," Mike said. "He's been linked to the reunion. I'd hoped to hold them off, but it's now the hot story of the week. That and Blake's funeral."

Harvey looked out the window and down to where Terry Lemieux and two patrolmen were roping off an area for the journalists. Terry'd had enough of holding press conferences in the foyer. The sky had cleared overnight, and the sun was out, although several puddles shimmered on the tarmac.

Mike, Arnie, Pete, and Eddie pretended to be reporters and fired questions at him. They deliberately exaggerated their reactions, because they all knew it would be rougher than the average media moment.

"The P.D. is slow," Arnie said. "You haven't arrested anyone in Blake's murder yet, and now you've got another one. What are you doing about it?"

"What were the divers out at Stroudwater looking for Tuesday? Did they find anything?" came from Pete.

"How much of the city's money did that cost?" Mike asked.

Eddie piped up, "Was Frederick actually at the reunion? Was he stabbed the way Blake was?"

"Will you arrest someone at the funeral?"

"Were Blake and Frederick friends?"

"You've been harassing Blake's classmates all week. Do you intend to make an arrest soon?"

"Turn and face the camera, Harvey," Mike said.

Harvey answered their questions as straightforwardly as he could. Finally, Mike said, "You'll be okay."

The other men drifted off to their desks.

"Stand beside me during the conference, Mike."

"No, you're heading this investigation."

"Why?" Harvey asked. "Why did you give it to me?"

"I knew you could handle it."

"But you knew this was a huge case. Why didn't you take it yourself?"

Mike shrugged. "I'm going on vacation next week. I don't want to postpone it."

Harvey had forgotten he was taking two weeks off.

"Are you serious? You're still going upcountry, with this going on?"

"We sure are. Sharon would have my head if I changed my vacation now. Two weeks in the Allagash."

"Mike, I need you."

"No, you don't."

Harvey looked out the window again. Reporters and camera crews were staking out their spots on the pavement below.

"What if I need help while you're gone?"

"Just take your time and think things through. Because I'm going where there aren't any phones, Harv. I'm not taking the cell phone, either."

"Sharon's orders?"

"No, mine. I need to get away."

Harvey knew it was true. When Mike took a case, he drove himself until it was over. He spent more evenings at the office than anyone else. But Mike also had high cholesterol, and his blood pressure had been fluctuating lately.

"Your tux is all set?"

"I made an appointment for the twelfth. That's the day I'll come back to work. Don't worry, Harvey. You've started out well on this, and it will all come together. Now, we'd better go downstairs. Eddie can back you up. I'll stay by the door to abet you in your getaway."

"What if I need to refer a question to you?"

"You won't."

Somehow Harvey got through it. They asked some of the same questions his friends had thrown at him, and others they hadn't thought of. He told them Frederick had been at the reunion early and had spoken to Mr. and Mrs. Blake and other class members, but had not been seen at the luncheon or after. He told about Frederick's car being left in the lot at the state park, and that he'd had a blow to the head before he went in the water, but no stab wounds. A reporter asked if that could have been accidental. Harvey said he didn't know.

They asked him again about Blake, and Harvey said, "We have some new evidence that we hope will pinpoint the scene of the murder."

"Does this have anything to do with the divers that were out at the bridge at Stroudwater Tuesday?" Ryan Toothaker, from the *Press Herald*, asked.

"They found some evidence," Harvey said carefully. "I can't tell you more than that at this point."

In response to a question about Blake's estate, Harvey said he couldn't discuss it because the will hadn't been read to the family yet. The new book would be published. The police were working toward solving the crimes. The Portland P.D. had no jurisdiction over the Luke Frederick case, but were cooperating with the state police, as it looked like Frederick may have died at Fort Point and the body washed down to Islesboro.

One female TV reporter threw him for a loop. "Detective, I understand Patrol Officer Tony Winfield is working on this investigation."

Harvey stared at her. "Yes, the governor's nephew has worked on this case."

"Are you happy with his work?"

"Yes, Winfield has done fine. But so have several other officers. He's a rookie here, and he's learning procedure for a homicide case." He wasn't sure why she was so interested in Wonder Boy, but he didn't want to make it sound like Tony was special, or better than the veteran cops.

He glanced over at Mike. The captain nodded slightly, with a little smile, and turned to the electronic pad by the door. Harvey shut off the questions and got back upstairs just after nine.

"Great job, Harv," Arnie said as he walked into the office.

"Thanks." Harvey pulled his tie off and sat down.

Eddie brought him black coffee, and he sat for a minute, just letting the adrenaline dissipate. Mike got his own mug and pushed his chair over near Harvey's. He glanced toward Eddie's desk, but Eddie was bringing in his e-mail.

"Harv, you know I'm grooming you," Mike said quietly.

Startled, Harvey tried to read something in his eyes. "For what?"

"To take over."

"What are you saying?"

Mike shrugged. "I won't always be here."

"You're not—" Harvey stopped.

"Come on, I told you I want to retire."

"You've been saying that for years."

"I'm serious."

"When?"

"I dunno. This Allagash trip is kind of a test. *Can* I stay out of it?"

"Sharon wants you to quit."

"Oh, she has for a long time, but I'm getting to where I can have a pretty good package. If I wait 'til I'm sixty-five, I may drop dead first. I want to be able to enjoy it, Harv."

"You can live on your pension?"

"I've got thirty-four years in. I think if we're frugal we can."

Harvey eyed him closely and leaned toward him. "Why me? Why not Arnie?"

"He's older than I am. He'll be retiring, too, before you know it. Besides, I'd never say this to anyone else, and certainly not to Arnie, but he doesn't have your instincts."

Harvey looked down at his steaming coffee. What could he say? He liked Arnie, and he knew Mike did, too.

Harvey had never aspired to management. He liked field work and had made a niche for himself as a computer person within law enforcement. But could he parcel out cases to other people and sit in the office preparing budgets? If he turned it down and they got a new captain, could he take orders from someone other than Mike? Mike had stayed very active, handling a lot of cases personally, and maybe Harvey could, too.

"I don't know, Mike. Your job isn't part of the future I'd pictured."

Mike sipped his coffee. "Who do you think is going to run this unit if I, A.) retire, or B.) have a heart attack?"

"I've never thought about it. You *are* this unit."

"No, I'm not. You guys are. Every detective in this unit keeps it going. But you're the best."

That was hard for Harvey to listen to. He sent up a quick prayer. Was this a temptation of some sort?

Mike said, "Listen, I don't know if you realize it, but Pete won't stay here long, either."

"Why not?"

"He's been taking law courses at night for ten years."

"So? He's good at legal work."

"He took the bar exam Saturday."

Harvey was stunned. Pete always studied law. He'd never thought he would actually become a lawyer.

"You mean he's going into practice?"

"If he passed the exam, and, knowing Pete, I'm betting he did."

"When will he know?"

"By the end of July." Mike started to get up.

"But you are coming back after your vacation?" Harvey sounded a little desperate, even to himself.

"Oh, sure. I wouldn't dump it on you that

suddenly. I'll probably work at least until next spring. I'm just telling you. When the time comes, as far as I'm concerned, you're it. If I have any sway at all with the chief, you'll step into my job."

Harvey shook his head. "I can't deal with this right now. The funeral and the Portland High School alumni, and the wedding . . . it's too much."

"Well, I thought it was time for you to start thinking about it, my friend. It won't be for a while yet."

When Mike walked away, Eddie was watching him. Harvey wondered if he'd heard anything.

He took off his jacket and checked the e-mail and crime updates. Frederick and Blake's names were both in the updates, because evidence had been entered in the records. He and Eddie spent the rest of the morning going over everything they had so far and preparing to question the alumni. They had a brainstorming session with Arnie, Pete, and Mike, to make sure they covered everything.

"Nate and Tony are doing funeral traffic this afternoon," Harvey noted.

"Do you need them here?" asked Mike.

"No, if we get too many people up here, it will be mayhem."

He explained his plan to question five people at a time. Harvey would use his desk area, Eddie would use the interview room, Mike the tiny observation room, Pete the break room, and Arnie his own desk, which they decided was far enough from Harvey's that they wouldn't interfere with each other.

They didn't have an area big enough for all the witnesses to wait in, so Harvey reserved the conference room downstairs as a waiting room. The unit secretary, Paula, would bring them in as the detectives were ready.

They discussed whether husbands and wives should be interviewed together and decided to separate David and Alison Murphy, but let the other couples go in together. Harvey would handle the congressman, and Arnie would turn on the charm with his wife. Harvey handed out the lists he had made for each man.

At five minutes before noon, Eddie asked, "You ready, Harv? We'd better get over to the funeral."

"Just a sec. Let me give Jenny a quick call."

"No lunch today?" She was mournful.

"We need to get over to the church. If we eat first, we might get caught in traffic."

"You need to eat, Harvey."

"We'll get something later."

"You're not taking care of my fiancé."

"It's just one of those days."

When they got to the parking garage, Jennifer was waiting there. She handed them each a package of cheese crackers with peanut butter and a can of juice.

"Best I could get from the machines," she said. Harvey tossed Eddie his keys, so Eddie could unlock the Explorer and get in while he kissed Jennifer.

"Come on, Harv," Eddie said through a half-open window.

Harvey let her go with a wink. "Catch you later." It was the happiest he had ever felt heading for a funeral.

The traffic officers had their hands full. Eddie parked three blocks down, heading up a side street, so they wouldn't get caught in the procession afterward.

Every local and state-level dignitary arrived. The security unit was caught unprepared when Stephen King, his wife Tabitha, and half a dozen lesser-known Maine authors showed up. The crowd burgeoned, and the huge church was not big enough. The two detectives were jammed into a pew with too many other people, two thirds of the way back. With much shuffling, they managed to keep the two aisle seats.

"They should have moved it to the Civic Center," Eddie said.

People were standing in the back, and more stood out on the sidewalk.

Two clergymen spoke, followed by the mayor,

Blake's editor, and Marty. Ellen Blake Trainor read a passage from one of her father's books, describing the death of an old friend. It made Harvey think of Chris, his former partner.

When they left the church, the crowd outside was enormous. Officers had to escort the family members and the Kings to their cars. Camera crews were everywhere. David Murphy improvised a p.r. moment on the sidewalk. The reporter from the *Press Herald* deigned to notice Harvey.

"Detective Larson, anything new on the case?"

"I just saw you a few hours ago, Ryan."

"Yeah, but you've been working hard since then, right?" He was young, about thirty, but a veteran of the police beat. He went to the police station every day to check the logs and try to pick up tips. He treated the officers more or less fairly in print.

"Come see me tomorrow morning," Harvey said.

He and Eddie opted out of the graveside service and went straight back to the station. They waited an hour for the first alumni to show up. Harvey was getting nervous. He paced to the window, to Eddie's desk, back to the window. "What if they all just go home?"

"They won't." Mike was sitting with his feet on his desk, drinking coffee. "You've made it clear this is required."

"I hope so."

"These graveyard jaunts can take longer than expected," Arnie said.

At three-fifteen, Jennifer, Beth, and Leeanne came up the stairs.

"Three beautiful women visiting the Priority Unit." Mike jumped up with a grin. He gave Jennifer's hand a courtly kiss. "The lovely bride-to-be." He had met Beth, and Jennifer introduced her sister to him, Eddie, Pete, and Arnie.

"We can't stay," said Jennifer. "I'm on my break, but I wanted Leeanne and Beth to see you guys in your habitat."

"We've got people from the funeral coming in for questioning any minute," Harvey said, "but I can give you the nickel tour."

"I'll do it," Eddie offered.

Jennifer stayed with Harvey while Eddie showed Beth and Leeanne everything from the interview room to the locker room. Mike, Pete, and Arnie drank coffee and laughed near Pete's desk. Harvey got in some hand holding with Jennifer.

"You and Jeff will have supper at our house, right?" she said.

"I don't know when we'll be done here."

"Well, Jeff called, and he's coming over at 5:30. Just show up when you can. We need to work on the invitations."

He glanced over at his boss and decided he

could steal a kiss. Jennifer blushed and looked over her shoulder. The guys were oblivious, or pretended they were.

"I want to send an invitation to Chris Towne's widow."

"Your old partner?" She wrapped the ends of his tie around her hand.

"Yes. I just felt it at the funeral today. I need to keep contact with her. Chris and I were really close."

"Okay."

His desk phone rang. It was Terry. "We've got a few people in the conference room."

"I'll send Paula right down."

Eddie and the girls came back into the main office. "So where do you book the prisoners?" Beth asked.

"Oh, that's done downstairs," Eddie said.

"We've got to clear you gals out," Harvey told them. "Our witnesses are here."

Paula went down the stairs, taking the guests with her, to bring back the first interviews.

David and Alison Murphy came directly to Harvey.

"Is this really necessary?" Murphy asked.

His wife sat down meekly.

"Would you folks like some coffee?"

"No, we'd just like to get home," Murphy said.

Alison looked up at Harvey. "Actually, I'd love a cup."

Good, Harvey thought. She wasn't a total doormat. After they had the coffee in hand, he smiled his best smile, the one that had bulldozed his mother a thousand times.

"You know what, Mrs. Murphy, I think I'll send you over there to Detective Fowler." He nodded toward Arnie, who was waiting patiently at his desk. "That way, he can talk to you while I talk to your husband, and the two of you will get out of here faster."

Murphy looked a little uncertain, but Alison seemed to think it was a great idea. Harvey took her to Arnie and made the introduction. Arnie was courteous, even flattering. The senior detective had a distinguished air, direct brown eyes, hair whitening at the temples, and a little scar by his left eyebrow. He always treated women respectfully, and with a hint of admiration that won them over. Mrs. Murphy warmed to him quickly, and Harvey thought she was in good hands.

He returned to her husband and took him back over the events of Sunday.

"You were late getting to the reunion."

"A little," Murphy said. "Most of the others were there when we arrived."

"Where did you go first?"

"They were starting the potluck, so we went right to the picnic area."

Harvey said, "You were seen on the shore below the picnic area, before the luncheon began."

"Somebody's mistaken."

"At least two people saw you."

Murphy didn't answer.

"You and Luke Frederick," Harvey said.

Murphy's eyes flicked over to Arnie and Alison.

Harvey said, "You told me yesterday that you hadn't seen Frederick at the reunion, but my witnesses say you did. Had quite a conversation with him on the shore, as a matter of fact."

"Perhaps. I had forgotten about Luke."

"Start remembering."

"It seems like I met him in the parking lot. My wife spotted a couple of old friends going up to the fort site, and she went to join them."

"And you and Luke Frederick went down to the shore together?"

The congressman hesitated. "There are paths on the other side of the parking lot. Near the picnic areas."

Arnie left his desk and walked to the coffeepot with two cups in his hand.

"Would you excuse me just a minute, please?" Harvey grabbed his mug. Arnie went back to his desk and gave Mrs. Murphy her cup. On the table beside the coffeemaker was a piece of paper. Harvey picked it up. "Met TN in pkg lt. DM & TN went to beach. AM went to ft. LF came there after." It was nearly as cryptic as Martin Blake's plot notes, but he deciphered it.

Puzzled, he looked over at Arnie, and Arnie

nodded slightly, but continued talking affably with Alison. Harvey could count on him to keep her busy as long as he needed. Pete came through with his interviewee and turned him over to Paula, to be escorted downstairs.

"Could we get on with this?" Murphy asked when Harvey sat down again.

"Sure." Harvey opened the flat desk drawer in front of him and scanned the list of reunion guests quickly. The only TN was Thomas Nadeau. He closed the drawer and smiled at Murphy.

"So, when did you see Thomas Nadeau?"

"Tom Nadeau? Oh, yes, he was there. We ate lunch together."

Harvey consulted his list. Nadeau had indicated he would attend the funeral, and he was on Mike's schedule. He said, "And Nadeau also met you first thing, in the parking lot. Is that accurate?"

Murphy eyed him speculatively, weighing something.

"It's not worth lying about," Harvey said, turning the page on his notepad.

Murphy's eyes grew stormy. "I don't remember very well when I first saw Tom. That may be correct."

"So you and Nadeau walked to the beach, and your wife went to visit with her old chums."

"Yes, Patricia Lundquist and Carol Harper. I'm not sure what her married name is, but her maiden name was Harper."

"You don't seem to have any trouble remembering who your wife talked to."

Murphy's jaw moved a little.

"Look, I want to let you go home. Just tell me what happened." Harvey waited.

Mike came through, chatting with the couple he had interviewed, and entrusted them to Paula. Turning back toward the interview room, he threw Harvey a questioning glance. Harvey gave the tiniest shrug and waited some more. Arnie was listening to Alison as if he was minutely interested in the recipe for the three-bean salad she'd taken to the picnic.

"Tom is an associate of mine. He works on my campaigns. Luke came along while the two of us were talking," Murphy said at last.

"On the shore."

"Yes. Luke said he wanted to speak to me privately, so Tom walked off up the beach and around the point, toward the lighthouse. I didn't see him again until lunch."

"So you didn't meet Frederick in the parking lot. It was on the shore."

"I guess so."

"What did he want?"

"There was something someone had said to him. He didn't like it. Wanted my opinion." Murphy sat back in the chair.

"What was it?" Harvey asked.

"I can't—"

"Yes, you can."

Murphy gave him a stony stare. Eddie's new people were going in, looking impatient.

"Why did Frederick come to you with this thing?" Harvey asked. "Did it concern you?"

"No." He was too quick. "It was someone spreading a rumor about him. He thought it would ruin his business. He's an accountant, and people have to trust him."

"And what? He thought you were good at burying rumors?"

Murphy's face reddened. "Look, I don't have to sit through this." He started to rise.

Harvey said quietly, "Yes, you do. If you want to drag it out, we can."

The congressman sat. "My lawyer's here."

"You brought your lawyer along?"

"He was a class member."

"You must mean Mervin H. Dawes of Belfast. We'll be interviewing him shortly."

"Yes. We spoke in the waiting room."

"And?"

Murphy's eyes narrowed. "Should I ask him to come up here?"

"You tell me. Do you feel like you need a lawyer?"

He held Harvey's gaze a few more seconds, then looked down at his hands. "What else do you want to know?"

"I want to know exactly what Frederick told you."

"He wasn't specific. No names. Just wanted my advice on how to deal with it."

"And you told him . . ."

"To be up front with his clients. I said he could drop my name if he wanted to. I'd vouch for him."

"So you two were friends."

"Well, I suppose so. Not close friends."

"But you trusted each other."

There was a pause before he said, "Yes."

"So then you split up? Or did you go up the path together?"

"No." He twisted his wedding ring. "I went around the shore the way Tom had gone, and Luke stayed there."

"Just stood there when you left?"

"I'm not sure. I thought he was going up the path to the parking lot."

"You didn't look back?"

"No."

"Did anyone go down to the shore later?"

"I don't know."

"You didn't see him again that day?"

"No."

"And at lunch, you and Thomas Nadeau ate together."

"Yes, he sat on one side of me, and Alison on the other. Martin and Thelma Blake were across the table. Michael and Patricia Lundquist were there, and a couple of others."

"Who brought up the school break-in, when you climbed through the air duct?"

That startled Murphy, and his eyes narrowed. Harvey glanced toward Arnie. He was looking a little strained.

"I guess that was Tom," Murphy said. "It was a stupid thing. Didn't matter. But at the time we were scared we'd get caught, and it seemed like a big deal."

"You and Tom Nadeau broke into the school together."

"Well, yes. It was after a football game. Tom had left his wallet in his locker, and he needed it because his driver's license was in it. We decided getting caught sneaking into the school was preferable to getting caught driving without a license. We'd explored the roof before and knew about the duct, so we did it. We didn't think anyone else knew, though."

"But someone did."

"Yes, Martin said he'd known it all along. I don't know how he knew. Maybe Tom had told him at some point and forgotten about it. Maybe I told him myself way back when, but I don't think so."

"Martin was an investigator, even then."

"Seems like it. He made a name for himself writing exposés."

"He said he knew all your secrets. Did that make you nervous?"

Murphy laughed a little. "Everyone has secrets."

"Worse than the air duct?"

He shrugged. "Politicians are constantly scrutinized, Detective Larson."

Harvey flipped back over his notes. "Mr. Murphy, I'm going to let you go, but I may need to contact you again soon. I'll expect you to keep yourself available to me."

"I can't come over here at the drop of a hat."

"Just take my calls."

He nodded.

They stood, and Arnie brought Mrs. Murphy over. They said goodbye cordially, and Paula took the couple downstairs. It was almost five o'clock, and Harvey was tired.

"Thought I'd go nuts prolonging that conversation," said Arnie. "You get anything?"

"Maybe. I'd like all of us to compare notes."

"There's still a lot of people waiting."

Mike and his subject came into the room just then, and Harvey asked for a quick conference. Mike took the woman to Paula and asked her to hold off on the others for a few minutes. When he came back, they got Pete and Eddie to excuse themselves from their interviews and join them near Harvey's desk. Harvey got to the point.

"Murphy changed his story. He told yesterday he hadn't seen Frederick, and today he admitted he did. He said he met Thomas Nadeau in the parking lot and went to the beach with him, then Frederick joined them. Nadeau walked around the shore to the lighthouse. Murphy says he left Frederick healthy and walked the same direction Nadeau did, but I don't know. He made up a story on the spot, to explain what he and Frederick were talking about. Oh, and Nadeau was the kid he broke into the high school with, way back when."

"I know all your secrets," Eddie quoted.

"Yeah. I'm wondering if Blake knew more secrets than that."

Mike said, "Okay, we're over half done, and these people are getting sick of waiting. Anyone who's done with his list, take some of Harvey's or Arnie's people, and everybody hit the Nadeau-Frederick thing hard."

"If Frederick was killed before lunch," Harvey said, "or even if he slipped and hit his head on a rock, why didn't anyone see the body? Other people must have gone down to the shore during the afternoon."

"Ask them all," said Mike. "We need a list of people who went down there, and we need to know what time, and what they saw."

Harvey gritted his teeth. "Tomorrow we'll have to call the ones who didn't come for the funeral."

They took Nadeau from Mike's list and put him on Harvey's, swapping him for Dawes, the lawyer. Nadeau answered his questions succinctly, without emotion. Harvey couldn't get a handle on him.

"You and David Murphy were on the shore when Luke Frederick arrived?" Harvey asked.

"Yes, David and I were discussing his next campaign. Luke Frederick came down the hill path and said he wanted a private word with David."

"What was his manner?"

"Maybe a little agitated."

"And you left?"

"I walked around the point toward the lighthouse. I left the shore just below the bell tower and walked up to where the other people were looking at the historical sites."

"You didn't see Frederick again?"

"No."

"And at lunch, Blake said something that upset Murphy?"

"I can't think what."

"Secrets. He knew Murphy's secrets."

Nadeau raised his eyebrows. "A metaphor, I thought."

"Really? I talked to David Murphy, and he seemed uneasy about that."

"Politician. They never want anyone to know their secrets."

"Does Murphy have secrets? Other than high school pranks, I mean?"

"I'm not the right person to ask," Nadeau said.

"But Frederick was healthy when you left him and Murphy."

"What are you saying?"

"Nothing."

Nadeau looked at him belligerently. "Yes, he was healthy."

They finished the interviews by six-fifteen. Most of the people weren't happy, although a few were mildly excited to be part of the investigation. The detectives conferred again when the last of them had gone.

Mike said the lawyer, Dawes, had been polite, but not much help. "He's done some minor legal work for Murphy in the past, but he's not his main lawyer."

"He made that up to rattle me," Harvey said.

"Well, Dawes claims he didn't go down to the beach. It was too steep. He talked to Murphy, Nadeau, and Blake, but didn't remember seeing Frederick."

"None of mine went to the beach," said Pete. "They're getting older, and apparently the path was almost vertical."

"Guess that's why Murphy and Nadeau took the long way around to get back up," Harvey said. "I wonder how far it is around to the lighthouse." He had looked at a map, but at that scale, he couldn't tell where the picnic area and the beach were.

"We can measure it Saturday," said Eddie.

Mike arched his eyebrows at Harvey.

"We're going up to Fort Point. Recreation for Jennifer and Leeanne and me. Eddie's going along."

"Good," said Mike. "Seeing it should help you."

They all started getting ready to go, and Harvey called Jennifer's house.

"Hi! Where you been?" she asked.

"I got stuck at the office interviewing the Class from the Black Lagoon."

"You'd better come over here for some left-overs. We're eating now, but I'll save you some lasagna."

Eddie was watching him and listening.

"How about Eddie?" Harvey asked. "He's hungry, too." Eddie grinned at him.

"Sure, bring him along."

Jennifer prepared plates for the men, and Harvey beamed as she waited on him and Eddie. They tucked into the lasagna and salad.

"This is great." Harvey closed his eyes for an instant. "Tell me my future wife made this."

"Sorry," Jennifer said. "Beth and Leeanne had it all made when I got home from work."

"Can you make lasagna like this?" he asked hopefully.

"I'll give her the recipe," said Beth. They had

held dessert, and everyone settled down in the living room for the chocolate cake with peanut butter frosting.

"You should have Patricia Lundquist put peanut butter frosting on the wedding cake," Eddie said. No one else seemed to like the idea. Jennifer refilled their milk glasses.

"How'd it go at the fire station?" Harvey asked Jeff.

"Pretty well, I think. I'm supposed to go back in the morning."

"When will you know?"

"They said they'd call me by next Wednesday."

"So, are we playing Trivial Pursuit?" asked Beth.

"Oh, let's." Leeanne jumped up.

Jennifer hated to put a damper on things, but she knew she had to take advantage of the available labor. "Guys, that's great, but we have to address the invitations first."

Groans all around.

"Oh, come on. With six people, it won't take long. Of course, Jeff's handwriting is so bad he can't do any addressing, but he can stuff the envelopes."

Harvey smiled in resignation. "Let's get to it, gorgeous."

She got the box and the address lists, and they all started working.

"Why do wedding invitations need two envelopes?" Jeff asked.

"Don't ask me," said Eddie.

"Then there's this stupid little card and envelope. What are they for?" Jeff held one up.

"That's the response card," Jennifer said. "It's vital."

"You coulda told me."

She gritted her teeth. "How many envelopes did you seal without one inside, Jeffrey?"

"Oh, I'm supposed to seal them, too?"

She picked up a patchwork throw pillow and stuffed it over Jeff's face.

Beth snatched the pillow away. "Easy, Jennifer. The mania will be over in twenty-three days."

"It's going to cost you a fortune to mail all these," Harvey said. "I'd better give you some cash."

"Daddy's paying. He sent a generous check down with Leeanne."

Harvey frowned, and Jennifer could read the signs of guilt. When something wasn't perfect, Harvey felt responsible. He was stewing about the money her family was spending on the wedding, for sure.

Jeff came to the rescue. He grinned at Harvey. "Hey, don't worry about it. Dad's so glad to finally unload Jennifer, he can't write the checks fast enough."

Leeanne grimaced. "Knock it off, Jeff. Mom and Dad want to do this for Jennifer."

"And you and Abby someday, I suppose," Jeff said.

"I don't think I could stand having two hundred people stare at me," Leeanne said. "When I get married, I'm eloping."

"I hope not." Jennifer frowned at her in dismay. "I want to be at your wedding."

They finished the job in about forty-five minutes, with only two spoiled envelopes. Jennifer gave Harvey one invitation to take home for Marcia Towne, because he didn't have the address with him, and one to post at the police station.

The Trivial Pursuit board came out a little after eight. They played men against women. Jennifer wished she could be on Harvey's team. No one could possibly stand a chance against him, with his encyclopedic knowledge.

Jeff sat beside Beth and handed her the dice with great care. Eddie was splitting his attention between Beth and Leeanne. Leeanne's eyes glowed, and she began bantering a little with him. Jennifer wasn't sure the way she watched Eddie was good. Beth was cool as always, and impartial in her attentions to Jeff and Eddie, and to Harvey, too, as far as that went.

"So, you guys are looking for a house," Eddie said between questions, while Leeanne was trying to "roll again," until she could get the girls' token on a spot that wasn't orange for sports. The men were killing them in sports.

"Haven't really started," Harvey said.

Beth looked up. "Ask Pastor Rowland."

Leeanne moved the women's token. "Pink."

"Does he know someone?" Harvey asked.

Jeff pulled a card out of the box.

Beth said, "I think Mr. Bailey is putting his house up for sale."

"He's the older man whose wife died?" said Jennifer. "Back pew on the right?"

She and Harvey had met the homeowner in question, a polite man in his seventies, quiet but intelligent, a retired engineer. He'd been widowed about six months.

"Okay, here's the question." Jeff held up a card. "In 1952, Gary Cooper starred with Grace Kelly in what western?"

Jennifer stared at Harvey, trying to read his mind. She was positive he knew the answer. He seemed to cache information about old movies in the far corners of his mind. He also liked Grace Kelly, to whom he'd said Jennifer bore a slight resemblance, but Jennifer couldn't see it.

"*High Noon*," said Beth.

"Is that your final answer?" Jeff teased.

"You sure you girls don't want to network a little?" Harvey asked.

"No, we trust Beth," Jennifer said gravely.

"Well?" Beth grinned at Jeff.

He sighed. "Get your little piece of pink pie."

The women won in the end, mostly because

Jeff couldn't get the men's token to land on the spot for literature, but Jennifer didn't care. Eddie made a big fuss, saying they'd have to have a rematch sometime.

Harvey's fatigue was showing, and the men left soon after the game ended. Jennifer, Leeanne and Beth cleaned up a little and headed for bed.

Jennifer had just turned off her bedside lamp when her phone rang.

"Hey, gorgeous. Did I wake you up?"

"Almost."

"Jeff was just telling me you were a pyromaniac in pigtails nineteen years ago," Harvey said. "Almost burned the family home to the ground, he said."

Jennifer laughed. "Oh, he'll never let me forget that. I put something in the stove, and it fell out on the hearth. Mom came and stomped on it. It was no big deal, but I'll never live it down."

Harvey chuckled. "Maybe that's why he wanted to be a fireman. Hey, I suggested Jeff might want to take the lease on my apartment if he gets the job down here."

"That would be great." She snuggled down beneath the quilt her mother made.

"All right, kiddo, you sound tired. Just wanted to say goodnight, and I love you."

Chapter 7

Friday, June 25

Jeff dragged out of bed at six and ran with Harvey and Eddie. Harvey ran the three miles with only a little pain.

"You going home today, Jeff?" Eddie asked as they went up to the apartment for breakfast.

"Yeah, after my interview."

"Let me give you a key before you leave," Harvey said. "And call me when you know about the job."

Ryan Toothaker was at the front desk checking the police log when Harvey and Eddie entered the station, and he followed them upstairs. He sat beside Harvey's desk and took his notebook out.

"What can you give me?"

"We interviewed most of Blake's high school classmates who came to the funeral yesterday," Harvey said.

"Any suspects yet?"

"Not that I can tell you about."

"Can you tell me what those divers found in the river?"

Harvey hesitated. Would it hurt the case at all to tell him about the knife? "Let me think about that."

"The second dead guy—Frederick—was at the reunion, too," Ryan said. "Is there a connection between the two deaths?"

"Not that we know of so far."

"All right," Ryan said. "But you'll tell me when you have something I can use?"

"Sure. Hey, let me ask you a question or two."

"Shoot."

"What was Blake working on for the paper?" Harvey asked.

"Oh, some big story."

"Hadn't run yet?"

"No, he was writing it, I think."

"Did he do his writing for the paper at home?"

"No, I'd see him at a computer in the newsroom lots. He didn't keep regular hours like the other reporters, though. I heard he pretty much came up with his own story ideas. They were so glad to keep him, they let him write about whatever he wanted to, whenever he wanted."

"And this big story was something he came up with?"

"I guess."

"Who could tell me?"

"The managing editor, John Russell."

"Was he at the funeral?"

"Oh, sure," Ryan said. "You got a paper?"

"Eddie, we got a paper?" Harvey called.

Eddie went to Arnie's desk and came back with that morning's *Press Herald*. The funeral story started on page one, with a photo of the family going out of the church. On the first page of the second section was a photo essay on the service.

"There," said Ryan, pointing to a picture of the pallbearers. "That's Russell."

"Got a number?"

Ryan gave Harvey the phone number and Russell's extension. "Is there anything else you can tell me?"

Harvey hesitated. "Hold on." Mike had come in. Harvey went to meet him outside the locker room for a quick consultation then went back to his desk.

"This is your lucky day, Ryan. The divers found a knife in the water, a little downstream from the bridge. A hunting knife."

"Wow." Ryan stared at him for a second then scribbled in his notebook. "Do you know whose it was?"

"Nope. Don't know yet if it was used to stab Blake, either."

"Did you check to see if anyone bought a new one last week?"

"That only works on TV. This was an old knife, Buck brand."

"So, do any of your suspects go hunting?"

"Probably eighty percent. This is Maine, Ryan."

"Yeah, I suppose. So, what else can you tell me?"

Harvey scratched his jaw, thinking. "Check back with me after the weekend."

"For sure. Thanks!" Ryan hurried toward the elevator.

It was Mike's last day on the job before vacation, and he had cleared his schedule so he could help with the Blake case. The whole unit would man the phones that morning, contacting reunion guests who hadn't attended the funeral, asking if they knew of any connections between Blake, Murphy, Frederick, and Nadeau. Harvey was almost sure Luke Frederick was killed during the reunion, and he'd been seen with Thomas Nadeau and David Murphy. Martin Blake was murdered that night. He had to find out why.

He called Mrs. Blake for an appointment, then drove Eddie's truck to her home. Marty had left, but Ellen Trainor was still there, and she sat in on their session in her mother's sitting room.

"What was your husband working on last?" Harvey asked.

"The book about Mexico, *Border Feud*," Thelma said.

"How about for the paper?"

"Oh, I don't know. He didn't usually discuss his news stories with me. He did all that at the office."

"Kept it separate from his fiction books?"

"Yes. He filed his clippings here and did some research, but he would go in to the office and work on their computer system."

"We interviewed his classmates from the funeral yesterday."

"I heard. Some of them were upset."

"Are you making any progress?" asked Ellen.

"I think so. It takes time. This isn't public knowledge yet, but it soon will be. We found a knife in the water."

"Was that what killed him?" Tears glistened in Thelma's eyes.

"The medical examiners said he drowned, Mom," Ellen reminded her.

"I'm sure the knife wound contributed," Harvey said. "It could be the weapon that wounded him. I'm sending it to the medical examiner. Mrs. Blake, your husband didn't own a hunting knife, did he?"

"Yes, he did. Now, where would it be?" Thelma left the room for a minute and returned with a knife. Harvey pulled it from its leather scabbard. It was a Schrade, with a bone handle.

"That's a nice knife." He handed it back to her, glad Blake's own knife was accounted for. "Better give it to Marty. I wanted to ask you, Mrs. Blake, you're certain it was Luke Frederick you saw talking to David Murphy on the beach?"

"Now I am, but I didn't recognize him that day."

"What was your husband's attitude toward Frederick?"

"I didn't ever see them together, so I don't know. He didn't say anything about him."

Harvey nodded. "And the will was read yesterday afternoon?"

"Yes. Martin made some donations and settled a million dollars on each of our children, leaving the rest of his estate to me. Satisfactory all around, I think."

Harvey would have called forty million dollars something beyond satisfactory.

"We were wondering about Daddy's things," said Ellen.

"We returned his ring and watch."

"I know, but the other things. We never got his clothes back, for instance."

"I'll have someone call the medical examiner. The clothing should have come back before this." Harvey thought about the small items that had been in Blake's pocket. The pocketknife, key ring, and wallet seemed like the only things worth having. Maybe his notebook.

He sat very still and pictured the notebook, damp and disintegrating, and the inked runes, "M confronts TN—TN is defiant." He inhaled sharply, and Ellen Trainor said, "What is it, Mr. Larson?"

"Mrs. Blake, after you and Martin saw the men down on the shore, did you both leave that area and go to where you couldn't see the shore anymore?"

"I went to help set up the lunch buffet. It was potluck, and we used one picnic table to hold all the dishes."

"Where was Martin during that time?"

"Let me see . . . He may have stayed where he was for a few minutes. Then he came over and helped Patricia and me with the tablecloth. We couldn't make the little clips stay on the edges. After that, he went back over near the head of the beach path. I think he actually started down, but when we called that lunch was ready, he came back up."

"He didn't go all the way down?"

"I don't think so. It's a steep path there. I think he started down to see David, then thought better of it when the lunch call was given."

Harvey went around to see John Russell at the *Press Herald* office.

"Martin's latest work? He'd started an article on corruption in government. We were going to run it next week."

"Corruption in local government?" Harvey asked.

"No, it concerned a member of Maine's delegation to Washington."

"Interesting."

"Very. It was going to be great. I've got his

rough draft, and I may still run it. It's a huge story. He was trying to verify everything. Sources are cagey on something like that. You have to have them nailed, or you get accused of libel."

"So this story was in that category? Someone might call it libelous?"

Russell shrugged. "I told Martin, 'If you can't prove it, I won't print it.' We've had lawsuits before. Even if you win them, they're expensive, in cash and reputation."

"I wonder if I could have a copy of his article?"

"Oh, no. It's too sensitive."

"I promise I'll keep it confidential."

"You don't understand. This story belongs to the *Press Herald* right now. If one word leaks out before it hits print, we lose our advantage. I am talking a major scandal on the national level, with roots right here in Portland."

"Murphy," Harvey said.

Russell swore.

"You may as well give it to me now," Harvey told him.

The editor eyed him with something between admiration and loathing. "You ought to be a reporter."

"I like my job."

"I guess you're good at it."

"I'd have guessed Murphy anyway. They went to school together. At the reunion on Sunday, somebody overheard a remark Blake made. He said he knew Murphy's secrets."

"Martin was usually more discreet than that."

"They weren't talking politics. An old high school thing had come up in the conversation, and Blake said he knew about it."

Russell sighed and turned to his computer. "The article's in the system, in Martin's private queue." Harvey waited while he found it and copied the file to a thumb drive for him. Russell hesitated, then handed him the drive.

"If this weren't important to my investigation, I wouldn't ask you for it," Harvey said.

"What, you think this is the motive?"

"Any chance Murphy got wind of it?"

"I don't see how. Martin was very good at covering his tracks. Not even the staff here knew what it was about. We didn't discuss it in meetings. Secrecy was paramount."

"I'll keep my word. You were paying him for this?"

"We paid Martin big bucks for every word he wrote for us the last fifteen years. But I guess Thelma will get the check this time."

"What day will you run the article?"

"Not sure. I think I'll hold off a few days. It's something that needs to be made public, but I've got to go over Martin's documentation scrupulously first. We can't afford to mess up on something this big."

When he got back to the station, it was nearly eleven o'clock. Harvey logged Blake's notebook out of the evidence room and took it upstairs.

It was dry now. He opened to the last entry.

"Eddie, look at this."

"M confronts TN—TN is defiant. We saw that before. Notes for his next book." Eddie stopped suddenly, then grabbed the reunion list from his "in" box. "Thomas Nadeau and who? Martin?"

"Murphy."

Eddie nodded slowly. "On the beach."

"David Murphy confronts Tom Nadeau, and Nadeau is defiant."

"You sure it's not for the book?"

"I checked. There are no characters in the new book with the initials TN. There's a Maria and a Mateo starting with M, but no TN."

Eddie chewed the end of his pen. "But Nadeau and Murphy are chummy."

"Maybe not." Harvey checked his stocks. They were looking good. Not enough to buy Martin Blake's house, but it would certainly get him and Jennifer a comfortable home, even within the city limits.

He and Eddie met Jennifer for lunch at the café.

"What's Leeanne up to today?" Harvey asked.

"Beth was taking her to the art museum," Jennifer said. "Did Jeff get off all right?"

"Yes, he left early."

They ordered sandwiches, and Harvey arranged to pick Jennifer up for their counseling session with the pastor that evening.

Sarah came and stood by the table. "Is it all right if I sit here?"

They all welcomed her, but Eddie seemed a little stand-offish. A red flag went up in Harvey's brain. Eddie never shut off the charm around women, especially women he liked.

"Sarah, I haven't seen you for a couple of days," he said.

"We've been really busy. I caught traffic duty for the cemetery yesterday. Today we had an abuse call from a daycare center. Big mess. We had to call in Social Services. I'm so glad it's Friday." She started eating her salad.

"What are you and Cheryl doing tomorrow?" asked Jennifer.

"I told her I'd go to her parents' for the day. Wish I was going with you guys." She shot a glance at Eddie, but he was looking inside his sandwich.

"Maybe another time," Harvey said.

It was getting a little depressing. Eddie and Sarah usually struck sparks off each other.

"You're coming to the wedding, right?" Jennifer asked. "We mailed the out-of-town invitations today. Yours is right . . . here." She fished it out of her purse and handed Sarah the fat envelope that read, "Ms. Sarah Benoit and guest." Harvey had posted the one for the other officers on the bulletin board in the roll call room and distributed those for the men in his unit, plus Nate Miller and Tony Winfield. On Mike's advice, they had mailed one to the police chief.

"I wouldn't miss it." Sarah finally cracked a smile, opening the two envelopes and sliding out the white embossed card.

The conversation lagged. Eddie was the best man, so he couldn't take Sarah to the wedding. He'd be squiring Abby that day. Sarah knew that, and Harvey thought she was pining for him.

Jennifer's blue-gray eyes were trying to ask him something. Harvey smiled a little and wondered if the wedding ceremony gave couples mental telepathy.

"Harvey's taking me to an auction Tuesday," she said brightly to Sarah. "You ought to come with us."

That was what she wanted to ask. Another double date.

"That would be fun," Sarah said eagerly. She brushed her short, dark hair back, and didn't look at Eddie. "What are you guys shopping for?"

"Just stuff for the house," Jennifer said.

"You found a house?"

"No, but we're hoping."

Harvey decided he'd better step in. "Eddie, can you go? I might need you if I start buying furniture."

"For you, *mon ami*, but of course," he said, with the Maurice Chevalier accent. They all laughed. Eddie only lapsed into French when he was trying to be funny, when his grandmother was around, or when the job demanded it.

The ice was broken, and soon Eddie was eating chips off Sarah's plate and keeping the repartee flowing. She shook her head at him but came back with smart remarks, her eyes bright.

Harvey raised his eyebrows at Jennifer and tried to communicate mentally what he was thinking. This could be serious. Jennifer nodded solemnly and squeezed his hand.

"Gonna be strange without Mike for two weeks," Eddie said.

"Yup." Harvey didn't want to think about it.

"I heard him say he's retiring."

"Not yet. At least not until spring." Harvey shot him a glance sideways. "You hear anything else?" That was the conversation where Mike had talked about Harvey stepping into his job.

"Yeah. You want me to forget it?" Eddie asked.

They had reached the top of the stairs, and Mike was leaning over Arnie's desk, looking at a file with him.

"We'll talk about it sometime."

"Sure."

Eddie set to work on the interview notes. Harvey had asked him to compile a coherent narrative of the events from the first arrivals of alumni at Fort Point Sunday morning, through the discovery of Luke Frederick's body two days later. It was slow work, picking out the significant details from the witnesses' statements.

Harvey put the flash drive John Russell had given him in his computer and began reading Blake's article. When he'd finished, he sat for a long time, letting things settle in his mind.

"How's it going, Harv?" He jumped. Mike was standing beside him.

"Sit down for a minute." He bumped the mouse so the screen saver went away and the text showed on the monitor.

"What's this?"

"A story Martin Blake was writing for the *Press Herald*. It's pretty explosive."

Mike read intently, chewing his wad of gum. He whistled softly and scrolled down a screen, scanning the text. After a couple of minutes, he looked at Harvey.

"And they were going to print this?"

"They still might. Think anyone would want to stop it bad enough to kill him?"

Mike squinted at the screen again. "Blake had proof?"

"His editor was adamant he had to have documentation for everything. The paper's afraid of a libel suit. They're very strict about proof, but the managing editor still wants to publish it. If it's true, it will come out sooner or later, and he wants the *Press Herald* to break the story."

Mike shook his head. "Don't kill yourself over this one, Harv."

"Like you wouldn't." He sighed. "I hope we can wrap this up before the wedding." He was beginning to envy Mike his Allagash trip. No phone. No case. No press. Just the woman he loved and a few billion mosquitoes.

Jennifer hated to leave Leeanne that evening when Harvey picked her up for their counseling session at the church. "I've hardly seen her!"

"We'll only be gone a couple of hours, and we'll spend all day tomorrow with her," Harvey said.

Leeanne was enjoying her trip to the city, and Beth had taken over as hostess. They'd been to the Maine Mall after the art museum, and Leeanne had come home with a new pair of shoes and sunglasses. Jennifer was jealous of the time Beth had spent with her sister. Maybe after she and Harvey were settled, both her sisters could visit.

Pastor Rowland focused on communication that evening.

"Harvey, you're an intelligent man, and an independent thinker. However, I think it would benefit your marriage tremendously if you'd talk to Jennifer more."

Jennifer smiled at that. Many times she wished Harvey would spell out what he was thinking.

"I guess I needed that," he admitted. "I tend to assume Jennifer knows how I feel."

Pastor Rowland nodded. "You've had to do some joint decision making already, but there'll be a lot more after the wedding. People who have been single for a long time tend to be independent. That's not necessarily bad, but you need to remember you're half of a team now." He handed them each a sheaf of papers stapled together, containing eight pages of questions.

"You need to discuss these things," the pastor said, "and this is just a start." Jennifer leafed through the pages. The topics were wide ranging and detailed. Some of them she and Harvey had already dealt with, but others hadn't entered her mind. In-laws, housing, working wives, children, finances, household chores, submission, sex, and dozens more. She swallowed hard.

"You expect us to talk about all this tonight?" Harvey asked.

"No, but over the next few weeks. Talk, talk, talk. You don't need me there, but you each need to get an idea of the other's opinions in these areas. If you hit a snag, you can come to me. Some things we'll go over together."

The pastor talked about God's view of marriage then, and Harvey listened gravely. Jennifer sat quietly, her hands folded in her lap, feeling woefully inadequate.

They discussed the vows after that. Did they want the traditional wording? Harvey looked at Jennifer.

"I'd like it," she said.

He smiled. "You don't have to obey if you don't want to."

"I want to. I mean, I want it in the vows."

They prayed together. Jennifer's heart soared when Harvey prayed, asking God to help him lead their family and never to put her in the situation where she felt uncomfortable letting him. Her tears were near the surface by then.

The pastor brought out a stack of books for them to take home.

"Harvey," he said, "I'm not going to give you the sex lecture, unless there's something you want to talk about."

Harvey smiled. "I appreciate that."

"But Jennifer—" Rowland turned to her, and she blushed and looked at her hands. "I was wondering if you might like to talk to my wife sometime."

She took a shaky breath. "Maybe that would be good."

"There's a lot in these books," said the pastor. "They're all from a biblical perspective." He looked at Harvey. "You'll find this marriage is different from a secular one. You have the love of Christ now, and you'll love Jennifer in ways you never knew about before. Unselfishly."

Harvey nodded and looked over at her cautiously. Jennifer smiled, and he reached for her hand. *This is right,* she told herself, as joy shot through her. *This is the smartest thing I've ever done, and also the scariest.*

He took her home and left her at the door with a prayer and a sweet kiss.

Chapter 8

Saturday, June 26

Harvey picked Eddie up in the morning for the expedition to Fort Point. Eddie was well outfitted, with a tape measure, binoculars, a coil of rope, and his regular gear. The air was cool, and he and Harvey both wore light work shirts over their holsters.

On the way to Jennifer's house, Eddie said, "Only three more weeks."

Harvey smiled. "And five hours."

"You nervous?"

"Just a tad."

"Yeah?"

"Yeah. I messed up my first marriage. I really want to do things right this time."

"You're older and wiser."

"Well, older for sure."

Eddie looked over at him. "Hey, Harv, am I supposed to throw you a bachelor party?"

"No. Absolutely not."

"Okay. Pete said it's part of the best man's job."

"Well, he's wrong. Imagine how Jennifer would feel."

"Guess you're right. Or we could all get together without the other stuff."

"Don't forget, Mike's away. Why don't we just skip it?"

Eddie nodded, then asked slowly, "So, what exactly is my job?"

"Just hold the ring until we need it, and be there to catch me if I pass out."

"You wouldn't."

"You never know."

"What about at the reception? Do I dance with Abby?"

"Eddie, we're not having dancing at the wedding."

"No dancing? I've never been to a wedding without dancing."

"Well, brace yourself, buddy, because there won't be any champagne, either."

"You're off of champagne, too?"

"I'm off everything, and so is Jennifer."

"Okay. Is it because you're having it at the church?"

"Partly, I suppose. You know I've had a problem with alcohol in the past."

They were passing the church, and Eddie looked at it solemnly. "I don't get it, Harv. You're so different all of a sudden."

"I'm still me. I'm still your friend."

"I know, but . . . is it God or Jennifer that did it?"

"Maybe both." Eddie was pensive, and after a minute Harvey asked, "Do you not want to do it?"

"What? Be your best man? Of course I do!"

"Well, you don't seem comfortable with it."

"Just give me some time. I'm getting used to the new you, but you keep surprising me. Like the dancing thing."

A memory of his first wedding, with the reception at a posh Boston hotel, flashed through Harvey's mind. He'd called cabs for several people who drank too much, including his father-in-law, and he hadn't been exactly sober himself. As for dancing, after five or six drinks, Carrie had taken that to a new level with one of his Harvard buddies. He shook his head, trying to banish that memory.

"It's just better this way, okay? For Jennifer and me both."

"Okay."

Harvey turned in at Jennifer's driveway and shut the engine off. "There are just some things that we can do without now."

"Like drinking?"

"Yeah. When you drink, you're not in control. I want God to control me now, not alcohol."

"I can understand that."

"You know I quit drinking before I started dating Jennifer," Harvey said.

Eddie nodded slowly. "Yeah. When Carrie died. I remember."

"Well, Jennifer's family are nondrinkers, so it works out pretty well."

"What about the dancing? It's tradition."

Harvey blew out a breath. "That's a personal request on my part. It's got nothing to do with Jennifer, but she agreed."

The door opened, and Jennifer and Leeanne came outside. Harvey got out of the SUV. Jennifer had her hair in two long braids. On the lower part of each braid was a leather wrap with green wooden beads securing the thongs that laced them.

"Hey, Pocahontas." She made a face at him, but he kissed her anyway. "Better take a jacket. It might be chilly at the park."

"All right. The lunch is inside."

He followed her in and carried the picnic box to the SUV. She had packed food enough for an entire squad of detectives.

"Where's Beth? Would she like to come?" he asked.

"She's already left for her parents' in Freeport for the weekend," said Jennifer. Her tomboy ensemble consisted of jeans, a Portland SeaDogs sweatshirt, sneakers, and a blue Civil War campaign hat. Leeanne's dark hair was in a ponytail, and she wore a navy zip-front sweatshirt over a yellow T-shirt and jeans. She and her sister didn't look very feminine that day, but definitely cute.

Leeanne's luggage went in the back of the Explorer, along with the lunch. She climbed in and buckled up, demure and perhaps a little nervous beside Eddie.

Traffic was already heavy on coastal Route 1, and Harvey had to pay attention to his driving. In the back seat, Eddie began telling Leeanne a story about one of the unit's undercover jobs. He had her laughing in no time. Jennifer pulled out the pastor's list of questions and scanned it.

"What's the topic today, gorgeous?" Harvey asked.

"Number 48," she said.

"What's that?"

"Who will make the final decision when you disagree on a minor matter? And an important matter?"

Harvey said, "Well, if it's not important, then whoever feels most strongly should have their way."

"What if we both feel strongly?"

"For example?"

Jennifer smiled. "Oh, I don't know. How about the flavor of the wedding cake?"

"We compromised."

"Yes, but I was willing to have it your way."

"Wasn't I willing to have it your way?" he asked.

"I guess so, as long as it wasn't chocolate. Until you tasted the chocolate, that is."

"Well, you wouldn't want an all-chocolate wedding cake, would you?"

"Of course not." Jennifer watched him warily. It had started out as light teasing, but a knot tightened in her stomach, and she wasn't quite sure where the humor ended and the anxiety began.

"Is this your first fight?" asked Eddie.

Jennifer said, "No, I think we've had this fight before."

"It wasn't a fight," Harvey said.

"Well, I don't want to fight." She blinked furiously, determined not to cry over something so frivolous.

Harvey looked over at her and then put the turn signal on, pulled into a parking lot, and threw the gearshift into park.

"Why are we stopping?" she asked a little shakily.

"Your first lesson in making up." Harvey put his arms around her and kissed her, lingering over the embrace. She sighed and relaxed. The back seat was very quiet.

"Do you know where we are?" he asked.

"Searsport?" Jennifer guessed.

"No, only about halfway. Thomaston."

She craned her neck and looked. They were near the entrance of a bookstore she recognized. "Oh." She sat very still, looking at it.

"One of my favorite spots. Want to go in?"

165

She nodded. He got out of the Explorer and went around the back.

"A bookstore?" Eddie asked.

She smiled. "Not just any bookstore. This is where Harvey proposed. You guys will love it."

Harvey opened her door, and she got out. He put his arm around her shoulders, and they went inside. He led her down the book-lined hallways and through History, Biography, and Cookbooks, into Fiction. They went through Westerns, Sci-Fi and Suspense, and into Romance. Three women were in the room between the floor-to-ceiling shelves, talking and comparing authors. Harvey sighed and stepped back into the adjoining room, which was empty at the moment, and pulled Jennifer close.

"What, you're keeping me in Suspense?" she said.

He shook a little, then his laugh broke out. "Jenny, let's don't ever fight."

"It wasn't really a fight." She choked a little on it. "I didn't mean it to be."

"Me either. And if it's something that doesn't matter, then you can do whatever you want. I mean that. Even a little bride and groom on the cake, if that's what you want."

"It's not. But if you care about something, I want to do it your way, even if it doesn't matter. And if it does matter, you definitely get the final word." He tipped her face up and kissed her, then kissed her again.

"Excuse me. Romance is in there," said a woman, coming out of the room in question with an armful of paperbacks. She sounded a little bemused, but not severe.

As they stepped aside so she could wend her way out via Suspense and Sci-Fi, Harvey said, "In this store, ma'am, Romance is where you find it."

When the other two women came out, he and Jennifer stepped in and looked around at the historic room.

"There should be a brass plaque on the wall in here," he said. "Detective Harvey Larson asked for the hand of Miss Jennifer Wainthrop on this site, and received a favorable response."

"That's not romantic enough," she said. "It should read, 'Detective Harvey Larson passionately declared his love on this spot, and coaxed his sweetheart, Jennifer Wainthrop, into a whirlwind engagement.' Or something like that."

Harvey smiled, "I thought courting you was hard, but being engaged is a lot more tiring."

"Think so?"

"Yes. I've never been so happy or so stressed. I'm sorry about the cake and anything else I've been obnoxious about."

"You weren't obnoxious. I need your input,

and I appreciate the way you've put up with everything. I know you never wanted a big wedding."

"It's okay." He kissed her beneath the spot where the brass plaque should have been. "Are we ready for Fort Point?"

"I think so."

They ambled back out through the maze of alcoves and crannies and found Eddie in Automotive. They split up to look for Leeanne. She emerged from Juvenile with shining eyes, holding up a pair of hundred-year-old children's books.

"G. A. Henty," she said to Jennifer.

"Oooh! Let me see!" Jennifer was as excited as Leeanne. They'd loved the author's books as children. Leeanne paid for her finds, and they went back to the SUV.

As they drove on, Leeanne and Eddie talked like friends, and Jennifer felt at ease. Whenever Harvey didn't need two hands to drive, he held on to one of hers.

They found the state park a little before eleven o'clock. A young woman in a Parks & Rec uniform stood in the booth at the gate, and when Harvey gave her the entrance fee, she handed him several brochures. He parked in the lot and looked around, trying to visualize Martin and Thelma Blake's arrival on Sunday. A dirt road led up an incline from the far end of the lot, and a sign beside it said, "Fort and Lighthouse."

Harvey opened the door and got out, still surveying the layout.

"It's not like I thought," said Eddie.

"Nope. Can't see the water or the lighthouse from here."

Harvey pushed the automatic lock button, took Jennifer's hand, and led the way down a path toward Penobscot Bay. Restroom cabins were just visible in the woods to the right of the path. They went through the trees, and soon several picnic tables came into view. He and Jennifer walked past them and came to a rim, where the ground suddenly fell away about thirty feet, in a very steep slope to the shore below. Bushes and small trees grew on the slope, and the tops of the trees came up above it, partly obscuring the view. A narrow path zigzagged down between rocks and bushes, ending on a rocky strip of beach below. Waves rolled in over boulders, and water splashed within five yards of the foot of the path.

"Not much of a beach," said Jennifer.

Eddie and Leeanne came up behind them.

"Can't see much from here," Eddie observed. He put his binoculars to his eyes and trained them on the bay.

"Let's find out how much you *could* see." Harvey started down the path. It was rugged, and he had to place his feet carefully. Jennifer followed, holding on to branches as she went.

"Careful." Harvey got to the ground, and called up to Eddie, "Can you see us?"

Eddie leaned out over the rim and said, "Now I can."

They walked out away from the hillside, picking their way carefully on the rocks.

"How about now?"

"Clear view."

They went as far as they could without getting their feet wet.

"Now?"

"Yep." They walked back in. Eddie and Leeanne scrambled down the slope.

"I think the tide's pretty high," Harvey said. "The Blakes were up there looking down a little later, but that was six days ago." He calculated the difference a week would make in the tide schedule.

"So there might have been a little more beach showing," said Eddie.

"Yeah. Tide was high at two-thirty in the afternoon that day, so about halfway in when they were here."

They looked out at the bay, then to the right, at a strip of coarse gravel. They walked to it, and Harvey wondered if they could be seen from above. Beyond it, the shore curved around a point. In the other direction was a rocky stretch, then the water came nearly to the trees.

"The lighthouse is that way." Harvey gestured toward the point.

"Should we go back up, or walk around to the lighthouse?" asked Jennifer.

"I'm not sure that's possible at this stage of the tide. But the longer we stay, the lower it will get. How about if you girls go up the hill, and Eddie and I try to go around on the rocks?" Harvey gave her his car keys.

Leeanne and Jennifer climbed slowly, grabbing bushes to pull themselves up the path. He and Eddie stood below, watching them, in case they had trouble.

"I can't see a bunch of 50-year-olds taking that path," said Eddie.

"Me either. It was hard enough on *my* knees."

"Maybe there's another path."

When the women were safely up, Jennifer waved.

Harvey called, "We'll walk toward the point. If we make it, drive up to the lighthouse and meet us there."

He and Eddie started along the shore. When they got around the point, the strip below the hillside was narrower, and they had to climb carefully over slabs of rock. The cold waves splashed up, soaking Harvey's sneakers and pantlegs.

"Do you think they could have done this?"

"They could have. But did they?" Eddie asked.

"Well, if the tide was lower, it wouldn't be so dangerous," Harvey reminded him.

"Maybe Frederick slipped on one of these rocks and hit his head."

Harvey said, "Then why did David Murphy deny seeing him at first?"

"Maybe he knew he was dead."

"Hm. If Frederick died accidentally and somebody knew it, they'd raise an alarm and try to pull him out of the water. Murphy could come out a hero for even trying to save him. But if he knew Frederick was dead and didn't want anyone else to know, he would have lied."

"Which he did," Eddie said.

They rounded the point at last, and could see a pyramid tower ahead.

"Is that the lighthouse?" Eddie asked. "Kind of small."

They kept walking, and another structure appeared beyond it, a lighthouse tower with the keeper's house at its base. When they got to the first building, the girls were waiting.

"What is this thing?" Harvey asked. The grassy slope was much more gradual here, and they climbed it with little difficulty. A large bronze bell hung in the wooden tower on the side that faced the bay, but it wasn't up in the top like a steeple bell. Its base was only two feet off a recessed deck. The white pyramid-shaped tower was about fifteen feet high and had a locked door on the back of it.

"It's called the bell tower," said Jennifer, looking up from her brochure.

"What's it for?" asked Eddie, climbing into the front of the tower where the bell hung. He reached up inside it, grabbed the clapper and tapped it gently against the side of the bell.

Bong! The sound was so loud, he jumped back and looked around quickly. A few people stood in the field between them and the parking lot, and more near the lighthouse. They all turned and looked toward the bell tower.

"Am I in trouble?" asked Eddie.

Harvey shook his head. "I don't think so." *Just like a kid.*

"Maybe it's what they used before they had foghorns," said Leeanne.

"What's over there?" Harvey nodded toward the parking lot and barely visible signs.

"That's the fort." Jennifer held out the brochure.

"You're kidding."

"No. It was wood, built in 1759, before the Revolution. Only the earthworks are left."

They walked closer, and Harvey studied a diagram of the fort, comparing it with what was left in the ground before him. Fort Pownal had been in the shape of a four-pointed star, with a moat the same shape around it. They stood outside the ridges of earth that formed the outer wall of the moat. Harvey walked to the berm and surveyed the stone foundation that was left in the center, where the wooden garrison had stood. He wished he could have seen it in its original condition. The drawing in the brochure intrigued him.

At last he turned away. "So all the class members were up here looking at this."

"Sounds that way," said Eddie. "Most of them looked at the fort and the lighthouse and the bell tower before lunch. Then later some of them came back up here with lawn chairs and sat around talking."

"It's a better view than at the picnic area," Leeanne said.

"And the mosquitoes wouldn't be as bad here in the open as down there in the woods," Jennifer added.

Harvey stared out over the bay. "If Frederick was in the water, they might not have seen the body. At some point it had to wash down to Islesboro, but it might have been out from shore far enough that they wouldn't notice it."

"Or it might have hung up in those rocks until high tide," Eddie said.

"Someone must have gone down to the shore after lunch," Harvey insisted.

"It's a difficult climb," Eddie reminded him.

Harvey didn't want to give up the idea. "This

path is easier than the one we went down. I can't believe no one would see the body if it was below this place. I'm pretty sure this is where Thelma said they sat around and talked."

"Maybe there's an easier path farther down the shore," Leeanne said.

Jennifer wanted pictures for her scrapbook, so they took a few near the fort and the lighthouse. Eddie and Leeanne scrambled down into the foundation of the old fort, where rock walls stood chest-high.

Eddie said, "I wonder if people find old bullets and things here." They started looking around the ground.

After a while Harvey called them out of the hole, and they took the Explorer back to the first parking lot and followed the path on foot, to the spot they'd been to before on the rim. A family of five was eating at a picnic table close to the head of the shore path.

Harvey nodded to them and kept going. After a short way, another path branched off toward the water. He followed it until he found another dirt track heading down toward the rocky strip below. It was at least as steep as the first trail.

He turned back. Eddie was right behind him, and Jennifer and Leeanne were farther back, heading their way.

"I don't think they'd go any farther than this,"

Harvey said. Beyond that point, the main path faded to a faint trail with no markers.

"I doubt it, too," Eddie said.

"So they were all over there near the picnic tables. Why didn't one of them see the body?"

"Maybe it was never within sight from up there," Eddie said. "If he started around the rocks and slipped . . ."

"Or maybe someone did see it, or thought he saw something in the water," Harvey said, thinking over the options.

Eddie looked a question at him.

"Blake. Thelma said he started down the path."

"Find anything?" Jennifer called.

Harvey grinned at her. "Not yet."

"What else can we do?" Jennifer asked.

Eddie said, "We can put a body down by the rocks and see if you can see it from up top."

Leeanne stared at him, her blue eyes dark in the shade.

Harvey said, "Eddie and I will go down this path and walk over to where we were before, below the first path. You girls go back near the picnic tables and wave when you can see us."

"Wait a sec." Eddie took off his binoculars and hung them around Leeanne's neck. "Jennifer, do you have your phone?"

"Yes."

"Harvey?"

"Yes."

"Okay, so we can communicate without yelling in front of those people."

"Good." Harvey stepped over the edge onto the dirt path and nearly fell. The footing was tricky. Eddie, behind him, sent loose pebbles down on him. This path was more treacherous than the first, and he went on cautiously. At the base they walked over the rocks, looking along the edge above them for the girls. The strip of shore was a little wider now. Harvey saw the girls, and Leeanne had the binoculars to her eyes. Jennifer waved.

"They see us." He and Eddie hopped from rock to rock, then stopped on a flat rock. The waves skimmed the top, washing over his sneakers. "This would be out of the water at low tide." The girls waved.

"That day, while they ate lunch, the tide got higher. Today, it's getting lower." Harvey turned toward the bay. "Mrs. Blake said Murphy and Frederick were standing on the rocks, close to the water."

"This place is as good as any." Eddie looked back at the path. "If you were standing here and you got mad at me, what would you do?"

"Throw you in the drink."

"No, I mean really mad," Eddie said.

"You mean, murderously mad?"

"Precisely."

Harvey looked around. Seaweed and mussel

shells dotted the gravel between the bigger rocks, and little tide pools lay in depressions. He bent and picked up a rock the size of a softball, and hefted it in his left hand.

"This would do it."

"Can't hope to find any evidence." Eddie scanned the shore. Thousands of rocks lay within sight.

Harvey took his phone out and speed-dialed Jennifer.

"Hello down there," she said in his ear.

"Hey, gorgeous. Can you see what I'm holding?"

"Your phone?"

"No, in the other hand."

"No. Let me ask Leeanne."

They leaned toward each other, and Leeanne brought the binoculars up again.

"A rock?" guessed Jennifer.

"You got it."

"We couldn't see it without the binoculars."

Eddie wiggled his eyebrows. "Hit me with it."

Into the phone, Harvey said, "Watch closely."

He and Eddie turned toward the water. Harvey raised the rock behind Eddie's head and brought it gently against his skull. Eddie sat down on the rock, and Harvey dropped his hand that held the stone.

"What just happened?" he asked Jennifer.

"You hit him?"

"A-plus."

"But we can see Eddie, and he's sitting up," she protested.

Eddie was taking his shoes off.

"You'll get all wet," Harvey said. "You can't go all the way back to Portland soaking wet."

Eddie peeled off his work shirt and his holster. "Hold these." His T-shirt, with his badge pinned to it, followed, and his watch. He was starting on his belt buckle.

"Eddie! You can't undress in front of the girls."

"No worse than a swim suit." He stepped out of his pants and handed them to Harvey, shivering in his plaid boxers. "Careful, my wallet's in there. Besides, they're fifty yards away. They can't see."

"Leeanne has binoculars."

Eddie turned and waved up at them. They waved back, and the binoculars were hanging in front of Leeanne's sweatshirt.

"They're good, modest girls," Harvey said.

"And you're a prude."

Eddie lowered himself over the edge of the rock into the water with a gasp. He tried to lie down, but the seaward side of the rock was slimy with algae, and he slipped and went under. He resurfaced immediately, sputtering, but Harvey's adrenaline surged as he crouched on the rock and reached toward him.

"You okay?"

"Yeah." It wasn't very deep, and Eddie got his legs under him and maneuvered close to the rock. He clutched a rough edge, with his head above the water. The waves came up over him, but he was mostly above the water line.

"Jennifer, can you see him?"

"No. Is he okay?"

"Yes, but he's turning blue. Get out, Eddie."

Harvey grasped his wrist and he scrambled up, shivering. Harvey looked along the shore. "I wish I knew if this was where they were standing."

"We'll never know, unless we get Mrs. Blake up here to show us."

"A picture," Harvey said. He spoke to Jennifer again. "Can you girls take some photos with your phones?"

"Sure," Jennifer said.

"You see those big rocks over there?" Harvey asked Eddie, pointing a little toward the point of land. A cluster of large boulders was mostly above the tide now.

Eddie nodded.

"If they were over there, a body could be lodged between the rocks, and I'll bet nobody would see it for hours. Not unless some kids were climbing around. It might stay between the rocks all afternoon, and wash out at high tide that night."

"Let's take a look."

When Jennifer reported by phone that she was

finished, Eddie pushed his clothes into Harvey's hands and started walking toward the large boulders, stepping gingerly on the rocks in his bare feet. Harvey followed cautiously. In his dripping boxers, Eddie stood shivering, four feet above the shingle on a rounded rock that sloped down to the water. The chain of his crucifix glittered against the back of his neck.

"Jenny, can you see Eddie?" Harvey said into his phone.

"Plain as day. Leeanne wants to know if he works out."

"Take another picture."

Harvey picked up another rock, this time a little smaller, baseball sized, and climbed up beside Eddie with the bundle of clothes under one arm.

"Hit me," Eddie said.

"I don't know. It looks like a drop-off here. What if you can't get back up? Should we get the rope?"

"I'm not going in the bay."

"Okay." Harvey waved at Jennifer, and she waved back. He brought the rock up and gave Eddie a gentle tap on the back of his head. He collapsed and rolled off the side of the rock, down between the boulders into a tidal pool.

"Ouch."

"You all right?"

"Stupid clam shell," Eddie said.

Into the phone, Harvey said, "Can you see him?"

"No. Is he okay?"

"I think so. He's freezing, though. We'll be up soon."

He put the phone in his pocket. Laying Eddie's clothes on his shoes on top of the rock, he bent down and looked over the side.

"Are you good?"

"I cut myself on a clamshell."

"How bad?"

"It'll be okay. Hurts, though."

Eddie was sitting in the pool with a pair of glasses in his hand. He held them up to Harvey. They were a man's glasses, Harvey thought, wire rimmed with plain gold metal bows. The bow on the right side was bent and scratched.

Eddie hoisted himself up and sat on the rock beside him, shaking.

"You'd better get dressed." Harvey looked up at the hill. The picnicking family had joined Jennifer and Leeanne. While Eddie pulled his clothes on, Harvey put the glasses in an evidence bag from his pocket.

"Did you notice where they're bent?" Eddie asked, working his socks on.

"Yup," Harvey replied. "It reminded me that his head wounds were on his temples, not the back of his head."

"So Murphy couldn't have hit him from behind."

"How can you hit someone with a rock from the side?" Harvey asked. "He would have seen it coming."

Eddie was getting his sneakers on. "What if he was turning around when Murphy hit him?"

Harvey picked up his rock and looked at it and the glasses. He took his driving glasses out of his shirt pocket. "Put these on."

Eddie stood up and put on Harvey's specs, then turned to face the sea. Harvey got behind him and prepared to strike. "Okay, just start to turn toward me."

As he turned his head, Harvey brought the rock up against the bow of his glasses.

"I think it would work, if Frederick was about the same height as Murphy."

"How did he get the bump on the other side, though?" Eddie asked. "He didn't get hit with two rocks."

Harvey looked down into the tide pool. "Must have hit his head on the left side when he fell off the rock."

"His glasses might have fallen off when he was hit," said Eddie.

"Frederick's son lives in Portland. Shall we pay him a visit?"

"The glasses are probably not his."

"Probably not," Harvey agreed. He knew he wouldn't rest if he didn't follow up on it.

Eddie was still chilled when they got up the

path, and Harvey ran up to the Explorer for his bomber jacket and made him put it on. The picnickers were packing their lunch things.

"A little chilly for a swim, isn't it?" the mother asked.

"Yeah, it is," Harvey said.

They walked up to the parking lot. "Put Eddie in front," Harvey told Jennifer, and she got in back with Leeanne. He turned the heat on and watched Eddie. He was still shaking. After a few minutes Harvey was sweating, but Eddie had stopped shivering.

"You gonna be okay?"

Eddie nodded, and Harvey shut the heater off.

"My foot hurts."

"Better let me check it."

"It'll be okay."

"Well, you want to eat?"

"Sure."

Jennifer suggested they eat in the car to keep Eddie warm. She and Leeanne reached behind the seat and lifted the lunch box over the back. Harvey asked a brief blessing, and they ate sandwiches, grapes, and chips. Jennifer had packed a thermos of coffee, and it was still hot. Eddie drank two cups. The rest of them had soft drinks.

"Did you learn anything from all this?" Jennifer asked, handing Harvey a bag of cookies.

"One thing, at least." He brought out the zipper bag with the glasses in it.

Leeanne beamed at him. "A real clue!"

"Eddie found them between the rocks in that last spot where he pretended to fall. We need to ask Frederick's son if he recognizes them. Mrs. Blake said he wore glasses that day."

They drove down Route 1 to Belfast, then left the coast for the run to Skowhegan. They descended on the Wainthrops at three o'clock.

"I hope you can stay for supper," Marilyn greeted them.

Jennifer looked at Harvey, and he smiled regretfully. "I'm sorry. We really need to get back to Portland and check out a lead in the case we're working on."

"Well, have a piece of pie, at least."

They took Leeanne's luggage in and sat down. Jeff and Abby were at work, so only George and Marilyn Wainthrop and their two teen-aged sons, Travis and Randy, were there to visit with them. The boys soon had Eddie telling about the Blake investigation and the trip to Fort Point. Eddie made it sound like he'd nearly died of hypothermia. The boys wanted to know if they'd found any clues.

"We did," Harvey said, "but we can't tell you what they are while the investigation is open."

"Solving a case like this takes a lot of time and hard work," said Eddie.

"Hard work," Randy scoffed. "You guys take

picnics with girls and call it hard work."

"Hey," Eddie said with mock offense, "I nearly froze to death on that picnic."

Harvey leaned toward Marilyn and said confidentially, "You did teach your daughters to make pies, didn't you?"

"Well, Jennifer was a little slow in that department. She was always on the computer. But I think she could make a passable apple pie."

Jennifer grimaced at him. "Has Jeff heard about the job yet?" she asked her father.

"Not yet. He's hoping."

"We're praying about it," she said. George looked at her, but said nothing.

"We thought we'd go to church tomorrow." Marilyn looked from Jennifer to Harvey.

"Oh, great. Where?" asked Jennifer.

"Well, your father said your church has had a good influence on you both, and he wanted one like yours, so we found a Baptist church out on Fletcher Road."

George pushed his chair back and went for the coffeepot.

Leeanne said, "I'll go with you, Mom."

"Do you go there, too, Eddie?" Marilyn asked.

"No. Well, I've been a couple of times." Eddie scraped his dessert plate with his fork, and Leeanne jumped to get him another piece of pie.

Harvey could see that Jennifer's father felt

uncomfortable. "So, George, how's the garden coming?"

George lost the hunted look and refilled his coffee cup.

They headed out soon after that. Leeanne was a little wistful in her goodbyes, especially when Eddie chucked her under the chin and said, "See you at the wedding."

When they found Luke Frederick's house, it was nearly six o'clock. Harvey and Eddie went to the door, and Jennifer stayed in the vehicle. Frederick's son answered the doorbell. He was six feet tall and thin, with a long nose and straw-colored hair. Harvey showed his badge and made the introduction.

"Mr. Frederick, I'm sorry about your father. Have you had the service yet?"

"Yesterday."

"I've been working with the state police on this thing. My partner and I are investigating the Blake death, and we see a connection."

"You think the person who killed my father killed Martin Blake?"

"Well, I wouldn't go that far," Harvey said, "but they were together on Sunday, saw each other, talked to each other shortly before your father disappeared."

Ben Frederick frowned. "The trooper who was here this morning says they think it was an accident. Dad slipped on the rocks and hit his head and ended up in the water."

"There are one or two things that make me doubt that," Harvey said. "I can't elaborate right now, but could you tell me if your father wore glasses?"

"Yes, he wore them all the time."

"Did the police return them to you with your father's personal effects?"

"No. They said they were probably lost in the bay."

Harvey took out the evidence bag and held it up so he could see the glasses clearly.

Frederick's face paled. "Where did you get them?"

"On the shore at Fort Point."

He stared in amazement. "The police said they searched the beach after they found his car there."

"It was between some rocks. My partner found them today, but they weren't in plain sight. You recognize them."

"They look like my father's."

"You see the dent here, and the scratches?"

"Yes."

"Were those there the last time you saw your father?"

"I don't think so."

"Could you show us some pictures of your father wearing his glasses?" Harvey asked.

"Of course."

They followed him inside. The house was small, but had big windows facing the harbor on the back of the living room. Frederick walked to a bookshelf and selected a photo album. He flipped through it and pointed out several pictures of his father. One, taken a month earlier, showed Luke Frederick in profile, holding up a fish on a stringer. Harvey compared the glasses in the bag and those in the picture.

"They sure look alike," said Eddie.

"What does it mean?" asked Frederick.

"We'll try to determine that. May I have the name of your father's optician?" Harvey asked.

"Yes. Whatever you need." Ben Frederick went to a desk and opened an address book. "They probably won't be open until Monday." He handed Harvey a slip of paper with the name and telephone number of an eye care office on Forest Avenue.

Chapter 9

Sunday, June 27

Harvey was still tired the next morning when he joined Jennifer at the church. He'd stayed up until 1 a.m. rereading Martin Blake's article and writing himself notes on things to check into. He tried to put the case out of his mind for a couple of hours, but he nearly fell asleep during the missionary speaker's slides.

At the end of the service, Everett Bailey stood at the end of his usual pew, waiting to merge into the aisle.

"Mr. Larson," he said, when Harvey was even with him.

"Good morning, sir!" Harvey stuck his hand out, and Bailey shook it.

"I heard you folks are looking for a house. Beth Bradley gave me a call."

Beth hadn't returned from her visit to Freeport yet, and Harvey had forgotten about her recommendation.

"Yes, we are. We haven't really started looking, but we need to. Is your home for sale?"

"Yes, I've decided to move in with my daughter's family in Saco. I've been alone six months now, and I'm tired of it. I'll miss the

190

place, but it's too big for me now, and I can't keep up with the yard work. Are you folks interested? I was going to list it tomorrow, but if you want to take a look . . ."

Harvey looked at Jennifer. She had been listening, and she returned his look with wide eyes.

"I guess we would," Harvey said. "When would you like to show it?"

"Today? Tomorrow? What suits you?"

They were due at Carl and Margaret Turner's for dinner at one o'clock. Harvey said, "We've got a lunch date, but we could come later this afternoon."

"That's fine," Bailey said. "Four o'clock?"

Jennifer nodded, and Harvey noted the address. They went out to the Explorer and left her car in the parking lot.

Jennifer had met Carl, but not Margaret. The idea of rubbing elbows with two doctors seemed to intimidate her. She was wearing a gray tailored suit she'd worn to work when she was presenting computer programs to important clients. It was a sophisticated look, not her normal, less formal style. She looked good, but less approachable than usual. In honor of the M.D.'s, Harvey decided.

Before starting the engine, he turned to face her. "Jenny, these people are really down-to-earth. They're my friends."

"Okay." She was feeling the back of her hair, which was up in a Grace Kelly do. A few tendrils had escaped at the back of her neck, and he leaned over and kissed her there. She looked around the parking lot quickly.

"Don't be so nervous. Everyone knows we're engaged. They expect me to be romantic around you."

She gave him a little smile, but the nerves were definitely showing. How had she ever made it through their first date?

"What is it?" He put his arm up on the back of the seat.

"You're all forty, and I'm twenty-five." She wrapped the strap of her purse around her hand.

He laughed. "I thought we went through that already."

"We have, but have they?"

"They're happy for me. They'll love you."

She sighed.

He put his driving glasses on, started the motor, and pulled out into the street. "What do you think about Mr. Bailey's house?"

"I don't know anything about it, but I'd like to see it. Where is Van Cleeve Lane?"

"Pretty posh neighborhood. It's a couple of miles from here. I haven't been over there much, and I can't picture the street."

"Sounds like it has a big yard."

"Yeah. Me mowing a lawn weekends."

"Maybe you don't want to do that," she said. "You've lived in an apartment so long. Maybe the maintenance wouldn't fit with your schedule."

"I think it would be a great outlet. I'm tired of climbing stairs when I get home and having to go over to the park if I want to sit outside."

"It might be expensive."

"We'll see."

"Well, what do we want in a house? Shouldn't we have an idea before we see it?"

"Okay. I'd like a house with a yard, size optional, and at least two bedrooms. One for us, and one for a guest room." He glanced sideways at her. "Or a nursery."

"Sounds good." She wasn't looking at him.

"Maybe we need to talk about some more of the questions on Pastor's list," he said.

"Maybe."

He drove for a block in silence. He had shut her out of one abandoned room of his life, and he didn't like that. He didn't want to foist his pain on her, but he didn't want secrets between them, either. He ventured, "We haven't talked much about kids. I know we both want them."

"Yes."

He drove another block.

"How many?"

She looked out the side window. "Two at least. What do you think?"

"At least. But I'm not getting any younger. I

don't want to be tottering around with a cane at their high school graduations."

"So we should have them soon."

"I guess." He knew he couldn't leave it there.

They were only a quarter mile from Carl's house. Harvey glanced at his watch. They had fifteen minutes, and he pulled over to the curb and took off his glasses.

"Jenny."

She turned and looked at him.

He said, "I'm not very good at this. I'm sorry."

She came into his arms, street or no street. Her eyes glistened with tears. He kissed her. "Maybe we should quit by the time I'm fifty? We could have three or four kids by then."

She smiled and turned his face to the side and kissed the corner of his eye. He knew she was kissing the wrinkles. She said, "You've waited a long time."

He should be calm now, but his stomach was churning. "Look, I told you about Carrie."

She nodded, apprehension clouding her eyes. "She didn't want kids."

"It was more than that." He sat still for a moment. Why inflict needless pain on Jennifer?

"What is it?" she asked.

"There, uh . . . there was a baby. Would've been a baby."

Jennifer said slowly, "Carrie was pregnant?"

He nodded. "She didn't want it."

Jennifer caught her breath.

"She didn't tell me 'til after. I didn't know if I could forgive that."

"Oh, Harvey!" Jennifer put her arms around him and pulled his head down on her shoulder.

After a minute, he pulled in a deep breath and sat up. "I don't want to make you all sad and weepy. We'll have fun with Carl and Margaret. I shouldn't have said anything."

"No, Pastor Rowland's right. We need to talk about it."

"Later, then. My timing's lousy."

"Can we pray?" Jennifer asked. "Do we have time?"

"Okay." Harvey closed his eyes.

"Dear Father, please help us with this," Jennifer said softly. "Please take away Harvey's hurt and his feelings of guilt. And please bless that baby. Amen."

Harvey dashed away a tear. "Amen." He didn't trust himself to say any more.

Jennifer found a tissue in her purse and handed it to him.

"Thank you. You sure you're okay?" he asked.

"Yes. We can ask the pastor about this at our next class."

He nodded. Jennifer kissed his cheek and they drove on to Carl and Margaret's.

Eight-year-old Julia Turner was riding a scooter in the driveway, and she greeted them enthusiastically and escorted them through the open garage, into the kitchen.

"Mommy, Harvey and Goldilocks are here!"

Jennifer faced him with arched brows.

"Don't look at me," Harvey said. "Carl has a way . . ."

Margaret was coming to meet them with a huge smile. She'd had her dark hair cut short since Harvey had seen her, and she wore a white apron over her pink sundress.

"Jennifer! At last I meet Harvey's bride-to-be!" She kissed Jennifer on the cheek. "Carl described you to a T."

"Where is the galoot?" Harvey asked.

"In the back yard, grilling steaks." She took them through to the family room, where she opened the patio door for Harvey, and he stepped out onto flagstones surrounded by lilies and foxglove in bloom.

"Harvey!" Carl was manfully dealing with the grill. "Where's the gorgeous blonde?"

Harvey looked behind him and realized Jennifer had stayed inside. "I guess Margaret kidnapped her."

"You're looking good. Feeling okay?" Carl asked.

"Yeah, I think I'm back to about 98 percent. Maybe you could take a listen to my lung?"

"Sure." Carl went inside immediately and returned with a stethoscope. He listened, and

Harvey breathed. "Sounds good. Any problems?"

"No, just a little twinge the first time I ran."

"That will go away. You should be all set to face married life."

Harvey smiled. "If we just get through the wedding, I think the rest will be easy."

"Got the jitters?"

"Not me so much as Jenny. Everything's got to be perfect."

"Really? She didn't strike me that way." Carl laid down the stethoscope and went back to the grill.

"She's not exactly a perfectionist." Harvey tried to clarify it in his mind. "Maybe it's just that she's afraid something will be wrong, not that it has to be right. It didn't seem as though it took this much work to get married the first time."

"I'm guessing Carrie's mother took charge, and you didn't have to lift a finger."

Margaret, Jennifer and Julia came through the patio door carrying dishes of salad and a pitcher of fruit juice.

"Harvey, you look happier than I've ever seen you," said Margaret.

"I take that as a compliment."

"It is. I've been wanting to meet Jennifer. She seems like a good match for you."

Jennifer looked as though she wished Margaret wasn't talking about her when she was right there.

Harvey said, "I didn't know if I'd ever find the right woman, but here she is." He slid his arm around Jennifer, and she smiled.

Carl brought the platter of meat over, and they all sat down. They started serving the food, so Harvey didn't say anything. Jennifer looked at him, then took some potato salad and passed it on. They'd been praying over their meals for a month, and it already felt strange not to do it.

"So what are the honeymoon plans?" Margaret asked.

"Big secret," Harvey said.

"Oh, come on."

"Jennifer doesn't even know yet."

"Oh, all right."

"Where do doctors vacation?" he asked.

"We're going to Japan in August," said Carl.

"Whew." Harvey was impressed. Jennifer had an out-of-my-league look. He said, "Jennifer's asked for a passport renewal. I'm waiting for it to come in before I buy the tickets."

"Don't cut it too close, or you'll pay more," said Margaret.

"Ever been out of the country?" Carl asked Jennifer.

"Just to the Maritimes."

"So, this should be an adventure."

"Oh, I can't wait," Jennifer said. Then she looked confused and started blushing.

"Will you send me a stamp?" asked Julia.

"Of course," Harvey said. Stamp collecting was a recently acquired hobby for Julia.

"Are you working, Jennifer?" asked Margaret.

"Yes, at the police station, in the records department. I've only been there two weeks."

"Oh, so you didn't meet at work, then?"

Jennifer looked at Harvey. He smiled, to encourage her to tell the story herself. After a second she said, "Harvey and his partner came to the place I used to work on business."

"He told me about that," said Carl. "Wasn't it when that fellow was murdered?"

Jennifer winced, and Harvey said quickly, "Yeah, but we didn't know he'd been murdered then. He was missing, and it turned out Jennifer was the last person to see him. Well, the last one to admit it, that is."

"That must have been horrible," said Margaret.

Harvey was afraid Jennifer was too rattled to keep her composure, but she managed a weak smile and said, "So, how did you two meet?"

"In med school."

Carl grinned. "Margaret was at the top of the class. We men were so mad that a woman was outdoing us, we all tried to sabotage her. Then I started rooting for her. I figured a mind like hers in a body like that was not something I wanted to see sabotaged."

Margaret laughed. "He ended up with the top honors at graduation. I was second."

Harvey was glad they were safely off the subject of the murder, which was still fresh in Jennifer's mind. "That's the kind of doctor I want," he said. "not some guy who passed anatomy with a D minus."

"You have a family practice?" asked Jennifer.

Margaret said, "Carl's is family practice. We share an office. I'm in OB-GYN."

"That reminds me," Harvey said. "Jennifer's going on my insurance at work in a couple of weeks. She's a temporary employee, and I guess the HMO covers her now. But she needs a primary care doctor."

"Who's your doctor, Jennifer?" Margaret asked.

"Dr. Marks, but I don't like him."

"Keith Marks? I know him," said Carl. "I don't think he's in your HMO, Harvey. You'd have to check to be sure."

Jennifer blushed. "I don't have anything against him personally, I just don't feel comfortable with him. He's the doctor my old company recommended when I first came here, and I never took the initiative to change."

"He's not a bosom buddy of mine," said Carl.

"So you don't have to like him," Margaret said with a wink.

Harvey said, "Why don't you put Carl down for your PCP, and he can refer you to Margaret for girl stuff."

"Girl stuff!" Margaret's voice dripped acid. "You are such a chauvinist."

"Am not."

"They never admit it," she said knowingly to Jennifer.

Jennifer smiled a little. "I think I'd like having a female doctor."

"Daddy, may I please have more potato salad?" Julia piped up. She'd been quiet, listening to the conversation.

"What are you doing this summer, Julia?" Harvey asked.

She started telling him about an upcoming bike rodeo. In the background, he heard Jennifer say quietly to Margaret, "I made an appointment with Dr. Marks for a checkup before the wedding, but I'm sort of nervous about it. Do you think I could switch that quickly?"

"When's the wedding?" Margaret asked. "July seventeenth? Sure. Call my office tomorrow. I'll make sure we get you in. Kristy will tell you I'm not taking new patients, but tell her I've approved it personally. I'll have her request a referral from Keith Marks. Unless you want to switch to Carl? Don't feel you have to, just because Harvey suggested it."

There was quite a pause. Julia said, "And then you ride zigzag, in and out, around these red cone thingies, and if you don't hit any, you get a prize."

"I'll bet you'll get one." He looked over at Jennifer. She was looking at Carl. Harvey asked Julia, "What happens if you hit one?"

Jennifer said to Margaret, "I'm not sure. Your husband is so . . . well . . . gregarious."

Margaret laughed. "He is that. Stay with Marks if you want. Or find somebody else."

Jennifer said something Harvey couldn't hear, because Julia was now imitating the siren of the ambulance that would come for her if she fell off her bike.

The next thing he heard in the women's conversation was Margaret whooping, "Not really! Skowhegan Area High School! What year?" It turned out Margaret had grown up in Canaan, a little town in the same school district as Skowhegan. Of course, she had graduated 15 years before Jennifer, but they soon discovered some mutual acquaintances, including one English teacher they had both studied under, and they knew the same cheers for the Skowhegan Indians.

Carl nodded toward them and said to Harvey, "Thought they'd hit it off."

Harvey said quietly, "Jenny was a little apprehensive about the generation gap."

"You wouldn't be marrying an adolescent."

Harvey smiled. "Most of the time, she makes me forget the age difference."

"Well, you look like the cat with cream on his whiskers. She must be taking care of you."

"She's the best."

"Hey, you two, are you going to do the dishes?" Margaret was stacking plates.

"No way," said Carl. "The squaws of Skowhegan do that."

Margaret threw a pot holder at him.

They all cleaned up, then sat in the family room. Harvey and Carl discussed the fine points of buying a house, and Margaret pumped Jennifer for wedding details. When Harvey heard Jennifer telling the cake story without embarrassment, he knew the friendship was established.

Carl paused in mid-sentence to hear Jennifer tell about Harvey saying no chocolate, then yes chocolate. "Harvey, you're incorrigible. Women are supposed to be the ones who change their minds."

Harvey grinned but kept quiet.

Carl leaned back lazily. "How's the Blake case going?"

"All right."

"David Murphy told me he'd had a run-in with you."

"Oh?"

"He's a patient of mine."

"Am I supposed to be impressed?"

Carl chuckled. "I'm not. He's as mortal as the rest of us."

"Is he in good shape?"

"Not bad for his age. Why?"

"Just wondering if he'd go skipping over rocks on the shore."

"You're serious?"

"I shouldn't have said anything. Really, Carl, this is hush-hush."

"No problem. Like I said, he's pretty healthy. If he could quit smoking, he'd be healthier. It might help his image, too."

At three-thirty they said goodbye and left to look at the house.

"I think I'll switch my doctor," Jennifer said, as they pulled out of the driveway.

"I thought Carl made you nervous."

"At first he was a little overpowering, but he's not so bad."

Harvey nodded. "He has that personality, but he's a great doctor."

When they got to Van Cleeve Lane, she started paying attention to the houses. A stone cottage, an ivy-covered mansard, a large modern with glass covering the entire front. Apprehension pricked at her.

"These houses look expensive."

"Just keep an open mind," Harvey said.

Bailey's house was a Cape Cod with weathered shingles, and dormer windows upstairs. A white board fence enclosed the front yard, which had some lawn but ran mostly to flowers and bushes, with paths among them, a stone bird bath, and a sundial. They approached the breezeway between the house and attached garage.

Jennifer hesitated. "I don't know, Harvey. It looks like a lot of upkeep."

Mr. Bailey opened the door. "Hello, folks! Glad you made it."

He took them down a short hall with a bathroom, utility room and coat closet opening off it. The kitchen was large and sunny, with windows on the back of the house. In front of it was a dining room filled with massive cherry furniture—table and eight chairs, sideboard, and hutch. Even Harvey looked a bit intimidated. The living room was also on the front of the house. The pleasant room had a fireplace and a wall of built-in bookshelves. A piano sat to one side, away from the sofa, settee and arm chairs. Jennifer didn't see any electronics, and she wondered if he had any. Mr. Bailey kept up a commentary, saying most of the antiques his wife had collected would go to his daughter.

From the living room, a door opened into the front garden. At the back of the house was a family room, or sunroom as Mr. Bailey called it, with wicker chairs and a library table, bookshelves, and the TV at last. A French window opened onto a deck, and a large back yard was visible beyond. On the extreme left of the deck, a wall from another room jutted out behind the main house.

"This house is bigger than I thought," Harvey said.

"There's more. When my wife was incapacitated, we had a bedroom built on the back. You can't see it from the street." Bailey moved to the far side of the family room and opened a door. It led into a large master bedroom with a roomy attached bath.

"Flossie needed an accessible bathroom," Mr. Bailey explained.

"How long was your wife ill?" Jennifer asked.

"About seven years. We built this the first year. She couldn't go upstairs. We slept in the dining room while the builders were here." Jennifer wondered where the cherry furniture had spent the duration.

"It's lovely," she said. "It's obvious you thought a lot about what she needed before you built this room." One of the closets held a low rod and shelves that could be reached from wheelchair height, and the bathroom had rounded corners, several handrails, and a shower with no ridge where the door opened.

The bedroom walls were papered in pale gray, with pink rosebuds climbing trellises. On the wall opposite the bed was a Georgia O'Keeffe print of a larger-than-life poppy blossom, and over the headboard hung an original Maine harbor scene in oils. The woodwork was pristine white, and sheer curtains covered the large, low windows.

"She could sit in here or in the sunroom and look out at the back yard," said Mr. Bailey. "Her rose garden is just out there." He pointed through a window, and Jennifer went to stand beside him.

"Oh! How beautiful!"

"Over twenty varieties." He shook his head. "I've tried to keep them healthy, but it's too much for me. Do you like roses, Miss Wainthrop?"

"Yes, but I don't know how I'd be at tending them."

"I've had a man coming in this summer. Flossie started that garden thirty years ago. It brought her great satisfaction in her last few years."

Harvey came to stand beside her, looking out at the roses, a wide expanse of grass, and a small vegetable garden in the far corner. The lot had to be at least half an acre, maybe more. She glanced up at him, and he smiled.

Bailey took them back to the living room, where the staircase went up.

"I'm not too good at climbing stairs myself anymore," he said apologetically. "Perhaps the two of you could go up by yourselves. There are four bedrooms up there and a bathroom."

"Four—" Jennifer swallowed hard and looked at Harvey. He took her hand and led her up the stairs.

Two of the rooms had beds and dressers and a few other furnishings. One was empty, and the fourth held boxes and luggage. The bathroom had attractive green and white tile and gleaming white fixtures.

They stood in the hallway, and Jennifer looked at him helplessly. "It's too much," she said.

"Too much money?"

"Too much house."

"We could fill it up." He put his arms around her. "It's a terrific house."

"I know. I love it, but it's not a starter house, Harvey. We'd have to work and save for years to afford a house like this."

"I've done that, gorgeous." He pulled her close and kissed her forehead. She laid her head against his chest. Slowly she slid her hands in under his jacket and around his waist.

Softly, she said, "I know you said you had some money from the stocks, but even a down payment for this would be . . ."

"Let's find out." He stood still, holding her. She leaned away, to look at him, the smile she couldn't resist lit his face, and she melted back against his chest.

"I thought if we got a house, it would be little, like the one Beth and I are living in. This one is huge! I don't know if I could keep it clean, let alone pamper the roses. It would be a full-time job."

"If you couldn't handle it, I'd get someone to help you."

"Yeah, right."

"I'm serious. This is a great house. Besides, it's something that matters, so I get the final word." He kissed her, and she kissed him back, but she was still a bit uneasy.

He said, "I think it's time to talk turkey with Mr. Bailey."

Jennifer shook her head. "I don't want to listen. I'd be too disappointed."

They found him sitting in the living room. He started to get up, and Harvey said, "Please sit, Mr. Bailey. I think we're ready to talk price." He smiled and sat on the sofa.

"Do you mind if I take another look at the sunroom?" Jennifer asked.

"Go right ahead," Mr. Bailey said, and Harvey gave her a reassuring smile.

She walked in there and looked out at the beautiful, big back yard. Her heart was pounding so hard, she heard the men's calm voices in the other room but couldn't distinguish what they said.

She dared to open the glass door and step outside, onto a ramp leading down to a flag-stoned patio. She could picture Harvey mowing the lawn, and a swing set near the fence.

Their voices grew louder, and she went back inside. Harvey and Mr. Bailey had come into the sunroom.

"Sir, if we decide we want the house, when would you need to know?" Harvey asked.

"Well, of course I'd like to know as soon as possible, but . . . a week?"

He looked at Jennifer, smiling. "I think that's more than enough time."

The older man nodded. "You talk it over."

"I'll get back to you soon," Harvey said.

They all went back through the kitchen. Jennifer looked around again, taking in the maple cabinets with glass in the upper doors, ample work space, and textured steel appliances. A small round table and two chairs sat to one side, and she pictured them eating there in the kitchen, not the big dining room. It wasn't that far from Eddie's place. He could come for coffee in the morning, when it was his turn to drive Harvey to work.

"The plumbing and heating are all good," Mr. Bailey said. He told Harvey what the taxes were. As they passed the utility room, he said, "I wouldn't want to take the appliances. If you wanted them, I'd leave all the kitchen appliances and the washer and dryer."

Jennifer gulped and went out at the breezeway. Harvey thanked Mr. Bailey and followed her.

He opened her door on the Explorer. "Do you want to eat supper out?"

She shook her head. "I'd rather go home and see if Beth is back, if you don't mind. I'll make you a sandwich."

Harvey headed back toward the little yellow rental house.

"So, what do you think?" he asked.

"I think we can't afford it."

"What else do you think?"

"I think it's a dream house. It's what I would hope for years from now. When you're retired and the children are through college."

"It would be too big for us then, just like it is for Mr. Bailey now. I'd be seventy years old, and too crippled to climb the stairs. It's the house we want now, Jenny."

"Well, what did he say? We can't go into debt. Remember our first counseling session, about finances?"

"I can do this," Harvey said calmly. "He told me what it's appraised at, and then he offered a generous reduction. When he heard I could pay cash, he lowered the price even more."

Jennifer swallowed hard. She wanted to ask why he would do that, but she thought she knew. Everyone respected and loved Harvey.

"You can pay cash?"

He grinned. "I could, if I liquidated all my stock. But he doesn't want it all at once. He asked me to make one payment a year for five years, for tax purposes. It will help us both."

She couldn't say anything. She had almost expected that she would have to keep working if they bought a house and took a mortgage.

He turned in at the driveway to her house and shut the engine off. Beth's car wasn't there. He laid his glasses on the dashboard and put his arm around her shoulders, looking her in the face. "Jenny, I can do this. Please let me."

She sat very still.

"Say something."

"I . . . you . . ." The breath went out of her in a little puff. "How much do you have, if I may ask."

"As of Friday, almost a quarter of a million."

"That's . . . I can't cope with this." She fumbled for the door handle. He reached over and laid his warm hand on her arm.

"Sit still, gorgeous." He put both arms around her and cuddled her on his shoulder, the way Rick Bradley held his two-year-old when she went splat on the aisle rug at church. They sat for a few minutes without saying anything, then he asked, "Do you like the house?"

"You know I do. But—"

"But what?"

"You can't—well, even if you can, you shouldn't."

"Why not? It's my dream. A home for the woman who loves me. A comfortable home that's beautiful and has plenty of room for the little ones God will give us."

"It would take all your savings, and you wouldn't have a cushion."

"Not quite all, but by paying in installments, my investments won't be wiped out. They'll recover some in between. Sweetheart, the one thing that would make me stop considering it would be if you said you'd rather live out in the willywacks, on a farm or something. We can do that if you want to."

She pulled in a ragged breath. "The back yard is huge. There's room for a swing set."

He kissed her, and she didn't object. It was part of the fantasy come true. A few moments later there was a knock on the passenger side window. Beth had driven in and was standing just outside. Harvey turned the key part way and put the window down.

"You'd better come inside," she said. "You're fogging up the windows."

Jennifer jumped out and threw her arms around Beth.

"It's the most wonderful house, Beth! Thank you so much for telling us about it!"

Harvey got out and walked around the vehicle, smiling at Beth.

"You're buying it?" she asked.

"Harvey says we can. I can't believe it. It's fantastic! Have you ever seen it?"

"Yes, I was over there twice, before Mrs. Bailey died. Her rose garden was beautiful."

"It still is. What if I kill her roses?"

Beth laughed. "There was some ugly dark furniture in the dining room."

"It's still there," Harvey assured her.

They went in, with Harvey carrying Beth's luggage. She and Jennifer made sandwiches, talking as they worked about the house and the wedding.

Beth went to her room to change after supper, and Harvey helped Jennifer clean up. As he wiped off the table, he said, "I think we should both sleep on this house thing, and pray about it. If we both still want it tomorrow night, I'll call Mr. Bailey."

Jennifer stopped drying the plate in her hand. "Be honest. Don't you hate to spend all your money like that?"

"No, it would make me very happy. I'm thankful that I can do it, and that I didn't just waste it all over the years." He looked steadily into her eyes, and a thrill of joy shot through her.

"Jenny, let's pray about it now," he said. "I feel like I want the house, and you want the house, and we'd be happy there."

"Anyone would be happy there. But with you—" She gave him a fierce hug.

Chapter 10

Monday, June 28

Mike's chair was empty on Monday morning, and the top of his desk was bare of paperwork. His empty coffee mug sat near the coffeemaker.

Arnie and Pete came over to Harvey's desk.

"So," said Arnie, "we don't seem to have anything new this morning. Pete's got a hearing this afternoon, but if you need us for the Blake case, we're at your disposal."

"Thanks." Harvey gave them a brief rundown on Fort Point and the glasses Eddie had found. "We've got to move on this thing. Eddie will call the state lab and see if there's anything on the bloodstain. Can you call Frederick's optician and ask if he'll try to identify the glasses?"

"Sure," Arnie said.

"Thanks. I've got a feeling that if we find out how Luke Frederick died, we'll be close to finding out how Martin Blake died."

Eddie was on the phone, but he pushed the mute button and said, "Harv, line 2."

Harvey picked up his desk phone. "Detective Larson."

"Please hold for the chief of police." The adrenaline started pumping. He had a feeling the chief wasn't calling to ask him what bridal registry Jennifer picked.

"Larson?"

"Yes, sir."

"How are things looking on the Blake case?"

"Progressing, sir."

"Can you come to my office for a few minutes, please?"

"Yes, sir. You want me to brief you personally?"

"There's another matter. I'll expect you."

"Yes, sir." He had already hung up.

Eddie's brown eyes were huge, like a Labrador retriever's.

"I've got to go to the chief's office," Harvey told him.

He had been in Chief Dwight Leavitt's office twice with Mike. It was on the top floor, in a corner with glass on two sides like their own office, but a floor above, and much more plush than the Priority Unit. Carpet on the floor, thick drapes, pictures on the walls that were real art. The detectives just had maps and wanted posters and a framed display of different caliber cartridges one of the ballistics guys had made years earlier. The chief's office suite was the penthouse of the police station, and all the men were in awe of it. Most patrolmen had never been on the top floor.

"Go right in, Detective," the private secretary said gravely, after she buzzed him into the outer office, so he walked slowly to the door of the chief's sanctum. Even the secretary had art, he noticed. A watercolor of pastel flowers hung behind her desk.

He knocked, sort of a medium timbre knock, not so soft as to be construed as timid, but not loud enough to be presumptuous.

"Come in, Larson."

Leavitt sat behind a wide federal period desk, one Jefferson would have been proud of. On the gleaming top were a telephone, a brass model T, and a dish of Sugar Babies. Two file folders lay exactly in the middle of the desk. The rest was clear. Harvey didn't see a computer monitor anywhere in the room. He looked over his shoulder to see what kind of art the chief stared at every day. It was a Turner seascape. A print. At least, Harvey hoped it was a print. The city couldn't afford art like that if it was real. On the side wall was a print of a big-eyed whitetail doe licking her fawn. The chief was a Bambi lover.

"Have a seat." Leavitt held his gaze with serious brown eyes. His hair was dark, but thinning, and a little white showed. He had a mustache, and his fingers were long and thin, like the rest of him.

"Bring me up to date on the Blake case, please."

Harvey told him what they had so far, and that he hoped to come at Blake's killer through the Frederick case. Leavitt was skeptical.

"That's not your jurisdiction, Larson. Have you

shared this information with the state police?"

"Most of it, sir. There was some confusion at first over who was investigating the Frederick case. Now the state police have taken it over."

"That's right. You need to work with them, if you really think this will help with the Blake case. But I'd rather see you concentrate on the Blake matter."

"We're doing everything we can on this end, sir."

"Dave Murphy called me this weekend. You think he's embroiled in this?"

Harvey wondered if Dave and the chief were pals. "Well, sir, Blake wrote an article Murphy wouldn't like much, and his editor is planning to publish it. And he lied to me during our first interview. Changed his story later."

Leavitt put a Sugar Baby in his mouth and sucked it for a second. "Do you think this story of Blake's could result in criminal charges?"

"It might. Murphy will at least be sweating pretty badly the day it comes out. It's . . . the editor made me swear it wouldn't get leaked, sir."

Leavitt's eyes narrowed, and he chewed. "Then make certain it's not. Keep me apprised of this case. Call me before five this afternoon and let me know how it's going."

"Yes, sir." Harvey was thankful he hadn't asked for details on the news article.

Leavitt picked up a pen and tapped it on the

desktop a few times. "Now, this other matter. I know Mike Browning has talked to you about his retirement."

"He's mentioned it a few times. But he's not retiring yet."

"Within a year, he says. He thinks someone should be training to take over, and I agree." The chief was watching him. Harvey tried not to squirm. "I've talked it over with the department heads. I'll tell you up front, we discussed bringing in someone fresh from outside. Browning disagreed vehemently. He rightly pointed out that the team he's had for several years has done the city proud. And he says you're his replacement."

"Is it up to him?"

"Not entirely." Leavitt tapped the desk with the pen. "Browning has run the Priority Unit since its inception. When he goes, the unit could lose prestige and backing, unless a man with a strong personality steps in."

Harvey didn't think that described him, but he didn't say so. "If Mike really retires, he'll be missed badly," he said.

"I've been watching you for a while, Larson." Leavitt looked him in the eye and nodded. "You've done good work. There was that spy software thing a few weeks ago, and last winter you broke that Internet fraud ring. You've built a name for yourself in the computer field."

Harvey shrugged. "It's one of my interests. I've had training, and I guess I have aptitude."

"Exactly. I hate to take you out of the front line and put you in management, because you're good."

"Mike is very active in field work, sir. I'd expect to do the same if I were in his position." It struck Harvey as odd that he was arguing in favor of a job he might not want.

"Hmm. Yes, I suppose you would," Leavitt said. "It comes down to this, Larson: when you wrap up the Blake case, you'll be promoted to lieutenant, as a temporary position. You'll be Browning's assistant, training as his replacement. It will give you a little rank and authority, and a hundred dollars more a week."

Harvey cleared his throat. "Sir, that kind of a raise isn't necessary. The city budget was tight this year."

"True, but I poked around and found where you and your partner confiscated over sixty thousand dollars in drug money during the month of May." Harvey remembered the case. Under Maine law, the police department got to keep part of any money they took on drug-related cases. "Part of that will go for new equipment downstairs, but I think part of it should go back into the Priority Unit. It will fund your raise. You'll have the same duties you have now, but Browning will give you some training, too."

"Mike's trained me for eight years, sir. I couldn't have had a better mentor."

"Yes, but there are administrative duties that you haven't had to deal with." Leavitt leaned back in his chair and chewed a Sugar Baby. Harvey wondered if his teeth were real. "I expect you'll solve the Blake murder soon. The day that happens would be a good time to announce your promotion."

Harvey wasn't sure what to say. What would happen if he never cracked the case and made the arrest? And did he really want a promotion that brought with it hours of boring paperwork? Maybe if Mike got rested and ate enough oat bran, he'd stay on a few more years.

"What about my spot, sir? Would you bring in a new detective?"

"Yes, when Browning retires." Leavitt shifted in his chair and held the pen between his hands. "Actually, the Priority Unit may see some new faces before that. Arnie Fowler wants to retire at the end of the year, and Peter Bearse, I hear, is thinking of bailing out and practicing law. We'll watch for candidates to fill those vacancies."

He was further inside the loop than Harvey had realized. On his way out, he leaned in for a closer look at the seascape. The Turner was definitely a reproduction. He was glad about that. He liked good art, but he didn't want their drug money to go for that when they needed new equipment. He wasn't sure he wanted it to go into his paycheck, either.

The police chief's sour-faced secretary showed him out of the suite, and he went down the stairs to his office.

Eddie greeted him with a frown. "The lab says they don't know yet if the blood is Blake's. The DNA test will take a few more days."

Arnie came to Harvey's desk. "I got the optician. He says if we take the glasses to him, he should be able to tell us if they came from him, and if so, whose they are."

"All right, you take them over. Eddie, how about those pictures from Fort Point?"

"I can ask Jennifer to send me hers and make you a slide show of hers and mine together."

"Sounds good." It was after ten o'clock, and Harvey felt he hadn't accomplished much that morning. His cell phone rang, and he rifled his jacket until he got the right pocket. It was Jennifer.

"Harvey, Beth just called me. My passport came in the mail at home!"

"Fantastic."

"So, where are we going?"

"You sure you want to know?"

"Well, I at least need to know whether to pack a swimsuit or a parka."

"I'll tell you later, when you can thank me properly."

She chuckled. "I also heard from the probate court."

"What about?"

"They're distributing Coastal Technology's assets."

The lilt in her voice told him it was a relief to finally hear something about the defunct software company that had employed her for two years.

"Terrific. What are you getting?" Jennifer's contract at the ill-fated Coastal Technology had given her royalties on the sale of software she had developed.

"Everybody's getting the last paycheck they owed us, and they've given me a choice on the program rights. Either a lump sum of five thousand dollars, or keep the five percent interest and collect that if anyone continues to market the programs. Or I could sell my rights to someone else."

"So what do you want to do?" he asked.

"I don't know. I'm leaning toward the lump sum. Too much hassle otherwise."

"Do it. I'll invest the five grand for you in a separate account."

"We could put it toward the house."

"No, that's okay. It's good for women to have money in their own names. You can use it for something later, if you want, or fund an IRA or something. Now, how about lunch? Are you available?"

"Meet me in the garage in an hour." When they hung up, Harvey went to the airline's website. The price he wanted was still good, and he made the reservation. Tickets to London on July 18. He printed out the confirmation and went back to work humming.

Harvey drove through the drive-up at McDonald's, and they ordered salads and soft drinks. Eating in the Explorer would be much more private than having lunch at the café.

Jennifer watched him while he ate, and his brow stayed furrowed, as though he was thinking about something he didn't like.

"What's wrong?" she asked.

He let out a big sigh. "Something's going on in our unit that you need to know about."

"Besides the investigation, you mean?" She fought back a smoldering anxiety.

"Yes. Mike's thinking of retiring next spring."

"He's talked about it for a while, hasn't he?"

"Yes, but I think he means it this time. And he wants me—" He broke off and stared out the side window, and she tried to classify his mood. Anger? Fear? "He wants me to have his job."

She set her drink down. "Whoa!"

"It gets worse. The police chief called me to his office this morning."

"What for?"

"Same thing. When we close the Blake case,

they'll promote me and train me to take over the unit when Mike leaves."

"Congratulations!" She smiled eagerly, but he didn't say anything. She leaned over and pulled his glasses down. The lenses got dark in daylight, and she wanted to see his eyes clearly. "You're not smiling."

He shook his head. "I'm not sure I want it."

"Why not?"

"Mostly, I guess I want Mike to stay."

"Nothing stays the same forever."

"I know. But me in management."

"The men respect you."

"That's another thing. Arnie and Pete will probably be gone by then. I'll be left with Eddie and three new guys."

"So, you can mold the unit to be the way you've always wanted it to be."

"It is the way I want it now."

She sighed. Lending moral support to a depressed genius was exhausting. He had a pessimistic answer to everything. "Then tell the chief you're not interested."

"I'm not?"

"You're telling me you're not."

"I told you no chocolate cake, too."

She put the salad dish up on the dashboard and slid over near him. "I think you should let this percolate for a few days. You're short on sleep, and you're in the middle of a very stressful case.

Not to mention you're getting married in nineteen days. *That* doesn't add any stress."

He smiled, pulled the glasses off, and kissed her lightly. "So what's the up side to all this?"

"The up side is that you're getting married in nineteen days."

He kissed her again. "You're very convincing. Now tell me why I want Mike's job."

"Aside from you being the smartest, most qualified detective in the world?"

"Yeah."

"You're good at directing people. You've coordinated tons of investigations, and you always come out on top."

"Not always. I've blown a few."

"You work well under pressure, and you're always learning new skills."

"Such as?"

"Handling the press."

"Gag."

"So, if you're the boss, you can make one of your men hold the press conferences, like Mike makes you."

"That I could enjoy."

"It will give you higher rank."

"I don't care about that. I work better when no one pays any attention to me."

"More money?"

"We can live on what I get now."

"Prestige?"

"I don't care what other people think. Except you."

"Maybe I'd like being married to the captain."

"Would you?"

"I'll have to think about that." She stroked the back of his neck. "Let's think and pray about it for a few days."

"Okay."

She sank back, drained.

"I love you," he said softly. "Thank you."

She looked around the parking lot. There were only a few cars, and those nearby were empty. She leaned over and kissed him, sliding her arms around him. Her fingers brushed the leather holster strap, and she buried her face in the warm front of his pale blue shirt for a moment, then sat up. "If you change your mind, you'll be a terrific captain. And if you don't, you'll still be a terrific detective."

She put the lunch containers in the bag, and Harvey got out to put them in the trash can before driving back to the station. He parked in the garage, and before he could open his door, she said, "Tell me now."

"What?"

She could tell that he knew what by his innocent smile.

"Where we're going."

He drew a folded sheet of paper from his shirt pocket, opened it deliberately, and handed it to her.

"London? Really?" She stifled a scream.

"Unless you'd rather see Copenhagen . . ."

"No, no! This is fabulous!" She hugged him around the neck and kissed him, momentarily forgetting about the cameras.

"Are you sure you like it?" His smile was on high beam.

"It's perfect! For both of us!" She waved the paper like it was a semaphore and she was trying to signal her mother in Skowhegan.

"Well, sure. We can poke around and find where all your favorite authors lived."

"And see historical sites from the Middle Ages!"

"Right, from back when I was born."

She swatted him with the paper. "Maybe we can go over there and find a mystery to solve together, like Lord Peter Wimsey and Harriet Vane."

He laughed, and she caught her breath. He was happy, at least for that moment. She hoped she could always bring that look to his face.

Another car pulled in beside them, and he squeezed her hand, then got out and opened her door.

Harvey went to see John Russell that afternoon. The editor assured him Blake had had documentation for his accusations.

"Pretty interesting reading," Harvey told him.

"How could he turn up so much, all at once?"

"He started researching this months ago. The more he dug, the more he found. He put it together between stints of getting a new novel out."

"Could I see the documentation?"

"What do you need?"

"Anything that would be helpful to my investigation. If Blake's claims are true, Murphy might have a motive to stop him."

"Oh, they're true. You think he'd stab a guy like that?"

"I don't know. He could hire someone for it. I just want proof he had reason to hate Martin Blake."

"But Murphy didn't know about the story. Nobody does but you and me."

"What if he did?"

"I don't like that idea."

Russell got up and walked to the wall and pulled an ugly landscape to one side on a hinge, revealing a wall safe. "Off the record," he said with a wink and began opening the safe. "Martin had me lock up his proof. He has file cabinets that lock, but he didn't think they were secure enough."

He brought two large manila envelopes to his desk, where he sorted through the contents.

"There you go." He selected a piece of paper and shoved it across the desk.

Harvey whistled. He was looking at a very incriminating inter-office memo originating in Murphy's capitol office. It named a sum to be obtained in consideration for a vote.

"Murphy wrote this?"

"Yes, to a lobbyist. Check his handwriting."

"Was Murphy stupid?"

"Maybe too trusting. There's more." Russell produced document after document: printouts of e-mail messages, pages from Murphy's appoint-ment book, notes from associates, memos from lobbyists and other political hangers-on. Having read Blake's article, Harvey could see where it all pointed.

"How did Blake get copies of all this?"

"He had a source inside. Someone who loves his or her country, but didn't like Murphy much."

"So he left all his proof here, in the safe. Can I have copies?"

Russell considered. "I suppose so, if you swear it won't end up in the wrong hands. This is a coup for the *Press Herald*, and as Martin's last work, it will sell papers. I'll be ready to go with it Friday, I think. I don't suppose the P.D. would object? I mean, it wouldn't compromise your investigation?"

"No, in fact, it might bring it to a head. Go for it."

"All right, but this stuff stays confidential until we go to press."

• • •

"I've compiled those pictures from Fort Point," Eddie said when Harvey walked into the office.

"Show me."

Eddie went to his desk.

Harvey called to Pete Bearse, "So, Pete, I heard you took the bar exam."

"Yeah. Probably won't hear for a while."

"You'll pass."

"I think I did. But then, you can't be too sure on these things. I've heard of a lot of guys taking it three or four times."

"Kennedys, even," Harvey said.

Pete laughed. "So, you guys will get somebody new in here. I wonder if Mike's thought about it."

"He may have someone in mind." Harvey thought of Nate Miller or Jimmy Cook. Knowing city politics, they might end up with Wonder Boy. He just hoped the administration wouldn't put a pretty girl in there, or Eddie's work would go to pieces.

Eddie was at his elbow. "I set it up on my screen. Can you come take a look?"

Harvey went over and sat down in Eddie's chair. He clicked through the ones of them up around the fort and lighthouse, until he came to photos of himself and Eddie standing on the rocks near the ocean. In the first ones, they stood together on the flat rock at the edge of the water.

It was a distant shot, and their backs were to the camera. Thelma Blake might well question the identity of the men she saw.

In the next picture, Eddie was up higher, on the rounded rocks, wearing only his boxers. Harvey was below the rock, bending down to pick up a stone. Jennifer had snapped a couple of them standing on top of the rock together, facing the bay.

"Makes me cold, just looking at you." Harvey flipped to the next one. He was on one knee, looking over the side of the rock. Eddie wasn't visible. There was one more picture, Leeanne holding the binoculars in both hands, just below her chin, looking gravely at something in the distance. "That's a good picture of Leeanne."

Eddie smiled. "Yeah, Jennifer must have taken it while we were down on the shore."

"Well, get the personal stuff out of the slide show. Save that one for yourself if you want. Then call Mrs. Blake and ask her if we can bring these over. She may be able to help us."

In Harvey's vehicle on the way to Thelma's house, Eddie said, "Harv, was my behavior acceptable on Saturday?"

"Sure. I wouldn't have found the glasses without you."

"I mean with Leeanne."

Harvey glanced at him. "I thought you were fine. How serious are you about Sarah?"

Eddie hesitated. "I could be serious. What do you think?"

"I don't know her very well. I like her. She's smart."

"She's got some baggage. Family stuff."

"Doesn't everyone?"

Eddie shrugged. "I think I could live with it. But I'm not sure I want to tie myself down yet."

"Then don't. Wait until you're sure you won't have any regrets."

"You and Jennifer . . . she knows about everything from the past?"

Harvey shot him a sidelong glance. "Everything—even some stuff you don't know."

Eddie laughed. "And she still wants to marry you?"

"Strange, isn't it?"

Harvey presented the slide show to Mrs. Blake on a flash drive that she put into her laptop. She looked for a long time at the photos of the two detectives standing together on the rocks. First the flat rock, then the rounded rock. At last she tapped the second one.

"I'm sure it was here. They climbed up and stood talking. The waves washed around the bottom of these rocks. I remember thinking they would get their feet wet when they got down." She smiled. "My daughter left this morning, and I'm lonely. I'm glad you boys came around.

It hits you when you have to face the first day alone."

"Mrs. Blake, if there's anything we can do for you . . ." Harvey said.

"No, no. I've just got to get used to it. Barbara Heflin will be leaving soon. There's nothing for her to do, now that Martin's gone." She clicked through the photos again. "You think the Frederick man was killed there?"

"I can't say, ma'am. But your evidence is important."

"What does this have to do with Martin's death?"

"Maybe nothing," Harvey said. "They died the same day, and they'd talked to each other. We went up there to see if we could understand it better, find anything that had to do with either your husband or Frederick."

"But you didn't find anything that relates to Martin's death?"

"Not for sure."

"Come back and see me again," she said.

"We will."

Eddie went ahead of him out of her sitting room, and she called Harvey back. "Mr. Larson, I don't want whoever did this to get away with it."

"I know, Mrs. Blake. We'll get him."

She gave him a smile. "Nice looking young man, your partner."

Arnie was back from the optician when they returned to the office, with word that the glasses were definitely Luke Frederick's. Harvey called state police headquarters and told Captain Wadleigh about Eddie's discovery. Wadleigh was excited about the find, and a little miffed that his men had overlooked the glasses. He suggested an appeal to the public, in an effort to find people other than the reunion guests who had been at the park on the twentieth.

Harvey said, "I've been thinking of doing the same thing on the Portland case. Now that we've identified a possible murder scene in the Blake case, I'd like to hear from more people who were in the area that night."

Wadleigh was agreeable to letting Harvey ask for witnesses on both matters, since Blake had been in both locations the day of the murders, provided he would continue to share information about the Fort Point reunion with him.

Harvey called Eddie, Pete, and Arnie to his desk. "I hate to say it, but I need to hold a press conference. Appeal to the public."

"Sort of, anyone who drove over the bridge the night of June 20th call us?" asked Eddie.

"Right, and anyone other than Blake's class-mates who visited Fort Point that day."

"Tourists," said Pete. "There had to be other people there."

Harvey called the chief to update him on the case, and Leavitt seemed a little disgruntled that he and Eddie had found evidence for the state police's case, but not for their own.

"Sir, the Frederick murder is somehow connected to the Blake murder. I hope it doesn't upset you too much that some of the evidence points to Congressman Murphy."

"You have to go wherever it takes you, Larson."

Jennifer met Harvey at her door at six o'clock with a thick paperback book in her hand.

"Ready to visit Mr. Bailey?" Harvey asked.

"Yes, but first, I went to the bakery to pay Patricia for the cake," she said. "We were talking about Martin Blake's books, and she told me a lot of stuff in the first book really happened."

"His daughter said something like that to me, too."

Jennifer held out the book. "It's bad stuff."

"Like what?"

"Well, there was this robbery. Some kids from the high school were involved, but Patricia said it never was solved. In the book it was solved, but not in real life."

"Slow down. What happened in real life?"

"Some kids from the high school broke into someone's house and trashed it. Then the owner came home, and they beat him up and left him there. I can't remember all the details, but

Patricia said it really happened. The man died."

"And it's in this book?" He took the paperback from her and looked at the garish red cover with embossed gold letters: *MORRISTOWN*, by MARTIN BLAKE. It was a fat mass market edition. He turned to the publishing information. "The first edition was published 21 years ago. May I take it? I think it's time I read Blake's first book."

"Be my guest."

In the SUV on the way to Mr. Bailey's, he smiled gently at her. "Forget about that burglary stuff, gorgeous. You don't need to keep thinking about murders and mayhem."

She shook her head with a smile. "How did you know?"

"You had worry lines."

"Well, what worries you worries me."

He laughed. "I'm not worried about the case. At least, not when I remember who's really in charge."

She watched him carefully as he drove. "You mean . . ."

"I mean God. Old habits die hard, I guess. I've been stewing about it some, I'll admit. But God knows who killed Martin Blake. If he wants the truth known, we'll find it."

She reached over and touched his sleeve. "Thanks. I'll try to remember that." He clasped her hand, and she settled back, contented. "A guy from Coastal called me, one of the programmers. Remember John Macomber?"

"Sure."

"He's nice, has a family and is a normal person."

Harvey smiled.

"Well, you know," Jennifer said. "Not like the bosses at Coastal. He offered to buy my software rights."

"Really?"

"Yes. John was with Coastal quite a while, and he wrote a lot of programs. He's interested in starting his own company. The court will let him market the programs he has partial rights to. He offered me a job, too." She watched for a reaction, but Harvey's face remained neutral. She went on, "A partnership, actually. I'd keep my rights and work with him to start the new company." She swallowed hard.

He parked in Bailey's driveway then turned to face her. She knew he didn't want to come home to an empty house at night.

"I was hoping you'd enjoy just being Mrs. Harvey Larson," he said plaintively.

She squeezed his hand. "That sounds great, but buying the house might be more of a financial strain than you think. There are always expenses you didn't plan on. I wondered if I ought to keep working for a while."

"I don't think you need to."

238

She had hoped he would say that, and she smiled. "So, I should just sell him my rights?"

"How much?"

"Twelve thousand."

His eyebrows shot up. "Take it. But let me see the contract first. I'll show it to Pete Bearse and make sure everything's square."

They sat in the sunroom with Mr. Bailey and talked for a long time. They settled the timing of the payments, and Harvey said he could have the papers drawn up.

"If I should die before the contract is completed," Mr. Bailey began.

Harvey said, "I would just pay your daughter, sir."

Bailey nodded. "All right." He named a few pieces of furniture he would like to take to his daughter's house. "The rest I'll get rid of. I had the dining room set appraised. You folks don't want it, do you?"

Jennifer winced involuntarily, and Harvey fought back a smile. "No, sir, I don't think so."

"Then I'll call the dealer tomorrow. I'll sell my wife's piano, too, I guess. My daughter wants the living room set, and the bed from the master bedroom, and her mother's china. I'll take my desk and my recliner. That's about it. Can I just leave the rest and not charge you anything extra?"

Jennifer stared at Harvey.

He said, "Sir, you have some fine pieces. You should get what you can for them."

"It's too stressful to haggle and pack things. I'll have them come for the dining room set and the piano. My son-in-law is getting a truck for the things going to their house. But the rest . . . it would be so much easier to not have to deal with it."

"You may wish later you'd kept some things," Harvey said.

"Well, I'll have my daughter go through everything with me, but your paying cash will save me a lot of bother. Bring the papers by any day this week, and we'll settle it."

Harvey looked at Jennifer. She shrugged as subtly as she could, and he gave her a reassuring smile.

"When would you want occupancy?" Bailey asked.

"Our wedding is July seventeenth, and we'll be out of the country for a week. Is the twenty-fifth all right?" Harvey asked.

"Yes, that's plenty of time for Lucy to go through it all with me. We'll take away my personal things. They've arranged for me to have two rooms at their house. Their children are grown and gone. With my desk and my books and recliner, my sitting room will be pretty cozy." He waved toward an Early American portrait of a child. Jennifer had noticed it on their first visit, but hadn't gotten a close look. Could it possibly be real? "I'll take that painting, too, and the floor lamp."

"Just make sure you have everything you want," Harvey said.

"I'll be happy, knowing you're living here. I have great respect for you, Mr. Larson."

"Thank you." Harvey extended his hand, and Mr. Bailey shook it.

This is our home, Jennifer allowed herself to think. *Thank you, Lord!*

Harvey took Jennifer to dinner and then home. He didn't linger, but went back to his apartment and opened *Morristown.* It had over four hundred pages, and he wondered if it would hold his attention that long.

Jennifer was right. It was good. The seacoast town seethed with tension. Eighty pages into it, he came to the chapter about the home invasion burglary.

Three high school seniors, Binky, Danny, and Jason, were looking for trouble. Problem was, none of them had a car. They talked an introverted, unpopular kid into taking them for a ride in the heap his father had given him for his birthday. They cruised around for a while, assuring the poor kid, Larry, that he was now their best friend. They bought him a burger, then they had Larry drive them to an exclusive

241

neighborhood. They picked an upscale house where all the lights were out and there was no car in the driveway. Larry got nervous, because their talk told him they were up to no good.

They teased him a little, then pressured him to go with them. He refused. They needed the car, so the ringleader, Binky, at last told Larry he could stay in the car and they would be back in a little while. Larry parked down the street, under strict orders not to leave without them. He waited.

After fifteen minutes, he saw a car pull into the driveway of the house where the boys had gone. He was afraid, but he stayed. Another five minutes, and the three came running silently across the lawns.

"Drive!" Binky said when they got in the car, and Larry drove.

The next day it was all over the school. A man had been killed by burglars who ransacked his house and stole eighty-four dollars and a .22 caliber pistol.

Larry was sick. He had a hard time believing it, but after school the other boys were waiting by his car, and he knew it was true.

"You can't ever, ever say a word," Binky said earnestly. "We didn't kill him. At least, we didn't think we did. We roughed him up a little and tied him up."

"You put tape over his mouth," Danny said.

"So, he should have been able to breathe through his nose," Binky replied.

Another student walked past, and they all shut up.

When the coast was clear, Jason said they hadn't left any fingerprints. They'd been smart. If Larry didn't blab, everything was cool. Binky leaned close to Larry's face. If he did blab, he'd be charged as an accessory. Larry had never been so scared.

He thought about telling his father but didn't dare. His father, one of the book's main characters, was difficult to please, and Larry feared he would be abandoned if he admitted having a part in the episode. The police got to work and slowly began finding clues.

Harvey put the book down at midnight, halfway through, and went to bed, but he kept thinking about it and wondering who the boys were.

Chapter 11

Tuesday, June 29

Eddie came to pick up Harvey in the morning, and he was still tired. He took the book with him and told Eddie about it in the truck, then read more while they drove to the station.

The plots and subplots were intertwined, and he tried to skip parts that didn't have to do with the burglary. The fictional police eventually brought charges against Binky, and he withstood questioning without ever ratting out on his friends. Binky went to jail, and the other three boys lived in fear. By unspoken consent, they never mentioned the incident.

Eddie pulled into the parking garage, and Harvey took the book with him in case he had time to read after the press conference. Jennifer was getting out of her car one row over. Harvey opened his arms, and she ran to him.

"I'd better get out of here," said Eddie.

"You don't have to."

Eddie just shook his head and steered for the door. Harvey walked with Jennifer down to Records, soaking up her innocence and joy. He was happy because she was happy that he was there. She wasn't thinking about corpses and burglaries and dirty politicians. For three minutes, he had a carefree life.

Upstairs, he turned his computer on and went right to his market accounts.

"What are you doing?" asked Eddie.

"Liquidating stock. I'm going to make the first payment on a house."

"You didn't tell me!"

"Didn't know until last night."

"Where is it?"

Harvey told him. "Not too far away, Ed. And if Jeff gets this job with Portland Fire, he's going to take my lease on the apartment."

"Great. I like Jeff."

Harvey needed extra money for the rehearsal dinner and other wedding-related expenses, plus running money for the honeymoon, so he gave the order to sell $52,000 worth of stock. Eddie whistled, and Harvey realized he was still looking over his shoulder.

"You're loaded! Did you have a rich uncle that left you a bundle?"

"No, I just quit spending money and socked it away instead."

"Well, I took your advice a couple years ago," Eddie said. "I've got about eight grand in the mutual fund now."

"That's good, Ed. Keep it up. Someday you'll want to get married, and you'll be glad you did it." Harvey finished the transaction and looked up at Eddie. "Would you please call Patricia Lundquist? Ask her if she's still got her high school yearbook."

By then he was sure Binky was David Murphy. He was the brightest member of the class, the most likely to succeed. But in the book, he was convicted of the crime and imprisoned for life. Murphy hadn't done any jail time, or he would never have made it to Congress.

At nine o'clock, the four Priority Unit detectives went downstairs for the press conference, leaving Paula to tend the phone. Arnie took Mike's usual post by the door, and Eddie stood to Harvey's right. Pete took a spot against the outside wall of the parking garage, next to a few uniformed officers who had come out to listen.

Terry introduced Harvey, and he started out with, "Thank you for coming. The department has a little information to make public in the Blake murder case. Last week, our investigators found some human blood on the railing of the bridge over the Fore River at Stroudwater. The state lab in Augusta is checking it, to determine whether the blood was that of Martin Blake. We would like people to come forward to help us with the investigation. First, we would like anyone who drove over the bridge on the evening of Sunday, June twentieth, between 10:30 and 11:30 p.m. to please contact the

Priority Unit at the Portland police station." He gave the number that rang in on Paula's desk.

"My second request is for anyone who visited Fort Point State Park, near Stockton Springs, on June twentieth to please contact us." Again he gave the number. "All right, I'll take a few questions." He called on Ryan Toothaker first.

"Did you get any information off the knife that was found in the river?"

"Nothing new on that," Harvey said. He called on another reporter.

"Was Martin Blake stabbed on the bridge on Route 9?"

"We'll know more when the state lab completes the DNA test, but it's a possibility that his body entered the water there, from the bridge."

"Could he have been stabbed someplace else and the body carried there for disposal?"

"Remotely possible, but unlikely. He was seen walking in the area that night. The most logical scenario is that he was stabbed on the bridge during a lull in traffic and dumped over the railing. According to the autopsy, Blake was still alive when he hit the water, and the medical examiner has concluded that the stabbing took place a very short time before that."

From a TV reporter came the question, "Detective, what do you hope to gain by interviewing tourists who visited Fort Point the day of Blake's class reunion?"

"We have other lines of inquiry we hope to follow."

"Does this have anything to do with the second death that occurred that day, the drowning of Luke Frederick? Are you also investigating the Frederick case?"

"The state police are handling that. Anything we find, we'll share with them."

"Then why are *you* asking for information about Fort Point, instead of the state police?"

Harvey tried to stay calm, but that guy was pushing his buttons. "Both the Portland P.D. and the state police would like an explanation for some things that happened that day. We've agreed that one press conference is easier on you journalists than two. People who think they have information pertinent to the Frederick case may prefer to call the state police. That's okay."

A young woman with black-rimmed glasses called, "Could you elaborate on the things you want explained?"

Harvey was getting into deep water, and he knew it. He looked over at Arnie, but he was no help. He just stood by the door, frowning. Harvey said, "The class reunion was attended by both Blake and Frederick that day. They saw each other, spoke to each other. We'd just like to be sure we cover all the bases."

• • •

Harvey and Eddie walked the few blocks to the bakery in the warm sunshine. Pete and Arnie would handle any calls that came in while they were gone.

"Harvey, good to see you," Patricia said. A man was behind the counter, waiting on a customer. Patricia took them through to her office, and Harvey introduced Eddie.

"That was my husband, Michael, out front." She picked up a green high school yearbook and handed it to Harvey. "I think you wanted to see this?"

"Thank you. I read most of Blake's book, *Morristown*, last night and this morning. Stayed up later than I should have. But Jennifer said you told her the burglary incident described in the book actually happened thirty-five years ago."

"Yes, it did. You could probably get clippings from the *Press Herald*. It was pretty traumatic for our class."

"Could you tell me about it as it actually happened, and separate the fact from the fiction for me?"

"Well, it happened in the spring, early April, I think. It was a real sensation. Everyone talked about it for years. The man apparently returned home while the burglars were in his house, and they killed him. Martin wrote the details very much the way it really happened—the things that were done to the house, the amount of money that was taken."

"And the police accused a classmate of yours?"

"Yes, Philip Whitney was accused and stood trial for it."

"Philip Whitney? Who's Philip Whitney? I was sure David Murphy was Binky."

"Oh, no. It was Philip. He denied it and would never name the others, but the police knew there was more than one person involved. But they couldn't find any fingerprints, and the evidence against Phil Whitney was circumstantial. He stonewalled it all the way, and the jury let him walk."

"Was he guilty?"

She laughed. "You're asking me? I was a kid. Barely eighteen years old."

"But the kids at school knew, didn't they?"

"Not for sure. There were all kinds of stories going around."

"So, who else was involved?"

"We never really knew. Some people thought David Murphy was involved, but if anyone brought it up he would deny it flatly and walk away. After a while I decided maybe he didn't do it. He was never charged. The police never charged anyone but Philip."

"But they did question David?"

"I think they questioned half the boys in the

school. But there was never any proof. None of them ever told."

"Who else did you think was involved?"

"I don't know. At least twenty guys were named at the time. Nobody knew. Everybody had a theory."

"So, what happened to Philip Whitney?"

"I thought you knew. He committed suicide."

Harvey was stunned. "When did this happen?"

"When *Morristown* was published."

He and Eddie exchanged looks. Harvey felt like he was missing something. "You're telling me this guy who beat the rap on the burglary in real life killed himself when Blake published it as fiction?"

"That's right," Patricia said.

"How?"

"Shot himself."

"Why didn't he just keep quiet, like he had for—what?—fourteen years or so?"

"Well, in the book, Binky was left handed, and he dropped his ID bracelet at the man's house."

"I remember. That's how the police got a line on Binky."

"That's how they got a line on Philip. He dropped something. It wasn't an ID bracelet, though. I think it was a pocketknife. And he was left handed like the character in the book, so, I guess it was too direct for him. He left a suicide note, confessing to the burglary and tying the man up. He said they didn't mean to kill him, but he still didn't name the other boys."

"And the case has stayed unsolved all this time."

"Other than Philip, yes."

"Was there a renewed interest when the book came out?"

"Oh, yes, and I think the state police reopened it, but nothing came of it, and after a while it died down again."

Harvey thought about three men, now in their early fifties, free but haunted by a shared secret. He held out the yearbook. "Could you show me a picture of Philip Whitney?"

"Sure." She thumbed through the pages of senior portraits. "Phil was in custody during graduation. The whole class was upset. The trial didn't come up until the next fall. There." She pointed to the picture of a clean-cut young man looking over his shoulder at the camera. His gaze was direct, his mouth straight and firm. He looked like a decent kid.

"Did you like him?"

"Sure. Everybody did. When he was arrested, everyone said there was no way he'd done it. We all debated whether the pocketknife had been planted there, and whether there weren't thousands of knives just like it. But he wasn't released until fall, and most of us were scattered.

I don't think many of the class had contact with him after that."

"Did you have reunions before he died?"

"We had a five-year and a ten-year reunion. Philip didn't go."

She paged through the yearbook to the sports section. "That's him." She pointed to a photo of Philip Whitney, smiling with his arm around another boy. Both wore basketball uniforms.

"Who's the other kid?"

"Matt Beaulieu."

"Beaulieu. He wasn't at the Fort Point reunion."

"No. He never comes to our reunions. He was Philip's best friend."

"Where does he live now?"

"I don't know. I haven't seen him since graduation. He was going into the service. Cyndi Rancourt Reynolds might know. She organized the last reunion and sent notices to all the class members. If anyone has his address, she does."

"Do you think Matt Beaulieu was one of the other boys in the book? Jason, Larry, or Danny?"

"I honestly don't know."

"May I take this?" Harvey hefted the yearbook. "I'd hate to lose it."

"I'll take extra good care of it." She let him borrow it, and he and Eddie walked out onto the sidewalk. The sun was working overtime. It was eighty degrees and climbing.

"What now?" Eddie asked.

"I think we call Mrs. Reynolds for an address for Matt Beaulieu, and maybe the rest of the class members who skipped the reunion. We'll talk to some of the people who were there thirty-five years ago, but don't go to the reunions because they're too painful. And we'll get clippings from the time of the burglary."

Cyndi Reynolds shared the class mailing list with them, and Harvey began to realize what they were up against. The reunion goers were a small portion of the class. Many of the those who hadn't attended the reunion lived out of state. Three, including Philip Whitney, were known to be deceased. Eddie spent a while on the phone with her, going through Patricia's yearbook and checking off names on his list.

They divvied up the names with Nate and Tony, and they all began calling. Harvey tried Matthew Beaulieu's last known phone number, but got an out-of-service recording. He called Cyndi Reynolds again.

"Matt was in the Navy," she said.

"Career man?"

"I think so. He and Philip Whitney were going to enlist together, but Philip was . . ."

"In custody?"

"Yes, you know about that."

"Yes. So his buddy Matt joined up without him?"

"I guess so. I haven't seen Matt since graduation, but he was in San Diego last year. That's where I sent the notice in April, for the reunion at Fort Point, and it didn't come back."

Harvey searched on the Internet for Matthew Beaulieu in the San Diego area and turned up three.

Tony came over to the desk. "I've reached a Melissa Carter Duncan. She lives in Falmouth, Massachusetts. She said she would have come for the reunion, but it was too far, and she had to work. She also said she dated Philip Whitney a few times their senior year."

"Before the burglary?"

"Yes. She never saw him after. Tried to go to the trial, but her parents wouldn't let her."

"And?"

"She carried the torch for a while, refusing to believe he did it. When he was acquitted she sent him a note, expressing her undying support and devotion. She never got a reply."

Harvey rubbed his chin. "Make a note of it. We may want to talk to her again later."

Paula screened the calls, but the phones rang constantly, and the lines were tied up all afternoon. They asked a few people to come in the next day for interviews.

Harvey called John Russell and asked for copies of articles about the burglary and the time when Blake's first book was published and

Philip Whitney died. Russell agreed to ask the newspaper's librarian to search the archives, but he expected a scoop for Ryan in return, if their efforts helped solve the case.

"I can live with that," Harvey said, "but please do not publish anything connecting the old burglary to Blake's murder unless I give you the word."

"We're agreed," Russell said. "I'll have the librarian e-mail you the reports you want."

When the patrolmen's shift ended, Harvey told Tony and Nate to go home. "Do you guys mind if I request for you to work with us again tomorrow?" he asked.

Tony grinned. "That's great."

Nate nodded. "This beats traffic duty any day."

They still had about a dozen classmates they hadn't been able to reach, including Matt Beaulieu. Harvey had started asking the other class members about him and his family. He had Eddie look for Beaulieus in the phone book and call them one after another, hoping to find relatives, but there were dozens of listings.

Jennifer and Sarah came to the office at five o'clock.

"Hey, gorgeous."

"You look tired," Jennifer said.

"I am."

"Do you and Eddie still want to go to the auction?"

"Yeah, just about ready."

Sarah had changed from her uniform into dark pants and a cotton knit top. Jennifer wore gray pants and a blue shirt, her work clothes that day. Her hair was in braids that were bound to the back of her head, a cool hairdo for a hot day in a simmering office.

"Thanks for letting us come up," Jennifer said. "It's cool in here."

"They ought to get A.C. in Records," Harvey said. "The heat can't be good for your computers, let alone all that paper you file."

They ended up not buying anything at the auction. None of the furniture appealed to Jennifer and Harvey. He bid on a shotgun, but it went too high. They ate hot dogs and pie and came out at nine-fifteen feeling a little disillusioned with the evening.

"Let's get a drink," said Eddie.

Sarah said, "Let's."

"Okay," Harvey said cautiously, not sure what Eddie and Sarah were thinking of drinking.

"Sodas?" said Sarah.

"You got it."

After the Burger King, Harvey drove them back to the station to pick up their vehicles. He pulled into the garage and stopped behind Sarah's car. Eddie hopped out and unlocked the car for her. Harvey started to put the Explorer in gear, then stopped. Eddie was kissing Sarah. He looked at his watch, then at Eddie. His dark head was bent, and Sarah's arms were pale against his black shirt.

"What are we waiting for?" Jennifer said softly.

He looked at his watch again. "Seven seconds. Pretty serious." He shifted into drive, and they rolled quietly out of the garage.

"You judge people's relationships by how many seconds they kiss?"

"It's one indicator."

"You should have been a scientist."

He drove her home and gave her a kiss longer than Eddie's at the door. "Now, tell me this relationship isn't serious," he said.

"I never doubted it."

"Jenny, I don't think I want the promotion."

She stepped away from him and looked at his face in the light from the porch lantern.

"Do you want to talk about it?"

"I'm so stressed right now, I don't think I can add something else. The responsibility, and being accountable to the chief every day. It's really a burden, with Mike gone. I don't know if I could do this all the time." He took his glasses off, put them in his pocket, and rubbed his eyes.

She reached for his hand and squeezed it. "If that's the way you want it, it's fine with me. I just want you to be content."

"I will be, with you. I just don't know about at

work. Everything's going to be different when Mike goes."

"You could get a new captain who's harder to work for."

"I know."

"Maybe you could get reassigned if that happened."

"Maybe. I might be able to go back to Legere's detective squad."

"Is that what you want?"

"Not really. I like my unit."

"You and Eddie are so close."

"I know." He sighed.

"Wait until Mike comes back and talk to him."

"I guess I'll do that. The past two days have been really hard without him."

"But you're doing good work on the case."

"I guess so. It's slow going, but it is the kind of work I'm good at. We've got hundreds of potential witnesses. I hope we can solve this thing."

"You'll get there. Remember? God is in charge."

He kissed her.

"How many seconds?" she asked.

"Who cares? We know we're serious."

Chapter 12

Wednesday, June 30

Eddie arrived at Harvey's apartment the next morning in gym shorts and sneakers, and they set off to run their loop. The air was already warm, with the promise of crippling heat later. By the time they got back to the park, they were both dripping wet.

"Breakfast at my house," Eddie said, panting.

Harvey walked home and drank a cold Pepsi, then hit the shower. He took a couple of clean shirts and his sport jacket to the Explorer and drove over to Eddie's. He had cold cereal and juice ready. An air conditioning unit in the kitchen window pumped cool air into the apartment.

"You want coffee?" Eddie asked.

"No, maybe at the office." He told Eddie about the plans he'd made for the honeymoon. He and Jennifer would spend their wedding night in Portland, then take a plane to New York on the morning of July 18. They'd fly out of Kennedy at noon for London.

"Where are you staying Saturday night?"

"The Oakwood."

"Good choice. I'll go over in the morning and drive you to the airport."

"You wouldn't mind?"

"Nah. We can wash all the soap and stuff off your vehicle."

"Eddie, I really don't want the guys to decorate my Explorer."

"Well, they will. You can't stop them. It's a tradition for the groom's friends. And Leeanne will probably be out there helping."

"I'm sure Margaret Turner will be."

"Beth, too."

"And Abby," Harvey said.

"So you need a decoy." Eddie eyed him with some surprise. "You're supposed to know all this stuff. You've gotten married before."

"It's been a long time."

"Didn't anyone decorate your car the first time?"

"Yes, and it was awful. Streamers and shaving cream and tin cans, and rocks in the hubcaps. That's why I don't want you to do it this time."

"Let them think you're taking Jennifer's car, and they can decorate it all they want, then you take off in yours. Hide it somewhere until you're ready. Or better yet, let them decorate Jennifer's car, then throw your stuff in the back of my truck and I'll take you to the Oakwood in style."

Harvey laughed. "I'll talk to Jennifer about it. I'm not sure she'll want to begin her honeymoon in a pickup truck." At least Eddie was on his side.

• • •

The night dispatchers had taken messages from people who saw Harvey's press conference on the evening news, and his unit had two dozen calls to return. Nate and Tony arrived, and Harvey assigned calls to them and the four men of the unit. Most of the contacts weren't helpful, but Arnie found a couple who had seen a man walking toward the bridge around 10:50 on the night in question, and from their description, it could have been Martin Blake.

Harvey got a call from a woman who had been at Fort Point with her husband and children the day of the reunion.

"We didn't stay long. It was too crowded." They had looked at the lighthouse and the fort, but couldn't find a free picnic table, so they left the park. "I'm kicking myself for not recognizing Martin Blake or Congressman Murphy," she wailed. "To think, we were there at the same time Martin Blake was there!"

Harvey took her phone number and jotted a few notes.

Tony was interviewing a young man with long hair and a beard, and the other officers were on the phone. Harvey checked the crime updates and brought in e-mail.

"Excuse me, sir." Harvey looked up at Tony. "This fellow may have seen something."

Harvey went over and introduced himself to the young man.

He held out his hand. "I'm Charles Fotter. You're in charge of this case?"

"Yes. What can you tell me?"

"I went over the bridge that night about eleven. I'd been to the airport and was coming back. My girlfriend came in on a plane from Pittsburgh, and I picked her up."

"Did you see anyone on the bridge?"

"Yes. Two men. One of them was smoking."

Harvey's radar picked up. "Where were they?"

"About in the middle of the bridge, on the left-hand side. On the sidewalk, I mean."

"Okay. Can you describe them?"

"It was pretty dark. I know the one with his back to me was taller. I just glanced over when we came alongside them. The shorter man had a cigarette. He was wearing a dark jacket or sweater. I couldn't see his face."

"What could you see?"

"He was shorter than the other man."

"And?"

"Hmm. The taller man had white shoes."

"Could your girlfriend talk to us?" Harvey asked.

"She's gone back to Pennsylvania. If we'd known it was important, I'd have brought her in last week. But I called her last night after I saw the news, and she remembers."

"Can you give us her name and phone number?"

Harvey left it to Tony to try to reach Fotter's girl-friend and went back to calling all the Beaulieus in the phone book. Finally he hit pay dirt.

"Matthew is my nephew, but he hasn't lived in Portland for a good many years," the elderly woman said.

"He's been in the Navy, hasn't he?" Harvey asked.

"Oh, yes, all over the world."

"Do you have a current address or telephone number for him?"

"No, he retired recently, and I think he moved. But his sister could tell you."

"His sister? Do you have her phone number?" Finally. She gave him a number in Camden, and he dialed. No answer. Harvey sighed and went for coffee.

At noon he sent Tony to the café for sandwiches and cold drinks. It was too hot to eat on the sidewalk, where the heat bounced up at you off the bricks. He cleared off Mike's desk, and the men crowded around it to eat, talking over the bits and pieces they'd gained during the morning.

After they'd gone over everything and eaten the sandwiches, he told the others he wanted a fifteen-minute break. Pete took a phone call, and the others drifted away. Harvey went downstairs. Jennifer and the other women from Records were just returning from lunch, and he grabbed her hand, pulling her away from the group. The others were good-natured about it. They were getting used to him haunting the hallway in front of the records room.

He stole an extra minute and walked her slowly down the stairs.

"I'm taking you and Beth out to eat tonight," he said. "Someplace cool."

"All right, I'll call her." Jennifer straightened his holster strap. He'd left his jacket upstairs. "Are you going to wear this thing to the wedding?"

"Hadn't thought about it."

"I have. You and Eddie and Mike will probably be standing up there in the church with your guns and badges under your tuxedo jackets."

He smiled at that.

"I guess I'll be the safest bride in Portland," she said. Harvey kissed her, and she didn't fuss about the cameras.

"More calls about the bridge and the park," Eddie told him when he got back upstairs.

They stayed on the phones most of the afternoon and found several tourists who had been at Fort Point in the morning. Most had left when the reunion moved in. They turned up three people who had gone down to the beach after 11 a.m. but hadn't seen anything unusual.

Near the end of the day, Eddie had a call from a man who had seen a solitary pedestrian on the bridge about 11 p.m. He couldn't pin the time down any closer. The man was leaning on the railing, looking down into the Fore. He hadn't seen his face. Dark clothes. A cigarette? He didn't remember.

At four-thirty, Harvey called the chief and gave him an abbreviated report, updated his written reports, and went to the locker room to shave.

"Going out tonight?" Eddie asked.

"Yeah, but I'll take you home first."

"Okay. Where are you and Jennifer going?"

"Prayer meeting."

Eddie was silent.

"Do you want to come?" Harvey asked.

"No, I was just wondering."

"What?"

"Are you still praying for me?"

"Every day, Ed."

"Just me, or do you pray for other people?"

"We pray for lots of people. You, Jeff, the rest of Jennifer's family, my sisters, Beth—"

"How come you pray for Beth? She believes what you do."

"She has other things that need praying about. Like her personal life, that kind of thing."

"Could you pray for Sarah?"

Harvey turned around and met his gaze. "Sure. Anything in particular?"

"Just . . . stuff."

"Okay."

● ● ●

Jennifer and Beth were ready when Harvey got to their house. Beth had her hair up and was keeping cool in front of the fan in a sleeveless dress. Jennifer had changed to a skirt and sleeveless blouse and braided her wet hair. The Rapunzel-just-had-a-shower look.

They ate supper at an ice cream restaurant and then went to the church. After the Bible study, Harvey looked for Mr. Bailey. He joined the elderly man, Rick, and the pastor for prayer time. Harvey shared his burden for Eddie and Jeff with them, and they also had a few requests.

"I'll have a decision to make at work soon," Harvey told them.

"As if you didn't have any decisions to make right now, investigating the case of the century," Rick said.

"I've had some pressure lately," Harvey admitted.

"Everything's on track for the wedding, I hope," said Mr. Bailey.

"Yes, sir, and I've got the papers for the closing on the house right here. We can take care of it tonight, if you'd like to."

"Suits me fine."

They prayed together, and Harvey was very thankful for the things he *didn't* have to worry about. Money, Jennifer's love, and friends he could trust, for instance. The other things, he took to the Lord.

He rejoined Jennifer and Beth, and they went outside into dusk. Jennifer pointed to the west. "Heat lightning." They stood and watched it for a few seconds.

Beth asked, "Are you going anywhere this weekend?"

"Let's get out on the water if it's hot," Harvey said.

"We haven't been to Fort Gorges," said Jennifer. "It's close. You don't want to go very far right now, do you?"

"I don't know. Maybe we should wait and decide Friday. See where the case is going." He could very well be tied up over the weekend on this case.

At their little house, Jennifer and Beth had a screen in every window and fans pumping as hard as they could, but it was still too hot. The tiny yard behind faced a fence. They sat on the back steps and drank lemonade. Thunder rolled in the distance.

"Any leads today?" Jennifer asked.

"A few," Harvey said. "The book may have helped. Or confused things worse than ever."

"That old burglary?" Jennifer asked.

"Yeah. I'm not quite done with it, and I'm not sure yet whether it means anything to the case or not. I hope I'm not spending too much time on something totally unrelated."

"Do you think Martin Blake was involved in the burglary?"

"No, he was too smart to write about it if he was in on it. I think he figured he knew who did it. Maybe it was a catharsis for him to write about it."

"Or he had something against those guys and wanted them brought to justice, if only in fiction. But he didn't publish it for years."

"I know." Harvey looked up at the cloudy sky. "I wish I knew why."

"You don't think it was autobiographical?" Beth asked.

"If Martin's in the book, he was the quiet kid who saw everything and told nothing. But I did find out who Binky was, the kid who was arrested."

"Who?" Jennifer asked eagerly.

"His real name was Philip Whitney, according to Patricia. He's dead now."

She frowned. "Were any of your suspects in it?"

"I wish I knew."

"Forget it for a while. You've got to let your brain rest." Jennifer squeezed his hand.

"Want to go with us Saturday, Beth?" Harvey asked. She hadn't been on any of their outings yet.

"That would be fun. Are you sure you want company?"

"Yes and no."

Beth laughed.

"Come," he said.

Jennifer's phone rang in the house. She got up and went in.

Beth gazed upward. "I hope it rains after all this." They couldn't see the lightning from that side of the house, but every few seconds the sky lit momentarily, and the clouds had thickened.

Jennifer came running to the door holding her phone out to him. "It's Jeff."

Harvey took the phone and put it to his ear. "Hey, Jeff."

"Harvey, I got the job."

"Excellent. When do you start?"

"A week from tomorrow."

"Great! Make sure you have the seventeenth off for the wedding."

"I already checked, and I do."

"Terrific. Jennifer and I are buying a house. The apartment's yours if you want it. I checked with the landlord, and you can move in anytime."

"Thanks. That will save me a lot of hassle. I'll work here Monday, Tuesday and Wednesday next week, but could I come down this weekend? I don't want to put you out."

"No, that's fine. On Saturday, Jennifer and Beth and I are talking about taking a jaunt to one of the forts or something. Want to go along?"

"Sure. Sounds like fun."

"Do you want to bring some stuff down and leave it?"

"You sure you're ready for that?" Jeff asked.

"Yeah, I talked to the man we're buying the house from tonight. We signed the papers, and he says he'll be out before the wedding, so I may be able to start moving early, too."

"All right, I'll be down Friday."

"You've got the key. Make yourself at home. Oh, Jennifer and I have counseling Friday night. I'll come home first, though."

"Counseling? You guys are fighting already?"

"Not that kind of counseling." Harvey shot a glance at Jennifer. "Premarital counseling. With the pastor. You know, talk about all the things we don't want to fight over later."

"Is that normal?"

Harvey laughed. "We're finding it educational." He signed off with Jeff.

Beth had brought out the newspaper and was reading it by flashlight.

"They're going to shoot fireworks off from Fort Preble Saturday night," she said.

The Fourth of July had been on the edge of Harvey's consciousness, but he hadn't considered how it would affect their weekend plans.

"If we went out to Fort Gorges at suppertime and took a picnic, we'd have a great view," Beth said. "You have to have a boat to get out there, though."

"We could arrange it," he said.

"I could," Beth agreed. "I know someone from the school. Let me call him and see if I can fix it up."

"Uh—" Harvey stopped. This could be embarrassing. He realized he'd sort of set up a date for Beth without her permission.

"What?" asked Jennifer.

"Well, is this guy, uh, a friend of yours? Because I just told Jeff he could tag along Saturday."

"Oh, he's married," said Beth. "I just want to borrow his boat." She didn't say anything about Jeff. She looked at her watch. "I don't think it's too late to call him." She went inside.

Harvey slipped his arm around Jennifer's waist and pulled her up against his side. "Seems like we're spending less time together than we did before we were engaged."

"Maybe less time alone together." She looked up at him, and he took it as an invitation to kiss her. The day's stress began to slip away.

"We both have too many obligations right now," he said.

"Maybe we shouldn't go anywhere Saturday."

"It's too late to change it now. Besides, we'll enjoy being with Beth and Jeff."

"Do you think it's a good idea? I mean, Jeff . . ." Jennifer's gray eyes were dark in the twilight.

"Beth didn't complain." He sighed and leaned

272

back against the steps. Jennifer came with him and leaned her head against his shoulder.

"Where's your gun?" she asked suddenly.

"Locked in the Explorer."

"Have you decided where it's staying on the honeymoon? You can't fly with it."

"Probably in my locker at work." It would be strange to go a whole week without the holster.

Beth came back out. "We can have the boat after four in the afternoon. Charlie wants to take his family out early in the day, but it's all ours for the evening. You can drive a boat, can't you, Harvey?"

"Sure."

They made plans and decided to take in the batteries at Peaks Island first, then putter over to Fort Gorges for a picnic supper and fireworks viewing. The boat was a cabin cruiser with a ninety-horse outboard. They'd be fine if the bay was calm.

"If it's windy, it's off," Harvey told Beth.

"Of course."

They moved inside, and Jennifer brought her Bible. She and Harvey sat on the couch with it and went over the books of the Bible. Jennifer was learning them faster than Harvey was.

"I'm too old for this," he said.

"No, you're not. People who keep learning new things stay alert and active longer."

"Now I feel really old. You make it sound like I'll be senile tomorrow if I don't watch it."

"How did you learn the multiplication tables?" she asked.

"My mother bribed me. I got marshmallows if I said them right."

Jennifer smiled. "You want me to get a bag of marshmallows?"

"No, just kiss me."

"Say them right."

He started at Genesis and got through Proverbs. She kissed him.

"Feeling any younger?" she asked.

"I don't know. I think we need to repeat that experiment. Measure the recurrence of youth per unit of osculation."

She slugged his shoulder.

"It's for science," he said. She drilled him on Ecclesiastes through Daniel for a couple of minutes before she would give him any more rewards.

Beth came through with a pile of clean laundry. "Are you still here?"

"Watch your mouth," Harvey said. "I was just leaving, but I need to talk to you first."

She turned back expectantly, with the towels and socks and shirts in her arms.

"It's about Jeff."

"What about him?" Beth asked.

"Did I overstep the bounds when I told him he could go with us Saturday? I should have asked you first."

"I don't mind. You took Eddie and Leeanne last week, and that worked all right, didn't it?"

"Well, yeah."

"It's fine," Beth said, and disappeared into the hallway with her laundry.

"I'll talk to her," said Jennifer.

Harvey shrugged. "Maybe she's not interested in him."

"Maybe not."

They left it at that, but he thought otherwise. There had definitely been sparks of attraction between those two. He went home, but called Jennifer as soon as he got there.

"Did you talk to her?"

"A little."

"So?"

"She likes him, but she's keeping cool for now."

"Absolutely? Because I don't want to be the one who messed things up." He walked around his sparsely furnished apartment while he talked.

"How could you mess things up?"

"By putting people together when they shouldn't be. Matchmaking the wrong people. Like Eddie and Leeanne."

"You think Eddie's interested in Leeanne?"

"I don't know. He likes Sarah, but he's not wearing blinders yet."

"Well, I talked to Leeanne on the phone last night, and I told her to forget it."

"That means Leeanne thought Eddie was paying attention to her. I was afraid of that."

"He was," Jennifer said. "A little. How could he help it?"

"So how can Jeff help paying attention to Beth? He likes her, I'm sure of that."

"Beth can take care of herself. If she doesn't think it's right, she won't go out with him, even if he is my brother, and even if he is the best-looking guy in Portland, with the possible exception of Eddie."

"Eddie?" Harvey said. "What about me?"

"You're fantastic, but a totally different type."

"You think Eddie's cute?"

"Cute? Not exactly. He's good looking. Leeanne was a little awestruck, I'm afraid."

"Is she going to get over it?" Harvey asked.

"In time."

"So, let me ask you something." She had the ring on her finger, and the wedding was within sight, but his insecurity had surfaced anyway. "You met me and Eddie the same day. Why did you fall for me, not him?"

"Eddie?" Her voice was full of disdain. "Eddie's a great guy, don't get me wrong, but he's a long way from being you."

Harvey stopped walking in the bedroom doorway. "Could you elaborate? Because I think I need to know."

"He's immature in a lot of ways," Jennifer said.

"You're . . . well, you're right for me, that's all. I love you."

He smiled. "Can I come back over there?"

"Now?"

"Yes."

"No."

He felt a lot better than he had earlier, even though she was keeping him at a distance.

He sat down and skimmed the last two chapters of *Morristown*. In the end, Danny and Jason began promising careers, one a doctor and the other an actor. Larry, the wimp, died of alcohol poisoning.

Chapter 13

Thursday, July 1

On Harvey's desk the next morning he found a bag of marshmallows. He smiled and brought in his e-mail, which included a folder of archived newspaper stories. He started reading the accounts of the burglary and its aftermath.

The homeowner, Richard Fairley, had cashed a pension check that afternoon. A handgun and eighty-four dollars from the check were the only items the police could determine were stolen. When the young people attacked him, he was hit a few times and tied up. They put duct tape over his mouth and left him on his kitchen floor. He was found dead the next day.

The folder had no articles on the arrest and trial of Philip Whitney. Fourteen years later, Martin Blake's first book was published. A small notice appeared in the community news, followed by a feature story on Blake, the news reporter turned fiction writer. Philip Whitney's obituary was in there, too, but no news article. The papers didn't do news stories on suicides. The obit said Philip R. Whitney, 32, had died unexpectedly at his home, the standard euphemism for suicides.

Harvey forwarded the folder to Eddie. While

he parceled out the phone messages to the other men, Pete tracked down Whitney's family. The father was dead, and the mother in a nursing home. Philip's little brother owned a grocery store in Rosemont and had a family, and his younger sister was a registered nurse, never married, working at Central Maine Medical in Lewiston.

Jennifer came into the office and approached his desk with gleaming eyes. "Harvey, I have something that may interest you."

"What is it, gorgeous? More marshmallows?"

"Better. I dug out the police records on that old burglary, the one Martin Blake wrote about."

"Really? I didn't think anything that old was computerized."

"It's not. Marge says they're working backward on data entry. They hope to get to that era by the first of the year." She handed him a folder full of yellowed report forms.

"How did you find this?"

"By snooping around and asking Marge questions. It was in a box of old reports from that year in a storage room. There are boxes piled to the ceiling in there."

He leafed through the folder.

"There's something else," she said.

"What?"

"That suicide when *Morristown* was published?"

"Yeah?"

She handed him a printout. "Marge and the staff entered all that year's data into the computer system last month. The police responded to a call when Philip Whitney was found dead."

Harvey scanned the paper eagerly. "Pretty straightforward. Single gunshot to the left temple. Whitney's prints were the only ones on the weapon. I wonder if they gave the gun back to his family." He focused in on the information about the weapon. "I can't believe this!"

"What, that I found it?" Jennifer asked.

"No, that's terrific, but I can't believe what this says. The gun Whitney shot himself with was the same model as the gun that was stolen during the burglary."

"Was it the same gun?"

"I don't know." He sat down and pawed through the burglary report. Finally he found the serial number of the handgun Fairley's son had reported missing and compared it to the one in the report from the suicide.

"It was the same gun." He smiled up at her. "Thanks, Jenny. This is important. I'll reward you suitably at some opportune moment."

"I can't wait." Before he could come up with a snappy reply, she went back down the stairs.

Tony and Nate came in from the patrolmen's

roll call eager to help, and Harvey called all the men over to his area and told them what Jennifer had found.

"Why didn't anyone make the connection when Whitney shot himself?" Pete asked.

"I don't know, but the records weren't computerized, and the burglary was old. Fourteen years old. If the officer who responded to the suicide didn't know about the burglary and didn't bother to do a check on Whitney . . . well, it was sloppy, that's all I can say."

"Who was the investigator?"

Harvey looked at the printout on the suicide. "Arthur Corson."

"Never heard of him," said Eddie.

Arnie frowned. "I remember that guy. He would have been old then, close to retirement."

"I wonder what happened to the gun," Nate said.

"Probably gave it to Whitney's family," said Arnie.

Harvey gave them assignments and called David Murphy's office to set up an appointment. Then he and Arnie drove to the store owned by Philip Whitney's brother.

"I wondered when someone would dredge this up again." Reggie Whitney sat behind a cluttered desk in the manager's office at the back of the grocery store. He had close-cropped brown hair and the same aquiline nose as Philip, and he looked harried. "It's a long time ago, Officer. Better to leave it alone."

"Wouldn't you and your sister like to know what really happened?"

"Phil helped kill a guy. One way or another, he paid for it. A waste, that's what it was. Phil never should have been there." Reggie looked up at Harvey, his gaze seeking understanding. "You know, he was smart. He could have done anything with his life. He wanted to go in the Navy and come out an admiral. Instead he went to jail for four months and came out broken."

"He shot himself with the gun stolen during the burglary."

"You don't say?" Reggie tossed his pen onto the pile of paper in front of him.

"Did he have it all those years?" Harvey asked.

"I don't see how. Our family moved across town while he was in jail. If Philip had a gun in the house, we didn't find it when we moved."

"So if he'd had it before they arrested him, he must have hidden it someplace else, not at home?"

"I don't know. If he had it, I never knew about it. But then, I thought he was innocent until he shot himself over it. He claimed he was innocent, and he was my big brother. I believed him."

"Do you believe it now?"

Reggie's face crumpled. "He confessed in his

suicide note, so I guess he did it, but that doesn't mean I like it."

"Do you know what happened to the gun afterward?"

"I think the police took it away." Reggie ran one hand through his hair. "It was a long time ago. I think my mom said she didn't want it in the house. She and Dad insisted Philip didn't own a gun, and they didn't know where he got it."

"Do you remember the police officer who investigated?"

"Come on, I was fifteen."

"His name was Arthur Corson."

Reggie shook his head. "I think he was a big guy. Old. He smoked cigars and maybe wore glasses."

"That's him," said Arnie.

"Thanks for your help." Harvey took out a business card and laid it on the desk. "I'm very sorry about your brother. Please call me if you remember anything that might help us put this to rest."

He and Arnie went out to the parking lot, where the pavement sent up scorching waves of hot air. Harvey said, "Philip Whitney was in on the burglary all right, but something still doesn't add up. A gun doesn't just disappear for fourteen years and then conveniently show up for a suicide."

"Where do you think it is now?" Arnie asked.

"Probably in a box in some warehouse with other evidence from the Dark Ages."

"Sometimes they sell stuff like that, if the family doesn't claim it," said Arnie.

"If they were going to sell it, they'd run the serial number, and they wouldn't sell a gun used in an unsolved murder case. But we can check the computer just in case and see if a handgun with that serial number has been sold by the department in the past twenty-one years."

Ryan Toothaker arrived at the office with a large envelope soon after they got back.

"More clips for you. The ones from the trial you asked for were filed separately, but they aren't computerized, so the librarian copied them for you."

"Thanks. I didn't expect the star reporter to hand deliver them," Harvey said.

"I smell another front-page story."

Harvey glanced through the clippings. "It's too early, Ryan."

"Well, I know you're looking at a thirty-five-year-old burglary case."

"What if I am?"

"I read enough to know the only guy ever charged on it was acquitted. And he was a member of the ill-fated Portland High School class. Was he a buddy of Martin Blake's?"

"I don't think so."

"Then why the interest?"

"Can't talk about it yet."

"There were other kids involved in that burglary-turned-murder."

Harvey didn't say anything.

"Come on, Larson, you need to give me something."

"Can't. I'm just about to walk out the door. I have some appointments today."

"Give me one thing. Anything."

Harvey sighed. "Don't start on the burglary thing, Ryan. I'm not sure it's connected to what we're working on, and it could hurt a lot of people if I'm wrong."

"Something else, then."

"We're still gathering information from people who drove over the bridge the night Blake was killed." Harvey walked toward the locker room, and Ryan walked right behind him.

"That's old. Have you heard back on the DNA test?"

"Not yet."

"How about people at the park during the reunion?"

"A few have come forward. Nothing sub-stantial."

"Who are you going to see now?"

Harvey opened his locker and pulled out a tie. "A member of the class."

"May I ask who?"

"No."

"Somebody who was at the reunion?"

"No comment."

"I need something."

"I told your boss I'd give you something later."

"It's later."

"You're starting to annoy me, Ryan." Harvey knotted his tie.

"This Whitney guy."

Harvey glared at him.

"The suicide," Ryan said.

"Yes?"

"Well, I saw it in the clippings. So I talked to his sister."

"Thanks, Sherlock. What did she say?"

"That her brother couldn't have done it, and she's always thought he was framed."

"You're not going to print that?"

"It's a great story."

"It's trouble at this stage of the game. You could scare off our witnesses if you link that burglary to the reunion."

"So you're sure the burglary is related to Blake's death somehow."

"I didn't say that."

"Yet."

"You got it. Work with me here, Ryan."

Ryan didn't like it, but he promised to hold off. Harvey still felt uneasy when he left.

He got to Murphy's office at ten minutes to

eleven and was consigned to a chair in the outer room. After two minutes, he went into the hall and called Eddie on his cell phone.

"You got anything?"

"Maybe. A woman from Cape Elizabeth called. The family was at Fort Point at the right time. They've been camping for two weeks, and they just heard we wanted to talk to people who were there. They'll come in around four."

"Anything else?"

"Mrs. Blake called."

"She wants results?"

"Or just company. I told her I'd try to swing by there later."

"Don't talk out of school, Eddie."

"Would I blab something important?"

"No, sorry. It's just that this case is so complicated. Something's got to break soon, or I will."

"We're getting there," Eddie said. "I really think we are."

"No word on Matt Beaulieu?"

"Not yet."

Harvey went back into the office and sat down, praying for wisdom and a break.

"Congressman Murphy will see you now," the secretary said. Harvey followed her into Murphy's private office.

"Larson, I can't give you much time. I've just been told I have an urgent situation to deal with

287

this afternoon." Murphy didn't shake hands, but gestured toward a vacant chair.

"Then let's get right to the point," Harvey said. "You and Thomas Nadeau had words on the beach at Fort Point before lunch Sunday. An argument."

Murphy looked at him narrowly, but said nothing.

Harvey continued, "Martin Blake wrote about it in his notebook. It was another of your secrets he knew about, like the school break-in, when you and Tom went through the air duct."

"Martin knew everything," Murphy said. "I don't know how. He was lucky."

Harvey said, "I don't believe in luck. Martin Blake was observant. He looked down to the shore that day and saw what happened. He knew your secret, and now I know it."

Something surged in Murphy's eyes; anger, or fear? It was gone.

"What did he see?" the congressman asked.

"He saw Luke Frederick's murder."

Murphy sat forward in his chair. "Murder? Luke Frederick drowned."

"Really? We found his glasses between the rocks, in a tide pool. They have a dent in one bow that fits nicely with the wound on the side of his head."

"You've got a great imagination. I talked to Luke on the beach, it's true, but that's all."

"You and Nadeau couldn't have stood where you did, arguing, and not see Luke Frederick's body."

"Then it wasn't there. Not when I was there."

"What were you and Nadeau arguing about?"

"I don't remember any argument."

Harvey changed his tactics. "Tell me about the burglary thirty-five years ago."

"What are you talking about?"

"The night of April twenty-eighth, your graduation year. Philip Whitney stood trial for it and was acquitted."

Murphy sighed and sank back. "Yeah, I remember."

"You were there."

"No, I wasn't."

"I think you were."

"I don't have to listen to this. If you have something concrete, arrest me. Otherwise, get out of here. I've got a media crisis to deal with."

"A media crisis?" Harvey asked.

"Martin Blake strikes again. That man was a pain when he was alive, but since he died, he's caused me more trouble . . ." Murphy loosened his tie.

"Blake's work is your crisis?"

The congressman eyed him speculatively. "I just heard that the *Portland Press Herald* is carrying a Martin Blake exposé on the front page tomorrow, indicating my office was involved in wrongdoing."

"You have a source at the *Press Herald.*"

"Yes, I do. Why he couldn't have found out about this sooner, I don't know."

"So, you didn't know until today that Blake was doing this article?"

"I had no inkling. Apparently they were going to run it earlier, but when he died they kept it a few days. You knew about this, didn't you?"

Harvey shrugged. "I thought you did."

Murphy's eyes flashed. "This whole thing is ludicrous. A dead reporter making false accusations. I am not happy, Mr. Larson. Are we done?"

"No. I want to know what you and Tom Nadeau talked about."

"I told you."

"Tell me again."

Murphy was silent. Trying to remember what he'd said before?

"Mr. Murphy, I suggest you stay available." Harvey walked out, feeling he'd lost the round. It took him a while to find Nadeau's office, and he prayed for guidance before going in.

Tom Nadeau seemed surprised to see the detective, but he stayed calm. He wouldn't budge on the shorefront argument and said he had just found out about Blake's new exposé.

"Dave Murphy called me an hour ago. He and

I are getting together this afternoon to frame a statement for the press. Murphy's office is clean on that lobbying thing."

Harvey eyed him for a moment. "Martin Blake knew everybody's secrets. He knew about the burglary a month before your graduation, didn't he?"

Nadeau's lip curled in disdain. "Everybody knew about it. It was in the papers."

"But he had information the police didn't have."

"I don't think so," Nadeau said. "His story ended wrong."

The Cape Elizabeth couple came to the office, and Arnie took them into the interview room for twenty minutes. He came out dejected.

"They were there at the right time. Mrs. Dixon even thought she recognized Martin Blake, but her husband convinced her it wasn't him."

"Did they go down to the shore?" Harvey asked.

"No. Too steep, and too many people in the park. The reunion scared them off. They went somewhere else for lunch."

"So they didn't see anything?"

"They saw the fort and the lighthouse. There may have been a few people on the shore, but they weren't paying attention. Couldn't describe anyone."

The men were packing up to leave when Eddie took a call from the state lab.

"We've got a break, Harv. The blood from the bridge is Martin Blake's."

"Fantastic. Tomorrow we go to Stroudwater and interview the woman Nate and Tony found."

"Okay, but don't expect much." Eddie walked to a file cabinet and opened the top drawer, where they filed documents on their current cases.

"Better head home, Ed," Harvey said.

"You're not leaving now?"

"I didn't call the chief yet, and I thought I'd try Beaulieu's sister one more time."

"Call the chief in the morning."

"We've got to get hold of Beaulieu."

"Yup." Eddie put some papers in his desk drawer. "Do you really think Murphy had Blake killed because of the news article?"

"I was leaning that way, thinking it would topple Murphy from his position if Blake had proof. The documentation Russell had impressed me. But after talking to Murphy today, I honestly don't think he knew Blake was writing it until today. He and Nadeau were going into high gear damage control."

"If Murphy didn't know about the story, why would he kill Blake?"

"And why would he kill Frederick?" Harvey asked. He pulled out his pocket planner to make sure he wasn't forgetting anything important, then called upstairs, but Chief Leavitt was gone for the day, so he called Jennifer.

He said, "Hi! Where are you?"

"Just got home. It's hotter in here than outside. If you're coming over, bring some ice cream."

"I might stay at the office a little longer tonight."

"You must be working hard on the case."

"I am, and I can't just drop it right now. I'm sorry." He really wanted to go over to Jennifer's house and relax. "Maybe I can come by later?"

"Sure. And I know you," she said. "If you're working, you won't eat. I'll have something for you when you get here."

Harvey called Denise Beaulieu Marston's number, and this time she answered. She was reluctant to give him her brother's new telephone number. Harvey explained who he was and that he was investigating Martin Blake's death.

"Good riddance," she said.

"Really? What makes you say that?"

"His book hurt a lot of people, including my brother."

"Was your brother in the book?"

"I hope not. I was thinking of Matt's friend, Phil Whitney. He'd been through the wringer already over that burglary thing, and then when the book came out it started all over again. He shot himself, you know."

"I know. I'm sorry about what happened to your

friend. You knew him in high school, of course?"

"I was a freshman when it happened, but Philip was at our house all the time. He and Matt were best friends. Matt was devastated when Philip was arrested. They had enlisted in the Navy, but of course Philip couldn't go. Matt thought of resigning, but in the end he went alone."

"Did you ever see Philip after his acquittal?"

"Only once, but he wasn't accepting sympathy. He went to Bangor to stay, just to get away from the talk. He was such a smart kid, but he wound up pumping gas. And then Martin wrote that awful book."

"I read it."

"Then you know what I'm talking about," Denise Marston said.

"Not exactly."

"He tried Philip all over again, and convicted him."

"And you don't think he was guilty?"

"There was a suicide note saying he did it, so probably he did. I've always hoped that somehow it wasn't true. But even if we found out it wasn't, Philip is gone, and it would be worse somehow to find out now he was innocent."

She gave him her brother's new address in Oregon and his telephone number. Harvey tried to call him but got no answer.

He called a couple of the other classmates they hadn't been able to reach during business hours, but didn't get any new information. Arnie hadn't been able to find the missing handgun listed in any of the department's sales of weapons. Harvey put the serial number into the software he tracked evidence with, but there was no match. It had never been logged in as evidence, or at least not since the system went digital.

He went to the locker room and shaved, then tried Beaulieu again. Still no response. He stretched and rubbed the back of his neck. He'd had enough. Jennifer smiled at him from the picture on his desk, and that did it. He turned off the computer and went out to the garage, carrying her copy of *Morristown* and Patricia's yearbook. The air was stifling. He threw his sport coat in the back seat and turned on the air conditioning.

Harvey stood on the doorstep, and he handed Jennifer a bag from a convenience store.

"Ice cream," he said.

"Wonderful. Come on in."

Beth had her Sunday school book out and was sitting on the living room floor in walking shorts and a sleeveless blouse, studying in front of a fan. Jennifer had opted for shorts, too, but she was still uncomfortable in the stifling heat.

"This place is an oven." Harvey pulled off his tie.

"They make you wear ties to work in this heat?" Beth asked.

"Well, between the press conference and interviewing a congressman, today was a tie day. I get a lot of that lately. You don't mind if I lose this shirt, do you?" He started unbuttoning his cuffs.

"We should drive down to the Old Port," Beth said. "It might be cooler near the water."

Jennifer frowned. "I don't have the energy."

She took Harvey into the kitchen, and he made a pile of his holster, shirt, and tie on the counter. She took cold cuts and salad from the refrigerator and fixed a plate for him, then poured two glasses of iced tea. When she set the pitcher down, Harvey put his arms around her.

"Too hot to kiss me?"

"Never." His T-shirt was sticky, but she didn't mind.

"How are the wedding plans coming?" he asked.

"Under control, I think. If there's anything we've forgotten, I don't want to know about it."

"Good, because I need some T.L.C. tonight." He sat down, and she stood behind him and rubbed his neck and shoulders.

"You're working too hard," she said.

"Not hard enough."

"Don't say that."

"I've got to break this case before the wedding."

She leaned down and kissed the back of his neck. He said, "I can eat, or I can kiss you. Hmm . . ." He started to turn toward her, but she pulled away laughing and sat down beside him. "Hold that thought," Harvey said. He was hungry, but after a few bites he seemed to lose interest. He drank the tea down, and she went to the refrigerator for the pitcher.

"You'd better just forget about the case for tonight. We're calling a moratorium on work here."

"What do you recommend?"

"Ice cream." She opened the freezer for the carton he'd brought.

Beth came in from the living room. "Ice cream," she said, in a robot voice.

Jennifer got bowls and spoons and served it up generously.

Beth looked at the thermometer. "Eighty-eight outside and 90 in here. Let's take it out back."

Jennifer and Harvey sat on the back steps, and Beth produced a lawn chair. The sun was low over the trees and houses, but it would be light for at least another hour, a perk they got in summer for living so far north.

"You getting a new roommate?" Harvey asked Beth. He took a bite of mocha chip.

"Not yet. I haven't started looking." She didn't seem too concerned about it. "When are you moving into the new house?"

"Probably right after we get back from London. Jeff might move in with me the week before the wedding."

"It's coming right up."

"Yup." He took another bite. "I might be able to move some stuff before then."

Jennifer just let them talk, enjoying the ease and comfort of being with them.

"Is Jeff showing an interest in spiritual things?" Beth asked, and Jennifer's attention snapped to high level.

Harvey looked keenly at Beth. "Sometimes I think so, but we haven't gotten past the superficial yet. Jennifer and I are praying for him."

"He's on my list, too."

Jennifer smiled. "Thanks, Beth."

"He's a great guy," Harvey said. Beth didn't say anything.

They sat for half an hour or so, with the sun slipping lower. Jennifer rested her head against Harvey's shoulder, wishing this evening would never end. But then they'd never get to the wedding. Sweat formed on her forehead, and she sat up to get some air between them.

"Can we have a lawn swing at the new house?" she asked, feeling a little sleepy.

"We can have a swimming pool, if you want it," he said.

"Too much trouble."

"It would sure feel good today," Beth said.

Jennifer turned to Harvey. "We'll have an air conditioner, though, right?" She hadn't noticed any units in the new house.

He smiled. "That house has central air."

Her eyes flared. "That's a huge splurge."

"Lucky you," Beth said.

"You can visit anytime," Jennifer assured her.

A tiny breeze drifted past, ruffling Beth's bangs. Harvey put his arm around Jennifer, but the body heat escalated so fast she leaned forward, out of his embrace and he dropped his arm behind her.

"We won't sleep tonight," she said.

Beth stood up. "Want more ice cream?"

Harvey held up his bowl. Jennifer squeezed against him so Beth could walk past them on the steps. He held her there and kissed her, but sweat dripped off his brow. He sighed and let go of her.

"Beth likes Jeff a lot," said Jennifer.

They ate all of the ice cream, and the sun went down, but the air was still muggy. Jennifer walked with Harvey to the park, and he kissed her under the big pine trees, then walked her back home holding her hand. They read from the Bible on the back steps, discussed the trip to London, and prayed together.

"Guess I'd better go," Harvey said listlessly. They went to the kitchen, and he picked up his stuff. Beth was washing up the ice cream bowls.

"Goodnight, Beth," he said.

" 'Night, Harvey."

"Maybe tomorrow will be cooler," Jennifer said without much hope. They paused in the living room, in front of one of the fans.

"I hope so." He pulled her in close, and she wished he didn't have to leave. "I love you," he said, "but I need a shower and some sleep."

"Me, too."

Harvey's eyes twinkled. "Don't you just want to come home with me?"

She knew he was teasing. "Do you have an air conditioner?"

"Afraid not."

"Then, in sixteen days."

Chapter 14

Friday, July 2

The air was slightly cooler at 5:30 a.m., when Harvey met Eddie to run. When they got to the office, the detectives settled in for another day's work, but a few minutes past eight, the elevator opened and Terry Lemieux got off, accompanying Mayor Jill Weymouth.

"Gentlemen," she said, looking around at the four of them.

They all jumped to attention, and Arnie said, "Good morning, Mrs. Weymouth."

"I need your assistance," she said. "The chief of police was injured in an automobile accident early this morning."

They all expressed dismay, and Pete asked what had happened.

"It seems there was a raccoon on the overpass near exit 5, and he swerved to avoid it."

"How bad is it?" Harvey asked.

"He's in ICU, still unconscious. They don't know if he'll walk again. His wife, Patsy, was injured, too. She's serious, but not critical. Broken pelvis, some internal bleeding."

"For a raccoon," Eddie said.

"Well, it's a tragedy," the mayor agreed. "I've

301

had to make some executive decisions this morning, and one of them is to put Michael Browning upstairs in the chief's office, but I understand he's on vacation."

"Yes, ma'am," said Arnie. "He'll be gone another week."

"Well, we need him now. We'll compensate him, but we need him. That's why I'm here. Can you help me locate him? The deputy chief said he's gone on a camping trip to the Allagash."

"That's right," said Arnie. "He wanted to get away from it all. He said we couldn't reach him. I'm sorry, ma'am."

"Nonsense. You're Portland's elite. Surely you can find him."

Harvey shook his head. "He didn't give us any specifics, ma'am."

Arnie frowned. "Maybe his children could help. There's Mike Jr., in Gorham, and their daughter, Debbie. What's her married name? Well, anyway, she's in Vermont. Then there's the youngest one, Tommy. He lives up in Somerset County, I think."

"Can you get hold of one of them?" she asked. "We need to find the captain as soon as possible."

Arnie went to his desk and pulled out a phone book, and Eddie started tapping his cell phone.

"Do you want to wait, ma'am?" Harvey asked.

"No, I'll be in the deputy chief's office. There are some things I need to discuss with him."

Harvey was curious. She was passing over the deputy chief for Mike. It must have shown on his face.

She looked around at them. "The deputy chief has accepted a position elsewhere. As of the end of this month, he's the new chief of police in Framingham, Massachusetts. We were planning to announce it Monday. I guess we still will. He'll act as chief here until we get Browning back."

Nobody said anything. Things were happening too fast, and Harvey wondered if she knew about Mike's planned retirement.

"You're Larson."

"Yes, ma'am." He was glad he'd shaved that morning.

She looked him up and down, nodding. "You're in charge of the Blake case?"

"Yes."

"You've been tapped to run this unit."

He opened his mouth, then closed it again. She knew about Mike, all right.

She stepped toward him. "We've got to carry on smoothly. You keep things going here, and as soon as we get Browning back from the woods, we'll talk. Call me in the deputy's office if you find out where he is."

She turned and walked to the elevator. Terry entered the security code.

Arnie got Mike Jr.'s twelve-year-old daughter

303

on the phone. Her mother was out, but she gave him her father's work number. Harvey went over to his desk and sat down slowly.

Pete said, "Congratulations, Harvey."

"Thanks." He didn't feel very festive.

Pete walked away, but Eddie came closer. Harvey looked up at him and said, "I told Jenny the other night I don't want the promotion."

"You don't want it?" Eddie whispered, his eyes shouting his dismay. He sat down in the extra chair and leaned toward Harvey. "Why would you not want it? You can be the boss here, and Mike will be upstairs."

"That might change things, if Mike stays."

"Have you prayed about it?"

Harvey couldn't believe this was coming out of Eddie's mouth. "Yeah, I have."

"Well, maybe this is your answer."

He nodded. "Thanks, Ed."

Nate and Tony came up after their roll call. The patrol sergeant had told them about the chief, and both were somber. Harvey sent them to Stroudwater to talk to witnesses again. Arnie was still trying to get a line on Mike and Sharon's camping trip. Eddie and Pete started in on the messages that had come in overnight.

Harvey got out the folder of old news clippings and dialed the Oregon number Matt Beaulieu's sister had given him. A man answered.

"Commander Beaulieu?"

"Yes, who is it?"

Harvey hadn't really expected him to answer, and he quickly activated the tape recorder.

"My name is Harvey Larson. I'm a detective with the Portland, Maine, Police Department's Priority Unit. I'll be recording our conversation, sir. We're investigating the death of Martin Blake."

"What's that got to do with me?"

"Probably nothing, but we've been trying to talk to all his class members. Are you aware that Blake was stabbed the night after the class reunion?"

"I read in the *Oregonian* that he was killed and dumped in the river or something."

"That's right. It happened twelve days ago. We've interviewed all the people who attended the class reunion, but now we're expanding our investigation to include the class members who weren't there as well."

"Why?"

"I believe that events from the past may have had something to do with the murders of Martin Blake and another man in your class, Luke Frederick."

"Luke Frederick's dead?"

"Yes, sir, the same day as Martin Blake." Beaulieu was silent. Harvey said, "Sir, I need to talk to you about the burglary that happened the

305

spring of your senior year, and your friend Philip Whitney."

"Phil's been dead a long time."

"Yes, and I'm sorry about that. But he was involved in the burglary, and I need any information you can give me."

"How can it help now? Phil wrote it all down in his note."

"Not all of it," Harvey said. "He didn't tell who was there with him the night they broke into the house and beat the owner."

"I wasn't."

"Who was?"

Silence. Then, "How do I know you're really a cop? You could be anybody."

"That's true. I'm at my desk. Do you want to call the Portland P.D. and ask for me?"

He was quiet.

"Commander Beaulieu?"

"I'm thinking."

"Sir, if you know who was involved in that break-in—"

"Philip talked to me some."

"You were best friends in high school," Harvey said.

"Yes, but I went into the Navy before he was released from prison. They kept him until the trial. No bail. They were hoping he'd cooperate and name the others. He didn't. He was loyal the whole time."

"That's what I've been told, sir. But he's dead now. Are you sure his loyalty wasn't misplaced?"

"I've tried to be true to him, too. He asked me never to tell."

"But, Commander, if you had told, perhaps it would have helped him."

"Do you think I haven't thought of that?"

Easy. Don't scare him off now. Harvey said, "He did take part in the burglary, sir. We know that."

"His lawyer told him to hang tough and he'd walk. And he did."

"But he was in Fairley's house that night."

"Yes."

Harvey's pulse picked up. "Did you see him after the burglary?"

"I went home on leave the next spring, and I found him in Bangor. He told me then he wished he had confessed. Said he'd have felt better. He had a tremendous load of guilt."

"What did you do?"

"I tried to be there for him, but I only had ten days at home. It wasn't enough. I got to see him a couple more times."

"Why weren't you with him the night of the burglary?"

"It was a silly thing. My parents made me go to my sister's piano recital. I hated it. Philip and I usually spent evenings together if we could."

"Did you ever do anything like that?"

"Like what?" Beaulieu asked.

"Break into houses. I'm not going to have you arrested or anything. I'm just trying to understand why Philip did what he did that night."

"We never did. I think it was the other guys he was with that night. They'd done some things before. Hassled people in the parking lot at the A & P, stolen pumpkins at Halloween, stuff like that. Not felonies or anything, but they liked to see what they could get away with."

"So why did they decide to commit burglary that night?"

"How should I know?" Beaulieu asked. "They were bored, maybe, or needed a bigger thrill. Philip went with them that night. He was daring and bright. He would take risks, but he wasn't into breaking the law."

"What kind of risks did he take?"

"Oh, things like walking across the railroad bridge. If you got caught out in the middle, the train would get you. Or he'd dive into an old quarry. We weren't supposed to do that."

"Did you know he was going with these other guys?"

"No. I'd told him I couldn't get out of Denise's recital, and he was sympathetic and said he'd see me the next day."

"Did he?"

"Yes, he came to school."

Harvey looked at the masthead on a clipping and said, "It happened on a Thursday night. You usually went out on Thursdays?"

"No, but we were usually together at his house or mine. We'd study or just goof off."

"Did he tell you why he went with them?"

"He was outside, and they came by and kind of pulled him into their scheme."

"They planned it?"

"Not specifically, I think. Not that house. They were thinking about going into a house and maybe looking for beer and taking a little cash. Maybe messing things up. They thought it would be funny."

"And Philip thought it would be funny?"

"I don't know. I think he was apprehensive but wanted to seem cool. Then they got this kid who had a car."

"Who was he?"

Beaulieu paused. "I'm not sure I should say. Phil told me they played up to him, like they were going to be great buddies. Later the kid got scared, and they made fun of him and threatened him."

"He told you all this the first time you were home on leave?"

"Not until later. A lot later. I tried to see Phil every time I went home. It was six or eight years before he told me. I'd been out on deployment

309

six months. I went home to see my folks, and I called Phil and went up to see him. That's when he told me who it was."

"Can't you tell me, sir? It would help our investigation. The police never arrested anyone but Philip."

"I think they had suspicions, but Phil never broke. Not until Blake's book came out."

"Tell me about that," Harvey said.

"I went home right after it was published. Everyone was reading it and talking about it and trying to guess who the characters were. I knew. I was very uncomfortable, because Phil had made me swear not to tell. I just played ignorant. The last time I saw him, he was visiting his parents in Portland, and he was very agitated. He told me he was going to confess and take the consequences. He said he'd rather spend the rest of his life in prison than live with it."

Harvey looked down at the photocopied clippings. "But in the end, he opted for suicide over the state prison?"

"That's always bothered me."

"What? The suicide?"

"Yes," Beaulieu said. "I saw him the day before he did it. He told me he'd talked to the other kids."

"The three from the burglary?"

He hesitated. "He said they were scared. They

310

begged him not to tell. They made other threats, too, and Phil never told, even in the suicide note. If it was a suicide note."

"What do you mean?"

Beaulieu exhaled heavily. "He told me that one of the guys had said, 'Go ahead, spill your guts if you want to. But don't name us. Write it all down, and give it to the police, but if you tell on us, we'll kill you.' "

"But he killed himself," Harvey said. "Why didn't he tell on them if he was going to kill himself?"

"My question exactly. I don't think he meant to kill himself."

Harvey wished he could see his face. "Commander, what are you implying?"

"Phil Whitney wrote a confession implicating himself only. It didn't say he was going to end it all, or anything like that. Then he died. Was it a suicide note? Or did the guys threatening him make sure he could never wrestle with his conscience again?"

Harvey thought about that. It was time for Matt Beaulieu to stop thinking of them as messed up kids. "Sir, will you please tell me who those men are?"

"I'd like to come home and see my sister, and Phil's family. If I'm going to blow this wide open, I owe them something."

"You'll come to Maine?"

"Yes. This weekend if I can. I'll have to look into it and discuss it with my wife."

"Time is important," Harvey said.

"Give me your number. I'll get back to you."

Harvey gave him his work number and his cell phone number and asked him to call as soon as possible, day or night. "Sir, you won't disappear on me?"

"No. I won't do that. It's time this thing was cleared up."

Beaulieu broke the connection and Harvey hung up, frustrated.

Arnie came to his desk. "Harv, I got Mike Jr., but he was very vague. He thinks Mike and Sharon's jumping-off point was Eagle Lake."

"Talk about remote."

"Yeah. What do you suggest?"

"Call Fisheries and Wildlife." Arnie went back to his desk.

Harvey popped the tape out of the recorder and took it to Eddie's desk.

"You got Beaulieu," Eddie said, his eyes on his monitor, and his fingers moving on the keyboard.

"Yes. He knows who was in on the burglary, but he won't tell me."

Eddie whistled. "Was Beaulieu there?"

"He says not. His buddy Phil Whitney told him about it."

"Even if he told you, it's hearsay." Eddie closed his computer file and turned to face him.

Harvey said, "Dying confession."

"You think that will fly?"

"He told him the night before the suicide. It's all we've got so far."

Eddie cocked his head to one side, considering. "Well, it's the only thing we have that remotely resembles a motive for Martin Blake's murder."

"I recorded the whole conversation. Listen to it, okay?" Harvey laid the cassette on his mouse pad.

"Sure. I'll take it in the interview room right now."

Harvey's Bible lay to one side on his desk. He picked it up, opening to Romans where they had read Wednesday night at the church Bible study. They'd been in chapter three, and he skimmed down the next chapter. It was all about Abraham, and he didn't understand it all, but he got the message that it wasn't what a man did that justified him; it was what he believed.

He stopped on verses 20 and 21. *No distrust made him waver concerning the promise of God, but he grew strong in his faith as he gave glory to God, fully convinced that God was able to do what he had promised.*

He closed his eyes and asked God to help him grow strong in his faith. He knew quite a few of the promises by that time. God would never leave him. He would give peace and strength. He would answer prayer. It had taken Eddie to remind Harvey of that. He prayed for Eddie. When he opened his eyes, Arnie was standing beside him.

"You okay, Harvey?"

"Yeah, what have you got?"

"Mike got a fire permit at the ranger station in Eagle Lake on Saturday and put down three possible destinations. The wardens are going to try to locate him. They've got a plane in Ashland, and they can put half a dozen men in the field."

"I don't know if the state should spend so much money on this," Harvey said. "It's not like looking for a lost person who needs help."

"They said they can get volunteers to help them if he's not camping where it says on the fire permit."

"Can you call the mayor and tell her? It's an isolated area, and it may take a while."

Arnie nodded. "Sure thing."

Tony and Nate came in from Stroudwater and told him their witnesses hadn't been able to add anything helpful.

"Okay," Harvey said. "Do what you can on the other leads."

He went down the stairs, all the way to the basement. It was stiflingly hot. Jennifer looked up in surprise when he opened the door to Records. She glanced over at her supervisor,

Marge. Marge just shrugged and smiled a little. Jennifer left her computer terminal and came into the hall.

"I'm sorry," Harvey said, "but we're having a major meltdown upstairs."

"The chief?"

"You heard."

"It's pretty awful." Jennifer's gray eyes had the worried cast. "They're saying he might not be able to come back."

"You heard right. The mayor wants to appoint Mike as chief."

"Not Deputy Chief Neilsen?"

"He's out of here as of the thirty-first, moving south to his own kingdom."

"But Mike—"

"Tell me about it." He sighed and put one hand against the wall, leaning on it. "She's putting me in charge of the unit, Jenny. She knew about that little plan."

"Did you tell her you don't want it?"

"No."

She put her hand up to his forehead and wiped away a bead of sweat. "Things are changing."

"Big time. They're sending game wardens into the Allagash to find Mike and bring him back. He's gonna love that."

"Sounds like what happened when McKinley was shot and they had to go climb a mountain to find Teddy Roosevelt."

He pulled his tie off. "You girls are cooking down here."

"The computers keep crashing, and the copier won't make more than three copies without overheating. Marge finally got approval to requisition an air conditioner. We're supposed to have it by Monday. We'll see."

"Pray for me," he said.

"I am, and I will."

"I've reached a guy in Oregon who may help us a lot on the Blake murder, if he decides he feels like it. He says he'll come to Maine, but I don't know. He's a retired naval officer. I think he'll do the right thing."

She nodded. "Good. Lunch today?"

"Maybe." Food was the furthest thing from his mind.

"You need to eat, Harvey."

He was thinking about Mike Browning and Matthew Beaulieu and David Murphy.

"I'll get some sandwiches and bring them up to your cushy, cool office," Jennifer said.

"Do that." He pulled out his wallet and gave her a twenty. She was back through the door to Records before he could do anything else. He took the elevator back upstairs, something he never did. The stairs were always faster, but he didn't need that exertion today. As the elevator made its way slowly upward, he stood dripping with sweat and praying. The door opened at the third floor, and he stepped out into cool air. Tony was sitting at Mike's desk with the telephone receiver to his ear. He hit the mute button when he saw Harvey and called, "I've got the woman in PA. Fotter's girlfriend. She's giving me a better description of the men on the bridge."

"Ask her about the cigarette."

Nate smiled at Harvey as he poured himself coffee. "Terry says we're yours for the duration of the Blake case."

"Great. I won't have to keep asking for you and Tony every day."

Eddie came from the interview room. "I listened to the tape, Harv. You're right. We need this guy in the witness box."

Harvey blew out a measured breath. "I'll do everything I can to get him to talk."

Tony came over. "Fotter's girlfriend says the shorter guy on the bridge was wearing a jacket and had dark hair. He was definitely smoking. The tall man was leaning back with his elbows on the railing."

"Sounds like maybe they knew each other," said Nate.

"Blake didn't smoke," Eddie put in.

Harvey nodded. "Blake was the taller man. He was over six feet, wasn't he? Let's look at the autopsy report again." Eddie went to his computer.

"Did your suspects smoke?" Tony asked.

Harvey leaned back in his chair and closed his eyes, picturing Murphy's office, then Nadeau's. "There was an ashtray on Nadeau's desk, and somebody told me Murphy smokes. I don't remember seeing him do it, but—" Carl's words came back to him, the day he and Jennifer had eaten at his house. "His doctor's been after him to quit."

"Maybe he did quit," Tony said.

"Arnie," Harvey called. "Can you charm Alison Murphy again?"

"Maybe. What do you want to know?"

"If her husband still smokes. I'm not sure we should ask her about the burglary. She might tell David we asked, and that would upset him."

"Well, this has probably already sent him through the roof," said Pete, tossing the morning's *Press Herald* on his desk.

The banner headline screamed at Harvey: *Maine congressman implicated in kickback scandal.* The subhead said, *Martin Blake's last exclusive to the Press Herald.*

"Oh, boy," Harvey said. "This will heat things up. Arnie, call Alison, but be discreet." He frowned at the headline. "David Murphy didn't know about this until yesterday. His source was a little slow."

"Someone at the paper?" asked Eddie.

"He admitted to me that somebody there tipped

318

him off. John Russell told me that not even the newsroom staff knew about it beforehand. He was right to be cautious, but even so, several people had to learn about it yesterday, when they laid out the page. Tony, you and Nate picked up some butts on the bridge, didn't you?"

"Not us, the crime scene techs. Everything they got went into the evidence locker."

"I'll get it." Harvey went down to Evidence and had to hunt for the detective sergeant. He pulled him out of a meeting to get the bag of trash.

"Hear about the chief?" Sergeant Legere asked, opening a locker.

"Yeah," Harvey said. "It's too bad."

"Big mess."

"Maybe not."

"You know something I don't know?" Legere asked. "The deputy chief's leaving. They'll bring in someone new, and we'll all have to break him in."

Harvey shrugged. "That's life. Thanks." He took the bag and went back upstairs.

It didn't look very promising. Five cigarette butts, a wad of chewed gum, a candy wrapper, a Coors can, and a few scraps of paper. He wondered if he could get DNA testing on the butts and the gum. They already matched Blake's blood, but he'd need saliva samples from the suspects for a job like this.

He called the lab to ask about the logistics of

DNA testing on the cigarettes. The tech told him to call Augusta. The state crime lab was the only place that could do it.

Arnie called, "Okay, Harv, Murphy is trying to quit, but he's been unsuccessful so far. Smokes Camels. Chews gum only rarely."

"How's Alison?"

"Bored and lonely. Hubby's always at the capitol."

"Did she hit on you?" asked Pete.

"Would I tell?"

Harvey smiled. "Did she mention the newspaper story?"

"No. Did you want me to ask?"

"No, we're good."

They kept on, bit by bit. At noon, Jennifer arrived with sandwiches and cold drinks for two. Harvey sent the rest of the men away for lunch. She set the food out on his desk.

"It's really hot out," she said. Tendrils of her hair had escaped her braid and stuck to her neck.

"They've gotta get that A.C. unit for your office."

"Do you have any pull with the mayor now?"

"No, but when Mike gets back, I may have an in with the chief."

"They haven't found him yet?"

"Not as far as I know." Harvey envisioned the state plane buzzing Eagle Lake, and game wardens in canoes paddling furiously up Wallagrass Stream, stopping to feel cold campfire ashes and question moose and beaver.

He asked a blessing on their lunch, and Jennifer started eating her sandwich. Harvey looked at his and pushed back from the desk.

"Eat, Harvey."

"Not hungry."

"Eat anyway. Please."

He wanted to make her happy, and he'd said sincerely he would do anything for her. He took a bite. When he'd swallowed, he said, "I need to get back to work."

"Relax for twenty minutes."

"I can't." He stood and went to the file cabinet and pulled out Thomas Nadeau's file.

"Harvey, please, you're going to get sick."

He dropped the file on the desk and sat down, making himself not touch it. He picked up half the sandwich and took another bite. Jennifer was watching him.

"You want me to leave, don't you?" she asked.

"No."

"Yes, you do. But I'm not going until I see you eat that sandwich." He took another bite and a sip of Pepsi. She said, "I should have gotten milk for you."

"It would have soured by the time you got it in here." He made himself eat it all and said, "I'm sorry. I'm not trying to annoy you."

"I know." She smiled at him, but with a touch of regret. "I hoped I could make you forget all this for a while. I guess that's not possible without transporting you away from the office."

"I keep thinking about that gun," he admitted.

"The one from the old burglary, that the man shot himself with?"

"Yes."

"Someone else kept it," she said.

"Yes. But who?"

"Is it important?"

"Philip Whitney's best friend thinks it wasn't suicide. If he's right, that gun is a murder weapon. I checked the computer, but there's no record of it ever being entered into evidence by the officer who investigated the suicide. They don't usually for suicides, but Whitney's brother says the family didn't claim it, and I can't find that it was ever sold."

She put her hand on his cheek. "I'll go now. You won't rest until this is over, will you?"

"Probably not. But I'm not forgetting our counseling tonight. I'll pick you up."

She ruffled his hair and went away.

He called the Department of Fisheries and Wildlife and got through to the commissioner.

"Any word on Mike Browning yet, sir?" Harvey asked.

"No, but we've got a retired warden who's a

322

good friend of his. They've gone fishing together several times. He knows some of Browning's favorite spots. He's on his way up there now. Going to check Churchill, and on up toward Umsaskis. Maybe down the Allagash from there. If anyone can find him, Page can. And we've got some guides who are looking along the St. John and the Fish River."

As soon as Harvey hung up, his phone rang. "Please hold for the mayor."

"Mrs. Weymouth," he said.

"Yes, Larson, anything on Captain Browning?"

"I just spoke to the Fisheries and Wildlife commissioner. They've got a lot of people working on it. It's just a matter of time."

"And the Blake case?"

"We're getting closer."

"This is one case we want solved, Larson, even if we have to spend a little money. Martin Blake, for heaven's sake. Reporters are in my office every day."

"Here, too, ma'am."

"Could you give them something today, to take some attention off this police chief thing?"

"To be frank, Mayor, I was glad something was pulling the spotlight off the Blake case."

Jill Weymouth chuckled.

Harvey said, "We did get the report back from the state lab last night. The blood from the bridge on Route 9 was definitely Martin

Blake's. I've told a couple of reporters who have called, but I didn't want to hold another press conference."

"All right, Larson. Maybe we can work together on Monday. You announce an arrest, and I'll announce Browning's promotion."

"That would be ideal, ma'am, but it may take us a little longer to close this out."

When the men came back from lunch, Harvey brainstormed with them on how they could get information on Thomas Nadeau. "I can't call his wife like we did with Murphy," Harvey said.

"Why not?" asked Eddie.

"He's not married," Harvey said.

"Correction. He's divorced. Call the ex-wife."

Arnie's eyebrows shot up. "Didn't know there was one."

"I'm sure there is." Eddie stepped toward the file cabinet.

"I've got the file." Harvey held it out to him.

"You could try to charm his secretary," suggested Pete.

"Arnie's better at that than I am," Harvey said, and Arnie shrugged as though he was willing to make the sacrifice.

Eddie paged through the file, frowning. "I can't seem to locate it, but I'm sure there's an ex-wife."

"Maybe Patricia Lundquist would know," Harvey said. "Let's take her yearbook back."

He thought about walking over, but when they went out the door the heat drove them back in, and they went to the garage for his Explorer. The thermometer near the garage door showed 95. The bakery was well cooled, keeping the frosting from melting, but the store was empty.

Patricia came from the kitchen in her apron, her face flushed. "Hello, Detectives. Business is slow in this weather. People go for ice cream, not cakes, in heat."

Harvey held out the yearbook. "Thanks for lending me this. Could I ask you one more question?"

"Ask away." She set the yearbook down behind the counter and started putting cookies in a bag.

"Thomas Nadeau was married?"

"Yes, he married Cathy Perkins."

"But he's divorced now?"

"Yes, a long time now. Never remarried."

"Where does she live?"

"Out of state. Vermont, maybe?"

"She wasn't a member of your class?" Harvey asked.

"No, she was a year younger."

"So, she was a junior when this robbery thing happened?"

"Right." Patricia picked up the yearbook and ruffled through to the small headshots of the junior class. "That's Cathy."

Harvey gazed at the photo. "Were she and Nadeau dating then?"

"Oh, yes, childhood sweethearts. They were disgusting." She laughed.

Harvey frowned. "But they broke up later."

"They were married at least ten years. They had a couple of kids. She took them with her when they broke up."

Harvey looked at Eddie. The wheels were turning.

"Does Tom Nadeau smoke?" Eddie asked.

"Yes, he had a cigarette after lunch the day of the reunion."

"What brand?" Eddie asked casually.

She eyed him keenly. "This isn't just trivia, is it?"

"You've got to keep quiet about it, Patricia," Harvey said. "Please. Don't talk to anyone, especially not the press."

"I won't." She put a few more cookies in the bag. "Marlboro, I think. The pack had red on it, anyway." She held out the bag to Eddie.

"Oh, I can't take that, Mrs. Lundquist. Bribing cops, you know."

She laughed. "I'm not trying to bribe you, Detective Thibodeau. They'll go to waste.

Nobody's buying. And you two look like you could use a few cookies."

Eddie looked at Harvey helplessly. Harvey took out his wallet and gave her two dollars. "Token payment."

She shrugged and put it in the cash register. "Enjoy."

Harvey set Eddie to tracking down the former Mrs. Nadeau and got on his computer with a program to help him identify the cigarette butts in the bag. No generics. That was good.

Two Marlboro, a Camel, a Virginia Slims, and a Winston.

Eddie soon reported that Cyndi Rancourt Reynolds didn't have Nadeau's ex-wife's address. She only kept track of her own class, but she was sure Cathy Perkins Nadeau had remarried.

"Great," Harvey said. "She changed her last name again."

Eddie nodded. "No one seems to know what it is now. I did ask about her parents. Cathy's mother is still in the area."

"Give it a try," Harvey said.

Arnie, meanwhile, had chatted with Nadeau's office manager. Harvey heard him lie glibly, telling her he was a golf buddy of Tom's and owed Tom a pack of cigarettes. He wanted to have it ready when he saw him on the weekend. Harvey wished Arnie hadn't lied to her, but it hadn't been too long since he'd been lying as a matter of course on undercover jobs. He didn't say anything.

"Marlboros," Arnie told him when he'd ended the call. "Nadeau won't touch anything else."

"Now how are we going to get the DNA samples?" Harvey asked.

"How about waltzing in there with a warrant and emptying their ashtrays?" asked Arnie.

Harvey thought about that. "Maybe we could. What do you think, Pete?"

"Sure, get a warrant. But then we have to take the samples to the lab in Augusta."

Harvey called the judge's chambers and was able to talk to His Honor, who was agreeable, so he wrote a note for Pete to carry to the judge with his signature. When Pete left for the courthouse, it was already after three.

"It won't happen today," Arnie said fretfully.

"We can't sit on this until Monday," Harvey said.

"All right, as soon as Pete gets back, we go execute the warrants."

Harvey nodded.

"I'll run the stuff up to Augusta," said Arnie.

"You can't be there by five. Even if we get the cigarette butts tonight, the lab won't work on it until Monday."

"You're right," Arnie said.

"Call them," Harvey told him. "We can have a courier take it. Tell the lab it's a rush job for them on Monday. They can have someone accept the package from the courier tonight."

"I'll take care of it," Arnie said.

Pete came back just before four o'clock with the warrants. Harvey sent him and Arnie to Murphy's office and Eddie, Nate, and Tony to Nadeau's. He stayed in the office and went over everybody else's reports and typed up his own for the deputy chief, or whoever would read it eventually.

At 4:50, the commissioner of Inland Fisheries and Wildlife called.

"Just thought you'd want to know, Larson. A guide on the Allagash saw Mr. and Mrs. Browning at Umsaskis on Tuesday. We've checked the camp site, and they're gone, but we're looking in that area now, and down the Allagash. The guide had told Browning about a couple of good fishing spots. We're going to try to check them before dark."

"Have you got your plane in the air?"

"Yes, but we can't spend too much aviation fuel on this. It's not like a medical emergency."

"I know," Harvey said. "Thanks for what you're doing."

The men came back with their loot from the raids and tales of outrage from Nadeau and the administrator at Murphy's office. They packaged and labeled the ashtray contents from each office and the trash from the bridge. The courier arrived and signed for it. Harvey sank into his chair feeling drained.

They called it a day, and Harvey dropped Eddie off at his apartment.

"Try to relax over the weekend, buddy."

"If you don't mind, can I go to church with you Sunday?" Eddie asked. "We might need to talk about stuff before Monday."

"Of course," Harvey said. "You can come there anytime you want. Are you sure you want to?" Eddie's Catholic upbringing had made him leery of Harvey's faith, and Harvey was surprised he hadn't simply asked if they could get together in the afternoon.

"Yeah." Eddie didn't quite meet his gaze.

"Good," Harvey said.

He was dripping sweat when he went into his building. Mrs. Jenkins opened her door in the hall at the bottom of the stairs.

"You got a new roommate, Harvey?"

"Oh, yeah, that's Jeff, my fiancée's brother. He's going to rent the apartment after Jennifer and I get married."

"He's a handsome young man. Looks like his sister."

"You be good to him, okay, Rebecca?"

"I will." She smiled broadly. "We got the invitation. Thanks, Harvey."

"You're coming to the wedding, aren't you?"

"Oh, my, yes. I was hoping you would keep living here."

"No, sorry. We're getting a house a couple of miles from here."

"Well, maybe you'll come back and visit once in a while."

"For sure. Especially with Jeff here."

He walked up the stairs. When he opened the door, the kitchen was cool and it smelled great.

"Do I have the right apartment?"

Jeff turned from the stove. "Hi, Harvey! I hope you don't mind I brought an A.C. unit." The air conditioner sat in the kitchen window, pumping cool air out over the sink.

"Why would I mind? It's great. You didn't have to cook."

Jeff shrugged. "We cook all the time at the fire station. Thought I'd impress you tonight." He'd made a chicken dish and mashed potatoes and salad. The table was set for two. Harvey washed his hands and sat down with him.

"Do you want to pray, Harvey?"

Harvey was surprised at the question but pleased. He asked the blessing and realized he felt like eating for the first time in days. While they ate, they arranged to see the landlord together to transfer the lease to Jeff.

"I wanted to ask you something," Jeff said.

"Sure, what?"

Jeff went into the living room and came back with a Bible. "I got enough time off Sunday to go to church with the folks. Took my lunch hour then. The preaching was about how everyone in the world is a sinner."

"Yeah?" Harvey was surprised Jeff was going this route.

"Yeah. Do you believe that?"

"Sure."

Jeff opened the Bible to where there was a piece of paper stuck in it. "This is where he was reading."

Harvey looked at it. It was open to John 3. "I've studied that a little."

"So, do you think I'm a sinner?"

"Well, Jeff, I'd have to say yes, not because of any particular horrible thing you've done, but because, like it says, we're all sinners."

"Doesn't that seem kind of . . . I don't know, unfair or something? Do you think Mom and Dad are sinners?"

"Well, yeah. We all fall short of God's standard."

Harvey could see that thought made him uncomfortable. Jeff looked at the Bible and shook his head.

Harvey said, "The first time I heard it, I wasn't very happy, either. It took me a while to be ready to even think about it."

"Maybe I just need some time."

"Where did you get the Bible?"

"Saw it at a yard sale. Fifty cents."

"Good deal." Harvey helped himself to more chicken. He couldn't wait to tell Jennifer that her brother was thinking deeply about his spiritual state. Their prayers were bearing fruit.

"There are things I wonder about," Jeff said.

"If you want to talk about them, let me know."

His phone rang, in the pocket of the jacket he'd thrown over the back of a chair.

"Harvey, it's almost seven."

"Oh, Jenny, I'm sorry. I'll be right there. I didn't know how late it was."

"Just get over to the church, okay?" she said. "I'll meet you there."

Harvey managed to get to the church only three minutes after their counseling session was due to start. Jennifer waited for him on the front steps, relieved when his SUV rolled in. He got out and walked over to her and gave her a kiss.

"Sorry I'm late."

"So, Jeff got in okay." Jennifer turned and tucked her hand in his arm as they walked down the carpeted hallway to the pastor's study.

"Yeah, that's partly why I'm late. We were talking about God."

"You were? Oh, Harvey, I'm so glad!"

"He just started right in on it. And he had a Bible."

"Fantastic."

Pastor Rowland was waiting for them. Harvey apologized for being late and told him about Jeff.

"Let's pray for him now," said the pastor.

When they finished, Mr. Rowland guided their discussion of wedding preparations and family life. The pastor read the command for husbands to love their wives. Not a problem, Harvey assured him.

"Why doesn't it say, wives, love your husbands?" Jennifer asked. "Aren't we supposed to?"

"Yes, but I don't think you need to be told to do that," the pastor said.

Jennifer liked that.

The pastor read a verse that said older women should teach young women to love their husbands. "Christian mothers usually give their daughters that example."

"My mom's not a Christian, but I'm sure she loves my dad," Jennifer said.

"You have some examples here in your church family, too," the pastor told her. "Any of the ladies here would be happy to help you if you have difficulties, I'm sure."

"Your wife is a great model for me."

They went over some more of the questions on the list. The pastor knew they were buying Mr. Bailey's house, and he gave Harvey some advice on not letting the care of the house take over their lives.

"And what about children?" the pastor asked. "Did you talk about that one?"

"Uh, yeah." Harvey glanced at Jennifer, and she caught a flash of panic in his eyes.

She reached over and took his hand. "Harvey told me about some trauma in his first marriage, Pastor."

Mr. Rowland looked at Harvey. "Do you want to talk about it?"

"Maybe. Yeah." Harvey cleared his throat. "My ex-wife, while we were married, aborted a baby." He sat still for a moment, then went on. "I didn't know anything about it until it was too late. I wanted kids, and she didn't, so she made sure it didn't happen." He breathed out a shaky breath.

"You've been suffering over that for a long time," the pastor said gently.

Harvey nodded.

"How are you dealing with this, Jennifer?" Mr. Rowland asked.

She stroked Harvey's hand, knowing that talking about it was a huge step for him. "I've thought about it a lot since he told me. It wasn't Harvey's fault. We both want children. I can't see it being a problem in our marriage, but I think he could use some help coping with the painful memories."

Mr. Rowland nodded. "Harvey, I'd like to do a little research. Maybe I can find some resources for you. Would you meet with me, just the two of us, perhaps next week?"

"Yeah. I mean, I'm pretty stressed at work right now, but . . . well, Jenny's right. I would like to talk about it before the wedding, if possible."

They picked a time outside the regular sessions.

"If it's a comfort to you," Pastor Rowland said, "I believe you have a child in heaven."

"And I'll get to see it one day?" Harvey's tears were close, and he clung to Jennifer's hand.

"I think so. Just don't ever let this issue come between you and Jennifer."

"Never," Harvey said.

Jennifer nodded. "We can handle it."

When the hour was up, they left the pastor and went out to the parking lot. Harvey had parked beside Jennifer's car.

"Are you okay?" she asked.

"Come here." He hugged her fiercely. "You're too good to me."

"Don't ever say that." She looked up at him. "I love you."

Harvey said, "I'll follow you home."

"Part of me wants to run right over to your place to see Jeff."

"You'll see him tomorrow," Harvey said.

"You're right. But you don't need to see me home. Beth's there. Go back to Jeff."

He put a hand up to her hair. "I love you. We'll talk about this again."

"Yes. When you're ready."

She held him for another moment, hoping she could be the one to give strength for once. This old wound might never stop hurting.

"It's all going to be good when we're together, Harvey."

He pulled her tighter.

The outside light on the front of the church went off, and the pastor came out. Harvey released her and waved to Pastor Rowland. He opened Jennifer's car door and put her inside. When they drove out of the yard, she turned left and he turned right.

Chapter 15

Saturday, July 3

Harvey helped Jeff unpack some of his things on Saturday morning. Whenever Jeff emptied a box, Harvey put some of his books in it to move to the new house. When Eddie dropped in around ten o'clock, they were ready for a break. The three of them went over to the park and played basketball.

"You seeing Sarah this weekend?" Harvey asked.

"I don't think so," Eddie replied.

"Why not?"

"Well . . . I don't want to get too intense," Eddie said.

"Looked pretty intense Tuesday night."

"See, that's the problem. When I'm not with her, I think she's a nice girl and I like her a lot, but I don't want to commit, at least not yet. When I'm with her, sometimes I forget."

"Is she looking for commitment?" Jeff asked, taking a shot. He hadn't met Sarah yet.

Eddie went for the rebound and held the ball under his arm. "Maybe. This wedding mania with Jennifer is catching, I think. All the women at the P.D. are thinking diamonds right now."

"Sorry," Harvey said. "I didn't mean to cause problems for all the bachelors in the department."

"Are you praying for her?" Eddie asked. Jeff looked at him sharply.

Harvey said, "Yes, we are. Jennifer and I. You want to give me any specifics?"

Eddie dribbled the ball a few times and shot at the hoop. Harvey caught the rebound.

"Her parents are divorced," Eddie said. "She lives with her mom. Her sister lives with her dad. The two halves of the family fight all the time."

Harvey tossed him the ball. "Why doesn't she move out?"

"She doesn't want to leave her mother alone, I guess."

"Well, you don't want to marry her and her mother, if you get my drift."

"She's got a big grudge against her dad."

"Other than the divorce?"

"I think so," Eddie said. "She won't talk about it."

Harvey shook his head. "Too much baggage."

Eddie frowned and tossed the ball to Jeff.

"Do you think she needs help?" Eddie asked.

Harvey went after Jeff, trying to steal the ball. When Jeff put it up, he said, "You mean psychological help?"

"Well, you know."

Eddie got the rebound.

Harvey said, "Sounds like she might need

spiritual help. I'll keep praying for her. And you."

"Eddie, do you believe in God?" Jeff asked, tossing the ball from one hand to the other.

"Yes, but . . . yes."

"I'm starting to think I might," said Jeff.

Eddie considered that. "I'm going to church tomorrow with Harvey."

"With me, too, then."

Eddie slapped the ball away from Jeff and dribbled toward the hoop. They played a while longer, then Eddie left. Jeff and Harvey went home and showered and ate leftovers and did a little more packing-unpacking.

"At least Jennifer didn't rope me into being in the wedding," Jeff said. He seemed to have an aversion to tuxedoes. "So, Harvey, her roommate, Beth. Does she have a boyfriend?"

"Don't think so."

"She's a nice girl." It was almost a question.

"Yeah, very nice. But—"

"What?"

"Nothing." Harvey figured it wasn't his place. Beth could keep Jeff at bay. "Maybe you can run with Eddie and me when you move down here."

"I'd like that, when I'm not on duty. They have a three days on/two off schedule. Are you going to keep running after you're married?"

"Going to try. We'll be a couple of miles away. I'll have to drive over, but it won't kill me. I don't want to lose that time with Eddie."

"He's a good friend."

"Yeah."

Harvey's phone rang. Arnie was calling to tell him he'd finally gotten a phone number for Tom Nadeau's ex-wife, but she wasn't answering. "She's in Epsom, New Hampshire. You want me to keep trying?"

"No, Arnie, take some time off. But thanks. We found out what we wanted to know about the cigarettes. If we need her later, we'll get hold of her then."

"Any word on Mike?"

"No, but I think I'll call Augusta again," Harvey said. "He and Sharon seem to have gone way off the grid."

"That's something about Mike maybe going to be the new chief, huh?"

"We don't know that he'll take it."

"I know Mike," Arnie said. "He'll take it."

Harvey called Fisheries and Wildlife and talked to a part-time weekend dispatcher, who had no idea what he was talking about. He called Mike Jr.'s house.

"No, they haven't found Mom and Dad yet," he said. "I'm never going to let them do this again, you can be sure of that. If they're going to go off into the wilderness where nobody can find them, I want to be with them, not here, with the phone ringing off the hook."

"Sorry. We're just concerned."

"I know, Harvey. But it's getting so I'm real chummy with the mayor of Portland."

"I've got a surprise for you," Jennifer said when she met Harvey and Jeff at the door to her house.

"What is it?" Harvey asked.

"Come in and feel."

He stepped in, curious, and immediately guessed it. "You've got air."

"Beth's dad brought it to us this morning," Jennifer said.

Jeff came in and closed the door. "Nice and cool in here."

She grinned. "We've got the picnic mostly ready. Come on in the kitchen. Beth's making a jug of iced tea."

She gave them each a couple of cookies and a glass of cold milk while she and Beth worked. When the lunch was packed, they still had an hour before they could pick up the boat from Beth's friend, Charlie. They settled in the living room, where Jeff sat on the edge of his chair, talking earnestly to Beth. She sat in the rocking chair with her cross stitching in her lap; she held it loosely while she talked to Jeff, not stitching.

They drove to Charlie's house at four o'clock. He turned the boat over to them with good-natured admonitions about safety.

"It's really generous of you to let us take it," Harvey said.

Charlie shrugged. "Beth Bradley's word is as good as a bond. Besides, she told me the P.D. will garnish your wages if you wreck the boat."

"Aha."

Beth smiled sweetly at him.

It was a beautiful evening for cruising around the bay islands. On the water, the air was cooler, and they took their time with Harvey at the wheel. They checked out the two batteries on Peaks Island, then puttered in to Fort Gorges about seven o'clock, to stake out a spot. There weren't many people there, and they climbed up on top of the abandoned fort's wall and got a place facing across the water to Fort Preble.

The women spread out the picnic, and they ate as the sun began to sink toward the city skyline. Jennifer caught Harvey staring at her.

"What?"

"You and Jeff. You have the same hair."

She looked over at her brother. His hair gleamed golden in the bright rays. She smiled at Harvey. "Thanks."

The strip of clouds to the west went all pink and lavender. The air was still very warm, but a light breeze came in off the Atlantic. Jennifer took pictures for her scrapbook. There was still time before the fireworks would begin. Jeff and Beth poked around the parade ground inside the fort and went in and out of the stone arches, then up a corner stairway to the top, but Jennifer sat with Harvey, rubbing his back and neck. He told her Eddie and Jeff were coming to church the next day and suggested lunch out together.

"You don't have to take me out all the time," she protested, thinking of the price of the house.

"It's not a problem. And after we're married, we'll probably stay home a lot more." He pulled his knees up and folded his arms on them while she knelt behind him, continuing to rub his tense shoulder and back muscles.

Jeff and Beth were silhouetted against the sky on the opposite side of the fort. They faced each other, about a foot and a half apart, talking seriously.

"Think it's a match?" Jennifer asked.

"Man, I don't know when I've seen electricity like that."

"Not even with Eddie and Sarah?"

"I'm not sure about that one," Harvey said. "There's a charge, all right, but it may be more physical than anything. Eddie's concerned about Sarah's family situation and her emotional life. I told him to go slow."

"I'd hate to see him get tangled up with the wrong woman." Jennifer's concern for Eddie went as deep as it would for one of her brothers. "Sarah seems good for him in some ways, but there are things below the surface."

"Yeah, and Eddie might not be the one to deal with them," Harvey said.

Jeff and Beth walked around the fort toward them, not touching each other, but still deep in conversation.

"Jeff hasn't been serious about a girl for a while," Jennifer said softly.

"How long is a while?"

"There was a girl a couple of years ago, but it didn't last. She met someone else. He's dated some since, but Mom always said nothing major. If he'd had more than two dates with anyone, I'd have heard about it."

"He's thinking hard about God," Harvey said.

"And Beth, by the look of things. Don't you think she's encouraging him a little strongly? Before we got saved, she really laid it on the line to me about believers not marrying nonbelievers. I don't think she intended to feel this way about Jeff yet."

Harvey sighed. "Prayer time again, I guess."

Jennifer smiled wryly. "Seems like we've reversed roles with Beth, and we're her chaperones now."

The couple stopped ten yards away and looked out over the water. It was dusk, but Jennifer could see Beth's rapt expression. Jeff, taller by eight inches, leaned toward her to catch what she was saying and laughed a little. Jennifer felt an achy wistfulness for the two of them.

The heat had faded to comfortable as the twilight deepened. The sky lit up with a shower of color, and a muffled explosion made Jennifer jump.

She reached her hands around Harvey's neck from behind and clasped them in front of him. He held on to them as they watched the bursts of light, shapes that melted, with sparks falling toward the water. As the sky darkened, the colors became more brilliant. Harvey tugged on her arm, and she moved around to sit beside him on the cool granite.

A vivid shower of red, green, and blue burst above them.

"You're like that," he said.

"I'm a firecracker?" she hazarded, unsure where his mind had gotten to.

He slipped his arm around her. "No, you're unexpected and brilliant and—and a burst of joy."

She smiled and leaned over to kiss his cheek. "Thank you."

"God sent you when I'd stopped hoping," he whispered in her ear.

Tears filled her eyes, and she squeezed him lightly, in case his ribs were still tender from his injury in May. "I'm glad he brought us together."

Several rockets whooshed, sending tiers of dazzling sparks into the night. She sighed as the colors faded. They waited. Nothing.

"I guess it's all over," she said.

Harvey kissed her temple. "But not you. You'll stay."

Old wounds. She wrapped her arms around his neck. "Yes, Harvey. I'll stay."

After Sunday school the next morning, Harvey called Fisheries and Wildlife. This dispatcher was more on the ball and patched him through to the commissioner.

"Larson, glad you called. One of our wardens radioed in about half an hour ago. They've found the Brownings and will bring them out, but they're miles from the road. They figured the fastest thing will be to canoe down to the town of Allagash, at the confluence of the Allagash and the St. John, and drive them out from there. It's a long haul any way you look at it."

"What about Mike's vehicle?"

"He had someone drop them at Churchill on Saturday last week. If we'd known earlier, it would have saved us some headaches."

"So, what's the ETA?"

"In Portland? Probably late this evening. It'll be a long drive, even after they're off the river."

Harvey called the mayor's number, and she answered.

"Good morning, ma'am. I just spoke with the commissioner of Fisheries and Wildlife, and they've located Mike Browning."

"Where?"

"On the Allagash. It will take them a while to get out. He should get home late tonight."

"Well, that's something. You haven't talked to him yourself?"

"Not yet."

"Well, if you do, please ask him to call me right away, no matter what time it is. I'd like to make the announcement tomorrow morning."

"Yes, ma'am."

"How is your investigation going?"

"About the same."

"Keep me posted."

"Yes, ma'am."

The service had started when he walked into the auditorium and sat down between Jennifer and Eddie. On the other side of Jennifer was Ruthann Bradley, Beth's sister-in-law, and Jennifer was holding baby Ethan. He slept on her shoulder, and Jennifer cuddled him close, patting his back gently. A yearning touched Harvey's heart, and he put his arm along the back of the seat behind her.

He had to make himself focus on the sermon that morning. When Ethan started to fuss a little and Ruthann took him out to the nursery, it was easier. He needed to hear everything, for himself and for Eddie. He knew Eddie was taking it all in and would have questions later, so he got out his notebook. Jeff sat behind them with Beth, and he hoped Jeff was focused, too. They went out to eat after, not fast food. Harvey felt mellow and generous, and he treated everyone. Jeff talked some with his sister, but mostly with Beth. It was a good meal, with good company, and Harvey actually ate and pushed the case out of his thoughts every time it intruded.

His phone hummed, and he took it from his jacket pocket.

"Harvey!"

"Mike!" Everybody grinned when he said that.

"Harv, can you—this thing—Leavitt?"

Harvey winced at the static. "You're breaking up. Say again."

"Brief me."

"Where are you?"

"Saint Francis."

"Call me back when you hit Caribou."

"10-9."

"Call me when you're in civilization."

"10-4–couple of hours."

Mike hung up.

"This is great," Eddie said. "Things are looking up now."

Harvey smiled and ordered dessert all around.

Jeff was heading north that afternoon. His goodbye to Beth was as intense as Harvey's to Jennifer, although Jeff said it all with his eyes. Eddie came back to the apartment with them, and

Jeff carried down his duffel bag and tossed it in the back of his pickup.

"I'll be back Wednesday," he said. "I start the new job Thursday morning."

"Shouldn't you take a few days off in between?" Harvey asked.

"I'll be all right. It will probably be really late when I get down here Wednesday, though."

"That's okay. Use the key. I'll have your bed ready."

Jeff drove out, and Eddie came up to the apartment. Harvey broke out two bottles of Poland Spring water.

"Water?" Eddie asked.

"There's grapefruit juice in the fridge."

He took the water.

"I called the hospital earlier," Harvey said. "Chief Leavitt is still critical."

Eddie nodded. "Harvey?" His tone was different. "That thing the pastor said this morning, that Jesus Christ is the only way to get to heaven—"

"Yeah?"

"I thought I believed that. But then when he talked about how you can't do things to pay for your own sins, I thought about all the penance I've done, and the candles and stuff. I'll bet I've said ten thousand Hail Marys. For nothing."

Silently, Harvey prayed, *Lord, don't let me*

350

blow this one. Even if I can't solve the murders, let me do this one right. Then a conviction settled on him that God was doing his part right, and Harvey's part was incidental.

"You're right, Eddie. The priest can't give you punishment for your sins or a way to make it right. Jesus did it all on the cross."

"Do you think he'd save someone like me?"

Harvey nodded. He couldn't say anything then. He took out the handkerchief he always carried for picking up evidence, then got his Bible and tried to tell Eddie slowly and calmly the one thing he knew was crucial to salvation, unconditional belief.

"Harvey wants kids, doesn't he?" Beth asked Jennifer as they cleaned up the kitchen after supper.

"Yeah. A lot."

Beth smiled. "I could tell by the way he looks at Ethan."

Jennifer hesitated.

"I'm kind of surprised he didn't have kids before," Beth said.

"He wanted to, but . . . well, I guess Carrie didn't. It was a big disappointment to him."

"Is that why they broke up?"

Jennifer shook her head, knowing she couldn't tell the secret Harvey had kept so long. "There was a lot more to it than that. She left him very

351

abruptly, as I understand it. He came home one night, and she was just gone." She remembered hints Eddie had dropped. "Her and all their furniture."

Beth blinked. "That's pretty awful."

Jennifer hung up her dish towel and turned to face Beth. "I didn't realize it until last night at the fireworks, but I think part of him has been expecting me to call off the engagement and leave him alone again."

"No." That idea seemed to astound Beth.

"Maybe not consciously, but she did a real hatchet job on him."

Beth squeezed her shoulder. "Just love him. He'll get the message."

"Thanks." Jennifer looked at the clock. "He'll be here in fifteen minutes. I need to get ready."

She was surprised when Harvey landed on her doorstep that Eddie was still in tow. She called to Beth and let them in. "Hi. We're almost ready. Eddie, I didn't expect you back tonight. I'm glad you came."

Eddie looked at her with big, melting-chocolate eyes. "I wanted to come. I know Jesus for real now, Jennifer."

Jennifer caught her breath and looked at Harvey. He smiled and nodded, and she hugged Eddie and kissed him on the cheek. "I'm so glad!"

Beth came from her room, and Eddie made the

announcement again, and she hugged him, too. "Fantastic."

Eddie just beamed.

They sat near the back of the church, and Harvey slipped out to the foyer when his phone whirred during the song time. He didn't recognize the incoming number.

"Larson."

"It's Mike."

"Mike! Where are you?"

"Almost to Bangor. Close enough?"

"I hear you fine."

"Good. My battery died, and I had to use a warden's phone. So, the chief had a wreck?" Mike asked.

"Yeah, he's pretty bad."

"These guys said the mayor's been pushing them to bring me back."

"She wants you on the fourth floor, Mike."

"Acting chief?"

"Permanent."

Mike didn't say anything.

"You there?" Harvey asked.

"I'm here. She knows I want to retire."

"She's not thinking about you. She's thinking about the city of Portland."

"How noble."

"She wants to hear from you. Day or night, she said. Better call her now."

"I need to talk to Sharon."

"The deputy's leaving, Mike. If you don't take it, they've got to bring someone in. What do you think that will do to the department?"

"Maybe nothing."

"Ha, ha," Harvey said.

"How's your case going? The wardens haven't heard of anyone being arrested yet."

"Not yet. Can we talk tonight?"

"Come to my house," Mike said. "Eleven o'clock."

"I'll be there."

They took Beth and Jennifer home and drank milk and ate Jennifer's peanut butter cookies.

"You two have been baking again." Harvey was a little surprised.

Jennifer smiled. "It's the air conditioning. It makes me feel like doing things again."

"Be glad you don't live in Atlanta," Eddie said. "I heard it was a hundred and one there today." He reached for another cookie.

Jennifer caught Harvey's eye and smiled with a little nod toward Eddie. Maybe the telepathy was working, because he got the message. Eddie was even more cheerful than usual, and contentment seemed to radiate from him.

"Eddie, you made my day today," Beth said. "I'm so thrilled that you got saved."

"I don't know what my folks will say about me being a Protestant," he said warily.

"Don't put it like that," Jennifer said. "Tell them you've been learning what the Bible says Christ did for you."

"Make sure you remember that Jesus did all the work," Harvey advised. "That's hard for Catholics to understand."

"Hard for me," Eddie agreed.

Harvey looked at the three of them and let his spine relax. The pressure was fading away. Eddie believed, and Mike was coming back. He managed to sit in one spot for over an hour without fidgeting and ate without feeling self-indulgent.

At ten-thirty, he stirred. "Eddie, we'd better get over to Mike's."

"Do you and Jennifer need a minute?" asked Beth.

"Yes," he said, but at the same time, Jennifer said, "No, that's okay."

Beth laughed. "Go in the kitchen."

He took Jennifer's hand and pulled her through the door.

"Harvey!"

"What?"

"Beth and Eddie will be embarrassed."

"It takes more than that to embarrass Beth, and Eddie is pretty much unflappable." He pulled her close and kissed her. She sighed and let him hold her for a few seconds, then pushed him toward the door. "Get out of here!"

• • •

He and Eddie were waiting at Mike and Sharon's house when the game warden brought them home.

"The welcoming committee for the new chief?" asked Sharon.

Harvey wasn't sure how to take that, but Eddie had no qualms.

"Great! You're going to take it!" He wrung Mike's hand.

Mike said regretfully, "Not what I had planned. Let's get inside."

They carried all their gear in through the garage, and Sharon said, "If you fellows will excuse me, I'm exhausted. I know you have a lot to talk about, and I want to look my best on television tomorrow morning."

"So, you talked to the mayor?" Harvey asked when she'd picked up a duffel bag and headed down the hallway.

"Well, *she* mostly talked to *me*," Mike said.

"You're really taking it?"

Mike started making coffee. "I left here to get rested, and I am so tired! I wanted to take the Allagash in short stages, not in one day."

"Mike?" Harvey asked quietly.

He turned around and looked at them, then stuck the scoop in the coffee can. "Yeah, I'm taking it. Sharon has mixed feelings. The mayor made me an offer I couldn't refuse. I told her I'll stay with it at least two years."

Harvey's lethargy was gone. He and Eddie laid out the developments in the Blake case for Mike, drank coffee, and waited. Mike paced around the kitchen.

"You don't have enough," he said after a few minutes. "The DNA will help on Blake. If you find out where the gun was, that may help on the old homeowner. What's his name?"

"Fairley," Harvey said.

"Right. And if Whitney wasn't a suicide, it will help on that, too."

Eddie and Harvey looked at each other, but didn't say anything. Mike paced some more.

"Whatcha gonna do, Harv?" he asked at last.

"I was hoping you'd make a suggestion."

"Oh, no. I wouldn't pull you out of this, even if I could. You've got a brain. Use it."

"That's it?" Harvey felt tired again, and a bit stupid.

Mike said, "The mayor wants to hold an early press conference. You need to be there. Let's talk in the office at seven. Press conference at eight."

Dejection set in. Harvey looked back as he walked to the door.

"Mike—"

"Not my case, Harv."

"If you can help me—"

"I don't have any witnesses in my pocket. And besides, you can do this yourself."

"Right." Harvey managed a smile. "Glad you're back."

He dropped Eddie off and went home. The place was empty, and the boxes gave the rooms a forlorn feel. It was Jeff's place now. He went to bed and wished they'd been drinking decaf. It was too late to call Jennifer. He hadn't felt so alone since before he'd met her. He realized he was angry at Mike for not helping him, and he started to pray.

Chapter 16

Monday, July 5

The weather broke in the night, and rain moved in. Harvey and Eddie ran early, in a gray drizzle. When they got to the office, Mike was at his desk drinking coffee, making the room seem deceptively normal.

"Hey, I thought you'd be upstairs," Eddie said with a big smile.

"Not yet. You guys sit down and get comfy."

He'd called Pete and Arnie, too, and they came in and brought their mugs and chairs over.

"All right," said Mike, "the press conference will be held at city hall, and it's going to go something like this: The doctor will give an update on Chief Leavitt's condition, then the mayor will announce my appointment. She'll also congratulate the deputy on his new position and make it clear he's leaving the sixteenth."

"I thought he was staying 'til the end of the month," said Arnie.

"He's got two weeks' vacation coming, and Mayor Weymouth would just as soon have him take it to pack the moving truck as to pay him for staying on, doing nothing."

The men looked at each other, but nobody offered a comment.

"Then, Harvey, the mayor will announce that you're taking command immediately in the Priority Unit."

"Does she have to do that?"

"She and I talked, and we think it's best. City politics can be cutthroat. Right now there's enough of an administrative crisis that Jill Weymouth can make these decisions without taking a lot of heat. But if she postpones making these appointments, she might be forced to go through the regular channels."

"You mean, nominate you and have the city council rip you to shreds?" Pete asked.

"Something like that. And some bleeding heart would make a fuss and say the city had to advertise for months and take applications, and on and on and on. The mayor wants it settled now."

"Of course," said Pete. "She has to run for reelection this fall."

Mike looked at him. "You've never had a sarcastic bent, Peter. Something tells me you've heard from the bar, or you wouldn't express yourself quite so freely."

"That's correct, Chief Browning."

"Congratulations," Mike said.

"Thanks. How much notice would you like me to give?"

"Let's give Harvey a few weeks to get his feet wet."

"End of the month?" asked Pete. He looked at Harvey, not Mike.

"Whatever you want, Pete, but I'll miss you," Harvey said.

Mike nodded. "Okay, after all that, the mayor will probably allow some questions, and, Harv, you and I may have to answer them. Are you ready to be hounded some more about the Blake case?"

"Not really. We don't have much new information."

"Well, start thinking about it. If you can throw them a scrap, they'll be happy."

He dismissed the other three, but kept Harvey at his desk.

"You'll need two new detectives right away, Harvey, to fill your spot and Pete's. Have you thought about it?"

"Nate Miller, for one."

"Good man. He's qualified, and he was on my short list."

"Do you have any other suggestions?" Harvey asked.

"There are a couple of plainclothesmen downstairs that are pretty good. And you might think about Yeaton."

"Cheryl Yeaton? We've never had a woman up here except secretaries—I mean administrative aides."

"Exactly."

"Come on, Mike, you telling me I have to hire a woman? You never did."

"No, I won't tell you who to hire. I'm just saying, if it looks convenient, Yeaton's a good officer."

"How about Benoit?"

"Too green. She hasn't been with us long enough."

"Eddie came to us fresh out of the Academy," Harvey protested.

"That was an aberration that we won't get into. Besides, you're the first person to say you had to babysit him for a year." Mike took a sip of coffee then focused on Harvey's face. "Look, Eddie's a good cop, and he's a good detective now, but I think they need at least a couple of years on the beat before you start hauling them up here. Not only for training, but it causes jealousy. Officers can't make the detective squad until they've put in five years. Why should they be allowed to join this one?"

That was true, and Harvey had often wondered how Eddie had skipped the usual stint.

"Besides," Mike said, "there's another consideration on Benoit."

"What?"

"Isn't Eddie interested in her? You don't want that going on in the office all day. Calf eyes and spats and smooching in the break room. They haven't been real strict about dating within the department, but it can cause big headaches. Trust me on that."

"I know you're right, Mike. I just didn't think before I said it. Sarah wouldn't be a good choice. I actually had someone else in mind, but when you said that about hiring a woman, I thought she was the one I could get along with best. But Yeaton might be more professional, and I've never been on a double date with her. No question your advice is sound."

Mike nodded with a chuckle. "Spare me the details. So, who's your other pick?"

"Jimmy Cook. He's back on duty now."

"Hmm. I'll consider that one." Mike took a sip of coffee. "Don't know if he's had the exam."

"So, Mike, if you don't mind me asking, why *did* Eddie get put in here his first year? He's not related to the governor or anything."

Mike smiled and looked around warily. "Swear you'll never tell."

Harvey raised his eyebrows. "Of course."

"He was my punishment."

"No kidding?"

"That's right. Leavitt was mad at me for doing something not quite by the book, but I got results and the mayor—that was Mayor Green back then—loved it. I guess Leavitt tried to get me fired, and when that didn't work he wanted me demoted or censured, and finally did the only thing he could do without getting Mayor Green's approval—tried to make my life miserable. Giving me a green recruit was just one of several little tricks he played on me. Tore the unit's budget to pieces that year, for instance. Remember? We had to buy our own coffee."

Harvey shook his head. "I knew you and Leavitt butted heads, but I didn't realize it went so deep. You seem to have gotten along all right the last couple of years."

"We came to an understanding. And, by George, I took that gawky French kid and made a good detective out of him." Mike looked at Harvey apologetically and added, "Of course, you did most of the work, Harv. But wasn't Leavitt mad. He was just waiting for me to complain. Every time he asked me about Thibodeau, I'd praise him to the skies and tell Leavitt how much I appreciated him hand-picking my promising new detective."

Harvey laughed. "Maybe I should ask for Wonder Boy."

"Who?"

"Tony Winfield."

Mike threw back his head and guffawed. Pete and Arnie threw glances their way. Mike gasped a little. "Well, I'll tell you, Harv, I won't do that to you. I may give you some pointed advice, but I won't force a man—or a woman—on you if you don't want him."

"Tony's smart. If I knew he'd turn out like Eddie, I'd take him."

"Yeah, Eddie's all right now. I did wonder at first, though. Drove you to drink just a little, didn't he?"

"I was already there, I'm afraid." Harvey shook his head, remembering what a mess he'd been five years earlier. Mike had been patient with him. He looked up into his friend's eyes. "I'll need your help. Not on this case, I mean, but just in general."

"I won't desert you, Harv. You can climb those stairs anytime."

"Really?"

"Really. And one of my first official acts will be to start paperwork on a transfer for Nate Miller."

"Thanks. Could you do one more thing for me?"

"What's that?"

"Get rid of the Bambi picture in the chief's office?"

Sharon stepped off the elevator and came toward Mike, smiling. She had a first-lady look, and Mike grinned as he went to meet her. She wore a navy blue dress and gold earrings and necklace. Her hair and makeup were perfect for her. Hard to believe she'd conquered the Allagash River that weekend. Harvey pictured her next to Patsy Leavitt and decided Sharon won out easily.

She had brought Mike a newspaper, and after kissing her, he unfolded it, said, "That's interesting," and handed it to Harvey. The front page had an Associated Press story from Washington. The reporter speculated a special investigator would be named to look into the accusations of bribery against Murphy.

Mike let them all go to the press conference, leaving the phones to Paula. They'd been with him too long to miss the moment. A large crowd turned out at city hall.

"Chief Dwight Leavitt regained consciousness this morning," the surgeon said into a clutch of microphones. "He was able to move his arms and speak, but we're not sure yet if he will have full use of his legs. It will be a long, slow recovery." He threw the reporters some medical terms and said he expected Leavitt to be in the hospital for several weeks, then possibly in rehabilitation for months.

Harvey and Eddie sat to one side in the large city council chamber. Two on the aisle, as usual. Pete and Arnie sat behind them, and several other officers were sprinkled throughout the room. The deputy chief was noticeably absent. Mike and Sharon sat behind the surgeon, as did the mayor and the chairman of the city council.

Jill Weymouth walked to the bank of microphones after the surgeon had finished and looked out over the packed room.

"This is a sad occasion. The weekend has been very stressful for many. Our prayers are with the Leavitt family, and it's good to hear that Dwight is making some progress. It falls upon me as mayor of this city to step in when we have a situation like this. Chief Leavitt will not be able to fulfill his duties in the foreseeable future, and so I am appointing a new chief of police." She turned around and looked at Mike. He stood and walked to her.

Mrs. Weymouth held up a paper and pen. "This order makes Michael D. Browning the chief of the Portland Police Department." She signed the paper with a flourish, then turned to beckon Sharon to stand with Mike. All the officers from the P.D. clapped as she shook hands with them.

Then she said, "It saddens me to tell you all that the city is also losing its deputy police chief, Raymond Neilsen. He has accepted a position as chief of police in Framingham, Massachusetts, and will leave on July sixteenth. At this time, I'll allow the press a few questions."

Ryan was quick. "Mayor Weymouth, is this a permanent appointment for Captain Browning?"

"Yes, it is. In view of the police department losing its two top administrators in such a short time, I felt appointing an acting chief would only result in confusion and ineffectiveness. Michael

Browning has my full confidence. The city council may take some time looking for a new deputy chief, but the chief of police has been chosen and installed."

"Chief Browning," said the next reporter, taking the mayor's cue, and a faint smile touched Mike's mouth, "I understand you were on vacation when Chief Leavitt had his accident on Friday, and the Department of Inland Fisheries and Wildlife spent the weekend looking for you."

Mike was able to turn it into a funny story and make the game wardens look good, while downplaying the scale of the search. No one questioned the time and money spent, and Harvey thought Jill Weymouth was pleased.

"Sir, has there been any progress in the Martin Blake case?"

"Yes, there has been. I'll ask the chief investigator of that case to come up here and fill you in."

Harvey got up and walked slowly to the front of the room, praying that he wouldn't collapse or embarrass Mike too badly. About two hundred people were jammed into a room meant to hold a hundred and fifty. The crowed included a lot of policemen and reporters, but there were quite a few civilians, including Jennifer and Beth, seated near the back.

Before he reached the microphones, the mayor

said, "This gives me the opportunity to announce another promotion at the Portland P.D. Detective Harvey Larson will, as of today, be head of the Priority Unit, which has handled so many sensitive cases so well. He now has the rank of captain, and will continue as investigating officer in the Blake case. He's been with the Priority Unit since it was founded eight years ago, and has shown exceptional ability."

Harvey thought it was a little thick, but the applause from the guys was genuine, and Jennifer's smile beamed to him clear across the room. Her hair hung down loose for the first time since the hot weather began, and he drew confidence just from seeing her there.

He cleared his throat. "Thank you." The room grew quiet. "The Blake case is an extremely complicated one, but the investigation is moving forward. We received word late Friday that blood found on the bridge on Route 9, at Stroudwater Crossing, is the blood of Martin Blake. Blake's body was found about a hundred yards downstream, and our assumption at this time is that he was stabbed on the bridge, and either fell or was pushed over the railing on the night of June twentieth. We're still looking for people who drove over the bridge between ten-thirty and eleven-thirty that night, especially if they saw pedestrians on the bridge."

He paused, and a dozen hands shot up. He

swallowed and pointed at a woman he knew was from a local TV station.

"Captain Larson, do you have any suspects in the Blake murder?"

He took a deep breath. "Yes, we do." It was a tossup; say yes and they'd hound him for names, say no and they'd brand him incompetent.

"Can you tell us who?"

He couldn't help smiling a little. "What do you think?" A ripple of laughter went around the room.

"When do you expect to make an arrest?"

"We're waiting on some more lab tests that may lead to an arrest, but I expect it will be several days."

"Was Blake robbed when he was murdered?"

"No, he had cash and credit cards on him when he was found. We believe this was a case of premeditated murder."

"What was the motive?"

"I can't discuss that."

"You made a connection last week between the murder of Martin Blake and the death of Luke Frederick, a classmate of his," another reporter called. "Were they killed by the same person?"

"We are cooperating with the state police on that. The two victims were together early the day they died. They knew each other. Beyond that, I can't elaborate."

It went on, until finally someone asked Mike

a question about his plans for the police department, and Harvey was able to fade into the background. Mike shut it down, saying he was happy so many from the P.D. had turned out to support him, but they all needed to get back to work.

Jennifer lingered, and Harvey was able to walk out with her. He wanted to put his arms around her, but there were too many photographers in the vicinity. As a married man, Mike was able to leave city hall holding Sharon's hand. No doubt a picture of them hurrying down the steps in the rain together would appear in the *Press Herald* the next day, and reporters would pester Mike for interviews so they could write profiles of the new chief. Harvey hoped his own new position was still lowly enough for him to avoid that.

Jennifer said hurriedly, "I need to talk to you."

"What is it?" People were walking past, and she glanced around and leaned in so only Eddie and Harvey would hear.

"I looked at that suicide report again. The investigating officer was Arthur Corson."

"Right. He retired a long time ago."

"A very long time ago," she said. "Three months after Whitney shot himself, to be exact."

"And?"

"He's still alive. Lives out in Rosemont." She handed Harvey a piece of paper with an address.

He smiled. "I definitely need to reward you this time."

"Jewelry's good," said Eddie.

Harvey laughed. Jennifer scurried off to join Beth. He and Eddie drove back to the police station with the wipers squelching back and forth on the windshield. Upstairs, Paula met them with a concerned look.

"Mrs. Dixon called—the woman who was here Thursday with her husband."

Harvey looked blankly at Eddie.

"Arnie's interview," Eddie said. "The couple that was at Fort Point and had been camping."

"Oh, right. What did she want?"

Paula said, "They think their son may have seen something. I told her she could bring him in this afternoon. Is that all right?"

"Yes, that's fine."

In the locker room, they hung up their damp jackets.

"Are you going to use Mike's desk?" Eddie asked.

"Give up my desk?" That idea was abhorrent. Harvey had the corner with windows on two sides, and all his electronics laid out the way he wanted them. "Why would I want Mike's desk?"

"Middle of the room is all."

"I like being out of traffic. I think better. The new guy can have Mike's desk."

"Who's the new guy?"

"I asked for Nate."

"All right." Eddie sounded pleased.

"Pete's leaving. You heard him say it this morning."

"Yup. Who you getting to replace him?"

"Don't know. Any ideas?"

"Joey Bolduc."

Joey was one of the detectives downstairs. Harvey wondered if he was one Mike had short-listed. Joey was a little impulsive, but as far as Harvey knew, he had a good record.

"I'll think about it. You're not just hoping to get another francophone up here, are you?"

Eddie laughed. "*Mais non.*"

Pete, Arnie, Nate, and Tony were waiting when they went back into the main room. Harvey realized it was up to him to call the shots, so he parceled out assignments quickly. They had enough calls to return to keep them busy right up until lunch. He put Nate at Mike's desk. A few people came in for interviews, and Arnie went around to the courthouse.

Harvey found a minute to take Nate aside in the late morning, between phone calls.

"I mentioned your name to Mike this morning for a possible assignment in this unit."

"You mean permanently?"

"Yes. What do you think?"

"I'd sure like that."

"No more uniforms," Harvey said. "You'd get a small clothing allowance."

Nate smiled. "My wife would like that."

"I don't have the final word, but you're my first pick."

"Thanks. Would I have a partner?"

"Eddie, I guess. He's agreeable."

"Suits me."

Harvey was beginning to understand why Mike and Arnie stayed so close, and why Arnie had always seemed more like Mike's partner than Pete's. It would be strange to send Eddie out on the street every day with somebody else. Would the other men be jealous if he and Eddie continued to carpool? It was too complicated.

Jennifer was his usual antidote for worry. The rain had paused, and they ate lunch together at the café. Police officers kept coming over to congratulate Harvey, but none of them sat down until Eddie plopped down in a chair. Then Arnie came, fresh from court, then Sarah, then Terry Lemieux and Joe Clifford.

When Harvey walked back into the office, Pete was on the phone, and an 11-year-old kid was sitting at Harvey's desk, playing solitaire on his computer. No one else was in the room. Harvey went over and held out his hand as he would to an adult. "Hi, I'm Captain Larson."

"Joel Dixon." The boy shook his hand gravely. "Am I in the way?"

"No, but this is my desk."

"My parents are talking to another cop."

Pete got off the phone, and Harvey excused himself and went over to speak to him.

"Sorry about that, Harvey. I should have put him on Mike's computer. Arnie's got the parents in the interview room."

"Has he talked to the boy?"

"Not yet. The parents wanted to talk to Arnie first."

Harvey went back to the boy and sat in an extra chair. "So, Joel, you went camping with your folks?"

"Yup."

"Did you have fun?"

"It was okay."

"You visited Fort Point a couple of weeks ago?"

Joel let go of the mouse and looked at him. "I guess. We didn't stay there long. The fort is all wrecked."

"I've seen it." Harvey took a pack of gum out of his pocket. "Want some?"

Joel looked at him warily. "I'm not supposed to take stuff from strangers."

"That's right. But I'm a policeman, Joel. I think it's okay."

He reached out hesitantly for the gum.

Harvey asked, "Did you ring the bell?"

Joel smiled then. "Yeah. My dad got mad."

Harvey chuckled. "My partner Eddie rang it, too. It was really loud, and everybody looked at us."

Joel laughed. "Are cops allowed to ring it?"

"I think anyone is allowed to ring it. There wasn't any sign that said not to."

"That's what I said, but my dad was still mad at me."

They chewed their gum companionably.

"Did you go down to the beach?" Harvey asked.

Joe's eyelids lowered. "No, my dad wouldn't let me. We were going to have a picnic, but all these old people were at the park, so we left and went somewhere else to eat."

"So you didn't get to go near the water?"

"I was going to, but . . ." He was suddenly quiet, looking at Harvey from under his eyelashes.

"What, Joel?"

"Can I see your badge?"

It was clipped to Harvey's belt, and he pulled it off and handed it to him.

"Awesome."

"Did you see anything on the beach?" Harvey asked.

"Some guys." Joel turned the badge over and examined the pin.

"Guys? Boys?"

"Men."

"How many?"

"Three guys."

Harvey swiveled around to look at Pete. "The time was right," Pete said.

"Joel, excuse me just a minute. I want to hear more about this, but I want to check with your parents first, and make sure they don't mind."

Joel turned back to the solitaire game. Harvey motioned toward the boy, and Pete nodded.

At the door to the interview room, Harvey knocked, then stuck his head in. Arnie looked up. "Harvey, you're back."

"Yes. And this is Mr. and Mrs. Dixon?"

Arnie completed the introductions, rolling "Captain Larson" off easily, and they shook hands.

"The family was at Fort Point on the day of the reunion," Arnie said. "They looked around for twenty minutes or half an hour and left."

"My wife told me she saw Martin Blake, but I didn't believe it," said Mr. Dixon, adjusting his glasses. "Then we found out it really was him, and he was murdered twelve hours later. What a letdown."

"Well, I think it's exciting," said his wife. "At least I recognized him."

Arnie said, "After they were here Thursday, their son, Joel, told his mother he saw some men on the shore at Fort Point. They thought it might be important, so they brought him in."

"I've been having a few words with Joel,"

Harvey said. "I'd like to question him in an official capacity, if that's all right with you folks."

"We didn't actually go to the shore, except by the bell tower," said Mr. Dixon, "but Joel started down a path. I called him back. We'd decided to leave because it was so crowded."

"Do I have your permission to ask Joel about what he saw?"

They looked at each other.

"Can we be in the room?" Mrs. Dixon asked.

"It would be better if you weren't. I think he'd open up more."

"Well, I don't know," she said.

"They could watch in Observation," Arnie said softly.

Harvey nodded and waved a hand toward the large mirror on the side wall. "That mirror is one-way glass. It's clear on the other side. Detective Fowler can take you in the observation room next door, and you can watch the interview."

"Just like on TV," said Mrs. Dixon with a smile.

"Well, sort of. And I'd like to record what Joel says. If you'd like to speak to him first and tell him he has permission to talk to me, it might be good. I think we've made friends, but you've wisely taught him to be wary of strangers."

They went out into the main office, and Mrs. Dixon told Joel he could go with the nice captain and talk to him for a few minutes. Joel looked at him gravely and went with him to the interview room. Harvey started the recorder.

"You want a soda?" he asked, sitting down at the end of the table, with Joel next to him on the side facing the mirror.

"No thanks."

Harvey asked him his name and said the date and time clearly.

"So, Joel, you told me that when you were at Fort Point on June twentieth, you saw some men on the beach."

"Well, yeah."

"So where were you when you saw the men?" Harvey asked.

"On the path."

"By the picnic tables?"

"Well, down in the woods past the tables."

"That's a really steep path," Harvey said.

"Yeah. I wanted to go down there."

"What happened?"

"I got part way down and my dad yelled at me."

"And you went back up?"

"Yes."

"But you saw the men when you were on the path?"

"Yes."

"Were they standing on gravel?"

"No, they were on a big rock."

"Is this the place?" Harvey had transferred Eddie's and Jennifer's pictures to his phone. He pulled them up and held out the photo of himself and Eddie on the rounded boulder.

"Maybe. I was a long ways away. That wasn't the guys, though."

"No, that's me and my partner, Eddie."

"The one that rang the bell?"

Harvey smiled. "You got it."

"He got to go swimming?"

"Yup."

"My dad wouldn't let me."

"The water was pretty cold." Harvey flipped to another photo. "How about this place?" He showed Joel the picture of him and Eddie on the flat rock.

"No, it was the other one."

Harvey flipped back to the first picture.

Joel nodded. "There were lots of big rocks where they were."

"How many men did you see?" Harvey asked.

"Three."

"What were they doing?"

"Two of them were talking, like that." He nodded toward the photo.

"Could you hear them?"

"No, I was too far away, and the water made noise."

"Where was the third man?"

"At first, he was walking toward them, on the ground." Joel pointed to the edge of the picture, on the side nearest the point separating the beach from the lighthouse. "About here, I think. When he got over here," his finger stopped in front of the rock where Eddie and Harvey stood looking at the bay, "he stopped for a minute. Then he bent over."

Harvey's adrenaline surged. He swiped through the other photos and showed Joel the one with Eddie up on the rock and himself below, stooping to pick up a weapon.

"Like this?"

"Yeah, but the other two men were both up there."

"Okay. Did the third man pick up something?"

"I think so."

"What was it?"

"I don't know." Joel looked at him anxiously, like he wanted to please him.

"That's okay, Joel. What happened next?"

"My dad yelled at me."

"What did he say?"

"Get up here! I told you not to go down there!"

Harvey wondered what Mr. and Mrs. Dixon were thinking in the observation room.

"So what did you do?"

"I went up."

"Did you look back at the men anymore?"

Joel's gaze dropped. "Yes."

"What did you see?" Harvey asked.

"One man, the one that bent over—"

He looked at Harvey, then away.

"What, Joel?"

"He got up on the rock, too," he whispered.

"What did he do?"

"He—he—"

Harvey put a hand on his shoulder. "You can tell me. It's all right."

"It looked like he hit him."

"Which man?"

"He hit the one in the white shirt."

"Okay. And what happened to the man in the white shirt?"

"He fell off the rock. Just kind of—" He gestured with one hand, making it dive.

"What did the man who hit him look like?"

"I—I—" His glance met Harvey's, then darted around the room.

"Take it easy, Joel. Just tell me what you remember."

"I can't remember."

"How about his clothes? What color was his shirt?"

He shook his head, becoming more agitated.

"That's okay. Don't worry about it." Harvey flipped to the last picture. "Did the two men that were left look down over the edge of the rock, like this?" The photo showed him crouching at the edge of the rock, looking down at Eddie, but Eddie wasn't in the picture.

"Yeah, they looked down there like that, the other two. I thought the guy was maybe hurt down there. Do you think he hit him? Maybe it was an accident. I thought he hit the guy." Joel's eyes pleaded.

"Then what happened?"

"My dad yelled again, and I went up."

"Did you look back again?"

"No, I didn't see them after that. Do you think he really hit the guy?"

Harvey sighed. "Yes, Joel, I do. I'm sorry that you saw that, but I'm glad, too. It will help us catch the man who did it."

"My mom said a man died that day. Was that the man? The one in the white shirt?"

"Yes. I need to tell the state police what you saw, and later they may need you to tell a judge. Can you do that, Joel?"

The boy's eyes were huge. "I . . . guess so. If my dad will let me."

"I think he'll let you. It's very important, Joel."

"He was really mad at me that day." Tears flooded the boy's eyes, and he dashed one away with the back of his hand.

Harvey wasn't sure whether to ask, with the parents in the observation room, but he did anyway. "Did he punish you?"

"No, just made me get in the car."

"Did you tell him about the men?"

"No, I was scared."

"Scared of who?"

"Just scared that the man was hurt."

"Your dad will be proud of you today, Joel."

Joel looked at him skeptically.

"Is there anything else you remember from the park?"

He shook his head, then said, "My mom thought she saw a famous writer, but my dad said it wasn't him. They had a big fight about it in the car." Harvey tried not to smile.

"Can you tell me any more about what the three men on the shore looked like?"

"They were really far away. One had a white shirt. The one that fell."

"Right. Did any of them have a beard?"

"I don't think so."

"Glasses?"

"Maybe. I'm not sure."

"It's okay."

"One man had a blue shirt, I think."

"Which man was that?"

He frowned. "I'm not sure."

"Was it the one who hit the man in the white shirt?"

"I don't know. I don't know." His tears spilled over.

"Okay. We're done, Joel," Harvey said gently and turned off the recorder. He put his hand on Joel's shoulder as they went out into the office, and Arnie and the Dixons emerged from Observation. Mrs. Dixon put her arms around

Joel, and he pulled away, boylike, in front of the other men.

Mr. Dixon stuck out his hand to his son. "Joel, I'm sorry I yelled at you that day."

Joel looked at him, and slowly took his hand.

"We had no idea," said his mother. "Honey, you should have told us."

Joel ducked his head.

Harvey said, "We have your address and telephone number?"

Arnie nodded.

"If Joel remembers anything else, especially what the men looked like, or even what they were wearing, please call us. The state police may be the next to contact you. I'll send them a copy of the recording. This really bears on their case, not ours. The Frederick case."

"You think the same person killed him and Martin Blake?" Dixon asked.

"At this point, we don't know. But I'd like to ask you folks to keep quiet about this, please. It's imperative that the press doesn't get wind of it before we confront our suspects with this new information. Don't talk about it to your friends or relatives, or anyone except us or the state police. And please, don't make your son feel guilty. He's doing a good thing today."

When they had left, Harvey called the men to him. "Okay, we've got something to go on now. That boy saw the Frederick murder. There's no question any more of Frederick slipping on the rocks. There were three men on the beach, and unless I'm mistaken, they were Frederick, Murphy, and Nadeau."

"Fantastic! Can we make an arrest now?" Eddie asked.

"I don't think so. Joel wasn't sure. He saw three men, then two. Doesn't know who was who. One he *thought* hit another. But he wasn't sure if the man had something in his hand. He was too far away to hear anything over the surf. He's a good witness, as far as it goes, but he could be discredited. I say we wait. But we're going to keep at this thing until we find out exactly what happened. Eddie, call Pat Lundquist and Thelma Blake. I want detailed descriptions of what Murphy and Nadeau wore that day."

"Pictures would be better," said Tony.

Harvey stared at him. "How could I have been so stupid? Probably a dozen people took pictures at the reunion. If we can get pictures of Murphy and Nadeau from a distance that day, Joel Dixon may be able to ID Frederick's killer. Start calling the reunion guests. But whatever you do, don't call David Murphy or Tom Nadeau."

"How about Alison?" asked Arnie.

"Hmm. That might be like testifying against her husband."

"If she volunteers the photos, it's okay," said Pete.

"I'm going to miss you," Harvey said. "Call her, Arnie. Ask if she took her camera to the reunion or used her cell phone cam. She'd be bound to take pictures of her husband. Don't tell her what we want them for, just ask for reunion photos. Pete, you and Arnie divide up the list again. I want everybody on this. I've got to call the state police. They'll want the recording of the Dixon boy ASAP."

"It's late, Harv," said Eddie. "Do you want us to put in overtime?"

He looked at his watch. 4:40. He couldn't keep five men on overtime wages, even though the city wanted the case solved.

"Everybody call two classmates living in Portland and ask for photos. Tell them to bring them here tomorrow, or we'll send someone to pick them up. Then write your reports, and we'll pick this up first thing in the morning."

Eddie hung back while the others dispersed. "Harv, take your own advice."

"What's that?" Harvey asked.

"Go home. And lose the guilt. You're doing good work."

Chapter 17

Tuesday, July 6

In the Explorer the next morning, Eddie was ready to attack the case and pulled out his notebook and pen.

"What do you want to do first when we get to the office? Round up those reunion pictures?"

"Yes, and if we get some good ones, I'll call the Dixons to see if they can bring Joel back. I'll have one of the fellows make a copy of Joel's interview tape for the state police. I don't suppose there's a chance the state lab is finished with the DNA test on the cigarettes."

"That would be nice."

"Make a list for the other guys," Harvey said. "You and I are going to visit Arthur Corson."

By the time he parked in the garage, Eddie had the assignments ready. He tore out the pages and gave them to Harvey. "Let's pray about this. Do you think God would help us? We need to not make any mistakes."

It was a sweet reminder that, as muddled as he felt, God was still in control. Harvey prayed, and then Eddie said softly, "God, we need to get these guys. Help us to do it soon."

"Amen." Harvey opened his eyes, and Mike

was standing beside the Explorer, looking per-plexed. Harvey opened the door.

"What are you guys doing?" Mike asked.

"Praying," Harvey said.

"Praying? You I understand, but Eddie?" Mike shook his head.

"We're both praying now," Eddie told him.

"That reminds me of something Sharon said last night."

"What's that?" Harvey asked.

"She said she prayed to God for patience to help her wait for me to retire. But in the Bible, it says you get patience from troubles, or something like that. Me becoming chief of police is her trial now. She said next time she'll be more careful what she prays for."

Harvey clapped him on the shoulder. "Sharon's got her head on straight."

They went in and walked up the stairs together.

"Still taking the stairs, now that you've got three flights?" Harvey asked.

"I figure I need more exercise now," Mike said. "And, Harvey, you didn't get your administrative training yet. You'd better come up later today, and I'll start teaching you the joys of scheduling and performance reviews and inventorying equipment."

"Oh, great. Can we put it off until after we crack the Blake case?"

"And after the wedding? And the honeymoon?

I don't think so. Call me later, and we'll make time."

Within an hour, they had promises of photos from three of the reunion goers. Two would send them by e-mail, and Tony went for the other batch. Nate kept calling around looking for more, while Pete copied the tape recording and Arnie called the state lab. Eddie and Harvey headed for Rosemont, leaving Arnie in charge.

Corson's lawn had grown up in weeds, and a beat-up Pontiac sat in the carport of the small, neglected house. Old tires and car parts were piled around it. Harvey knocked on the side door, and a white-haired man opened it. An unlit cigar protruded from the side of his mouth, and his belly hung over his belt. He glanced at their badges and opened the door wide.

"Long time since any guys from the P.D. came to visit," he said.

They walked into the kitchen. It smelled like cats. The sink was full of dishes, and the table, counter, windowsill, washing machine, and every chair but one were covered with junk. Magazines, jigsaw puzzles, old lamps and pans and flower pots. A pair of whitetail antlers, a monkey wrench, a metronome, and books. Lots of books. Harvey quickly made the introductions.

"We'd like to ask you about an old case of yours."

"Oh, my memory's not so good, boys."

Harvey brought out a copy of the report Corson had made twenty-one years earlier. "One of your last cases, sir."

"Suicide," Corson mused. "Whitney, Whitney." He browsed on down the page. "I remember it vaguely."

"There was a handgun he had used. Do you know what happened to it?"

He looked up, startled. "The revolver. Yes, that's the one."

"The one what, sir?"

"In here."

Corson started through a doorway into another room. Harvey looked at Eddie. Eddie shrugged, and Harvey followed Corson.

He couldn't see him in the next room. Stuff was piled so high on the furniture and windowsills that light came in only at the tops of the windows. Years' worth of newspapers were bundled and stacked. Boxes and small pieces of furniture vied for floor space. A cat stretched and jumped down off a cabinet. Everywhere there was junk. Crocheted runners peeked out from under the edges of it. Coasters, sewing baskets, a slide rule, a shabby old briefcase, notebooks, cookie tins, and more newspapers. Paths wound through the house between the piles. Over the whole accumulation lay decades of dust.

Harvey came to a narrow place in the path. On his left, boxes were chest-high, and newspapers overhung the top of them, reaching above his head. On his right, a narrow cabinet with glass doors was crammed full of china, and on top of it a spindly candlestick crowded against a porcelain German shepherd and a tobacco tin. A pile of cigar boxes teetered near the edge. Harvey didn't dare move, for fear he'd be buried in an avalanche of newspapers and cigar boxes.

Arthur Corson came toward him with a shoe box in his hands. Harvey stepped back. Eddie was right behind him, and he stepped back, too. Arthur turned sideways and made it through the pass without setting off the avalanche.

They went back to the kitchen single file. He shoved aside a pile of dishes and crossword puzzle books on the table, and set down the box.

"There you go."

"Sir?"

Corson nodded toward the box. Harvey lifted the lid a little. His heart started pounding. He took the lid all the way off and lifted an oily cloth. He unwrapped it carefully, revealing an inexpensive .22 revolver, a nine-shot Harrington & Richardson. It was in fine shape.

"The gun that killed Philip Whitney, I presume."

"That's the one. Parents didn't want it. The mother said, 'Just take it away. I never want to see it again.' So I brought it home. Don't tell

392

me someone's making a fuss after all this time."

"No, sir. That is, it's a little irregular, but that's not why we need it. This gun belonged to a Richard Fairley."

Corson showed no recognition.

"Fairley was killed in a burglary fourteen years before the suicide you investigated."

"Really?" He shrugged. "I didn't know it. Suicide. I don't remember the details."

"Well, sir, we may want to use this gun for evidence now. Is it all right if I take it?"

"Sure. I never use it. Took it out for target practice a few times when I first retired."

"Thank you, sir." Harvey wrote him a receipt. He took the shoe box back to the police station and gave it to Eddie in the garage. "Just double check the serial number, then enter it in evidence."

"Right. We'd sure look stupid if he gave us the wrong gun."

"I'll be up in a few minutes."

Harvey went down the stairs to Records and lured Jennifer into the hallway.

"We've got the gun. Corson had it all this time."

"Fantastic. One more piece for your puzzle."

"Right. Thanks for the tip. You'll get your reward tonight."

She laughed.

"I'm serious."

• • •

"It's the right gun," Eddie said when he got upstairs. "Too bad Corson used it. We might have gotten Philip's fingerprints off the ammo."

"Or Fairley's," Harvey said. "But not the other boys. We need Beaulieu. He's the only one who can tell us who was in on the burglary."

"Except the burglars."

"Right," Harvey said.

Eddie frowned at him. "What if that whole thing is totally unrelated to the Blake murder, and the burglars are people we've never heard of?"

"Then we're back to square one."

Harvey called Oregon. It was only 6:30 a.m. there, but they'd waited long enough.

"Commander Beaulieu?"

"That you, Larson?"

"Yes. You said you'd call me."

"I've been trying to arrange things."

"Beaulieu, you're not skipping out on me, are you?"

"No, I just had to take care of things with my wife and make travel plans. I'm flying into Portland on Thursday."

"Good. I really need you. I'm close to solving two murders, maybe three."

"Blake, Frederick, and who?"

"The man who was killed during the burglary thirty-five years ago."

"What about Phil Whitney?"

394

"You want four murders? Okay, you got four. But you've got to help us."

"If you don't go after Phil's killer, I won't."

"What if it was suicide after all?"

"It wasn't. I've been thinking about it. It wasn't."

"I've got the gun, Beaulieu."

He was quiet for a minute. "You have it now?"

"Yes."

"There wouldn't be fingerprints on it now, would there?"

"If there ever were, they're gone."

Beaulieu swore.

"I have the police report from Philip's death, too," Harvey said. "They considered it a suicide, and the revolver's been cleaned since then. The serial number matches the gun stolen from Richard Fairley during the burglary."

Silence for a second, then, "I thought so."

"Commander, if Phil Whitney didn't commit suicide, tell me who pulled the trigger on him."

"I could be wrong."

"Then at least tell me the other three who were in on the burglary, and let us figure it out."

There was a pause, then he said, "One of them is dead."

"Luke Frederick?"

"Yes. He drove the car."

"Thank you. And the other two?" Harvey asked.

"I'll tell you when I get there. I'll land at two-ten Thursday afternoon."

"We'll meet you."

"My sister's meeting me."

"We'll be there, too," Harvey said.

Beaulieu didn't argue.

Harvey got the men together.

"Beaulieu's coming Thursday. Says he'll tell us the whole story then, but he gave me one very important thing today. Luke Frederick drove the car the night of the burglary, when the high school classmates killed Richard Fairley."

"Can we officially tie this to the reunion at Fort Point?" asked Pete.

"I'm not sure. We still don't know why Frederick was killed."

"I'd have said blackmail," said Arnie. "I was figuring Frederick for the blackmailer."

"Revenge?" asked Nate. "Somebody found out he was in on the Fairley killing?"

"I guess we need more facts before we can be sure," Harvey said.

Eddie leaned forward. "Frederick driving that car has got to be the reason he died. And the other two men Joel Dixon saw have got to be the other two who were in on it."

"We need Beaulieu," Harvey said.

Paula walked over to Harvey's desk. "There's a trooper here for some evidence, Captain."

"I'll be right there." Harvey looked around at the men. "Let's get more pictures."

The state trooper introduced himself as Brian Longley, in charge of the Frederick case. The interview room was empty, and Harvey took him in there for privacy and told him what he'd learned from Beaulieu.

"You're saying this case may be related to a 35-year-old unsolved murder?"

"That's what I think. The more we learn about that burglary, the worse it looks. I've got a timid witness who says he knows who the burglars were. Frederick drove the car, but didn't go in the house the others ransacked. One of the burglars supposedly shot himself fourteen years after the burglary with the stolen handgun, and the other two are walking around free. I figure one of those two killed Frederick at Fort Point."

Harvey gave him some background on Joel Dixon's statement, and Longley left with the tape of the boy's interview.

Eddie had obtained some pictures from Michael Lundquist, but they weren't much help. Martin and Thelma Blake were in two, and Patricia Lundquist and Cyndi Reynolds were prominent in others. There were some nice shots of the lighthouse, and one of Michael at the bell tower.

Tony's batch wasn't much better. David Murphy was in one, up close and toothy. As

Harvey examined them, Mike called and told him to report to the fourth floor.

"Now?"

"Now. Time for your lesson in being the boss."

Harvey wanted to protest but decided he'd better go. Leavitt's secretary sat at the same desk in the outer office. The door to the inner office stood open.

"The chief is expecting you," the secretary said somberly.

Mike was sitting with his feet up on the antique desk.

"Captain Larson." He laced his fingers behind his head.

"Is that desk Leavitt's or the city's?" Harvey asked.

"Oh, it's partly yours and partly mine and partly everyone else's. Sit down."

Harvey sat and looked around. The Bambi picture was gone, and a print by a local artist, with a fishing net, creel, and rod and reel, had replaced it. Sharon smiled out of a pewter frame on Mike's desk, and their children and grandchildren hung framed on the wall.

"Nice," Harvey said.

"Sharon fixed it."

Mike initiated Harvey into some of the mysteries of management, which was heavy on filling out forms and not telling the guys everything he knew. Staying active on field work, but letting the detectives handle their own cases. Not letting the administrative part get him down.

He had set Harvey up for a management seminar October first, and was sending him and Eddie to the Maine Criminal Justice Academy for two days in late October for advanced ballistics training on the IBIS system. After half an hour, they got onto the case. Mike said the new developments sounded promising.

"You keeping Leavitt's secretary?" Harvey asked.

"She's an administrative aide, and she has a name. Judith."

"I'll try to remember."

"She's okay. Knows where everything is, and she's old enough that Sharon isn't jealous. Yeah, I think I'll keep her. Don't let her intimidate you."

"She never smiles," Harvey observed.

"I'll tell her."

"How is it, having a private secretary? I mean aide?"

"Not too bad. Sometimes I get lonely up here. You and the boys will have to come up once in a while."

"You're still welcome in Priority anytime, too."

Paula and most of the men were out for lunch when Harvey got back to Priority. On his desk was a note from Eddie: *At diner with Jennifer.*

He went down the stairs and walked to the café.

It wasn't really a diner, but the officers persisted in calling it that. The sun was out, but it wasn't oppressively hot. Eddie and Jennifer sat at a table with Tony and Cheryl.

Harvey stopped a few yards away and watched Jennifer. Her ring glittered as she raised her fork, listening to something Cheryl was saying. She was more beautiful than ever. The sides of her hair were pulled back, and the rest hung down a mile. If he were closer, he'd be able to see her eyes reflecting the royal blue of her top. Eleven days.

He walked over, and Eddie hitched his chair to one side so Harvey could pull one in from another table, between him and Jennifer. She turned toward him and smiled that wonderful smile. He put his arm around the back of her chair and wished all the other cops would disappear.

"More pictures arriving this afternoon," Eddie said.

"Did you order anything?" Jennifer asked.

Harvey shrugged. Jennifer sighed and pulled her wallet out of her purse. She handed Eddie a five-dollar bill. "Eddie, would you please get the captain a turkey sandwich and a carton of milk?"

"Hey, none of that!" Harvey snatched the bill. "Eddie's not my slave." He held it out to Tony. "Winfield, get the captain a turkey sandwich and a carton of milk." They all laughed hysterically.

400

Harvey tucked the money back in Jennifer's purse before Tony could take it, got up, and went inside and ordered a sandwich and milk, just to please Jennifer. Then he went out and sat with his arm around her, watching little glints of sunlight bounce off her hair.

The waitress brought his food out, and Cheryl finished and left.

"I've been thinking about the motives," said Tony, his fork suspended over a piece of chocolate cream pie. He looked at Harvey self-consciously. "If you want to talk shop over lunch, sir."

"Sure."

Jennifer had finished her salad, and she sat back, leaning into Harvey's arm. He couldn't take his eyes off her.

"Well, why was Fairley killed?" asked Tony.

Her ears were perfect. No earrings. She'd told him her father had laid down the law to the three Wainthrop girls: no extra holes in their heads while he was supporting them. By the time she was out on her own, she hadn't wanted any.

Eddie kicked him.

"Oh, what? Fairley?" Harvey threw Tony a glance. "Accident, I guess. I mean, they killed him, but they didn't mean to do it, so it was manslaughter."

"All right, why was Whitney killed? His friend thinks it wasn't suicide, so why was he killed?"

Now Tony had his attention. "Because Whitney was going to tell on the others."

"Right. So why was Frederick killed?"

Harvey shook his head. "Because he drove the car?"

"No, no, no," said Eddie.

"No?" Harvey asked.

"They'd have done it long before if that were the reason," said Tony.

"Because he was going to tell, too," said Jennifer.

Tony pointed at her. "Yes. It has to be. They killed Philip so he couldn't tell on them. Then, twenty-one years later, they killed Luke Frederick so he couldn't."

Harvey looked at the sandwich he hadn't touched. "Then we'd better take very good care of Matt Beaulieu and Joel Dixon."

"There's one more question," said Eddie. "Why was Martin Blake killed?"

"Because he knew something," Jennifer said.

"But what?" Tony asked.

Even Jennifer had no answer.

"That woman in Epsom," Arnie said to Harvey late in the afternoon. "I finally got hold of her. Cathy Wagner."

"Nadeau's ex-wife."

"Yeah. There's something funny there."

"How?"

"She sounded really down. Wanted to know if she had to come up here."

"It's not that far, an hour or so." Harvey drove through Epsom every time he went to see his sisters. "Is she coming?"

"I didn't say she had to. But she was quite fatalistic. Said she knew it would all come out eventually."

"What would come out?"

"The burglary stuff, I guess," Arnie said.

"Did you tell her not to call Nadeau?"

"Yes. Told her not to talk to anyone about it."

"So, what did she give you?"

"Not much. She wanted to know if she had to answer my questions."

Harvey rubbed the back of his neck. "It's tricky, with her being in New Hampshire. Why don't you ask Pete about the legal fine points."

Arnie came back a few minutes later. "Pete says we can go down there and talk to her. We can't make her come up here unless we've got a formal charge. If she wants to come talk to us, that's another story."

"I guess I'll call her," Harvey said.

Arnie gave him the number, but no one answered his call.

"What kind of jewelry would you suggest?" he asked Eddie on the way home. "I want to get Jenny something special."

"Gold."

"Gold what?"

"Anything gold."

"Not sterling silver?"

Eddie's eyebrows morphed. "Her engagement ring is gold, doofus."

"Watch it, I'm your boss now."

"You'd pull rank on me?"

Harvey smiled a little. "No, you'll always be my equal now, Eddie. You're my brother in Christ."

"That's nice. Get her a locket."

"A locket? Isn't that old-fashioned?"

"Jennifer's old-fashioned. You've said so yourself. Put your picture in it, or a piece of your hair."

"Think so?"

"Stop here."

"Here?"

"Yes."

Harvey stopped.

"Park the vehicle," Eddie said with exaggerated patience.

Harvey nosed the Explorer down the street to an empty parking spot. Eddie got out, so he got out. They walked back up the sidewalk the way they had come, and Eddie stopped in front of a shop window.

"Antique jewelry." He nodded at the display.

Harvey patted him on the shoulder and went

inside. He walked out ten minutes later with a frilly, gold Victorian locket.

"You sure she'll like it?"

"Guaranteed," Eddie said. "Now take me to the Bible store."

"I think they closed already."

"You're probably right. I want to get a Bible like yours."

"Tomorrow," Harvey said.

Chapter 18

Wednesday, July 7

The next morning Harvey called Cathy Nadeau Wagner. She answered, sounding wary.

"Mrs. Wagner, it's very important that you talk to us about what happened back then," he told her.

"I've been talking to my husband."

"And?"

"He didn't know any of it," she said.

"So, will you talk to us?"

"I can't—you don't—"

"Mrs. Wagner, you knew Martin Blake was killed?"

"Yes, I heard it when it happened. What has that got to do with me?"

"It was the latest of four murders."

"Four?"

"Yes. You knew about Mr. Fairley, the night of the burglary thirty-five years ago."

"Y-yes."

"Then Philip Whitney."

"It was suicide!"

Too quick, too loud, he thought.

"Did you hear that Luke Frederick died early on the same day Martin Blake was killed?"

"No, not Luke, too."

"Mrs. Wagner, do you see a pattern here? You need to talk to me. Did Tom ever talk to you about the burglary?"

Long pause. Then she swore. "I think—"

Harvey waited.

"Should I get a lawyer?" she asked.

Harvey's pulse rocketed. "If you want one. Could you come up to Portland?"

"Do I have to?"

"No. We can come to you in Epsom. I'll need to make some arrangements."

She swore again.

"Mrs. Wagner, you won't go anywhere?"

"No, no, you might as well come."

"Tomorrow," Harvey said. "We'll be there as early as we can."

"I knew it."

"You knew what?"

"That this would happen." She hung up.

Harvey wanted to be the one to go to Epsom to interview Cathy Wagner, but he also wanted to be at the airport when Matt Beaulieu got off the plane.

"You can't do both," Eddie said.

"If I leave for Epsom first thing in the morning—"

"Send Pete and Arnie."

Harvey sighed. "You're right. We need to be here."

He briefed Pete and Arnie. "You might have to work hard to find out what she knows," he cautioned them. "She was Nadeau's girlfriend when the robbery happened, and they got married a few years later. She divorced him ten or fifteen years ago. That may be irrelevant to our case. Start at the beginning, with the cold case. Go wherever it takes you from there."

Arnie leaned back in his chair. "I was going to pick up Alison Murphy's reunion pictures in the morning. She had prints made. You'll have to send someone."

Harvey sighed. "We need some good pictures. I thought it would be easy."

The afternoon was filled with tedious detail. When Harvey got to the church that night in time for the Wednesday Bible study, he tried to put it all aside. After the service, Beth managed to pull him out of Jennifer's earshot and whisper, "Bridal shower for Jennifer, here, Friday night."

"That's our counseling night."

"Pastor will cut it short. Just have her here as usual. Mum's the word."

"Okay." This cloak and dagger stuff was so silly, he thought. They should just tell her.

"What do you need for the house?" Beth asked.

"You're asking *me?*"

"Who else would I ask?"

He shrugged. "Trash bags? Light bulbs?"

"Not disposable stuff. *Gifts.*"

"Towels, maybe? Sheets? That kind of stuff?" Jennifer was approaching. "You're her roommate," he said quickly. "You've lived with her. I haven't."

Beth launched into a story about her niece, Clarissa, just in time.

When Harvey's alarm went off, he smelled coffee. He'd heard Jeff come in after midnight and had gotten up long enough to say hi. He pulled his clothes on and staggered to the kitchen.

"I hope being married is like this," he said sleepily, pouring himself a mugful.

"Like what?" Jeff was clearly amused.

"Waking up to hot coffee." Harvey had nuked it by the cup for years.

"I'll put a bug in Jennifer's ear that you're not a morning person."

Arnie and Pete left for Epsom at eight that morning. Harvey called Matthew Beaulieu at 6 a.m. Pacific time, three hours earlier than Maine time, to make sure he was headed for the airport. The commander assured him that he and his wife were on schedule.

Tony came in with Alison Murphy's pictures. They were better than any they had so far of David Murphy. There was one of Tom Nadeau back-to. Harvey thought it might work for Joel.

"Let's go with it," he said. "Call the Dixons and see if they can bring Joel in here again. It may be hard for them to schedule it, but if they can come today, it would be good."

His desk phone rang.

"Mrs. Blake is on the line," Paula said. Harvey groaned inwardly. He and Eddie were too busy to do any hand-holding that day.

"I was just talking to Alison Murphy," Thelma said when he picked up the phone. "She says you've been asking for photographs of the reunion."

Harvey was alert then. "That's right. Did you take pictures that day?"

"Me? No."

"Oh."

"But Martin did."

"Are you serious?"

"Yes, he was a good photographer. It was a hobby of his. He had an old Pentax camera, not a digital, the one he used since he became a reporter, with real film and all."

"Did you have his film developed?" Harvey asked.

"Not yet. It's still in the camera. I don't know how to take it out. It's one of those old ones you have to rewind. I put his camera bag away in a closet after the funeral and forgot about it until Alison told me you wanted pictures."

"I'll be right there, Mrs. Blake. Don't touch the camera. Please let me remove the film."

It was an old camera, all right, probably forty

years old. It was all metal, no plastic, a nice 35-millimeter, and a telephoto lens was in the bag with it.

"Did Martin have the close-up lens on the camera that day?" Harvey asked.

"I'm not sure." Mrs. Blake chattered on, and he depressed the button on the bottom of the camera and wound the film back into the canister, then pulled the winding lever up, and the back of the camera swung open. He pocketed the film, thanked her profusely, and made a hasty farewell.

Not many places in town still developed film, but one of the men in the P.D. lab could do it. Harvey took it to him and paced the Priority Unit's office while he awaited the results. He made himself not check his watch.

Lord, give us a break, he prayed silently.

Finally, the technician came up in the elevator with an envelope of prints.

"Thank you."

"No problem, Captain. And congratulations."

Harvey smiled. "Thanks."

The other men left their desks and crowded around him. He prayed again as he opened the envelope. Patricia and Michael Lundquist in the earthworks. He handed it to Eddie to pass around. Carol Harper Hastings and Alison Murphy near the lighthouse. Luke Frederick and David Murphy standing on a large, rounded rock by the ocean. Harvey stopped breathing for several seconds.

Martin had used the telephoto. He must have stood in the exact spot Jennifer had stood in. Luke was turned three-quarters away from the camera, and David was in profile. His facial muscles were strained. The breeze lifted their hair. Luke wore the short-sleeved white polo shirt he'd been found dead in, and David had on a cranberry wool shirt over a lighter cotton sports shirt.

Eddie peered over his shoulder. "Now, that's something like!"

Harvey handed off the picture and looked at the next one. Tom Nadeau and David were standing on the rock. David looked angry. Tom's back was to the camera. The next one showed the two of them on the ground, walking away from the rock, toward the right of the picture. The angle was a little different. Maybe Martin had been partway down the path for that one.

The rest were of the picnic, with one at the end of an elderly couple he didn't recognize, in front of a yellow ranch house. Martin's cousin in Searsport and his wife?

Harvey checked the strips of negatives, to make sure of the order of the three photos of the men on the shore. They were in the order Blake had taken them; Frederick and Murphy first, then Murphy and Nadeau. He looked at the middle one again, with David's face livid. Harvey tried to imagine what he was saying to Nadeau. Luke Frederick was nowhere in sight.

"Martin Blake's last masterpiece," he said.

Eddie, Pete, and Tony passed around the prints.

"M confronts TN—TN is defiant," Harvey said softly. "That wasn't notes for the book. He was writing captions for the pictures. Too bad Martin went to help Thelma with the tablecloth."

"He almost caught the murder on film," Eddie breathed.

"Yes, but which one of them did it?"

The elevator opened, and Jennifer got out as Harvey's desk phone rang.

"Hey, gorgeous. Can you get that, Winfield?" Harvey looked at his watch, and Tony walked over to answer the phone.

Harvey took Jennifer's hand. "Eddie and I need to get over to the airport."

"The plane doesn't land until two-ten," said Eddie.

"We ought to be there early. Sometimes they come in early."

"You haven't eaten anything," Jennifer said.

He hadn't seen her that morning, either. "Sorry. Oh, Jeff came in at midnight."

"How is he?" she asked.

"He's good. Left for work when I did."

Tony came to stand beside him. "That was

Arnie. He and Pete are bringing the Wagner woman up here."

"I thought she didn't want to come," Harvey said.

"Arnie says she's got testimony we need on this thing, and they talked her into coming up here with them. They had to wait for her to square it with her husband and pack a bag. They should be here when you get back with Beaulieu."

"All right, let's get going, Eddie."

"You didn't eat," said Jennifer.

"I'll get something at the airport." He gave her a hasty kiss and followed Eddie down the stairs.

On the way there, they drove over the bridge where Martin Blake was killed. A blue heron stood among the tall weeds in the peaceful cove where the body had been discovered. Eddie turned into the airport entrance and parked in the garage, and they walked over to the terminal.

Harvey checked the information desk to make sure the plane was expected on time. The attendant told him the last leg of Beaulieu's trip would bring him up from Newark, and the plane was just leaving the ground in New Jersey. Beaulieu would come in on the lower level.

Harvey and Eddie ambled past car rental booths and snack shops to the escalator. Kiosks with displays for Maine shoes and Swiss watches were sprinkled around both levels. They had the better part of an hour to kill.

"You hungry?" Harvey asked. "I promised Jenny."

They found a small restaurant that served burgers and sandwiches. After a light lunch, they went back to a row of chairs near Beaulieu's gate.

Airport workers moved past them, and other people drifted to the chairs. Harvey's mind bounced between the case and the wedding.

Eddie stared out toward a de Havilland Twin Otter. "Lying is a sin."

Harvey frowned, trying to connect that statement with the airplane. "Yeah."

"Even if it's for a reason?"

Harvey looked at him. "Like an undercover case?"

"Well, yeah. Like that."

"Still a lie," Harvey said.

Eddie was silent.

Beaulieu's plane should be halfway from Newark to Portland. Harvey said, "I'm going to go check on him." He walked down to the desk for the airline and got in line behind two passengers.

When he got up to the counter, a slender young woman in the airline's navy-trimmed gray blouse smiled at him. "How may I help you, sir?"

He held his badge up. "I'm Captain Larson,

with the Portland P.D. I'm here to meet a passenger on your flight 1350 from Newark. Can you tell me for sure if he's on board?"

"What's his name, please?"

"Matthew Beaulieu."

She made a few keystrokes.

"Two Beaulieus are on board. Matthew and Brenda. They're seated together. Looks like the plane will be on time."

"Thank you."

He went back to where Eddie was.

"The plane's on time. Beaulieu and his wife are on it."

The chairs were filling quickly. Harvey looked carefully at each person waiting. Finally he thought he had spotted Denise Beaulieu Marston, Matthew's sister—a fifty-year-old woman by herself, wearing a wedding ring. She had long, tapered fingers. Piano fingers. Matthew had attended his sister's recital the night of the burglary.

He walked over to her chair. She was watching the gate anxiously, clutching a shoulder bag close beside her.

"Excuse me," he ventured, "I'm Captain Larson with the—"

She jumped up. "Matt told me you'd be here. I'm Denise. We spoke on the phone."

"Yes. Your brother and his wife should be here soon."

"I'm excited about it. Matt hasn't been home in three years."

"You've met his wife before?"

"Oh, yes, they've been married over twenty years. He's been in the Navy, you know. Met her in Norfolk, Virginia. It will be good to see them both."

"Are they staying with you?" Harvey asked.

"Yes. I've got the guest room ready."

"How long are they staying?"

"Until next Thursday."

Harvey excused himself and went to where Eddie stood.

"His sister?" Eddie asked.

"Yes. She's friendly."

"Good. There's a plane landing now. Not sure what airline."

Five minutes later, people began filing in through the gate. Harvey stood back, watching Denise Marston and the passengers. Eddie stood a few feet away, also watching the incoming queue. Those arriving either fell into the arms of loved ones or strode off alone toward the exit or the baggage area.

At last, Denise stepped forward with pleasure on her face, her arms extended to her brother and his wife. Harvey gave them a few seconds for greetings, but stepped up when they turned toward baggage claim.

"Commander Beaulieu? I'm Harvey Larson."

Beaulieu held out his hand. "I was expecting you. This is my wife, Brenda."

"Ma'am." Eddie came close, and Harvey introduced him to the three.

"Is this necessary?" asked Brenda.

"Yes, ma'am. We need to talk to your husband as soon as possible, and we also want to be sure he's safe."

"We're going to my house, in Camden," said Denise.

"We'd like to question your brother first. I'm sorry if that's an inconvenience, but it is very important."

They all looked at each other. Beaulieu said, "All right, where? Is there a place we can talk here?"

"We'd prefer the police station, sir."

"Wait a minute," said Denise. "You're not taking him into custody, are you?"

"No, ma'am. We just need a secure place to talk. We'll wait while they get their baggage, then we'll take him to the police station. If you and Mrs. Beaulieu want to follow us in and wait, you can."

"I'd better call my husband." Denise took out her phone. Harvey nodded to Eddie, and he followed her. Harvey stood behind the Beaulieus at the baggage carousel. By the time they had retrieved three bags, Denise and Eddie were back. Eddie shrugged at him, indicating he'd heard nothing suspicious, and they went over to the garage. Harvey firmly suggested Beaulieu ride in his vehicle, and he got in the front. Eddie sat behind them, and Harvey waited on the access road for Mrs. Marston to pay for parking and catch up.

At the station, they took the guests up the elevator. Eddie seated the women in the break room and detailed Paula to bring them coffee. Harvey took Beaulieu straight into the interview room. He turned on the tape recorder and spoke the identifying information.

"All right, Commander."

Beaulieu cleared his throat. "What do you want to know?"

"Everything. Start with the burglary."

"All right. I don't remember the date." Harvey gave it. "Yes. It was my senior year. My friend Philip Whitney went out with some other kids that night and took part in a burglary. They tied up the owner of the house and taped his mouth shut, and he suffocated. They didn't intend to kill him."

"How do you know that?"

"Philip told me several years later."

"Did he also tell you who was there?"

"Yes. Luke Frederick drove the car. It was his car. He didn't go in the house."

"Who went in with Philip?"

He hesitated only a moment. "David Murphy and Tom Nadeau."

A surge of relief washed through Harvey. He'd known it, but the fear that he was totally wrong had nagged him.

"Philip always felt guilty afterward," Beaulieu said. "He had taken part in it, although reluctantly. And he had lied about it and gone free. I think that bothered him the most. He was never sure if his own parents believed him. He wanted them to trust him, but he didn't want them to be gullible enough to believe a lie."

"Did he speak to you about confessing?"

"Yes. At that point, he said he should have admitted it and done his time."

"Why didn't he?"

"They had a pact. No one would tell, no matter what. And he didn't."

"What happened fourteen years after the robbery?"

"Martin Blake published his first book, and the story of the robbery was in it. He put a lot of details in it, and the boys, men then, were scared people would recognize them."

"Do you think Blake had inside information?"

"No, most of what he used was in the papers. Only, Phil Whitney had been acquitted. In the book, Blake had him convicted. He changed a few things, but Phil was obviously the one convicted in the book. I went home to visit soon after the book came out, and Phil told me then he was going to own up to it."

"He wrote out his confession instead of coming to the police station and making a statement," Harvey said.

"Yes. He told me the day before he died that he'd talked to each of the other three who'd been in on the burglary. Luke was really scared and asked him not to tell. Phil told him he should confess, too, that he probably would get a light sentence because he didn't go in the house. He told me that he and Luke were going to the police together the next day. But he died early in the morning."

"And Luke didn't confess."

"No."

"And the others?"

Beaulieu cleared his throat, but didn't say anything. Harvey knew Eddie was in Observation.

"Ed, could you bring us some ice water, please?"

Beaulieu looked startled. "Your partner is listening?"

"The world is listening, Commander." Harvey nodded toward the tape recorder.

Beaulieu put his head in his hands. A minute later, Eddie came in with a tray holding a pitcher of water and two glasses. Harvey poured a glass for Beaulieu.

"Thank you." Beaulieu took it and drank half of it down. Eddie went out.

"All right, sir. What happened when Philip Whitney talked to David Murphy and told him he was on the verge of confessing?"

"David told him not to. He was a lawyer and was running for the legislature at that time. It would have ruined him."

"Did he threaten Whitney?"

"I don't know. Somebody did. Murphy or Nadeau, or both. Phil told me they said they would kill him if he told the police they'd been involved in the burglary. He said he didn't care, he'd rather be dead than live the way he was. Then they said they would hurt his sister and his little brother."

"When you say 'they,' you mean either or both."

"Yes. I'm not sure if they both said it."

It was all hearsay, and Harvey wasn't sure there was a way around that. "Did anyone else know about this?"

"I don't know. They might have told somebody, but I doubt it. Philip said he hadn't told anyone but me."

"Did they also threaten Luke Frederick?"

"I don't know."

"So what did Philip do?"

"Well, Tom told him after a while that he could go ahead and confess but not name the others. He told him to write it all down so he wouldn't mess up. Tom wanted to go over it and make sure he didn't implicate them. Then, if it was okay, he said Phil could take it to the police. But Phil had to promise not to tell them anything, just give them the paper and stick with what it said."

"So, the paper wasn't a suicide note?"

"No. Phil showed it to me that day."

"The day before he was found dead in his parents' back yard."

"Yes. He wasn't planning to kill himself. He was planning to turn himself in."

"You actually saw the note, in Whitney's own handwriting?"

"Yes."

"Did he have the gun? The handgun that was stolen in the burglary?"

"I don't think so. He never said anything about it to me."

Harvey leaned over the table. "Commander Beaulieu, this can't be used as evidence, but I'd like your opinion on the day Philip Whitney died. You seem to be the only one he confided in. What happened that day?"

He closed his eyes and said slowly, "I think Thomas Nadeau or David Murphy brought the gun to Phil's parents' house and shot him and placed the gun in his hand." He looked Harvey in the eye then.

Harvey went back over everything, asked him questions on the details and Whitney's wording. Beaulieu's story was consistent. At last Harvey turned to the mirror and motioned Eddie to come in. Harvey gave him the tape, to take to Paula, who would type up the statement.

Harvey turned to Beaulieu. "All right, you're going to be at your sister's in Camden until Thursday?"

"Yes."

"We need you to stay available for the next few days. The state police may want to talk to you, to see if this has a bearing on the Frederick case. Please don't leave the area without informing us." Harvey gave him his business card. "If you think of anything else you can add to this statement, or if at any time you don't feel safe, call me. We can get you protection if you request it. Do you understand?"

"Yes." Beaulieu pocketed the card.

They waited another ten minutes, until Paula came in with the transcript. Beaulieu read it silently and signed it. He looked up at Harvey.

"I can go now?"

"Yes." Harvey hated to let him. As long as Beaulieu was in the police station, he had a living, breathing witness. "Just remember what I said, and stay available, and be careful."

He and Eddie sat down and looked at each other when they were alone in the office.

"What now?" Eddie asked.

"We need warrants for Murphy and Nadeau, for the death of Richard Fairley."

"Hearsay. Will it be enough?"

"I hope so," Harvey said, "in light of two of the participants being killed. Beaulieu swears he saw the note. That should carry some weight. But I also hope to have more when Cathy Wagner and Joel Dixon have been here."

"Murphy or Nadeau must have kept the gun," Eddie said.

Harvey sighed. "We can't convict them on speculation. I'm going to run this by Mike." He called, and Mike told him to come right up.

"Overall, Nadeau and Murphy look pretty black," Mike said, when he'd read Beaulieu's statement, "but if you break it down into four cases, every one of them is pretty thin."

"Joel Dixon saw Nadeau hit Frederick," Harvey said.

"He can only identify him by his clothing," Mike pointed out.

"Beaulieu placed Nadeau and Murphy at the burglary."

"Hearsay from a dead guy. Beaulieu wasn't there. That gun," Mike said, chewing his gum and squinting a little. "Where was it between the burglary and Whitney's death?"

Harvey didn't have an answer.

"And you've got nothing on the Blake murder."

Harvey knew it was true.

Mike said, "Hold off on your warrants. David Murphy isn't going anywhere. He's too public, and he's got this kickback thing keeping him busy."

"What about Nadeau?"

"He's in Murphy's hip pocket. Build your case. You don't want to lose them for lack of evidence."

Pete and Arnie came back at four o'clock without Cathy Wagner. Arnie was grouchy, complaining about traffic.

"What happened?" Harvey demanded.

"Her husband talked her out of it."

"You're kidding."

"No, I'm not."

Harvey sat down and called her.

"I'm not coming, so don't waste your breath," she said.

"Mrs. Wagner, please. We know now who the boys involved in the burglary were. We know your ex-husband was one of them. You need to help us."

A man came on the line. "Look, leave her alone. She is not going to Maine. She is never going within a hundred miles of Tom Nadeau again. Do you understand?"

"Yes, sir." Irate husbands could be very lucid. "Mr. Wagner, do you understand that your wife has information that could help us solve multiple murders? She's no longer married to Thomas Nadeau. She can testify against him. If necessary, we can have the New Hampshire State Police pick her up for us. We need her testimony."

"I thought it was about the burglary thing when she was a kid. She told me about it. One old man died. It was thirty-five years ago, for crying out loud!"

"There's no statute of limitations on murder, sir. But it's not just that. There have been three murders since then that we believe are related to this thing. Please. Let your wife come and give us her statement."

"Hold on."

He could hear them talking, but couldn't make out the words. Wagner probably had his hand over the receiver.

Finally she came back on.

"You said before that Philip Whitney was murdered."

"I'm trying to prove that. Can you help me?"

She hesitated. "He shot himself."

"Yes, we have the gun."

"It was a pistol."

"A revolver," Harvey said. "The same one the boys stole from Richard Fairley's house."

"I'll come tomorrow morning."

He relaxed. "Come straight to the police station at Franklin and Middle. Exit 7 on 295."

"I'll be there by ten o'clock."

"You won't change your mind?"

"No, I'll be there."

Harvey hung up and breathed deeply.

Pete and Arnie had been waiting.

"She's coming tomorrow, 10 a.m."

"I'll believe it when I see it," said Arnie.

"Still can't get the Dixons," Nate called from Mike's old desk.

"All right, let's tie up loose ends and get the reports filed." Harvey latched on to Arnie for a few minutes before he left. "I'll be looking for a new partner for you. Any suggestions?"

Arnie shook his head. "Get someone you want to be here a long time. I'm out of here New Year's Eve, so don't think about me. I can put up with anyone for five months."

"It's going to be strange to have Eddie my senior detective."

"Yeah," Arnie said. "Maybe you'd better get somebody older in here, give this unit some stability."

"What do you think about the detectives downstairs?"

"They're all pretty good, or they wouldn't be where they are. You worked with Wood and Parkhurst. What about them?"

Harvey frowned. "I always wondered why Mike picked me over Clyde Wood. He had seniority over me, and he's always been good in homicide."

"Mike wanted you, that's why," Arnie said. "You're the computer ace. Besides, Wood's a little ambitious. In a new unit, I don't think Mike wanted any contenders for authority. But Wood's over fifty. He might like spending his last few years before retirement up here, even if he had to answer to a whippersnapper like you. Parkhurst is good, too. Methodical."

"What about Joey Bolduc?"

"He's good. He's cocky, though."

"Sort of like Eddie?"

"Now, those two would make a pair. Don't put them together as partners. If it were me, I'd go for somebody older. Just my opinion. Maybe Lemieux. He's over forty, and he's steady."

"Terry? He's the patrol sergeant."

"So? That uniform isn't glued to him."

Harvey was due to pick up Jennifer that evening, after his final fitting for the tuxedo, so they could pay a visit to their new house together.

"It's so exciting," Jennifer told Beth as she helped Beth cut out the pieces of a dress she was making. "Mr. Bailey's moved out. He says we can take possession anytime."

"I'm excited for you." Beth pinned a pattern piece firmly to her soft challis material. "You'll have so much fun decorating."

Jennifer gritted her teeth. "That will be a challenge. Maybe you and Ruthann can give me some pointers."

The doorbell rang, and she went to open the

door. Harvey, standing on the steps and smiling. Beth took a straight pin out of her mouth. "How's it going, Harvey?"

"Good. We're getting close to solving this thing."

"You got some new clues today?" Jennifer asked.

"Yeah, we got some good stuff. You want to go with us tonight, Beth?"

"Maybe next time," Beth said.

Harvey had already received the keys from Mr. Bailey. When he unlocked the breezeway door, they entered the house solemnly. Jennifer looked around the lower rooms in awe.

The piano and the dining room furniture were gone. So were the living room set and the other pieces Mr. Bailey had mentioned. Most of the dishes and linens and all his clothing were gone. The bookshelves in the sunroom were bare except for one row of books on the care and propagation of roses. A note was stuck under them. "For Mrs. Larson."

"How sweet of him," Jennifer said.

"We'll have to buy some furniture, and I guess one of us can move in," Harvey said, surveying his new home.

"That should be you," said Jennifer.

"Think so?"

"Yes. I'd like to stay with Beth until the wedding."

"All right." When they went upstairs and peeked into the bedrooms, he said, "Say, have your parents booked a hotel?"

"Yes. For them and Grandpa and Abby and Leeanne and Travis and Randy."

"Tell them to cancel it. They can stay here."

"Really? Do you think we could do it?"

"I don't see why not. There are still two beds here. We'll work it out."

"I'll call them."

They were getting Mr. Bailey's small oak library table with four Windsor chairs in the sunroom, and the wicker furniture. Chairs, rugs, and baskets in the living room would be useful. A couple of side tables looked to Jennifer as if they ought to be in a museum.

"I wonder why Mr. Bailey's daughter didn't want this stuff," she said.

"Probably her house is full."

A small framed copy of Murillo's *The Divine Shepherd* hung in the living room, next to the doorway into the sunroom. "He told me that's our wedding present," Harvey said.

Jennifer gazed at the picture of a little boy who sat with a thin rod in his right hand, his left hand resting on a lamb's back. "I like it. Is it real?"

"No, it would be worth more than the house if it were."

"It's still nice."

"Very," he said.

They looked into the master bedroom. The Baileys' bed was still there.

"I thought he was taking that," Jennifer said.

"Changed his mind. You want the sleigh bed in here?" Harvey asked. She'd seen his bed a couple of times when he was injured, and she liked it.

"I think . . . yes." She couldn't quite look at him and talk about the bed they would sleep in.

He put his arms around her. "Jeff or Eddie can help me move this one upstairs." She only let him kiss her once, then pulled away and went into the kitchen. He followed her. She opened one cupboard door after another, finding a lot of pans and utensils that had been left behind.

"Mr. Bailey's daughter must not have needed any of this," Harvey said.

"My gain." She smiled, surveying her cupboards and her refrigerator and her dishwasher.

"So what do we need?" Harvey asked.

"Not much. You have a microwave. I have a coffeemaker. We may have to have a yard sale to get rid of extra stuff."

She bent to look in one of the base cabinets, and her hair hung down, almost sweeping the floor. She pulled out a bread pan. As she straightened, Harvey took it from her hand and set it on the counter.

"This is going to be perfect." His voice was husky. He stroked her cheek and slid his fingers under her hair, against her neck. She didn't look away this time, and he took his time kissing her. Anticipation shot through her. She sighed and cuddled in against him, but only for a minute. "Come on, we'd better get going."

They ate supper out, and she asked him about Jeff.

"He's good. I think he'll fix the apartment up and enjoy living there."

Jennifer smiled. "He called me. He told me that he's been talking to you about God and church and the Bible."

"Yeah, some," Harvey said. "We haven't had much time together, but it's been great. I'm glad I'm getting to know him."

When he took her home, they sat on the couch, and Jennifer showed him the basket full of RSVPs that had come in for the wedding. Over two hundred guests confirmed. She was a little nervous about that.

"The church is big enough," Harvey said.

Beth's phone rang, and she took it into the kitchen and didn't come back.

After a while, Jennifer went to the kitchen for ice cream. Beth was sitting at the table, still talking on the phone and laughing. "That's terrific," she said. "I'm so glad everything went well today."

Jennifer dished up two bowls of ice cream, keeping half an ear on Beth's conversation, and then took the bowls to the other room. "I think she's talking to Jeff."

"It might be somebody else," Harvey said.

"No, she's got that look."

"What look?"

"You know, sort of . . ." She looked right at him with a wistful sort of gaze, then smiled. "Your eyes are so blue."

"Blue is recessive." Harvey set down his ice cream. "Our kids don't stand a chance." He gave her a very unscientific kiss. "I'll be so glad when this case is over."

Jennifer said, "I'll be so glad when the wedding is over."

"You're not serious. I mean . . ." He eyed her suspiciously.

Jennifer laughed. "What?"

"Well, *I* think that. I've said it to Eddie a thousand times. But I didn't expect to hear it from you. I thought the wedding was your main focus in life."

"Only for the next nine days." Jennifer dug her spoon into the peppermint ice cream.

"What will you concentrate on after that?" Harvey asked.

"You, of course. I intend to make you supremely happy."

He took that as an invitation and set her ice cream bowl beside his on the table. By the time Beth came back smiling, Jennifer was sure her hair looked like a bird's nest, and Harvey was practically purring.

"How's Jeffrey?" He picked up his bowl of melting ice cream.

She smiled bigger. "Fine. He's just fine." She didn't tell him that visiting hours were over or call him names. She went over to Jennifer's CD player and put Vivaldi on soft, then went down the hall to her room.

"Wow," Harvey said.

"Yeah." Jennifer looked at him.

"I think our chaperone just copped out on us."

"Does this mean we're mature adults and can be trusted?" she asked.

He looked into her eyes and slid his hand along one of her long tresses. His eyes held that look she couldn't resist. To her surprise, instead of kissing her again, he stood up.

"Not me. Time to say goodnight."

Chapter 19

Friday, July 9

Mike came into the office at 8 a.m. Harvey was just turning on his computer.

"Hey, Mike! What's up?"

Mike tossed a folder on Harvey's desk. "Just came to tell you, Nate's transfer is permanent. Go over this with him." He looked around the room.

"Miss the Priority Unit?" Harvey asked.

"Maybe a little."

"Itching to get in on an active case?"

"Maybe."

"We're close, Mike."

He grinned. "Got someone you need arrested?"

"Not quite yet."

"Aw, too bad. See you later."

"Mrs. Dixon is bringing Joel in," Eddie crowed from his desk.

Mike back-pedaled. "Mind if I sit in, Harv?"

"Feel free."

Joel and his mother stepped off the elevator seconds before Terry Lemieux brought Cathy Wagner up the stairs. Harvey decided to take on Mrs. Wagner himself.

"Eddie, you and Pete show Joel Mrs. Blake's

pictures out here," Harvey said. "Mrs. Dixon can sit in if she wants to."

Mike and Harvey took Mrs. Wagner into the interview room. Harvey had been thinking of her as the girlfriend and wife of Thomas Nadeau, and seeing a 52-year-old woman anchored him in reality. She was still trim, wearing white slacks and a red-and-white-striped top, but she wore bifocals, and her dark hair had a few gray streaks.

"Mrs. Wagner, thank you very much for coming," Harvey said.

She looked around nervously. "Let's get it over with. My husband really didn't want me to come."

Harvey had set up the video recorder in advance, and Mike activated the cassette recorder, so they would have a separate audio record. Harvey gave the time, date, and name of the interviewee.

"Mrs. Wagner, could you tell me first about the burglary that happened your junior year of high school?"

She sat still for a moment, then began quietly. "I heard about it the night it happened. My boyfriend came to see me."

"What time was this?"

"Oh, midnight. He threw pebbles at my window. He did that sometimes. My parents didn't know. I snuck out and met him in the back yard."

"What was your boyfriend's name?"

"Tommy Nadeau. Thomas."

"So, what happened when you went out that night to see Tommy?"

"He told me he and his friends had broken into somebody's house. Nobody was home, and they thought they'd sneak in just for kicks."

According to the news clippings, Fairley's house had been royally vandalized, but Harvey let it pass. He said, "The owner came home while they were there."

"Yes. Tommy was laughing about it." She closed her eyes for a moment, and shook her head bitterly. "He told me they'd tied the old man up, but he'd get loose by morning."

"Who were the three boys who did that?" Harvey asked.

"Tommy and David and Philip."

"When you say David, you mean Maine's congressman, David R. Murphy."

"Yes. He was Tommy's best friend in high school."

"And Philip was . . ."

"Philip Whitney."

"Was there anyone else involved?"

She hesitated. "There was one boy who drove the car, but he didn't go in with them."

"Who was that?"

"Luke Frederick."

"And Tommy told you all of this the night of the burglary, before either of you knew Mr. Fairley was dead."

"Yes."

Mike stood up and motioned Harvey toward the door.

"Excuse me just a moment, Mrs. Wagner." They stepped out into the office. Nate, in his uniform, was sitting at Pete's desk. "Nate, would you please go in and stay with Mrs. Wagner while I talk to Mike?"

When the door to the interview room was closed, Mike said, "Do you want me to go to the courthouse for the warrants?"

"I think we're ready," Harvey said.

"I think you are. If I go personally, it should cut some red tape for you."

"Thanks, Mike."

Eddie came from his desk holding Martin Blake's pictures. He held out the one of Tom Nadeau and David Murphy on the rock. "Joel Dixon's identified the man who hit Frederick," he said.

"Who?"

"The man in the blue sweater, Nadeau. He recognized them all right away."

"Be ready to move on Nadeau and Murphy when I come back," Mike said.

Harvey went back into Interview. Cathy Wagner was drinking coffee, and Nate was sitting at the far end of the table. Harvey sat down near the tape recorder.

"All right, Mrs. Wagner, let's continue. Is there anything else you can tell me about the night of the burglary?"

"That night . . ." She looked up at him, then down again. "That night, Tommy brought me something. He asked me to keep it for him."

"What was it?"

"A box. A metal box. Like a small fishing tackle box. It had a padlock on it. He said to keep it for him for a while."

"What was in it?"

"He didn't tell me."

"Weren't you curious?"

"Of course. He said it was something they took from the old man. I thought maybe it was money."

"So you took it."

"Yes. I was a little scared, but I would have done anything for him then. I took it up to my room when he left, and I kept it."

"How long?" Harvey asked.

"Until we got married."

"How long was that?"

"Five years. Until I graduated from college."

"You kept this locked box for five years without knowing what was in it?"

"Yes."

Harvey supposed that was possible. He'd have

440

had it open within a week. "Didn't anyone else ever see it?"

"My sister did. She asked me about it a few times, but I just told her it was something of Tommy's, and after a while she quit asking."

"He never came and got it, or asked you to give it to him?"

"No."

"And the next day you heard the homeowner was dead."

"Yes, the whole school was shocked. When Philip Whitney was arrested, it was even worse." She stopped and sat staring at the coffee cup.

"Did your boyfriend talk to you about it?"

"He said they didn't kill him, just tied him up and left him. Tommy was scared. They all were. At lunch, David came over and ate with us, and Tommy kept saying, 'We don't know anything. We weren't there.' Alison brought her tray over, and David said, 'Shut up. She doesn't know.' She was saying how awful it was, and we all had to pretend we were shocked. Well, we were shocked, but . . . we had to make her think we didn't know anything about it."

"You, Thomas, David, Philip, and Luke were the only ones who knew?"

"I think so. David was really mad that Tommy had told me. When Philip was arrested, we all thought for sure the other boys would be. Philip must have gone through a lot. I know the police questioned Tommy at least twice, and lots of other guys, too. But they never found out who else was there. And Philip hadn't been a regular friend of theirs. I thought for a while they suspected his buddy, Matt Beaulieu, but I guess he was somewhere with his parents that night."

"What did Tom and David do when Philip was arrested?"

"They got hold of Luke Frederick in the hallway at school. David and Tommy kind of cornered him. They told him, 'We weren't there, and you weren't there. Get yourself an alibi. You don't know anything, and we never mention this again.' And they didn't."

"They never talked about it to each other after that?"

"I don't think so. I tried to bring it up once to Tommy, and he walked away and didn't speak to me for two days. I learned from that. He did say once to David that he'd gained a lot of respect for Philip. Because he didn't tell, I guess."

She didn't seem to see anything odd in that.

"So, when did you learn what was in the box Tom Nadeau gave you?" Harvey asked.

"When Philip Whitney died."

"How did you find out?"

"When we got married I asked Tom if he still wanted that old tackle box. He said he did, so I took it to our apartment, and later, when we bought a house, he took it there. I thought he would keep it in the tool shed with his fishing rods, but he didn't. He kept it on the shelf in the closet, with his hunting stuff. Then, after Martin Blake's book came out, we all read it. I mean, I'm sure everyone from our high school read it. You must have read it."

"Not until recently," Harvey said. "I grew up in New Hampshire, and I would have only been six when the burglary happened."

She looked a little disappointed.

"This hunting gear Tom had," he said. "Did he go deer hunting?"

"Every year."

"Did he have a hunting knife?"

"Yes."

"What was it like?"

"I don't remember. About this long." She held her hands eight inches apart.

"Can you describe the hilt?"

She shook her head.

"All right, the tackle box was in the closet for a long time. When did you learn what was in it?"

"It wasn't long after *Morristown* came out that Tom came in one night looking pretty upset. I asked him what was wrong, and he said, 'Nothing,' and went straight to the bedroom. I was fixing supper, I think. After a minute I went in there, and he had the metal box open on the bed, and he was taking something out of it." She turned and looked him full in the face. "A gun."

"So, then you knew you'd had this gun for fourteen years."

"Yes."

"What kind of gun was it?"

"I don't know much about guns. It was a handgun. You said it was a revolver."

"Can you describe it?"

She shook her head. "Not really."

Harvey thought about his next question. "Mrs. Wagner, tell me what Tom Nadeau did when you saw him taking the gun out of the box."

"He turned around and saw me, and he said, 'You didn't see anything, did you, Cathy?' and I kind of shook my head. He said, 'That's right. You didn't see *anything*.' Then he loaded it and put it back in the box. He took it and left. He didn't come back for a long time. I sat up and waited. Finally he drove in. I looked out the window, and he went in the tool shed before he came in the house."

She took a drink of coffee, and Harvey waited.

"The next day, I heard Philip Whitney had shot himself."

"What did you think?"

"That it was awful. Then I started thinking about the gun. After lunch, I went out to the tool shed. Tommy was at work. I looked in there and found the metal box. It wasn't locked anymore. It was empty."

"What did you do then?"

"I got scared. I packed a suitcase and took my kids to my mother's house. I told her we'd had a big fight. When Tommy called, she told him I wasn't there. He came around the next day. I told him I didn't want to live with him anymore."

"Did he make any sort of explanation?"

She closed her eyes for a moment. "He said, 'I had to, Cathy. Philip would have ruined us all.' I didn't know for sure what he meant, that he had given the gun to Philip to commit suicide with, or . . .'" Tears rolled down her face. "I said, 'Ruined you?' and he said, 'Us. You're an accessory. You kept the gun, and you knew about the burglary. David is a lawyer, and he knows these things. He's running for office, Cathy.' He said it like David had the most to lose."

"What else?"

She frowned. "I said his fingerprints would be on the gun, and he said, 'No, they're not. No one's but Philip's are.' I threw him out. I cried and I cried. The next day I went to New Hampshire to stay with an old college roommate of mine and filed for divorce. Eventually I got a job and met Jack Wagner. I was afraid Tom would come looking for me. I never told anyone about this until . . . until you called me. Then I told Jack."

Her tears were flowing freely. Harvey passed her a box of tissues. She pulled one out and stopped with it halfway to her eyes.

"I should have a lawyer in here, shouldn't I? Am I going to prison?"

"I don't know," he said honestly. "Do you want to call someone?"

"I wouldn't know who to call." She wiped her eyes and looked at him again. "You're not letting me go home, are you?"

"No."

"Are you arresting me?"

"No. We'll keep you here for a while, though." He looked toward Nate. "Officer Miller here will get you some lunch."

Nate stood up. "You want me to take her to the diner?"

All they needed was for Thomas Nadeau to drive by and see her eating on the sidewalk with a policeman. "No, I think we'll keep her out of sight. We'll order in for the two of you."

Nate nodded.

"If you want to call your husband, you can," Harvey told her. "Tell him you may need to stay in Portland overnight. And if you want to have a lawyer come in and see you here, you can do that."

"If I stay over, where will I stay? In a cell?" Her face was white.

"No," Harvey said. "We'll put you up some-where safe, if that's necessary. But you need to stay in this building until we execute warrants this afternoon. I'll try to get a female officer to come up here and stay with you. When the suspects are in custody, we'll talk again."

Harvey left the room. Arnie was coming from the stairway.

"Alison Murphy called me," he said. "Tony got her reunion pictures yesterday."

"Yeah?" Harvey asked.

"She wanted to know if they helped. Then she asked if we were behind this trouble her husband's in for financial irregularities, and I assured her we're not. Harv, he'd apparently said something to her over breakfast about the old burglary, because of all our questions."

"Oh, great."

Arnie nodded. "She was trying to convince me David wasn't in on it. She said he swore to her from Day One that he wasn't there, and she believed him. She never would have married him if she thought he could do something like that."

"Of course not," Harvey said.

"Of course not."

"You didn't tip her off, I hope?"

"Oh, no. Alison and I are still friends. But they're both aware we're poking into that."

"Harvey, the lab report is in," Eddie said, getting up from his chair. "The DNA on the cigarettes is a match for Marlboro Man."

"The ubiquitous Nadeau. Okay, Arnie and Pete, go get a quick lunch. Check with Nate and bring something back for him and Mrs. Wagner. When

Mike gets back here, we all need to be ready to roll."

Harvey called Jennifer on her cell phone. "Where are you, gorgeous?"

"Records. Just ready to go to lunch."

"I need to wait here for Mike. We're close to breaking this thing."

"Want me to bring you a sandwich?"

"Just bring yourself up here for a few minutes. That's all I need."

"That's an illusion. I'll bring you some food."

Tony was standing beside his desk when he hung up.

"Sir, do we need armor?"

"Yes. We're going after a killer. You and Eddie get yours now. Tell Pete and Arnie when they get back."

He called Terry and asked for a female officer. Eddie came out of the locker room wearing his vest and handed Harvey his.

"I hate these things." Harvey unbuckled his holster.

Eddie made a face at him. "It saved your life not so long ago."

"That's why I'm putting it on." Harvey fastened the vest and put his holster back on over it.

Jennifer came in with lunch, and her eyes widened. He should have waited and put it on after she'd left.

He said, "Don't be that way, gorgeous. We're

448

just being cautious. And God is in control here."

"I didn't say anything." But her eyes said plenty. He pulled a chair over for her, and they sat down. Uncomfortable. He pulled open the right side of his vest. Eddie went back to his desk and sat down. Sarah came in from the stairway.

"Hey, Sarah, how you doing?" Harvey said.

"Fine." She didn't sound fine. "Where's the witness?"

"In the interview room."

Eddie stood up. "Hi, Sarah."

She cast him a baleful glance and turned away, heading for the room where Mrs. Wagner waited. Eddie frowned.

"Do we want to know what that was about?" Harvey asked him as he sat down again.

"I tried to tell her how I've been finding out about God, and how we're all sinners and we need Jesus. She didn't like it."

"Oh, Eddie, I'm sorry," said Jennifer.

Harvey nodded. "Me, too. You can't expect everybody to accept things like that the first time they hear them."

"I know. I thought you were nuts at first," Eddie admitted. "I need to learn a lot more, though, so I can tell it better. I've been staying away from my mother's because I don't know how to tell her."

Jennifer gave him a sad smile. "We'd better pray about that."

Pete and Arnie came in and distributed sandwiches, and Harvey sent them to the locker room for their vests. A few minutes later, Mike came up the stairs waving the warrants.

"Hi, Jennifer."

"Hello, Chief."

He looked around at them and grinned. "Oh, boy, body armor."

Harvey stood up. "You think it's unnecessary?"

"No, not considering what you're dealing with."

Harvey lowered his voice. "Should I make Nate and Pete call their wives?"

"What for?"

"Well, you know, Mike, the widows cry all over the captain and say, 'I never got a chance to say goodbye.' "

Jennifer put down her sandwich with a stricken look.

"Come on, Harvey," Mike said. "That's a little melodramatic."

It wasn't. Marcia Towne had said it the night Chris was shot, and Mike had tried to comfort her.

"I've never been in this position before. I could lose somebody today."

"You gotta quit thinking like that." Mike glanced at Jennifer. "You never got the jitters like this before. If it will make you feel better, take Eddie and Jennifer in the break room and have a prayer meeting, but you've got to show some confidence here, Harv."

"Are you coming with us?"

"What's your plan?"

"Half of us go for Murphy, the other half for Nadeau. Pick them up at the same time. I really don't expect any trouble."

"You'll do fine. Just go get them and bring them in. I'll be upstairs." Mike went to the stairway and disappeared.

Harvey started closing his vest. Jennifer stood up. She gazed at him with a look he didn't ever want to see.

Eddie came over and said quietly, "What about that prayer meeting?"

Arnie and Pete were still in the locker room. Tony was wolfing his lunch. Nate had turned Mrs. Wagner over to Sarah and was adjusting his vest. The door to the interview room was closed. Harvey drew Jennifer into the tiny break room, and Eddie followed and closed the door.

Harvey prayed, just a short prayer. Jennifer's arm crept around his belt at the bottom of the bulletproof vest while he had his eyes closed. When he said amen, she launched herself at him.

"Don't cry, Jenny. It's nothing. We'll be back in half an hour."

"I'm not," she choked.

"I'll take care of him," Eddie said. He went out and shut the door. Harvey tipped Jennifer's chin up and kissed her.

"You didn't eat again," she said.

He'd only taken a bite or two, it was true. He tried to say something, and just shook his head. This was why Mike didn't want the wives to know. It was too hard on the men.

When he'd put Jennifer into the elevator, all of his men were ready. Harvey tried to follow Mike's advice about showing confidence. Tony was his rookie, and he had to keep him close. But he wanted Eddie at his back.

"Arnie, you, Pete, and Nate go for Nadeau. Eddie, Tony, and I will visit Representative Murphy." Maybe they should switch it around. He hesitated with the warrants in his hand. Nadeau might be more likely to resist. Harvey knew he had to quit second guessing himself. He huffed out a breath and handed Arnie the warrant for Nadeau.

He stopped at the aide's desk. "Paula, please ask Com to track all of us."

"Of course." She picked up her phone.

"Thanks."

They all went down the stairs. Terry Lemieux looked after them a little wistfully as they passed his desk.

"Call me as soon as you've got him," Harvey told Arnie.

"Right."

Eddie, Tony and Harvey got into Tony's car, a new Mustang convertible.

"Nice car, Winfield."

"Thanks. I figured it was my turn to drive." Tony seemed a little embarrassed. The car probably cost nearly what Harvey made in a year. He drove to Murphy's office and parked beside the white Lincoln with congressional license plates.

Harvey went in first. He had his sport coat over the vest and holster, and he was hot. Eddie and Tony were in their shirtsleeves, but they were sweating, too.

Two men in suits were waiting in the outer office. Harvey walked up to the receptionist's desk. "I need to see Mr. Murphy, please."

"He's in a meeting."

He held up his badge. "Portland P.D. I think he'll see me."

The door to the inner office opened, and Alison came out. Her brow furrowed when she saw Harvey, and she stopped.

"Mrs. Murphy." He tried to be as suave as Arnie. "How delightful to see you again. I just came by to have a chat with your husband."

She looked beyond him at Eddie and Tony, taking in the body armor and holstered weapons. "Not a social call, I think."

"Will you just step back inside with us, ma'am?" Harvey put his hand on her arm, and she turned around and walked back to the door of the inner office and opened it.

She said, "David, Captain Larson is here."

Murphy was halfway up out of his chair, but froze when he saw the officers.

"Good afternoon, Mr. Murphy." Harvey stepped forward.

He sank back into the chair.

"Sir, you are under arrest."

Murphy didn't move.

"Please stand up and put your hands behind you."

Very slowly, he obeyed. Alison stared, glassy-eyed.

"What's the charge?" Murphy asked in a hoarse tone.

"Manslaughter, in the death of Richard Fairley."

Alison gasped.

Harvey started the Miranda, "Anything you say may be used against you in a court of law . . ."

"No, he didn't do it. He swore he didn't do it!" Alison began to sob. Harvey kept on through the rule Murphy had learned years ago in law school, cuffed him, and patted him down.

Eddie said, "Mrs. Murphy, if you want to come over to the police station and wait, you can."

"Call Ned Baxter and have him come there," David said to her. Lawyers always had lawyers.

"It's my fault, isn't it?" Alison's voice rose higher. "They asked me for pictures of the reunion and things about that burglary. I thought I was being helpful, David!"

They went out through the waiting room, and the two men in suits stared, open-mouthed. Alison went to the receptionist and screamed, "Call Mr. Baxter. Quickly." Harvey was glad he hadn't sent Arnie there.

He radioed the marked unit he had arranged to have waiting nearby. When it arrived, he put Murphy in the back seat and buckled his seat belt. From Tony's car, he called the office and instructed Paula to move Sarah and Cathy Wagner to the break room, so Murphy wouldn't see them when they came in.

They took Murphy in the back door of the police station. Ryan Toothaker was leaning on Terry's desk in the foyer. He straightened up when they came in, and his jaw dropped. Harvey punched the security code for the elevator. They didn't have prisoners climb the stairs in handcuffs. Ryan was beside him before the door opened.

"Captain Larson—"

"One hour," Harvey said.

"My story?"

"This is big, Ryan. We have to tell everyone. Have Terry let you upstairs in an hour, and I'll see you first."

"What are the charges?"

The elevator door opened, and Eddie moved Murphy inside. Tony and Harvey followed. As the door closed, Harvey said, "So far, manslaughter."

Ryan whipped out his phone.

They stepped into the office a moment later. Harvey caught Eddie's eye and nodded toward the interview room. Eddie and Tony took Murphy, and Harvey stopped at his desk and called Records.

"Jenny, Eddie and Tony and I are back. Everything's okay. Just didn't want you to worry."

"Thank you! Thank you! I love you!"

"Ditto." He hung up and peeled off his jacket and vest and dropped them on his chair. His cell phone rang, and he scrambled to get it out of the jacket pocket.

"Harv, it's Arnie. Nadeau's skipped on us."

"He isn't just out for lunch?"

"No, he ate early. The secretary says he got a phone call and went rushing out. He didn't say where he was headed."

"Great. We've got to find him. Come on in."

He called upstairs to Mike. "I've got Murphy, but Nadeau ran. He was tipped off."

"Get what you can out of Murphy, and start a manhunt," Mike advised. "That guy's four up on you already. And protect your witness."

"Put her in the Motel 6?"

"Too obvious. What about one of those little bed-and-breakfasts? If she wants to call home, have her do it from here, and don't tell her where she's staying tonight. I can activate the manhunt on Nadeau if it will help you."

"It would. I've got my hands full with Murphy, and the other team's not back yet."

Harvey went into Observation and looked through the glass. David Murphy sat stoically at the table in the interview room, and Tony and Eddie stood at opposite ends of the table. They had their vests off. He went to the break room and said, "Sarah, we're going to move you and Mrs. Wagner to a more comfortable place. You'll stay with her until the end of your shift, then another officer will relieve you."

Sarah nodded.

"May I call my husband?" Cathy Wagner asked.

"Yes, you can tell him you're staying up here overnight. If you need anything, we'll send someone to the store, then Officer Benoit will drive you to your room for the night. Sarah, she can use the phone on my desk."

Finally he opened the door to Interview.

"Eddie," he said.

Eddie came out. "Could you please arrange lodging for Mrs. Wagner and a female officer for tonight at a little B and B within the city limits? Don't tell anyone but me where they're going. Not even Mrs. Wagner, or Tony, or *anybody*. Don't tell the B and B it's a police matter, either. They might spill it."

He raised his eyebrows, and Harvey leaned close to his ear and whispered, "Nadeau's loose." Eddie scowled at the ceiling. Harvey said, "Tell

Terry we'll need another female officer for the next shift, but don't say where. Tell him to have her come up here when she comes on duty."

Paula came over to him. "Captain, the patrol sergeant says Mrs. Murphy is downstairs."

"Have her wait down there, please."

Finally he went in and faced Murphy. The video cam was rolling, and Tony started the tape recorder and reeled off the interview data.

Harvey faced David Murphy. "Are we ready to talk?"

Murphy sighed. "Can you take the handcuffs off, please? I won't do anything."

"That depends. Are we talking?"

"I know my rights. Better to surrender to you than the federal agents, I guess." He was thinking about the kickbacks, expecting to be arrested for that, Harvey realized. The manslaughter charge was a surprise.

He was handsome, but starting to show his age. A little gray. A smile too perfect to be natural. Caps in front, at least. Dark smears of fatigue under his eyes.

"What do you want to know?" he asked.

Harvey walked behind him and unlocked the handcuffs. Murphy shook his arms and rubbed his wrists while Harvey put the cuffs in the case on his belt.

"Let's begin thirty-five years ago," Harvey

said. "Your senior year of high school. A burglary at the home of Richard Fairley."

"Philip Whitney was arrested for that."

"Let's not play games. Philip Whitney was there. Thomas Nadeau was there. You were there. Luke Frederick was out in the car waiting."

Murphy slumped a little. "Maybe I should wait for Baxter."

"Up to you," Harvey said.

"My wife—"

"She's downstairs."

"Can I see her?"

"Not now."

Murphy sighed. "She came to the office this noon and told me she gave your man photos from the reunion yesterday. She also said she'd asked someone about that old burglary."

"That's right. But you're wandering from the point, Mr. Murphy. I asked you about the burglary. We know you were in on it. No shadow of a doubt."

"Then you've got Tom or Cathy."

Harvey kept quiet, but Murphy was ready to talk once they got past that.

"We didn't intend to kill that man. He walked in on us in his house. Tom got behind him and hit him. We were scared he'd identify us, but we had ski masks. It was the end of snow season, and we thought we were pretty smart. Gloves and everything. Oh, we were smart. Top

459

ten percent of the class. Even Luke Frederick. He was what they'd call a nerd nowadays. He didn't do anything. We made him go along, just for the car. He had no idea what he was getting into. But then, none of us did. When I heard the next day the man was dead, I was just sick. My whole future was going down the drain. College and law school and Alison." Murphy looked up quickly. "She never knew. I told her I was nowhere near that house, and she . . . she trusted me." He laughed bitterly. "She trusted me so much it didn't bother her when your detective started asking questions about it. She thought there was nothing to hide."

"Did you tell Nadeau we were asking?"

"When Alison told me, the first thing I thought was that I had to call Tom." Murphy shook his head. More damage control.

"What did Tom say?" Harvey asked.

"He was pretty upset. I told him to come over to my office, but he said there was something he had to do first."

"Who put the tape over Fairley's mouth?" Harvey asked.

"Philip did."

"You're not just saying that because he's already dead?"

"No. He said it would keep the guy quiet until we were out of there. I think that's how they caught Philip. He dropped his knife after he cut the tape or something. I'll own up to the vandalism, but not to killing the guy. I didn't do it."

Someone knocked on the door. Harvey opened it, and Mike and Eddie stood outside. Harvey went out, leaving Tony with Murphy.

Eddie said, "I sent Sarah and Cathy away. Here's the location." He handed Harvey a folded piece of paper. "Arnie and the guys are back." They were clustered near the door to the break room.

Mike said, "The search is started. I put the description of Nadeau's car and the plate number out. You want to send your men out on this?"

"Do we have a chance of getting him that way?"

"You got a better idea?"

Harvey told them what Murphy had said, that he wanted Nadeau to meet him at his office. "But Nadeau said he had to do something else first."

"Destroying evidence?" Eddie wondered.

"What's Murphy told you so far?" asked Mike.

"The burglary. You can watch the rest if you want."

"Let's put these men out on the street. We'll have someone watch Nadeau's house, his office, and Murphy's office, just in case. But he's probably gotten wind of Murphy's arrest already."

"Bad news travels fast," said Eddie.

"Take Nate," Harvey told him. "Tell Arnie and Pete to go out, too. Who's coordinating the search?"

Mike said, "Charlie Doran in the com room. They're bringing in an extra dispatcher. I'll have them track your detectives."

"Thanks." Harvey went back into the interview room. Tony started the tape recorder again.

"Mr. Murphy, we've established that you took part in the burglary at Richard Fairley's house. That may result in a manslaughter charge. Let's move on to the death of Philip Whitney."

Murphy swore softly. "You know everything, don't you? I couldn't believe it when I heard about it. Tom and I had talked to him the day before. Philip was going to confess. He said he couldn't stand it anymore. He was going to the police. Tom had it all worked out to protect us. He had Philip write this elaborate confession that wouldn't incriminate us. Told Philip that if he really wanted to go through that again, so be it, just don't drag us down with him. I relied on Tom a lot. It was my first big campaign. I told Tom that if the press got hold of it, my career was over, and he knew it was true. He said it was all set, Philip wouldn't tell, but I kept saying, 'How can you be sure?' Then the next day, Philip was dead."

"Did you confront Tom about it?"

"You bet I did. At first he tried to tell me he

couldn't help it if Philip killed himself. I asked him where Phil got a gun, and after a while he told me it was the gun from the burglary. I knew Tom had taken the gun at the beginning."

"So, he admitted killing Philip Whitney?"

Murphy hesitated. "Not in so many words. But he didn't deny it after that." He swung around and faced Harvey. "Look, Tom has been my friend all these years, practically all my life. He's done a lot for me. I can't just . . ." His voice trailed off.

Harvey didn't say anything. Murphy put his elbows on the table and clasped his hands, leaning on them.

"My lawyer should be here."

Harvey looked at Tony and jerked his head toward the office. Tony got the message and went out.

"Let's talk about the death of Luke Frederick," Harvey said.

"What do you want to know?"

"He came down to the shore to talk to you the morning of the reunion. It wasn't about his business."

"No. He insisted on talking to me alone, so Tom walked away, up the shore toward the lighthouse. Luke said he'd had enough, and he was going to the police. It was the same nightmare all over again. Only now I had more to lose. I begged him not to. He said I couldn't stop him, and he wasn't writing any white-washed confession the way

Philip had so Tom could kill him. Only by that time, Tom had come back and was standing right behind him." He closed his eyes. "I just . . . I was totally in shock."

"What was it that shocked you so?"

Murphy looked at Harvey, then at the tape recorder. "Tom hit him with a rock, and he fell down in the water. I wanted to pull him out. Tom said I was crazy, and to just walk away. We looked around, and there was no one else on the beach. I looked up the path, and I thought someone was up there."

"Who was it?"

"I didn't know then. His back was to us. But later I recognized Martin Blake by his clothes. He said to me he knew my secrets. When he said that at lunch, I was scared, I admit it. I said to Tom after, 'He knows,' but Tom said, 'No, he doesn't.' But Martin had a camera with a long lens. I said to Tom, 'What if he's got pictures?' I was just sick. Alison thought I had a headache. It was all I could do to stay and talk to people. I kept looking toward the water, wondering if the body would go floating past. I started once to walk back to the picnic area and look to see what showed from up above, but Tom said, 'Don't be stupid. Stay away from there. If someone goes down there and finds him, you act surprised. If not, so much the better if he floats out to sea.' "

"So, what did you do?" Harvey asked.

"I went home." Murphy covered his face with his hands.

"And Tom went after Blake," Harvey said.

"I don't know. I swear I don't know."

"But you've thought about it."

"Of course."

"Sir, I can let your wife come up here to see you for a minute if you wish, with an officer in the room. Then I'll send you down to the booking area. They'll place you in a holding cell. When your lawyer arrives, he can see you down there."

Murphy swore softly. "I can't go through with this."

"Your statement is videotaped, sir. I'll have it typed up so you can sign it, but we'll need to have you testify, too. You might get consideration for your cooperation. I can't guarantee it. There may be conspiracy charges."

"I never did anything. I was in that house that night, but that was all."

"Thomas Nadeau did a lot of damage control for you, sir. He may have taken your words at Fort Point as instructions to do away with Blake."

He swore again.

Harvey said, "Then there's Luke Frederick. Conspiracy to conceal a crime. He might have lived if you'd raised the alarm immediately. He had water in his lungs, sir. Have you thought about that these last three weeks? About how you might have saved his life?"

Tony came in. "Mrs. Murphy and the lawyer are here."

Harvey told Murphy, "You can see your wife. When she goes, Officer Winfield will put the handcuffs on you and take you down to booking." Tony nodded.

Harvey went out, and Alison Murphy and the overpaid lawyer went in past him.

The lawyer immediately asked for privacy with his client. Harvey told him he could have it downstairs, as soon as Mrs. Murphy left. Baxter went back in, and soon he and Alison came out, with Alison sobbing. Tony led Murphy out in handcuffs, and they all went to the elevator. Harvey called Terry to tell him they were on their way down.

Mike came out of Observation.

"Nice job, Harvey."

"Except the killer's still loose."

"You'll get him."

The office was empty then, except for Paula, Mike, and Harvey.

Mike said, "Ryan Toothaker was up here. I sent him away with a scrap. Told him we were tying Murphy and Frederick to the cold case burglary. Didn't mention Nadeau. Hope you don't mind. It'll give him something to write up tonight."

"Sure. Guess I'll go check with Charlie in the com room," Harvey said dejectedly. Mike went upstairs.

It was twenty minutes to five. Harvey hung around the com room for a while. Charlie assured him they would overlap all the stakeouts and field units when the shift changed. Harvey went down to Records and waited in the hall. When Jennifer came out, he told her he might not make it for counseling.

"Should I call Pastor and cancel?" she asked.

He remembered the bridal shower. "No, don't do that. I'll try to get there. If I'm late, maybe you can have that session with Mrs. Rowland."

She blushed a little. "Call me if you're going to totally miss it."

"Okay. I'd better get upstairs now."

The night patrol sergeant, Brad Lyons, flagged him down as he passed through the foyer. "Officer Bard was just going up to your office for her assignment."

Harvey walked over to Elaine Bard, who stood by the elevator. He knew the patrol officer by sight, but not well, since they worked different hours and units. She was nearly Harvey's height and attractive, with reddish hair and green eyes.

He fished in his pocket for the paper Eddie had given him and put it in her hand. "Here it is. You're prepared to stay all night to protect the witness?"

"Yes, they called me. I brought a bag."

Brad said, "Her relief will come on at 2 a.m., and we'll change it again at 8 a.m. You'd better give me the location, unless you want me to call you at two in the morning."

"Mill Pond B and B, Room 7," said Elaine, before Harvey could say anything. He had planned to tell Brad to have the relief call him at 2 a.m.

"This is strictly confidential," he said, looking hard at them.

"Of course," said Brad.

"Definitely," said Elaine. "Now, what am I dealing with?"

Harvey walked out to the garage with her, explaining that Sarah had settled the witness at the B&B an hour or two previously. "It's a very important witness for a sensitive case," he said.

Elaine nodded soberly.

Harvey decided she needed fair warning. "Her ex-husband, whom we believe is a four-time murderer, is at large. So far as I know, he's not aware that the witness is here in the city, and we need to keep it that way."

"No problem," she said.

"Elaine, be extra careful. Don't open to anyone. And don't use the house phone or let the witness use it."

"Got it."

She unlocked her car door.

"Maybe we should put another officer with you."

"I'm already late relieving Sarah."

Harvey let her go with some misgivings. He went back upstairs and drank coffee and watched the tape of Murphy's interview. Then he went over Joel Dixon's and Cathy Wagner's and Matt Beaulieu's statements. He was sure they had Nadeau cold, if they could just find him. Mike came in at quarter to six.

"I just came from the com room," he said. "Nothing yet. You ought to send the Priority guys home. You may need them tomorrow."

Harvey called Charlie Doran, and the dispatcher told him they'd had a lot of complaint calls because they had the highway buttoned up tight, with road checks at all the exits and entrance ramps. Harvey smiled. Finally he had a case important enough to snarl up the traffic on 295. The chief had ordered it, not him, so he didn't have to take the blame. It felt good.

"Can you contact my guys and send them home?" Harvey gave Charlie the list: Eddie and Nate in Eddie's truck, Pete and Arnie in Arnie's car.

"I'm heading out," Mike said. "Sharon will be hopping mad because I'm late again."

"None of us wrote our reports tonight."

"Get them to me Monday. I'll expect Nadeau's arrest to be the highlight."

As Mike left, Harvey's cell phone rang. Eddie.

"I'm staying on this thing, Harv."

"Better go home, Ed."

"Nah, we're going to get him tonight. Nate's staying, too."

"Where are you?"

"In my truck, at the subject's house."

"Real exciting surveillance, I'll bet. If I get wind of anything better, I'll call you."

Harvey sat down with a mug of coffee and started typing his report. The phone rang.

"Harvey, this is Lyons. Are you working with the state police on this thing?"

"We're sharing information on the Frederick case. Why?"

"No, I mean on the witness protection thing. Were they going to send another officer over there to help Bard?"

"No." The hair was rising on the back of his neck.

Lyons swore. "We may have blown it."

Harvey jumped up, picking up the telephone. "What happened?"

"Loose lips, that's what. Apparently one of the clerks heard Bard tell me the 10-20 when you were down here. She said the state police called a minute ago to check on a Mrs. Wagner's location because they were supposed to send a trooper over to get her. The secretary said something like, 'Is that the witness they're protecting?' "

"Don't tell me," Harvey said. "I don't want to hear it."

Lyons told him anyway. "She said it. Mill Pond

B and B, Room 7. Just like that. I heard her, and I couldn't believe it. I grabbed the phone and said, 'Who is this?' and they hung up. Harvey, I'm sorry."

"That clerk is fired, you hear me? Fired!" Harvey slammed the receiver down.

He took three deep breaths. He didn't even have the phone number. He grabbed the phone book and started looking, but his fingers and his eyes wouldn't coordinate, and he dropped the book on the floor. He pulled out his cell phone and punched Eddie's code, praying while he waited for him to answer.

"Thibodeau."

"Eddie! You remember the witness location you gave me?"

"Yeah."

"Get over there now! Someone's breached security."

"On the way."

Harvey sat down and looked up the address. He called Charlie in the com room. "Charlie, send units to 114 Bingley Lane stat."

"That's near the chief's house."

"Send anybody close over there. And alert Officer Bard her location may have been leaked."

Harvey hung up and speed-dialed Mike.

"They blabbed the location downstairs, and I think Nadeau's got it. It's on Bingley Lane. Are you near there?"

"What, the Mill Pond B and B?" Mike asked.

"Yes, yes, Room 7. What's your ETA?"

"Thirty seconds."

Harvey shoved the phone in his pocket, picked up his jacket and vest, and ran for the stairs. Even he was closer than Eddie had been, but Eddie would have quite a start on him by now. Lyons looked up anxiously when Harvey entered the foyer.

"Give me a car," Harvey said.

"Are you driving?"

"I don't think I can right now, I'm so mad."

Brad yelled, "Clifford!"

Thirty seconds later, Joe Clifford and Harvey were in a marked unit, heading for Mike's neighborhood. Charlie Doran's voice came over the radio, telling Captain Larson to call in.

"Larson," he said a moment later. "What's up, Charlie?"

"Officer Bard isn't responding to my page."

Harvey clenched his teeth. Joe had the blue lights flashing, but sirens up close gave Harvey a headache, so they kept that off. The radio band was full of noise now. Charlie had called the closest units to the target area and was pulling the outlying ones in tighter. The checks on the highway entrances closest to the target were turned into blockades.

Mike came on the radio. "This is Chief Browning. Officer down at the Mill Pond on

Bingley. 10-57. Subject has been here. The owner reports a male went upstairs. They heard a shot, and the man came out with a woman four minutes ago. No description of the vehicle."

Charlie instructed all units to watch for Nadeau's car, describing it again. Joe drove as fast as he could safely. Harvey decided to trade speed for the headache and switched the siren on to clear the street ahead.

The sun was still well above the horizon, and visibility was good. He had his glasses on, and he made out a blue light ahead, coming toward them. A black Mercedes with tinted windows came tearing along in the other lane, way over the speed limit. Nadeau's car. Right behind it was Eddie's truck, with the siren screaming and the light going.

"That's him!" Harvey yelled, and Joe made the first safe U-turn he could and took off after Eddie and Nate. Harvey cut the siren so he could hear the radio better. Nate's voice was on the air, calling in a chase in progress, with the location. Nadeau got on Route 25 and headed west out of town toward Westbrook, and Eddie's truck followed. Charlie Doran called ahead and got Westbrook police out in front of them.

Harvey and Joe stayed on Eddie's back bumper until they heard that Westbrook was throwing spike mats down up ahead, then they backed off. Eddie kept hounding Nadeau, but Harvey knew he was prepared for a quick stop. Several other units were behind them now.

Oncoming traffic disappeared, and he knew Westbrook's road block was in place. They gave Nadeau some space between the spike mats and the blockade beyond them.

He saw the police vehicles and the row of mats at the last minute. Eddie's brake lights came on. Harvey couldn't see past his truck very well, but Nadeau hit his brakes and swerved toward the shoulder, hitting the mat with the driver's side tires. Harvey prayed he wouldn't flip the Mercedes. He hadn't seen Cathy Wagner when the car whizzed by, but he was sure she was in there.

The black car fishtailed and came to a halt just short of the blockade, passenger side to them. Eddie parked with his tires inches from the spike mat, and he and Nate got out, shielding themselves behind the truck doors. Joe parked beside Eddie. Harvey got out and ran to Eddie's position. The Mercedes just sat there.

"Think he's hurt?" Harvey asked.

"Dunno. Better put your vest on," Eddie said.

Harvey had thrown it in the back seat with his jacket. "Wait," he said.

Three more patrol cars nosed up behind them. Nate and Eddie both had vests, and they started folding up the nearest mats. A couple of Westbrook guys on the other side started yelling at Nadeau over a speaker, "Get out of the car. Get out of the car."

Harvey yelled, "Joe, get on the radio and tell them this guy has a hostage, and to back off!" Joe waved in acknowledgement.

Nate had the mat out of the way enough so Eddie could drive closer to Nadeau. They both got in the truck, and Eddie eased it to within ten yards of the Mercedes. Harvey had his vest on and the holster over it, and he instructed Joe to follow Eddie.

"Does this car have a speaker?"

Joe reached up and switched it on. Harvey took the mouthpiece and said, "Nadeau, give it up."

The passenger window went down about four inches.

"Nadeau, let Cathy go. You can't gain anything here."

A gun barrel eased out the gap at the top of the window and Harvey told Joe, "Get down!" He and Joe ducked below the dash. They heard the shot. Harvey sat up. The Mercedes window was up. His cell phone rang.

"Harv." It was Eddie. His vehicle was closer to Nadeau's than Joe and Harvey's was. "I think I've got a bullet in my radiator."

"You guys okay?"

"Yeah."

"Did you see Cathy Wagner?"

"I didn't see anything but the gun and some movement."

"Stay low."

Eddie said, "Do we need a negotiator?"

"I don't know what we need," Harvey said. "Are you praying?" Joe shot him a glance, then looked forward again.

"Yes," Eddie said. "You know Mike has training. Or Cranston or Wood."

"Okay, let's sign off, and I'll try to get Mike."

Mike answered his phone immediately.

"I'm right behind you, Harv."

Harvey looked back, and behind six or seven squad cars, he saw Mike's vehicle.

"Can you come up here?"

"10-4." Mike drove up as close as he could and came the rest of the way on foot because police cars completely blocked the road now. Harvey got out and walked behind the car to meet him.

"Nice situation here," Harvey said.

Mike peered ahead. "Has he got the woman?"

"Didn't see her, but he must. We've got a speaker."

"Got another vest?"

"No. Take mine."

Harvey held Mike's holster while he put the vest on.

"Officer Bard gonna make it?" Harvey asked.

"Got her in the shoulder. She was bleeding a lot."

"Did you call Sharon?"

"Yep. About ten minutes ago. She was mad, all right."

Mike took the microphone, and Harvey stayed behind the car.

"What do you want, Tom?" Mike called.

No answer.

"Tom, this is Chief Browning. What do you want?"

The window slid down again. Four inches. Six. Eight. Cathy Wagner's head became visible. Nadeau's left arm was around her neck, and his right hand held a gun to her right temple.

"Throw the gun out, Tom," Mike said.

"Go to hell."

Somebody's going to, Harvey thought, and he started praying again.

"All right, Tom, keep the gun. Just let Cathy go."

"No way."

"What do you want?"

No answer.

"Come on, Tom, you must want something."

"Just let me go."

"How far do you think you'll get?" Mike asked.

"I was thinking maybe Brazil."

"Not going to happen, Tom. You know that."

"I'm not giving you this witness."

"We've got other witnesses," Mike said. "We've got your pal David Murphy in a cell right now. He told us everything. We've got another witness who saw you kill Luke Frederick. Cathy won't do you any harm. Let her go, Tom."

Harvey walked up behind Mike. Mike looked at him, then back at the Mercedes. The front door of the black car opened just a crack.

"Get down, Harv," said Mike. Eddie and Nate crouched behind the truck doors. The car door opened slowly. When it was halfway open, Cathy Wagner's body, in the white slacks and red and white shirt, fell out, limp, to the pavement. Harvey thought she was dead, but then she moved her arm.

"Okay, Tom," said Mike. "Now throw the gun out. Nice and slow."

The car door closed. Cathy lay on the tar. Her head moved very slowly. She raised it a tiny bit, and looked toward them. Her face was bloody. Her left arm reached out toward them, and she hitched her body an inch closer.

Mike said, "There's an ambulance behind my car, Harvey. Go back there and try to clear things enough so they can get up here. We can't let her lie there long."

Harvey turned away and heard a muffled shot. He spun around. Mike was looking hard at the Mercedes.

"What was it?"

"Nadeau, I think."

Eddie ran crouched toward the black car, with

478

his gun in both hands in front of him. He flattened himself low against the rear fender. Slowly, he reached forward and pulled the rear door handle. The back door swung open. He ducked quickly down to look inside, the gun in front of his face, then ducked back out again. He did it again, slower this time, then waved.

Harvey said, "Joe, get that ambulance up here," and ran with Mike and Nate to the Mercedes.

Eddie was bending over Cathy Wagner on the pavement. He looked up at them. "Shot himself in the head."

Mike went around the car and opened the driver's door. The Westbrook police were walking out to meet them.

Harvey knelt beside Cathy. "Mrs. Wagner, can you hear me?"

"Yes." It was barely a whisper.

"What hurts, Cathy?"

"My neck and my back and—" She turned her head and laid her cheek on the pavement.

"We've got an ambulance here for you." Harvey stood up. The EMT's were running toward them, carrying their gear.

"Jeff!"

"Harvey! What happened? Is she shot?"

"I don't think so. She said her neck and her back hurt. He was choking her, I think. There's blood on her face, maybe from where she hit the tar."

They backed off so Jeff and Mark Johnson could work.

Harvey walked around to the other side of the Mercedes.

Mike straightened. "Awful mess, Harv. We need the M.E."

Harvey sent Nate to call for the medical examiner.

Harvey was late, and he knew it. It was almost eight o'clock when he was able to leave the scene.

Jeff had said he thought Cathy Wagner would stabilize, and he and Mark had put her on a back board and taken her in the ambulance. The M.E. had come and gone, and the hearse had followed. The Mercedes sat on the shoulder, awaiting the tow truck they'd called. The road had been cleared of police cars. Westbrook's contingent had loaded up their spike mats and gone home. Only two units remained, tying up the loose ends.

They held an impromptu press conference on the side of the road, with Mike and Harvey giving the basics of the chase. Mike had shooed the reporters off to their computers, promising complete information at the police station at ten the next morning.

Word came over the radio that Elaine Bard was at Maine Medical, serious but stable.

"I'll go over there," Mike said.

"I should go."

"No, Harv, you have other places to be tonight. Stop by the hospital in the morning."

Harvey nodded reluctantly.

"Come into the office at nine," Mike said. "We'll go over the presentation for the press."

Eddie offered to drive Harvey to the church. The bullet had missed his radiator, and the truck seemed none the worse except for a scar on the front bumper. Harvey sent Nate back to the police station for his car with Joe, telling him to rest well over the weekend and lose the uniform.

"There's blood on your jacket," said Eddie. "Want to go change?"

Harvey looked down. Cathy's blood. "No, I'll just take it off. Can I leave it in the truck?"

"*Mais oui*. It's not good to show up for a date with blood all over you."

By the time they arrived at the church, the pastor's study was empty, and a party was in full swing in the fellowship hall. Harvey and Eddie walked down the hallway. Fifty women and the pastor. Mr. Rowland was eating cake and cracking jokes. Jennifer sat in the seat of honor, holding up a toaster. Now they had three.

"The groom has arrived!" Beth shouted when she saw Harvey, and all the ladies turned to look at him and Eddie and clapped.

Mrs. Rowland put a paper plate with a piece of cake on it in Harvey's hand, and at least three single girls went to get one for Eddie. Harvey looked at it and decided he didn't want to dump that much sugar into an empty stomach.

Neither of the two detectives had been to a bridal shower before, but Harvey decided that if the pastor could, they could. Someone placed a chair beside Jennifer for him, and he sat down and smiled at her.

"Everything all right?" she asked.

"Yes, fine."

She was struggling with silver ribbon. He managed to hand off the cake to somebody behind him, then brought out his pocketknife and sliced through the ribbon for her. The package was wrapped in paper covered with umbrellas and flowers. Jennifer peeled the paper off and opened the box. Trash bags.

"That's got to be from Beth," Harvey said.

Jennifer laughed. "It is. And we now have towels in every color of the rainbow."

"Great. You'll only have to do laundry once a month."

"It doesn't work that way."

He couldn't believe all the stuff she got that night, and this was only the prelim. Glasses, clothespins, dishrags, a wastebasket, pillowcases, steak knives, a jam kettle, and a teapot.

At last she had opened everything.

"Did you eat?" she asked.

He opened his mouth, then shut it again.

"Thought so." She made him go over to the food table with her. They were in the cake stage, but there were little sandwiches left, and chips and pickles and carrot sticks. Jennifer filled a plate for him and asked Mrs. Williams if they had any milk. They did, for the coffee, and she emptied the last of it into a paper cup for him. He ate a little bit and drank the milk. Eddie was stuffing the cake down and drinking red punch. Cast iron stomach on that kid.

The guests began to leave, and Beth took charge of packing up the gifts.

Eddie picked up a clothesbasket full of pans and said, "Did you know this church has a singles class during Sunday school?"

"Yes," said Harvey.

"And you didn't tell me?"

"Eddie, it's been there all the time."

"I didn't know. Three people told me about it tonight."

"Let me guess. Three single women."

"Well, yeah. You think they just want more men in there?"

"Probably eighty percent of the class is female."

"This is bad?" Eddie asked.

Harvey picked up a pile of boxes and followed him out toward Jennifer's car. "No, you're right. It would be a good place for you to meet Christian girls."

"So, how come you and Jennifer don't go to this class?"

"Two reasons. One, we won't be single after next week. Two, I'm old."

"So it's for young singles? Are we talking high school here?" Eddie handed him a cookbook and a throw pillow.

"No, I think you'll be right at home. You should try it. Go Sunday morning, and tell me what you think."

They loaded presents into Eddie's truck and Jennifer's car and Beth's car.

"We ought to take all of this right to the new house," Beth said as Eddie fit the last box into her trunk. Instead, they unloaded it at the little house, and she and Jennifer piled it all up in the living room.

Jennifer said, "Tomorrow, instead of chasing a lighthouse, we'd better do some moving, don't you think?"

"I have to go to the station in the morning," Harvey said. "Mike's orders, but after a briefing with him and a press conference, I'm free."

"I think we'd better move you over to Van Cleeve Lane and take all of this stuff, too." Jennifer surveyed the pile of boxes. "I wish I didn't have to work next week."

She had signed up for the twelve-week summer job before they set the wedding date, and she was getting Week 6 off for the honeymoon, but had felt she couldn't ask for more. Harvey was starting to wish they both had two weeks off after the wedding, but it was too late to change any of that.

When they'd unloaded everything, Jennifer pressed him for the details of their day's work. She had told Beth of David Murphy's arrest, but the later happenings were news to them, and Harvey let Eddie tell it. He sat back, half listening and half watching Jennifer's reaction.

Beth and Jennifer were a good audience, but Harvey was getting sleepy. He'd been tense all day, and finally was able to relax. He nodded off on the couch and awoke to hear Eddie saying, "Don't mind him, he's old." He roused himself, and Eddie reluctantly said goodbye to the girls and took him home.

Chapter 20

Saturday, July 10 and beyond

Harvey slept dreamlessly his last night at the apartment. Jeff called him from the fire station the next morning and told him Cathy Wagner would be all right in time. Her husband had come up from Epsom, and Jeff had met him at the hospital. He was furious with the police department and would no doubt pay the captain a visit at the police station to vent his wrath.

"How do you like the new job?" Harvey asked.

"Great," Jeff said. "They threw me in with my clothes on last night with that shooting, but I think I'm really going to like living down here."

Harvey smiled. "Your sister had a bridal shower at the church last night, and we now have enough household goods to open an emporium. If you need a toaster or towels, see Jennifer."

"How's Beth?" Jeff asked.

"What, you haven't called her yet this morning?"

"No."

Harvey held back his laugh. "She was fine last night. But she's quit sassing me. Funny. She was always so mouthy."

"Beth? Mouthy?"

"The worst. But for the past few days she's been almost feminine."

"Must be the weather."

"I don't think so."

"Maybe you've been more polite to her, and she's responding," Jeff suggested.

"No, I'm still giving her what for."

"She's never mouthy when I'm around."

"Oh, maybe that's it. Do you think?"

After Mike's briefing at the station, Harvey prepared for the press conference. He opened it by giving the solution of the old burglary and Fairley's murder to the reporters, along with background on the four teenagers who had committed the crime. Then he worked his way up through the revolver concealed fourteen years until Philip Whitney's death, the reunion, Luke Frederick's death, and the murder of Martin Blake because Murphy thought the author saw too much.

Mike took over to elaborate on Friday's events and gave medical updates on Elaine and Cathy. He had consulted the district attorney, and it looked like Mrs. Wagner would not be charged if she continued to cooperate.

With Thelma Blake's permission, Harvey gave Ryan Toothaker a bonus, copies of her husband's last photos. The *Press Herald* ran them on the front page the next day, with Ryan's sidebar on an 11-year-old boy's identification of Luke Frederick's murderer.

Harvey stopped at the hospital to see Elaine. She was groggy, but doing all right. Flowers and balloons vied for space around the bed.

"How are you feeling, Elaine?" he asked.

"Sore. I let you down, Captain."

"Don't talk that way."

"You gave me the location on paper. I shouldn't have said it to Lyons the way I did."

"It happened. Next time you'll be more careful."

"I'm thinking I did a lousy job of protecting Cathy Wagner."

Harvey shook his head. "I made a poor decision. I should have insisted on two officers with her. I knew Nadeau was out there, and you shouldn't have been alone."

"He busted in the door," she said.

"Yeah. That was not your fault." He held up a paper bag. "I brought you something."

"Not one of Martin Blake's books, I hope."

Harvey laughed. "No, it's chocolate."

Elaine smiled. "Thanks, Captain. That's almost as good as what Sarah Benoit brought me."

"What was that?"

"A picture of Cathy Wagner in her room down the hall. I'm so glad she survived."

After lunch, Harvey, Rick, and Eddie came to Jennifer's house to help move furniture.

"We've already put my bed and bookshelves in

the new house," Harvey reported. "I'm leaving the sofa at the apartment for Jeff, at least until he gets his old bed down here from Skowhegan."

"What about the kitchen table?" Jennifer asked, remembering the day he had bought it.

"Well, yeah, I guess Jeff can keep that if he wants it," Harvey said soberly. "We've got one at Van Cleeve Lane."

"No single man should live without a table," Eddie said. "It warps you somehow."

"Watch it," Harvey said.

Jennifer smiled. "I guess the shower presents should go first."

She had a great time with Beth and Ruthann, putting away utensils and linens with Ruthann and Rick's babies underfoot. Beth ran to the grocery store while the men went for another load from Harvey's apartment, and when they returned, she was taking hot muffins out of the oven.

The location for setting up the computers was a quandary. They all discussed it over muffins. Upstairs there were four empty bedrooms, so Harvey and Jennifer could each claim one for a study, but Harvey said that seemed rather isolationist.

Eddie jerked his head toward the dining room. "What's in there?"

"Nothing," Harvey said.

"Nothing? Just nothing?"

"No, it was the dining room, but Mr. Bailey sold all the furniture."

Eddie walked to the doorway and looked in. "Are you going to buy more dining room furniture?"

"Not right away," Jennifer said, looking at Harvey.

Harvey nodded. "We like to eat in the kitchen."

"What about when you have company?" Ruthann asked.

"We have company right now, and we're eating in the kitchen," Harvey pointed out. "Are you insulted?"

They ended up turning the dining room into the computer room, and Eddie and Rick helped them get everything up and running. By this time, Harvey's apartment and Jennifer and Beth's house were starting to look a little bare. They both had CD players, so Jennifer's went in the living room and Harvey's in the bedroom. Her TV and DVD player went in the living room, too, and they put Harvey's in the sunroom.

"This is obscene," Beth said. "You have two of everything."

"Maybe I should leave some of it for you," said Jennifer. "You have a TV, though."

"Hold it." Rick held up both hands. "This is normal for two adults who've lived alone for years. No guilt necessary."

Harvey had claimed he didn't have much

stuff, but once they started moving it, it kept expanding. Even so, his clothes took about a fifth of the closet space in the master bedroom. Jeff had brought Jennifer's bike from home, and he put it in the garage. Harvey's tools looked lonely out there, with the wide workbench around them nearly bare. Mr. Bailey had left the lawnmower and various other gardening implements.

"I'm starting to feel like a homeowner," Harvey told Jennifer. "For the first time in my life, I have my own hose and wheelbarrow."

They transported more of Jennifer's things—her desk, rocking chair, CDs, and books. When she took Harvey and Rick into her bedroom to show them the bookcase she wanted moved, Harvey stopped and stared at the wall. She had requested a photo of Harvey in his Kevlar vest after he'd been injured that spring, and a poster-size copy hung in her room.

Rick laughed when he saw it. "I guess we know who your hero is, Jennifer."

"That's not going to the new house, is it?" Harvey asked.

"It most certainly is," she said.

Her Van Gogh print found a new home in the sunroom, and they agreed Harvey's coffee table was ugly, so they kept Jennifer's. He hung a small shelf on the wall near the kitchen table, and the flow blue plate he'd bought for her went there.

Beth turned on the evening news at six o'clock. Harvey and Mike starred in the lead story, with clips from that morning's press conference. Beth recorded it while they unpacked. In the next half hour, she also caught a shortened version on national news. The arrest of the congressman and his henchman, along with the unraveling of the famous author's murder, was a huge story. The police station had received calls from news agencies all over the country.

"Does it still bother you to watch yourself, Harvey?" Beth asked.

"Not as much. Our side won this one, and the reporters aren't casting aspersions on the P.D.'s competence."

The Bradleys, Eddie, and Jennifer took a straw vote and agreed he projected confidence during the press conference, and he and Mike looked sharp.

When the national broadcast was over, Jennifer kissed him on the cheek. "You did great."

"Thanks." Harvey stood. "Show's over, folks. Eddie, I think it's time we fed these people."

"I saw a pizza place a few blocks from here," Eddie said.

They brought back three pizzas and cold drinks, and they all crowded around the kitchen table once more. Harvey's cell phone rang while they were eating. He looked at the screen then put the call on speaker with a wink at Jennifer.

"Hello, Mrs. Weymouth," he said. Ruthann's jaw dropped, but the rest of them weren't shocked.

"Excellent job, Larson," the mayor said. "Blake's murder solved, and some old cases to boot. I knew I made the right decision last week. You and Browning have exceeded expectations."

"Thank you, ma'am," Harvey said. "It was hard work, but it all came together in the end."

"I understand you're getting married soon."

"Yes, ma'am, a week from today."

"Congratulations!"

"Thank you." He smiled broadly at Jennifer.

"My invitation must be in the mail."

"Uh—" The smile slipped.

The mayor laughed.

"Would you want to attend, Mrs. Weymouth?" Harvey asked cautiously.

"I'd be honored. I'm told the bride is lovely."

"She's—"

Harvey gazed at Jennifer, and she was glad the mayor couldn't see her, sitting on a stool, bare-footed, in her cutoff jeans and dust-smeared Piglet T-shirt, with her hair in long braids and probably pizza sauce on her chin. She held her breath, waiting for his reply, her cheeks flaming.

"She's perfect," Harvey said, and Jennifer exhaled. "I'll hand deliver your invitation Monday morning," Harvey added.

Jennifer nodded, but she hoped the wedding

wasn't turning into a circus. She puffed out a breath when he'd signed off. "Wow."

"Double wow," Ruthann said. She turned to Rick. "Honey, can I get a new dress for the wedding?"

"Why not?" Rick shrugged. "It's not every day you socialize with the mayor."

He and Ruthann packed up the kids and left soon after. Eddie, Beth, and Jennifer stayed a little longer with Harvey. This would be his first night at the new house.

"We forgot to bring the games over," Beth said. "The next Trivial Pursuit tournament can be held here."

Jennifer smiled. She looked forward to evenings in front of the fireplace with their friends. The four of them prayed together, and she knew it would be a happy house.

Eddie and Beth went out, and she lingered in the breezeway with Harvey, seeing them off.

"I saw Margaret yesterday," Jennifer said softly.

"Margaret Turner? Where?"

"At her office. My checkup."

"Oh, right."

Eddie and Beth drove out, and they waved. Harvey put his arms around Jennifer, and she said, "She had me make another appointment for September."

"Something wrong?"

"No, just . . . she thought I might need it.

Her office is really busy, and it's hard to get appointments at the last minute." She had her sandals on now, and she kicked at the cocoa mat. Surely she didn't need to spell it out for someone as brilliant as Harvey, the man who wanted children while he was semi-young.

"You had me worried, Pocahontas." He tugged one braid gently so she'd look at him.

"Where are we staying next Saturday?" she asked.

"I made a reservation at the Oakwood. Eddie will take us to the airport Sunday."

"We could stay here."

His eyebrows lowered in a frown. "You don't want to go to London?"

"I mean just Saturday night. It would save us a hundred bucks or so."

"A hundred seventy-five," he said. "You want to come here instead? No room service."

"You can buy cereal and milk and coffee."

"You'd really rather stay here?" He sounded eager.

She looked deeply into his eyes. "I'm really looking forward to being here with you."

He smiled. "You got it, gorgeous. Come on, I'll drive you home."

The Wainthrops descended en masse on Thursday night. Jeff was working again after his two-day hiatus, but would have Friday and the wedding day off. The Wainthrops parked Travis and Randy at the apartment. The boys helped set up Jeff's bed and move the couch to the new house.

Abby and Leeanne and their luggage went to Beth and Jennifer's, and their parents and Grandpa Wainthrop would stay at Van Cleeve Lane with Harvey. He and Jennifer had managed to have the two furnished rooms upstairs ready for them. Beth, enjoying her summer vacation, saw that the family had what they needed while the bride and groom went off to work on Friday.

Jennifer's father had promised Harvey he would visit the police station, and he and Grandpa went that afternoon. They seemed very impressed with the setup in the Priority Unit. Paula brought coffee to the break room for the three of them, and Nate and Pete came in to politely update Harvey on their cases.

"So, you're the boss here now," said George, stirring sugar into his coffee.

"Make sure you boss Jennifer at home, too," said Grandpa. Harvey had never met him before, but he liked Grandpa Wainthrop. In his late seventies, he was still active and witty.

"I get enough bossing in around here," Harvey said. "I think I'll just want to be coddled at home."

"Coddled or cuddled?" Grandpa hooted.

Jennifer was waiting for them in the parking lot

when they arrived at the church that evening for the rehearsal.

"Harvey, we got twenty more RSVPs today."

"Wow. Okay."

"Do you think we'll have enough cake?" she wailed. Her gray eyes looked a little panicky. "I think every cop in Portland is coming, and bringing his family along."

"Good day to rob a bank," observed Eddie.

"Oh, shut up," said Jennifer. They both stared at her.

"I'm sorry, I'm sorry." She was crying now.

"My exit line," Eddie said, and high-tailed it into the church.

Harvey took her in his arms and gave her his handkerchief. "It's okay, baby. We'll figure everything out."

When the tears abated, he took her inside to seek advice from her mother and the Rowlands.

"How many people?" Marilyn Wainthrop asked.

"Around two hundred seventy-five, at the last count," Jennifer said.

"Seating's not a problem, but you might need more ushers," the pastor said. "Maybe a couple of our church ushers would help out."

"They won't match the other guys," said Jennifer.

"They don't need to. They won't be standing

up front. They can just help seat people, then disappear."

"My brother will do it," Beth said.

"Get Dan Wyman, too," Eddie suggested. "I'm sure he'd do it."

Beth went to call Rick and Dan.

"The mayor is coming," Jennifer quavered. "I've never even met her, and she's bringing her husband."

"Just pray Tony Winfield doesn't bring his uncle," Harvey quipped. Jennifer started crying again.

"Let's call the bakery," said Marilyn.

Mary Rowland, the pastor's wife, nodded. "Good idea. And the church ladies making sandwiches and salads can just make more. I'll go to my house and start calling from there."

"And call the florist, please," Jennifer yelled after her mother. "We'll need extra boutonnieres for Dan and Rick."

The rehearsal went forward, and Marilyn emerged from the pastor's study halfway through. "Mrs. Lundquist has extra cake layers frozen," she announced. "A customer broke her engagement at the last minute, and she'd already baked the layers. They're thawing as we speak, and she'll frost them to match the other cake."

"We're going to have two cakes?" Harvey asked. Dollar signs were ringing up in his brain.

"Yes. She and her husband will be here by

8 a.m. to set them up and do the final decorating."

"We should have invited her to the wedding," Harvey said.

"Your baker?" Marilyn was startled.

"She helped us out a lot on the Blake case. She was his classmate, loaned us her yearbook and everything."

"Why don't we just invite the whole class?" Jennifer said, her voice rising impossibly high.

"Well, Thelma Blake asked me if she could come, and I said yes," Eddie said.

Jennifer put her hands to her temples, her eyes wild.

Pastor Rowland said, "Stay calm, everyone. Let's have the wedding party back on their marks and get through this."

Harvey and Eddie found their masking tape markers at the front of the church, and the women practiced coming down the aisle again. Beth, then Leeanne, then Abby, then Jennifer on George's arm.

Eddie, as the only bachelor in the wedding party, divided his smiles among the bridesmaids. He had met Abby only briefly, and he seemed a bit awed by her. She had a strong resemblance to Jennifer, and she wore a long braid that night, the same hairstyle Jennifer often chose. Leeanne's dark hair was loose, and she was beautiful in her own way—the kind of dilemma Eddie relished, but Harvey hoped the sisters weren't headed for hard feelings. Beth got her share of Eddie's attention as well, but he understood Jeff was staking out that territory.

They practiced stepping up on the platform for the vows, and Jennifer practiced handing Abby her flowers. Pastor Rowland made Harvey repeat the vows until he could do it without stumbling. He just had to think about it. It would have been simple if Jennifer hadn't stood there, looking him expectantly in the face.

They lit the candles to make sure they'd light. He practiced blowing out Jennifer's candle, so she wouldn't catch her veil on fire. They even practiced kissing, so it wouldn't be messy the next day. Pastor Rowland approved the three-second version.

Finally, the pastor declared they were ready for the wedding, and they all went to eat a late supper at a Chinese restaurant.

People started arriving shortly after noon, an hour before the wedding was supposed to begin. Harvey paced the dressing room. Mike and Carl had their tuxedoes on and were ready. They were assisted by Rick Bradley and Dan Wyman, who stood by in the entry in their best Sunday suits to help seat people.

The photo session had taken place earlier. It had taken some persuasion to overcome Jennifer's bias about Harvey seeing her in the wedding dress before the ceremony, but George was on Harvey's side in the interest of efficiency, and he had convinced Jennifer it was best to get the pictures out of the way.

Jennifer had been gorgeous at the session, wearing the traditional white gown, the gold locket Harvey had given her hanging at her throat. Her eyes were like the stars in the Van Gogh painting, and her hair braided and wrapped on top of her head like the bridesmaids'.

After the photographer was done, Eddie made Harvey stay in the room they had dressed in. They peeled off their jackets, vests and ties to keep from getting all sweaty before the ceremony. A fan hummed before the screened window. Somebody had left sandwiches, cookies, and soda in the dressing room, but Harvey couldn't eat anything. After twenty minutes or so, he started the pacing.

"You're doing the right thing," Eddie said.

"Of course." No doubt about that, but his stomach was still rioting. Harvey took a deep breath and looked out the window. The parking lot was jam-packed.

Finally Pastor Rowland came in. "Better get dressed, guys."

"How many people?" Harvey asked.

"It's filling up fast. We're having the men bring more chairs up from the fellowship hall."

"Is the mayor here?"

"Not yet." Rowland went out.

Eddie helped Harvey with the vest and bow tie, and Harvey helped him. Eddie started putting his holster on over the vest.

"You're not really going to, are you?" Harvey asked. It suddenly seemed inappropriate.

"Well, what am I supposed to do? Leave it in the Sunday School room for an hour or two?"

Mike came in. "You guys ready?"

"Mike, are you wearing your gun?" Eddie asked.

He opened his tux jacket and displayed his badge and holster.

"See?" said Eddie.

"There are about fifty officers out there in uniform, anyway," said Mike. "They're all wearing their sidearms."

"Okay." Harvey had left his in his locker the night before. He pulled his jacket out of his garment bag and put it on. "Just don't tell Jennifer."

"You've got backup." Eddie took his badge off his discarded shirt and pinned it to his vest, where it wouldn't show under the tuxedo jacket.

Mike looked Harvey up and down. "You look great."

"Thanks. Where's the mayor?" Harvey asked.

"On the groom's side with most of the cops and your sisters and your ex-grandmother-in-law. Oh, and Thelma Blake and all the Thibodeaus."

Eddie grinned. "This is going to be a great party."

Mike handed Harvey a folded piece of paper. "Gotta run."

He unfolded it and saw Jennifer's handwriting. *Today and always.* He smiled and tucked it in his pocket.

"You want to send a reply?" Eddie asked.

Harvey got his notebook and pen and stood there, thinking. "It's got to be something romantic, but not silly."

"How about, *You're my top priority now*?"

"That's corny."

The pastor came in and told them it was time to follow him to the anteroom. Harvey scrawled, *I love you.* When they stepped out into the hallway, he saw Leeanne in her royal blue gown, peeking over the railing where steps went up to classrooms and the balcony. She looked grownup with her hair up, but childish hanging over the railing. Maybe all the Wainthrop girls had that knack.

He stepped over and handed the note up to her. "Take this to Jenny?" She nodded and disappeared up the stairs. Eddie watched her go.

Carl came striding over and took Harvey's pulse with exaggerated concern. "If you live through the next hour, you should make a good recovery. Just remember to breathe."

They went through hallways and past the

entrance to the baptistry, into a small room that opened into the sanctuary at the side of the platform. Pastor Rowland peeked out. The music was changing.

"Mrs. Wainthrop is being seated," he said. "Ready?"

Harvey and Eddie followed him out and found their marks, and Carl and Mike joined them.

The candles were lit, and the church was packed. Church members filled the back half, and uniforms dotted the crowd.

Harvey's sisters, Gina and Rita, were grinning and crying at the same time. Gina's 12-year-old, Alissa, gave him a tiny wave, and Harvey smiled back. Mayor Weymouth and her husband sat behind them, next to Thelma Blake, who was resplendent in a platinum wig and a silver lamé dress. In the next row sat Marcia Towne and two teen-aged boys. Those couldn't be Chris's boys. On second glance, Harvey guessed they could. Grandma Lewis was smiling contentedly, and he caught her eye and smiled. Over on the other side, Jeff, Travis, and Randy looked well-scrubbed and formal in neckties, in the row behind their mother.

Beth was starting down the aisle.

Eddie inhaled sharply, and Harvey looked at him.

"Sarah," Eddie whispered.

"Where?"

"Six rows back, on the aisle."

Harvey spotted her as Beth reached the front and Leeanne started down. Sarah was wearing a bright pink dress, not her uniform, and beside her was a tall, dark-haired man.

"Who's the guy?" he asked, but Eddie was watching the bridesmaids now.

Leeanne was striking, and if anything, Abby was more so. She looked so much like Jennifer, Harvey almost put his glasses on.

When Jennifer and George stepped into the doorway, he had trouble breathing, like the day he'd been shot. Her white dress was demure and lacy, and her mom's lace-edged veil swept the floor. But under it, her hair fell loose to her hips. No braids. No hairpins. No elastic bands. She'd taken it down during the last hour, and he knew it was just for him.

"You okay?" said Eddie.

"No."

"You gonna pass out?"

"No. I can't in front of the mayor."

Beyond Eddie, Carl was looking anxiously at him. He whispered something to Eddie, and Eddie relayed to Harvey, "Carl says, breathe!"

Jennifer smiled at him, not looking at anyone else. Harvey breathed.

George was looking a little shaky himself as he handed Jennifer over to him. When the ring slid onto her finger, Harvey just about burst.

"Mr. and Mrs. Harvey A. Larson." He grinned all the way down the aisle and out the door of the church. Cameramen and reporters thronged the walkway.

"Who invited you?" Harvey asked Ryan Toothaker.

"This is a big event," Ryan said.

"You're doing stories for the society page now?"

Video crews from two TV stations had set up on the pavement. Harvey couldn't believe it. He looked at Jennifer, afraid she would cry again.

"We can get mad, or we can laugh," he said.

"Let's laugh and forget about it!"

He squeezed her hand, and they walked down the sidewalk and into the fellowship hall door. He wished they had gone through the halls inside, but the press loved it. They chased after them, asking how they'd met, who designed Jennifer's gown, and where they were honeymooning.

They got inside and took up their spot for the receiving line. Harvey thought Jennifer would collapse before it ended. After half an hour of it, he asked Jeff to bring her a stool. She kicked off her shoes and perched on it for the duration. Harvey told Rick to make sure the guests knew they could eat.

He met so many Wainthrops that day, his head whirled. Grandma Lewis was adopted by Carl, Margaret, and Julia, and was having a great time.

She kissed Jennifer and whispered something to her that made her smile. Marcia Towne told Harvey she was thinking of remarrying, and that she was glad Harvey had found the right woman after all these years. He was happy for her, too. It had been really hard on her when she'd lost Chris.

Jennifer's old working pals, Jane Morrow and John Macomber, came around to chat with her for a minute and compare software settlements. Harvey's sisters cried on him a little bit. He'd talked to them both on the phone after the Murphy-Nadeau story hit the airwaves, but he wished that he'd had more time to spend with them. All of the police officers brought their families through the line. Harvey met Nate's wife and children for the first time.

Finally they got to go to their party. Jennifer took her veil off, so Harvey wouldn't step on it as they went from friend to friend. They were supposed to eat, but even Jennifer seemed too keyed up to sit down and look at food.

Jeff was hanging around Beth, and Harvey glimpsed Sarah and her escort talking with other cops. Sarah had introduced the man in the receiving line, with no explanation. Eddie didn't seem worried about her, but was carrying on a stereo flirtation with Abby and Leeanne.

"How soon can we leave?" Jennifer whispered in Harvey's ear.

"Uh, don't we have to eat cake or something?"

She took his hand and pulled him quickly out into the hallway. As soon as they were out of sight of the doorway, she threw her arms around him. "I love these people, but I've about had it, Harvey."

He kissed her. Not the altar kiss, the other one.

When they went back toward the fellowship hall, Jeff was talking earnestly to Beth just outside the doorway.

Harvey said to him, "We've got to do some fast cake eating and flower throwing so we can get out of here."

"Sure," said Jeff.

Beth said, "Go to it." Harvey wondered if that was their cue for car decorating.

They cut the first slice amid dozens of clicking cameras and left the rest of the cake for Mrs. Williams to deal with. Harvey thought his eyes would never recover from all the camera flashes. Reporters had somehow been absorbed into the crowd and were eating cake.

Arnie came by with two cups of punch in his hands. "How you holding up, Captain?"

"Okay," Harvey said, "but I don't understand what makes this event so interesting to strangers."

Arnie laughed. "Enjoy it."

"Who's that guy?" Harvey asked Jennifer, nodding toward a tall young man with a cake plate in his hand.

"I thought you invited him."

"How can this happen?"

"I have no idea," she said.

They went to the table where her parents and grandfather were seated, eating cake with the mayor and her husband. Mike and Sharon were telling them all about their trip in the Allagash. Jennifer whispered in her mother's ear.

"Already?" said Marilyn.

Jennifer shrugged.

"My dear, you haven't danced with the groom yet," said Mayor Weymouth.

"We're not dancing today, ma'am," Harvey said.

"Oh, I was looking forward to it," the mayor said.

Jennifer said to her mom, "I'll get Beth and Abby to help me with the dress."

"What, I don't get to come?" Harvey asked.

She halted in confusion. "Well, it takes two people to get me out of this dress."

He smiled and squeezed her hand. "I'll meet you in the entry in fifteen minutes."

That seemed to please her, and she went after her bridesmaids.

Harvey walked over to the guy neither of them could claim and stuck out his hand.

"Hi, I'm Harvey. You must be a friend of Jennifer's."

"No, actually, I've never met her before. I'm Dave Veilleux, Eddie's cousin."

"Oh, right. We played basketball once."

"Yeah. Congratulations!"

"Thanks," Harvey said.

He collared Eddie and dragged him away from a girl he'd never seen before. "Come help me get ready."

Eddie followed him down the hall to the room they had changed in.

"Boy, you Thibodeaus are literalists, aren't you?" Harvey asked, shaking his head.

"What do you mean?"

"I just met your cousin Dave. I guess when the invitation says, '*M. et Mme. Thibodeau et famille,*' you figure it means the whole clan."

"That would be my mother," said Eddie. "I'm sorry, Harv, but this wedding turned out to be the event everybody wanted to be at. My mom included Dave and Marie and the kids in the RSVP."

Harvey peeled off the tuxedo jacket. "What is this phenomenon? Rick says he and Dan counted three hundred-plus guests, and reporters on top of that. I *hate* going to weddings. And this is just an ordinary wedding. A cop and a records clerk. What is the big attraction here?"

"Come on, Harv, you're a local hero. You personally arrested a congressman and solved the Blake murder the same day."

Harvey turned on him. "The press has been after Mike and me at the station all week. Mike is going to be interviewed on national TV Monday. If I weren't going to be in London, the mayor would make me do it, too. Doesn't it ever end? It's my wedding, for crying out loud!"

"Breathe, Harv."

He breathed. "Okay. You're taking my tux back, right?"

"Right," Eddie said. "Hey, wasn't Jennifer extra beautiful coming down the aisle?"

Harvey smiled. "Yeah, she was." He was ready. They stepped out into the hallway, and a video camera appeared in their faces, the man operating it walking backward before them.

"The best man was your partner as a detective, wasn't he, Captain?" a reporter asked.

Harvey blinked and kept walking. "Get them out of here," he said to Eddie between clenched teeth.

Jennifer gasped when she saw her car. Streamers fluttered in the breeze, and "Just Married" was lettered on the back window in shaving cream and on a sign on the back bumper. A string of Moxie cans dangled behind. Eddie's truck was parked next to the car. She was thankful that Harvey's Explorer was hidden in the garage at Van Cleeve Lane.

"Ready to toss the bouquet?" Abby asked her.

"Yeah." She moved to the middle of the church steps. A sea of young women clustered below her, jostling each other and laughing. Had there really been that many single women at the wedding? The breeze ruffled her hair and the skirt of her new pale blue "going away" dress. She waited until Abby had joined the others and threw her bridal bouquet in Beth's general direction. Several women crushed together and dove for it. Sarah Benoit surfaced holding the roses.

Eddie was watching from the side, but his expression didn't change when Sarah waved her trophy. Jennifer turned for kisses all around from her parents, Grandpa, Beth, Leeanne, Abby, Jeff, Travis, and Randy. Harvey was waiting for her, smiling and dashing. Jennifer placed her hand in his. They ran toward Jennifer's car, but detoured to Eddie's truck and got in, and he drove out of the parking lot, honking the horn. Then he practiced his elusive driving, to make sure he lost any ambitious reporters.

Harvey sat with both arms around Jennifer, and she leaned her head on his shoulder.

"What do you think about Sarah?" Harvey asked Eddie over her head.

"I think she hates me."

"No, she doesn't," said Jennifer. "That guy she brought was a friend of her sister's. She dredged him up as a date at the last minute."

"She told you that?" Eddie glanced at her.

"No," Jennifer said. "She told Cheryl, and Cheryl told Candi in Records, and Candi told me."

"So, what does that mean?" Harvey asked. "She's too insecure to go to a wedding without a date?"

"I think it means she wants Eddie to be jealous."

"Doesn't matter," said Eddie.

"It doesn't?" Harvey asked.

"Nope. I'm not going out with her anymore. I decided it's not a good idea right now."

Jennifer reached out and squeezed his arm. "Take your time."

"I'm meeting a few girls at the church." Sometimes he had an attractive air of shyness.

Jennifer smiled. "I saw you talking to Amanda Driscoll today."

"Who's Amanda Driscoll?" Harvey asked.

"The Driscolls' daughter that's home from college," Jennifer said. "Auburn hair, blue eyes, five-foot-eight, beige dress."

"Okay."

Eddie grinned. "Jennifer, you'd make a great court witness."

"Thanks, but I don't want to witness any more crimes for a while." She was on tap to testify against her old bosses from Coastal Technology, but she'd rather not think about that on her wedding day.

"Do you think Jeff would want to run with me while you're gone?" Eddie asked.

"That wouldn't surprise me," Harvey said. "Ask him."

Eddie was quiet for a moment, then he said,

"Abby sure looks like you, Jennifer. She's really pretty."

Jennifer looked at Harvey, trying not to laugh. "Thank you. She's very special."

"Of course, Leeanne is special, too," Eddie said soberly.

"Yes, she is." Jennifer thought it was probably a good thing for Eddie's sake that both sisters would go back to Skowhegan the next day.

Harvey built a fire in the fireplace that night, a small one that wasn't too hot, but big enough to snap and flicker, throwing shadows on the ceiling. George and Marilyn and Grandpa had moved out that morning, and Marilyn had made sure the refrigerator was stocked. Jennifer ate yogurt and her mother's banana bread in front of the fireplace with Harvey so he would eat. "I saw you take exactly three bites at the wedding," she said.

"You fed me cake."

"That doesn't count. Fortify yourself."

He'd been in the house for a week, and it was starting to feel like home. Jennifer made the feeling complete. He turned off both their phones. If somebody died, Eddie and the Wainthrops knew where to find them.

Eddie came the next morning, not ringing the doorbell but knocking softly on the breezeway door at seven-thirty. Harvey opened it with a cup of coffee in his hand.

"Come on in, Ed. We're almost ready."

Eddie handed him the morning paper and sat down in the kitchen with the coffee Harvey poured him. The suitcases already sat near the door.

Harvey opened the paper.

"Oh, man!" On the front page was a picture of him and Jennifer, coming out of the church. She was gorgeous, and Harvey looked rather smug. The headline was *Priority cop's wedding hot ticket*. He said, "They're really hard up for news for the Sunday paper, aren't they?"

"At least it's below the fold," Eddie said.

"Well, I should hope so!" The lead story beneath the banner was, "Kansas tornado kills 14." There was also a follow-up on the Murphy scandal and an update on Elaine Bard, released from the hospital and gone home to recuperate.

Eddie said, "You didn't watch the late news last night, did you?"

"Uh, no. I was otherwise occupied."

"Well, the reporter on Channel 3 said you'd married a woman half your age. And on Channel 7 they called it a May-December romance."

"Oh, man. Did they call her my child bride and say I robbed the cradle?"

"No, but the paper says you're 45."

"Do *not* tell Jennifer."

"Okay, but Beth taped all the news reports. The reporters all thought it was sweet and romantic, for an old guy like you."

515

"It was. It still is." Harvey skimmed Ryan's story. He'd been to the morgue for background clippings and had tied in the Coastal Technology case with the romance and reprised Harvey's promotion and the Blake case. It was mostly nonfiction, but Ryan had used a little creativity.

"Mrs. Wainthrop had us take all your wedding presents over to Beth's for safekeeping," Eddie said. "You can open them when you get home."

Harvey was still reading the paper. "Nova Scotia?" he asked incredulously. "Ryan says we took the ferry to Nova Scotia yesterday for our honeymoon. Where on earth did he come up with that?"

"After you guys left the reception, Mike sort of let the reporters get the impression you were heading for Canada. If they'd known you were still in Portland . . ."

Jennifer came into the kitchen, wearing a green-and-white print sundress with a white bolero sweater. She smiled hugely at Eddie. "Good morning!"

"How you doing?" he asked, smiling.

"Spectacular!" She bent over and kissed the back of Harvey's neck, and half her hair floated over his shoulder. Harvey had never seen Eddie's face so red.

Discussion questions for *Fort Point* for Book Clubs and other groups

1. Harvey loves getting a new case, but is often conflicted over that, since it usually means someone has suffered a tragedy. How does he temper his satisfaction in compiling the evidence and slicing to the truth with his innate compassion?

2. Harvey and Jennifer do some mild bickering over the wedding details, and this causes Jennifer some grief. She can't take any disagreement lightly. How does Harvey handle this? What could he do to help Jennifer lighten up? And do you think wedding cakes should be chocolate?

3. The new house practically falls into Harvey's and Jennifer's laps. It seems almost too easy to Harvey. Why can he be confident that it will work out? Jennifer is afraid they'll go into debt or that she'll kill the roses. What do Harvey and Mr. Bailey do to reassure her?

4. Did you ever want to "unplug" for a vacation? How can you do that without possibly causing a crisis like Mike did?

5. As soon as Mike returns, Harvey begs him for help on the case, and Mike refuses. Why?

The next day, Mike practically begs to get in on the field work. Why?

6. Do you think Mike will be a good police chief? Why does Sharon go along with his promotion when she clearly doesn't want him to take it?

7. Harvey also vacillates on whether or not to accept a promotion. He likes their unit the way it is. When change becomes inevitable, he bows to it. What would you tell the man who carries around the key to his old car that blew up in Book 1?

8. Should the detectives call their wives before they go into a high-risk situation?

9. Jennifer nearly loses it in the 24 hours before the wedding, when the arrangements get out of hand. We've seen her fearful before, but not hysterical. Who's to blame for the chaos? Who helps smooth things out?

10. Who do you vote for as the future Mrs. Eddie Thibodeau—Sarah, Leeanne, Abby, or someone else? You'll have to keep reading the Maine Justice Series to find out who finally takes him to the altar, but we'll have a lot of fun getting there, and maybe a few tears and headaches.

About the author

Susan Page Davis is the author of more than seventy published novels. She's a two-time winner of the Inspirational Readers' Choice Award and the Will Rogers Medallion, and also a winner of the Carol Award and a finalist in the WILLA Literary Awards. A Maine native, she now lives in Kentucky. Visit her website at: www.susanpagedavis.com, where you can see all her books, sign up for her occasional newsletter, and read a short story on her romance page. If you liked this book, please consider writing a review and posting it on Amazon, Goodreads, or the venue of your choice.

Find Susan at:
Website: www.susanpagedavis.com
Twitter: @SusanPageDavis
Facebook: https://www.facebook.com/susanpage
    davisauthor
Sign up for Susan's occasional newsletter at
    https://madmimi.com/signups/118177/join

Books are produced in the United States using U.S.-based materials

Books are printed using a revolutionary new process called THINKtech™ that lowers energy usage by 70% and increases overall quality

Books are durable and flexible because of smythe-sewing

Paper is sourced using environmentally responsible foresting methods and the paper is acid-free

Center Point Large Print
600 Brooks Road / PO Box 1
Thorndike, ME 04986-0001 USA

(207) 568-3717

US & Canada:
1 800 929-9108
www.centerpointlargeprint.com